LAST DANCE WITH VALENTINO

Daisy Waugh

WINDSOR
PARAGON

First published 2011
by HarperCollins*Publishers*
This Large Print edition published 2011
by AudioGO Ltd
by arrangement with
HarperCollins*Publishers*

Hardcover   ISBN: 978 1 445 85750 3
Softcover   ISBN: 978 1 445 85751 0

British Library Cataloguing in Publication Data available

Picture Credits
p.434 © Apic/Getty Images; p.435 © John Springer
Collection/Corbis; p.436 © Imagno/Getty Images; © Bettmann/Corbis; p.437
top © Bain Collection/Library of Congress; p.438 © Harris & Ewing
Collection, Library of Congress; p.440 © From *The New York Times*, © 2011
The *New York Times* All rights reserved. Used by permission and protected by
the Copyright Laws of the United States. The printing, copying, redistribution,
or retransmission of the Material without express written permission is
prohibited.; p.440 © Topical Press Agency/Getty Images; p.441
© NY Daily News Archive via Getty Images

Printed and bound in Great Britain by
MPG Books Group Limited

For my mother, with love.

AMBASSADOR HOTEL

NEW YORK

Friday, 13 August 1926

I can still feel him.

I can still feel him, I can still smell him, I can still see the fold in my pillow where he leaned over to me . . . I can feel his tongue . . . his hands . . . his lips . . . his fingers in my mouth. I can still taste him. Only a moment ago he was here, with me, and I can still hear the sound of the latch closing softly behind him. I can hear his voice and his laughter fading as he moves away down the hall.

We made love for hours; all night and all morning and late into the afternoon. Mr Ullman must have telephoned him a hundred times, until finally he pulled the wire from the wall and sent the whole wretched contraption flying to the ground. And we lay quietly, talking in whispers, smoking cigarettes, covering our laughter, even while Mr Ullman was outside the door to the suite, imploring him to come out, to pick up the telephone at least, and to talk . . .

In any case he had to leave our bed eventually, of course. There were people waiting for him. Thousands of them—waiting only for him. What a feeling it must be! I can't even imagine—I'm not sure I really even want to. But that is his life now,

1

for better or worse. It was what he wanted, all those years ago. Or, at least, perhaps, it is the price of what he wanted—and today I see him carrying the burden of his extraordinary success with that sad, delicious grace, which is so much his own, and which so entirely melts me. Which melts us all, I think.

So—now what? I watched him dress. In evening clothes, for such a dazzling occasion. I lay in this enormous, sleek black bed, and watched him as he prowled, his footfall soundless, from dressing room to bathroom and back again. He stood before the glass at the beautiful Chinese dressing-table and told me about the time, only last week, when he had come away from an appearance like this evening's—a movie promotion of some type. At his arrival the crowds became so carried away that extra police had to be called. They had mauled him as he fought his way through from theatre to automobile, torn the buttons from his coat, and a great chunk from the lining of his jacket—one woman had clung to his tie and swung: '*And I wanted to say to them all . . .*' he told me, that soft, deep voice, smiling, talking only to me, '*. . . I wanted to say but, girls—ladies! Are you all quite mad? Can't you see I am only a man? Just another man. Go home to your husbands!*' That was when he turned, came across the room to me, lying here, and he leaned over the bed and kissed me once more, one last time; a perfectly tender, perfect kiss—'*. . . what you see is nothing but an illusion. Nothing but a dream . . .*'

'Not a dream to me,' I told him. 'I hope. You're

2

not a dream to me—are you?'

He shook his head. 'No, Jennifer,' he replied, his hand on my cheek, finger tracing my lips. 'I think *you* are the dream, *cara mia* . . . All this time I have been waiting, and wondering, and hoping . . . hoping against hope . . . and finally . . .' He sighed. 'But I wish you would stay tonight. Or at least let me get you a room of your own. You'd be far more comfortable. And safer. And closer. And then maybe you could accompany me tonight—if you wanted to. Or maybe you would let me come to you later and then—Jenny, if you were here, in the hotel, we could be quite discreet. Quite unobserved . . .'

Cara mia.

He has been waiting for me all this time.

But I can't let him get me a room. I can't go with him tonight. I think we both understand that.

'Will you be here for me when I return?' he asked.

I replied that I would be in my own hotel room on 41st when he returned, preparing for my meeting with Miss Marion. He nodded at that. So, I said to him, I would return to my hotel and sleep, and wait for him to telephone me there.

'Tomorrow, then,' he said. ' After you have seen Frances. I shan't distract you, I promise. And then, when you're finished, I shall send all sorts of messages. I shall inundate you with messages . . . I shall telephone you every half an hour. That is,' he stopped suddenly, 'if I may?'

If I may! I laughed aloud. And after a polite hesitation, he laughed too.

For I am his completely. We both know it.

Now, it is my turn to wait. Again. It is Lola

3

Nightingale's turn to wait. Or Jennifer Doyle's turn, I should say. Jennifer No-one from Nowhere must join the long line . . .

*   *   *

Last month he was voted the Most Desirable Movie Star in America by the quarter-million astute readers of *Photoplay.* Hardly a surprise, after all . . . He has lit a fire in us all. Every woman in America! But I have loved him since long before the others, I have loved him from the moment I first laid eyes on him—that airless night ten years ago . . . 11 August 1916 . . . Ten years, one day, nineteen hours and twenty minutes . . . It was my first night in America, and he was as lonely as I. Fighting, just as I was, only with better grace and a bigger, warmer, bolder heart, for a little space in this brash new American world . . .

And now I am alone in his bed, with our salt on my skin, the taste of him, the feel of him glowing, still, in every corner of my being—and he is returning to me because he loves me. *He loves me.* And I have always loved him.

*   *   *

I need to leave. I begin to think it's a little mawkish to be lolling here in this crazy, beautiful bed—now that he is gone. I should get the hell out of this beautiful, warm place before the maids come in and gawk at me, and imagine I am simply another of his little fans.

Only I feel too feeble. I feel so dizzy—I don't have any strength left, not to sit up, let alone to

4

stand . . . So I shall lie here, mawkish or not, and I shall do what I always do in times of confusion, disorder, disarray, complete and utter madness . . .I shall scribble it down on paper. On his own embossed writing paper, nothing less, since I have found it lying here . . . And then the mental effort of ordering my thoughts will force me to some sort of stillness, just as it usually does.

*   *   *

I heard a couple of ladies paid Mr John Barrymore's valet $2,000 in fresh new dollar bills a short while back so as to be let into his bungalow over at Warner while he was out; and they hid in his private bathroom until he wandered in from the set and then, in a great burst, the ladies jumped right out in front of him! Heaven knows how Rudy might have responded. In any case, the great John Barrymore was too well fizzed (*quel surprise*) to give it even the slightest notice. He simply looked at them, from one to the other, and smiled, and then as the poor girls almost died right there before him, he gave them a low bow, and said, 'Care for a little moonshine, ladies?' And, yes, as it happened, they did! Cared for a great deal more than a little moonshine, I understand. Cared for all sorts of things. So much so, indeed, that I believe the valet was even permitted to keep his job! But never mind that. Never mind them.

He loves me. Rudy loves me. And I am not just a fan. I am not just a lady in search of moonshine. I am a professional person, for God's sake! A paid-for professional writer of Hollywood photoplays. At least, I am about to be. Frances Marion has telegraphed to say they will surely buy the first one and with her recommendation they surely will, since all Hollywood listens to Miss Marion . . . And really, quite suddenly, everything in my crazy life is too unimaginably wonderful, and I have not the faintest idea what I may have done to deserve it.

But I should leave! I *must* leave! There is the new Marion Davies picture showing at the Strand, and Frances Marion says I must see it before our lunch together. But of all the movie theatres in New York, could it not have been showing at any other? It's where we saw the Mary Pickford picture, he and I, on that awful, terrible night.

And then afterwards we took a taxicab with all our winnings, and he came with me to surprise Papa for supper . . . And I suppose that was where it started. Not with the secret dance on the lawn that first warm night, and my mind spinning, and the sound of the Victrola seeping out through the moonlight . . .

You made me love you . . .
I didn't want to do it

Ha! How I remember that song!

. . . You made me want you . . .
And all the time you knew it

. . . Not with the secret dance that first night. Not quite. A little later, I think. Of course, it was at Papa's that it started.

6

SUMMER 1916

I must begin with leaving England, I suppose, and with my father, even if normally I try my best to avoid thinking of him. Only today, and yesterday—in the midst of so much happiness—suddenly I discover I can hardly keep him from my mind.

Papa must have drawn the sketch of me from memory, alone in that awful boarding-house. He must have drawn it at the very end, when I half believed he was capable of nothing. In any case, even if there had never been the sketch, and Rudy never *had* kept it all this time, and never *had* shown it to me as he did, only yesterday—and taken the wind from my lungs, so that I thought I might drown—I must still remember him. Because in spite of everything he was a wonderful man—and I loved him. I loved him dreadfully.

* * *

Papa and I were only ever meant to come to America for a short while. It was summer 1916, and since neither of us was much able to make a contribution of our own, we thought we would leave the war behind, which had already taken my brother, and my father could finally start to work again.

The trip was another of Papa's Big Ideas; it was the Big Idea, like all the others before it, which was finally going to rescue us. We believed it, he and I.

We embarked on that long voyage—the one that was going to save us—with only each other in the world to care for. I had no memory of having met our American benefactor, John de Saulles, whom my father assured me would be waiting for us at the other end. But Papa swore we had been introduced in the spring, at the Chelsea Arts Club, where my father and I used to spend so many evenings together. He tended to forget that during those long nights I often used to peel off on my own, hide away and read or, more often, simply fall asleep.

They were like peas in a pod, the two of them: utterly feckless, and hopelessly, faithlessly—lethally—addicted to a certain type of woman. Mr de Saulles had been in London the previous few months, on some sort of business, I don't recall what. It happened to coincide with a time when my father was especially desperate for money, having blown his last of everything, once again, on who knows what? Mr de Saulles had visited Papa's rented studio, and after plenty of bartering (something Papa took a great and uncharacteristic pleasure in), my father had made a painting of Mr de Saulles, in exchange for which Mr de Saulles had not only provided the paints (or so I assumed, since Papa was often so broke he was unable to finish a work for lack of materials) but also paid for his and my passage, second class, to America.

Mr de Saulles wanted Papa to paint his wife, a celebrated beauty. Also his mistress, a celebrated professional tango dancer (named Joan Sawyer. I was quite a dance fanatic back then and I had read about her, even in England). Since, by then, Papa had infuriated virtually everybody who might have been inclined to employ him in London, either by delivering botch jobs horribly late or—more

8

often—by taking the money but failing to deliver anything at all, and since, with the war, portraiture was not in very high demand in London at the time, and since Papa was almost certainly broken-hearted again, we took up the offer.

The tickets were hand delivered to Papa's rented studio on 27 July 1916. On 6 August, we had packed up our few possessions and boarded the great *Mauretania* for New York.

*   *   *

I shall never forget how the two of us stood on deck, quite silent, as that vast ship pulled slowly out to sea. Side by side, we stood, surrounded by noise: the ground-shattering bellow of the ship's horn, the whistling and weeping and the weeping and cheering of passengers on either side of us, and from the decks above and below us; and together we looked back at the Liverpool dock, where not a soul in the great waving crowd was weeping or whistling for us . . . It seemed unimaginable to me then that we would not return to England again.

In any case, we watched until we could no longer make out the faces on shore. I was tearful, feverish—half wild with every crazy emotion—grieving for my brother and my unremembered mother, and for England, and for myself a little.

I longed to speak, but couldn't quite summon the confidence. So it was Papa in the end, with one of his heavy, melancholic sighs, who finally broke our long silence.

Ah, well, he said.

And he turned away. From me. From the shore.

9

From everything he and I had ever known. My father presented himself as a man of the world, and he was, I suppose, in a way. But he had never left England before, so perhaps he was afraid. Or perhaps he already knew, as I didn't yet, that the wonderful, whimsical era of Marcus Doyle and his Big Ideas was edging ever closer to its tired and unfulfilled finale.

Or perhaps he might have been searching for somebody in the crowd, hoping until the last minute that some beautiful, familiar woman might appear from the midst of it and beg him to turn back again. Poor Papa. Since ever I can remember there was always a woman, always absurdly beautiful, always breaking his selfish, silly, fragile heart.

I said, impertinently, because usually it lifted him a little when I was pert, and in any case I needed to talk—to say anything, just to make a noise, 'You oughtn't to worry, Papa. I understand there are ladies galore in the city of New York. Some of them quite intelligent. And not all of them hideous.'

He smiled rather weakly. 'Thank you, Lola. You're very kind.'

Papa used to call me Lola. I never knew why. He didn't like the name Jennifer, I suppose. It's why I chose it, of course. When the choice was mine.

'But, Papa, you may find them alarming at first,' I continued facetiously. 'Mostly they are entirely fixated with the vote. So I read. Much more so than the average Englishwoman. You may have to become a "suffragist" if you're to make any progress with the American girls.'

He laughed at that. Which thrilled me. He

ruffled my careful, seventeen-year-old hair, which, I remember, thrilled me rather less. 'Come with me, my silly friend,' he said to me. 'Come and entertain me, will you, Lola? While I get myself a little stinko.'

It was how we spent the voyage. It was how Papa and I spent the greater part of all our time together actually, once my brother had died—or since probably long before: since Mother died and Marcus was away at school and it was always just the two of us, on our own, with him a little stinko, and me trying my darnedest to keep his melancholy at bay.

*   *   *

Dear God, this heat! This sticky, dirty, airless warmth. So much is different since I left the city all those years ago, but the New York summers don't change. They remind me of August at Roslyn. It reminds of everything I would most like to forget.

I am writing this in a wretched little café just a couple of blocks from my own flophouse . . . Oh, and what a come-down it is! The Ambassador Hotel has its own air-cooling system—of course. As one might expect of such an ultra fine and modern hotel. It lent Rudy and me a magic, secret climate of our own, up there in our private paradise. I had forgotten what the rest of Manhattan was enduring.—Not that I care! Nothing in the world could bring me down tonight—

Ah! The little dooge has come with my eggs at last. I thought I might die from hunger . . . devilled

11

eggs and buttered toast . . . I never saw a more welcome sight! And more coffee, too. And I have asked him to bring me a large slice of chocolate cake and some fruit Jell-O. And some ginger ale and some vanilla ice cream. And more toast. Good God, I'm so hungry I could swallow the whole of it in a single mouthful then order it all again—except I'm not sure I have enough money in my purse.

Is he thinking of me?
Is he thinking of me now?

But if I continue along those lines I shan't be able to eat a thing, and it's hopeless, because I must or I shall probably faint in this dreadful heat. I've hardly eaten for days. It would be too horribly embarrassing.

I must keep writing. About the beginning—when Papa was still here, and it was only the two of us, thrown together on that great big ship, setting off to start our new life together.

It's strange. I've not dwelled—purposely not dwelled—on the beginning, not for all these years, and yet suddenly, tonight, it comes to me in a rush, as vivid as yesterday. I remember what I was wearing—the little shirtwaist with the embroidered daisies at the buttonhole . . . I remember that, and how splendid I felt in it. I remember the feel of my new rabbit-skin stole, too hot for the day, but which I wore because Papa had only given it me the day before, when I was crying because we were leaving our home. (And I'm convinced, by the way, that he had always intended to give it to another girl entirely.

He looked quite rueful as he handed it over.)

I remember what Papa was wearing, too. He was a handsome man: tall and slim and athletic-looking, with eyes of dark blue and thick, golden-brown hair—speckled grey, by then, I suppose, but always golden brown in my memory. I've said he was a handsome man: perhaps it's an immodest moment to observe that he and I looked rather alike. We have the same colouring and similar build. The same nose—it looks better on a man—straight and long; the same square, determined jaw; the same dark blue eyes and angular face.

He was elegant—always. I remember the jaunty angle of his boater hat, and the familiar hint of his cologne as we stood side by side on that vast deck, and the smell of the crumpled pink azalea in his lapel. He had taken it from Chelsea at the crack of dawn that same morning, just as we were leaving our rented cottage for the last time—plucked it, with that roguish laugh, from the front garden of Mr Brampton next door. It was an act of half-hearted defiance, of course, of playfulness and sentimentality, which was somehow typical of my father. My wonderful, magical, wicked, feckless, faithless father. I miss him. God, I miss him still.

*   *   *

So, our vast ship slipped away from England and the war, and five days followed, surrounded by sea: long, strange, empty days they were; and while my father drank, and charmed our fellow passengers

13

with his usual elegance and wit, I talked too much—couldn't stop myself—and mostly sent them scurrying away.

The sixth morning dawned at last, not a moment too soon: Papa and I were setting each other on edge. I could feel his impatience—the suffocating coat of boredom that wrapped every word when he addressed me. And there was something else too, perhaps, now that I think about it. He had grown increasingly ill-tempered as the journey progressed. I would glimpse him sometimes, gazing at me as a prisoner might gaze at their jailer, as if culpability for everything—all his torment, all the little irritations of our journey, the sourness of his wine, pain in his toe, the ache in his heart and head—should be laid somehow at my door.

In any case I left him at his breakfast table that final morning, not eating, since he never much ate, mostly muttering to himself about the horridness of all things American. I left him alone and joined the other passengers on deck to catch a first view of land.

Oh! I will never forget it! That first thrilling glimpse of Manhattan—how it rose from the golden haze; glistening with boastfulness in the dawn light—it moved me in a way nothing in old England ever could . . . I had imagined 'skyscrapers'; Father and I had discussed them at length (he detested the mere notion) but to see them in reality, soaring triumphantly against that pink morning sky, so proud, so ambitious, so completely *extraordinary*—I had never in my life seen a sight so beautiful. Even today they take my breath away.

My father, when he finally emerged on deck, decreed them 'hideous', just as I had known he would: 'If the good Lord, in his infinite wisdom, had wanted us to live suspended in mid-air in that undignified fashion,' he said, scowling across the water, 'he'd have given us wings.' After I failed to respond to that, Papa wandered back to his empty dining-table, I think, and I stayed where I was until we docked.

And then what? A blur of everything, I suppose: a whole lot of noise and energy and mad confusion . . . Papa coming to life at last, striding importantly off the ship as if poor, wretched New York couldn't possibly be expected to survive without him a moment longer . . . And me, left behind again, organising our paltry luggage, coming ashore and searching desperately for him through the crowd.

It was a sweltering morning, and the pier was teeming; a monstrous, roaring jumble—or jungle, it seemed to me—of steam and smoke; motor-cars and carriages, porters, passengers and officials; and the clatter of horses' hoofs and the spluttering of automobile engines, and above it all, the constant hammer and crash of construction, here and there and everywhere, and far off in the distance, from towering metal skeletons, there were little men, like insects in a spider's web, riveting together more buildings to add to the madness of that crazy, beautiful skyline . . . So, we stood there, waiting, jostled this way and that: the failed English Portraitist, who drank too much, and the Failure's daughter; I was mesmerised by the little men in their metal webs— I was mesmerised by it all. But, of course, I was lucky. I was young and—unlike my father—I had never really shone, so could never feel the shock of my insignificance quite as he must have felt it that morning. I think perhaps it frightened him, to feel so utterly, infinitesimally small.

After what felt a long while, with the two of us standing there—dumb and simply staring—I dared to ask my father if perhaps our mysterious benefactor had provided us with an address. Papa began to rifle half-heartedly through the pockets of his linen coat. But he seemed to be on edge. Even more so than before. He kept glancing at me, as if on the point of saying something, only to lose his nerve and fall silent again. Finally I asked him what was the matter. Had he lost the address? Was his friend not likely to come? Did his friend, perhaps, not even exist?

He looked pained.

'Lola, old girl,' he said, at last (and I knew at once we were in trouble. He only ever called me 'old girl' when he had something dreadful to say). 'There's something I've been meaning to tell you. The, er . . . that is—the, er . . . *As you know—*' Abruptly, he stopped patting his pockets, straightened up and looked at me.

He looked—what did he look? What did you look, Papa, just that instant before? *Sorry*? . . . Yes, I think so . . . *Shamefaced?* . . . Gosh, yes. Like an animal caught in a trap. 'Dear girl,' he said— boomed, rather, over all the noise. 'I am not—that is to say, *we—we*, you and I, are not blessed with a pecuniary—pecuniary . . . How does one put it?' He took a breath and tried again. 'The time has come, old girl, now that you're—we're—now that we've arrived here, adults, and so on . . . The time has come for the two of us to address the *perennial*

16

deficiency of funds at Ranch Doyle, such ranch that it is. . . Peripatetic ranch . . . and so on. It is, or has been, as you may or may not be aware, a constant struggle for your old papa to keep ahead of things . . .'

Ahead of things! My poor father! I'm ashamed to say I laughed.

'It has been a *constant struggle* to stay ahead of matters. And now that you yourself are a young lady—and a *remarkable* young lady, I may add—I was rather beginning to think . . . that is to say . . . *What I have done* . . . Oh, Lord . . . Perhaps I should have mentioned it earlier . . .'

I began to feel a little sick. 'Papa, for Heaven's sake . . .' Over all the noise my voice was barely audible even to myself. 'For Heaven's sake, tell me—what should you have mentioned earlier?'

'Only I didn't feel it would be very pleasant to disrupt our very pleasant journey . . . What I have done, old girl, may take you a little by surprise. But I assure you in the long run it is with your own interests very much in my mind . . . at the *forefront* of my mind . . . that I have rather taken the matter of the, er, perennial *pecuniary deficiency* at our albeit rather peripatetic ranch into a new dimension . . . a new chapter, so to speak. That is to say . . . Lola, darling, when my kind friend Mr de Saulles offered to—ship us out here, he very sweetly made a suggestion regarding your own future, which I'm certain—I'm *absolutely convinced—*'

'Misster Doyles? Misster Marquis Doyles?'

A strange man was peering down at my father. He was pale and extraordinarily tall, with white-blond hair slicked back from a huge, worried face,

17

and a long chin that curved disconcertingly to one side. He was in his forties, possibly fifties; ageless, actually. And he was frowning—that eyebrowless frown with which I would grow so familiar.

There weren't many who could peer down at Papa. Justin Hademak, the crazy Swede, must have been six and a half foot or more. He was a giant. 'Misster Doyles?' he repeated. 'Iss it you?'

'Aha!' exclaimed my father, joyously, noticing him at last. 'Saved by the bell. So to speak.'

'You are Mr Doyles?'

'Marcus Doyle. At your service. Jolly clever of you to spot us. You're rather late. But no matter.'

'Of courses.' The giant bowed his head—it was absurdly formal—and flashed an unlikely smile. 'I apologise. Unfortunately, at the moment of leaving, the mistress suddenly required the motor-car . . . with utmost urgency . . .'

'Don't think about it for a second, old chap,' my amiable father assured him. 'When a lady requires a motor-car, she requires a motor-car!'

'I am sent by Mr de Saulles,' he continued, my father's charm or humour—or whatever it was—quite lost on him, 'but I am right to think you are indeed the portrait painter? It is important I locate him correctly. You are the renowned portrait painter from England, coming to America on the appointment of Mr John Longer de Saulles?'

'I do solemnly declare that I am he,' said my father. 'Back me up, Lola, won't you?' he stage-whispered to me, above all the racket. 'I'm not certain he believes me.'

'And you are the daughter?' said Mr Hademak.

I nodded.

'You know, I'm almost certain de Saulles sent me

18

a bit of paper, with all the particulars and so on, and I think he may even have mentioned you . . . a tall gentleman . . .' My father was patting his pockets again. '. . . only it seems to have disappeared. Lola, do you suppose I may have given it to you?'

There was no opportunity to reply. Mr Hademak had taken a brief look at our travelling trunk and, in one easy swoop, bent from his freakish height, lifted it onto his shoulders and lurched headlong into the crowd. We had little choice but to end our conversation and follow him.

'I am to put Mr Doyle into a motor vehicle and send him to Mr de Saulles in the city,' the man shouted behind him. 'Mr de Saulles is *most* impatient to see you again, Mr Doyle. You are to lunch together at Sherry's, and afterward to join Mrs de Saulles for dinner at The Box . . . And the daughter . . .' he glanced back at me, not with any hostility, or with the slightest hint of interest '. . . Mr de Saulles says you are to drive with me to The Box directly. The mistress wants . . . that is to say she doesn't want . . .' He tailed off. 'You are supposed,' he tried again, 'to begin your employment at once.'

'To begin my . . .' I think I may even have laughed. 'Papa?' I turned to him. He looked away. 'My employment . . . as what?'

'Not quite *employment* . . .' my father muttered sheepishly. 'Only the poor little chap's got a Spanish accent, Lola. Y'see . . . *That's* the thing. And he's only four. Or nine. Or something frightful. He terribly needs someone to talk to . . . And then there's dear Mrs de Saulles, hardly much older than you are, Lola, miles away from her

19

native land and *abysmally* lonely most of the time. It'll only be for a couple of months . . .'

I didn't say anything. I was too shocked—I had no idea what to say. I remember my silence seemed to annoy him. 'Really, Jennifer, darling,' he began to sound slightly peevish, 'there's no need to pull that long face. They're excellent people. My friend Jack de Saulles is . . . top notch. And Mrs de Saulles comes from one of the most spectacular families in Chile. In fact I have a feeling her uncle might even be President. For example. And if he isn't he certainly ought to be. In any case, darling, even if he *isn't*, I don't think you should complain when I arranged it all so nicely for you . . . Entirely because I was so utterly convinced you would enjoy yourself . . . '

'So . . . But we shall be living in different places?'

I could feel him itching to slide away from it all. How he longed for this conversation to be over! 'Yes and no. That is to say, I shall be in the city mostly, at their apartment. But it's all part of the *same family*. And I shall be travelling to see you during the week, of course. Or as often as I can . . . It's really not far at all from New York. Only an hour or so by the train, Jack tells me . . . In any case it's hardly up to me, is it?'

*   *   *

It seems ridiculous, I suppose, because I was a grown woman, with a father who was constantly broke, and of course I hadn't a penny of my own— but it had never passed through my head, never, not even for a moment, that I should play any role during our great American adventure beyond the one I had always played: that is to say, to be hanging about with Papa in a daughterly fashion and occasionally slipping off to fall asleep.

But it was not to be. And why should it have been? No reason. One cannot remain a child for ever. Only I had been his constant companion for as long as I could remember. And the news that we were to separate came as a dreadful shock. I suppose, if I wish anything, I wish he'd had the courage to break the news to me a little earlier, so that I might at least have had time to prepare myself . . . It's too bad. It doesn't matter now, in any case. In fact, I am grateful it happened, and not simply because it allowed me to meet Rudy.

However, I was not grateful then. As I stood there on that crazy, bustling, deafening pier, the thought of being apart not just from my home but from the only person in the world I loved, or who loved me, filled me with nothing but a clammy dread. I looked across at Papa—still hoping, I think, that his face might break into one of those wonderful, wicked grins, that he might slap me on the back, as he did sometimes, always much too hard, and laugh, and tell me he was teasing.

But he didn't look at me. Carefully didn't look at me, I think. 'Righty-ho!' he said. 'Jolly good. Well, take good care of my little Jennifer, won't you, Mr . . . Mr . . .'

'Hademak. Justin Hademak. From Sweden. . .'

'Hademak. Of course you are. From Sweden. How delightful. Lovely. Well, jolly good.'

Mr Hademak put my father into a taxicab. Papa and I kissed each other briefly, without eye contact. I was afraid I would cry. He muttered something—*good luck, old girl*—something feeble, and not in the least up to the occasion. I didn't reply. Couldn't. And then, as he was driven away, he turned back to me.

I remember his expression, I see it now: it was as if he was apologising, and not just for this unfortunate incident but for everything. He looked awful: like someone else entirely—someone so old and so exhausted with the disappointment of himself it allowed me, briefly, to forget my own abandonment, and wonder, for the first time, what might become of him without me. He needed me more than either of us realised, I think. The sight of him, shrinking into the chaos, tore at my heart. It still does. He lifted his hat to me through the glass, and I think he whispered, *Sorry*. If he did, it was the first and last time . . . He never apologised to me again. Never. And he left me there, alone, with the giant from Sweden.

*   *   *

After Papa had disappeared into the great cloud of the city, Mr Hademak became (if it were possible) even more frantic than previously. Afterwards, when I knew him a little better, I wondered if he hadn't done it on purpose, charged on ahead in that crazy way, yelling out instructions and so on, if not as a kindness to me then at least to avoid the embarrassment of having to witness my collapsing into tears. I might have done it too—collapsed, that is—if he'd allowed me a moment to pause. I'm not at all sure I would have held myself together.

'*Excellent*,' he declared, without looking at me—with the trunk still balanced high on his shoulder. 'We must get over to the island right away.' (Ellis

Island, he meant, of course: which island we had passed as we came in; and where the steerage passengers disembarked to have their immigration papers checked. And their hair checked, for lice, I think, too.) 'We must get over there *quickly*, though, Miss Doyle ... So *keep up*!' I had to run to stay apace. 'We have to pick out a new maid. You must help me with that, young lady. They're all rotten. Since the war we only get now the bad eggs. But we mustn't fuss. Madame wants her motor-car outside the home ... So we must pick out the first one we see who looks *at all* good. It doesn't matter a spot anyway. They never do stay long ...'

The journey to Ellis Island took our little boat back towards the great statue that had so exhilarated me only an hour or so before; the freedom it celebrated seemed to have taken on a more menacing significance since then. Liberty was more than simply an idea suddenly, and how I longed to have a little less!

In any case, we bobbed along, Mr Hademak and I. Mr Hademak was too impatient to wait for the little boat to dock and he disembarked, with those ridiculous spider legs, when there was still a yard or two of water before the quay. And then, even before his foot had touched solid land, he announced as loudly as possible to the milling crowd that he was looking for a housemaid.

Immediately the crowd surged forward but it only infuriated him. 'No, no, no!' he snapped. 'Get off! Get *away!* No gentlemen today. Are there any Irish about?' Then, momentarily cornered by the swell, he turned to me. 'Miss Doyle,' he bellowed over their heads, 'don't just stand there. Find us a girl! And a sweet one, mind. Madame hates them to look drab. *Over there! See?*' He pointed behind me. 'See the little group of Paddies over there? See the young one, with that terribly mad hair?'

The one with the hair—the unmissable, magnificent, golden-russet curls—was a girl of my age, maybe a little older. She was sitting on a black tin suitcase, slightly apart from the others, her sharp face turned towards us. She examined the blond giant, then looked at me. I smiled at her but she didn't smile back.

'*THAT one!*' he shouted at me, pointing irritably, batting the people away. 'With the mad, mad hair. YOU!' he yelled at her.

The girl looked back at him.

'*Ask her if she's looking for some work. DO IT!*' he shouted. 'Before someone else takes her! The good ones get stolen too quickly.'

So I turned to her, very embarrassed. 'The gentleman . . . you probably heard him. He wants to know if you're— '

'Is it board, too?'

'Why, *yess*! Most certainly it *iss!*' Mr Hademak cried, bearing down on us, his long white face sweating with the effort of having shaken himself loose at last. 'It *is* board. And a nice job, too. Twelve dollars a week. Better than you'll get anywhere else. With days off. Two days a month off! Do you want it, young lady? No or yes?'

She laughed. 'Do I want it?' She held out a hand to us, and I can picture her face now, the relief in her eyes, even while she was trying to hide it.

'You have family?'

'Back in Ireland. I'm here on my own.'

'Good. Like the rest of us, then.' He glanced at me, rather shyly, I think. Perhaps, even, with a

24

whisper of a smile. 'Welcome to America, young lady. You have your papers?'

She nodded. 'I was only waiting for a ride to take me to the city.'

'Well, come along, then. Follow me. Hurry now. We can tell ourselves about names and everything else like that in the motor-car. Only we must hurry.'

He drove us at breakneck speed. It was all so new to me and yet, at the time, I was too wrapped in my miserable thoughts to take much notice. I suppose, before long, we had left Manhattan—I remember nothing of it, only the three of us tearing over a long, straight, impeccably smooth road to Long Island; a road that Mr Hademak was pleased to tell us had been built by a rich man as a car-racing track—until, after however many deaths, the racing drivers had refused to use it any more. He had cackled as he told us this, shaken his head at their eccentricity, and proceeded to drive faster along that dangerous road than I had—or have—ever travelled. Mr Hademak spent most of the journey shouting at us over the din of the engine. It made the veins stick out on his neck.

'Well well well . . . it is quite a household you ladies are coming to. Miss Doyle—I don't know what you may know of it already?'

'Almost nothing,' I replied bitterly.

'*Quite* a household,' he continued blithely. 'We have some quite colourful individuals who come our way. Oh, yes, we are quite the entertainers at The Box—as our little house is called. You will be most amused!'

Amused? It seemed unlikely. *Amused?* To have

25

travelled so far, so full of fear and hope, only to be abandoned? To have arrived in that mythical new city at last, only to be whisked away from it? Actually, at that moment, I felt not so much amused, but as if a great wave of self-pity were enveloping me and, I'm ashamed to admit, tears were already stinging. I'm not sure I had ever felt so lonesome in my life.

Fortunately, neither Mr Hademak nor the Irish girl—Madeleine—seemed to notice.

'First, we have the *master* of the house,' he announced, as the car flew on, swerving aimlessly from one side of the road to the other. Mr Hademak, bolt upright at the wheel, smiled secretly to himself, and I wondered if, after so many trouble-free days at sea, I might finally be travel sick. 'Yes, indeed,' he said, 'and the master is truly quite some gentleman . . . And then we haf the little boy, of course—Jack Junior. Little Jack! Oh, but you will adore him! Quite the little man, he is! He is quite the little master! We all simply adore him. All the servants, and his papa and his mama too. He's *everybody*'s favourite! Every single body in our happy little big house just so simply *adores* him—'

Suddenly Madeleine, the Irish girl, gave a loud and derisive snort. I stared at her. Last she'd spoken, she'd been telling us, with eyes lowered and trembling lip, how she'd come to America alone because her husband had been killed in the French trenches (later she told me she'd never been married: she'd been found in bed with the priest and hounded out of town). She seemed to have forgotten her grief quickly enough. She glanced at me and rolled her eyes, and it goes to

26

show what sort of a hysterical mind I was in, because the next thing, with tears of self-pity still pricking my eyeballs, I was shaking with quiet giggles.

'But you mustn't think our life is only about the Little Man,' Mr Hademak continued cheerfully. 'Also we are quite the fashionable gathering. Though sometimes, when Madame is in the city, we are just the two of us: Father and Little Man. And then sometimes it is Mother and Little Man, when Mr de Saulles is in town. And then we have Madame and her *amusing* friends. Or Mr de Saulles and *his* amusing friends. Or Mr and Mrs de Saulles and *their* amusing friends. Yes, yes—it is all most amusing . . . We have counts and countesses of Europe. And Mr de Saulles sometimes brings along his Broadway—*connections*. And how lively they are! And even some of the stars from the pictures! No, no, not quite Miss Mary Pickford! Not quite yet! But we have an English duke. An English duke! And we have so many others. Dancers. Politicians . . . You might have read about them all quite often. In the yellow papers. Yess . . .' It was Mr Hademak's turn to laugh helplessly. He rocked on his bony backside, this way, then that.

'Sometimes,' he continued finally, 'I wonder if I know more about these fashionable individuals than they even quite know themselves . . . We are quite the *fast* set at The Box, you will discover. Oh, you will be *most* amused.'

'And if you'll excuse me for asking,' interjected Madeleine, suddenly, 'only I'm wondering—what's the mistress like?'

*   *   *

27

–Ha. And if I had known the answer to that—would I have stopped the car?

Would I have thrown myself out onto that racing drivers' rejected MotorParkway right there and then, hitched a lift with whatever vehicle came along, hauled my father from his delightful lunch at Sherry's, and taken whatever employment anyone offered me? Perhaps.

She destroyed my father—what there was left of him to destroy. And she haunts me still—there's barely a day goes by I don't think of her, of the part I played or didn't play, of what I saw and said, and didn't see and should have said . . .

On the other hand, without her, I would never have befriended Rudy. Or ever have travelled to Hollywood. Nor Rudy either. Imagine that! Then who would the readers of *Photoplay* be drooling over at nights? Perhaps, in spite of everything, I should be grateful to her. Well, and maybe I am, but I hope she burns in any case—if not at Sing Sing, then in Hell when she finally gets there.

*   *   *

'What's the mistress like?' asked Madeleine.
And I swear Mr Hademak blushed.

*   *   *

Dear God—three in the morning already, and still too damn hot to sleep! I have been writing all night so my arm is swollen. And my head is burning and my eyeballs ache . . . but I can't stop.

Not yet. Not until I reach the moment where Rudy and I are there in the garden, and we are standing in silence together, listening to the music, and I am wondering about Papa, and where he is, and worrying a little about his newest infatuation, but not as much as I ordinarily would because how can I when Mr Guglielmi—Rudy—is standing so very close beside me? And I don't believe I have ever glimpsed a more handsome, more dazzling man in all my life.

And then he turns to me and he says, 'It's beautiful music, isn't it?' And his voice—his Italian accent was much stronger then but his voice was the same: that low, dark, beautiful voice. I can feel it through me. I didn't recognise the music. I'm not sure that I had even fully noticed it was playing. And he smiled at me, and I thought how sad he must have looked before because the smile had such an effect, as if his face had been illuminated by a thousand million electric light bulbs, and he said, 'Do you like to dance, Jenny?'

> *You made me love you. . .*
> *I didn't want to do it*
> *. . .You made me want you . . .*
> *And all the time you knew it*

Rodolfo Guglielmi was a professional dancer then: a dancer-for-hire. When the papers wrote about him—because of the divorce—they called him a lot of hateful names, and of course they still do. And of course he was no angel then. He is a long way from being an angel now, I suppose. But, Hell, which of us isn't?

29

When he danced it was as if he moved through a different space from the rest of us: as if the air carried him; as if he had no weight at all. So I danced with him, still in my travelling clothes, in the moonlight, and with the music seeping through the warm night air. And I thought—I remember it so clearly—I thought, This is Life! Now I am truly alive . . .

What a gorgeous, magical place is this America!

*   *   *

Justin Hademak said it again, as we were turning into its long drive: 'We are quite the fast set at The Box you will discover.' It didn't surprise me, knowing my father and the people he normally consorted with. Actually I would have been surprised if they had been anything else.

Nevertheless there certainly wasn't anything very fast about Mrs Blanca de Saulles that afternoon. We arrived by a side door—Mr Hademak made us tiptoe into the back lobby, and he closed the door behind us as if a lion and her cubs were sleeping on the other side.

'Sssh!' he ordered. We hadn't made a sound.

Just then Mrs de Saulles herself tripped past us, like a ghost. We stood there, the three of us, fresh from our journey, huddled together in a knot. And maybe she didn't see us. *She* was a vision, at any rate; quite out of place in our whitewashed servants' lobby. Quite out of place—and a little lost, possibly, since it was the one and only time I ever saw her there.

She was dressed in the palest lilac: a shirtwaist of

30

lace and voile and a silk skirt, ankle length, with tiny mother-of-pearl buttons. I can see her now, floating by in that ghostly way, only five or so years older than I was, with that thick, black, shiny hair pinned demurely at the nape of her neck, and those vast, dark, unhappy eyes. She looked as pale as death, as feminine and fragile as any woman I had ever encountered. I knew right then how my father would adore her.

'*Oh! Mrs de Saulles!*' whispered Mr Hademak, his great big block of a body rigid, suddenly, with the dreadful possibility of interrupting her. She continued regardless, slowly, vaguely . . . 'Mrs de Saulles?' he tried again.

'Yes, Hademak?' she said. Sighed. It was the softest voice you ever heard.

'We are back!'

'So it appears.'

'This—this one—this is Miss Doyle,' he said, pointing at me, looking at Mrs de Saulles's feet. (Little, little feet.) 'The portrait painter's daughter. Just arrived from England.'

I think I bobbed a curtsy. God knows why.

'And this is the new maid, Madeleine,' he added. 'She's Irish. We took her from Ellis Island this morning.'

Mrs de Saulles spared us not a glance. She released another of her feather-sighs: a sigh I would grow quite familiar with. (She was tiny. Did I mention how tiny she was? Hardly above five foot, I should think, and so slim that if she stood sideways you could honestly hardly see her.) 'How lovely,' she murmured. She sounded more English than I did. 'Lovely, lovely . . .' and then, slowly, she turned to continue her journey.

31

She was, there is no doubt about it, a truly exceptionally beautiful woman. And *that*, by the way, even after so many years, and whether I'm grateful to her or not, is about the only pleasant thing I have to say about her.

*   *   *

The Box was near Great Neck, on the Long Island Gold Coast, not far from many of the finest houses of the richest folk in America (and just directly up from where handsome Mr Scott Fitzgerald has set his new novel, of course, which I have by my bedside as I write.)

The Box was a frame house, large and quite important and very graceful, but not vast. Not quite like Mr Gatsby's. It was painted white. There were wooden porches along the front, framed all round by wide, trellised archways which had been designed for flowers to grow along, I suppose, though there were none while I was there. To one side, rather like a church, there was a high, square tower, where Mrs de Saulles had her private sitting room. The house stood on its own land, with a drive of seventy yards or so, and space enough for a large, bleak garden.

In England, Papa and I had stayed in plenty of magnificent houses while my father (before they grew tired of employing him) painted portraits of their owners. And, really, it wasn't even as though The Box were particularly large, not compared to the houses I knew in England—and certainly not compared to some of the other houses in the area. Nevertheless there was something indefinably glitzy about it. Mr Hademak was right about that.

To my English eyes, fresh from all the deprivations of war, The Box seemed to offer comforts that in Europe had yet to be even imagined: as many bathrooms as there were bedrooms, for example, or not far off it, and hot, running water in all of them; and electrical lighting in every part of the house, even the servants' rooms. The kitchen was fitted with an electrical icebox—something I had never even seen before—and another electrical machine specifically for making waffles! And in the drawing room on the ceiling there was a wonderful electrical fan. The Box had all these things and more. In its construction, it seemed every possible human comfort had been pandered to.

Yet for all that it felt uncared-for. Cold. There was my father's—not especially good—portrait of Mr de Saulles, which hung importantly in the large white entrance hall, but other than that there were very few pictures. Nor even much furniture. And what furniture there was appeared ill assorted and unconsidered: a heavy leather couch here, a feeble rattan armchair there, and a hotchpotch of rugs across that great big, elegant drawing-room's floor. Luxurious—and yet unloved. From the moment I walked into it I could sense it was an unhappy house.

Madeleine was summoned to Mrs de Saulles's bedroom within minutes of our arrival, and I didn't set eyes on her again until the following morning. In the meantime Mrs de Saulles seemed to have no interest in meeting me. She had dispatched her young son and temporary nurse to spend the day in the city with his (and my) father. So, I wandered about behind Mr Hademak trying to prise from him what, exactly, my duties would be. He was terribly vague about it. 'Oh, just make the little soldier to giggle!' he said irritably. For which, by the way, I was to be paid twenty dollars a week, with Sundays off. A better deal than Madeleine, then.

Poor, sweet Jack. I miss him. He turned out to be the sweetest, gentlest little friend in spite of all the turmoil that surrounded him. Afterwards I wrote several times to him, care of his grandmother. I wonder if the letters even reached him. I never received any reply, not once. But I think about him often—his bravery, mostly. And the way he looked at his mother with so much love and sorrow on that terrible, awful day . . .

Mr Hademak took me to the little boy's nursery: the only room in the house that seemed to have any warmth to it. A jumble of Jack's drawings leaned against the mantelpiece, and there was hardly an inch of the place that wasn't cluttered with some new-fangled plaything: model cars and mechanical guns, circus sets and a doll-sized piano that really worked, and a steam engine that could puff around its own railway track . . . And aeroplanes that could be wound up and flown, and Houdini magic sets and . . . His father never came home without a carful of new toys for him.

'But he doesn't play in here much,' Mr Hademak said airily. And then, after an unusual pause, 'You'll be kind to him, I'm sure, Miss Doyle. He has many toys, but he has . . .' He stopped for a moment. 'Well . . . his parents adore him, of course. But—perhaps you have discovered it . . .' He flashed me the shyest of smiles and blushed. 'When you are young there are many ways to be lonely.'

34

I nodded. A pause.

'Tell me, are you fond of watching the flickers, Miss Doyle? I am very fond of watching the flickers. I can't keep away. Each Sunday, if Mrs de Saulles allows it, there I go to the movie theatre at Westbury, or at Mineola. Wherever they have a movie showing. And my favourite star—who is yours? My favourite of all the stars is, of course . . . Miss Mary Pickford! Do you admire her, Miss Doyle? I hope so!'

I would have liked to answer since, from what little I had been permitted to see of them, I was already quite a fan of the movies—and of Mary Pickford, too. But just then a telephone message came through informing us there were to be fifteen for dinner, and after that Mr Hademak had no time for me.

I would have preferred to stay up there in the nursery, but he insisted I come down to the kitchen, where I only got in everyone's way. I tried to make conversation with the cook. Unsuccessfully, since she was Spanish, and always surly. There was a kitchen-maid, too, whose name I don't even remember. She was from Mexico. Not that it matters. In all the long months I stayed at The Box I don't think I ever heard her speak. Certainly, she didn't speak to me that day. Nobody did much, except Mr Hademak, and only then so he could boast about the evening's guests. There was to be an Austrian count and his heiress wife, he said, and the Duke of Manchester, and various others, all of them amusing to Mr Hademak in one way or another.

'. . . and finally there is Mr *Guglielmi*,' Mr Hademak said regretfully. 'But he is not quite a

guest . . . Mr de Saulles only likes him to come so
the other guests have an opportunity to watch Miss
Sawyer dance. He comes once a week to teach Mrs
de Saulles the tango—I believe Mr de Saulles pays
his travel expenses . . .'

'He's a professional dancer?' I asked.

'A dance instructor. And recently a new
professional partner for Miss Sawyer. Not as good
a partner as her last, in my small opinion. He was
just a gardener not so long ago. And he iss a wop.
So although he eats in the dining room,' he said
again, 'he iss not *quite* a guest . . .'

*   *   *

They arrived—the guests and the not-quite
guest—in a noisy motorcade, four vehicles in all,
with Mr de Saulles, and the woman, Joan Sawyer,
whom my father had told me was our host's
mistress, in the front car. After them came a
second car, and a third, both crammed with dinner
guests, joyously attired. (After wartime London, it
was amazing to see how colourful and prosperous
they looked!) And in the final car—which stopped
directly in front of us—sat the temporary nurse,
who had earlier been dispatched to the city with
the little boy, and the not-quite-guest, Mr Rodolfo
Guglielmi.

That was the first time I glimpsed him, gazing
moodily out of the automobile window, smoking a
cigarette, with the boy, Jack, fast asleep against his
shoulder . . . And even then, when I was so
impatient to be reunited with my father, when
there was so much new to look at, the sight of him
made me stop. He looked quite detached amid all

the activity—all the noisy people in their joyous hats, clambering out of their cars, shouting and laughing. He sat very still. More handsome than any man I had ever seen. His thoughts seemed to be miles away.

Mr Hademak and I stood side by side at the front door. I think he was rather put out to have me there—as uncertain as I was of my not-quite-guest-like status. Actually, it was difficult for both of us to know where I was meant to fit in for there was my father, climbing out of the same car as the duke. ('There! I told you!' whispered Hademak. '*That* one—the great big chubby one—that is His Grace, the English duke!') There he was, my father, clapping His English Grace on the great big chubby shoulder, laughing and joking with an elegant woman in vibrant yellow dress. And there was I.

'Ah!' cried my father, looking up at me, with love and warmth and blissful forgetfulness, I truly believe, as to where the two of us had only hours before left off. 'There she is!' He left the yellow woman and strode towards me. 'My very own little Jane Eyre!' He laughed, enveloped me in his arms, lifted me off my feet and kissed me. The familiar smell of alcohol, tobacco and his cologne . . . I can smell it now—I can feel the wash of relief I felt then, as his great arms wrapped me in it.

'How is it, Lola, my sweet girl? Have you had a delightful day?'

The woman in the yellow dress shouted something at him. I didn't hear what, but it made him laugh, and before I had time to say anything much he had put me down and wandered back to

talk to her again. It didn't matter at all, really. I
was accustomed to his child-like attention span—
and I was just so happy to see him. In any case he
returned to me moments later, this time with our
benefactor, Mr de Saulles, in tow. 'Jack! I want you
to meet my beautiful, clever, delightful,
enchanting, charming, beautiful—did I already say
that?—*lovely*, courageous, extraordinary daughter,
Jennifer. Jennifer Doyle. Jennifer, this is Mr de
Saulles, our immeasurably kind benefactor.'

De Saulles was tall and powerfully built, a good
fifteen years older than his young wife, with hair
slicked back from an even-featured, handsome
face, a strong American jaw and startling bright
blue eyes. He stared at me.

I said something—thanked him, I suppose, for
all he'd done for us. He took a long moment to
respond, but continued to gaze at me with the
same strangely absent intensity. He said—and, like
his wife's, his voice was so clipped he might have
been English himself, 'Did they feed you well?'

I didn't know if he meant on the ship, or in the
house, or what he meant—or really, given the
heavy cloud of alcohol that surrounded him, and
the blank look behind his eyes, whether he meant
anything by the question at all. I said, 'Very well,
thank you.'

Still, he gazed at me. I felt myself blushing. I also
noticed Miss Sawyer beside him, fidgeting a little.
She didn't look so great—cheap, with the face
paint. It was before we all wore it. Nevertheless I
longed to be introduced to her—was on the point
of introducing myself, even. But suddenly Mr de
Saulles seemed to lose interest.

'Good,' he said abruptly. He put a careless arm

38

around Miss Sawyer, pulled her towards him and looked about vaguely. 'Has anyone seen my darling wife?'

*   *   *

After that Mr Hademak told me I should keep out of the way, so I wandered upstairs to my room at the back of the house—small and simple, but better than the room I had left in Chelsea—and while the music and laughter from downstairs grew steadily louder, I lay on my bed and tried to read.

I couldn't concentrate. It was such an airless night—and my first in this new and exciting place. It seemed preposterous to be spending it alone in that small, hot room. So around ten o'clock I put the book aside. Downstairs I could hear the booming, bawdy voices of the men (and my father's as loud as any of them). They were calling for Miss Sawyer and Mr Guglielmi to dance.

Only imagine it! In your own sitting room! I had read about the exhibition dances that were such a mad craze in America. In my bedroom at home in Chelsea I had attempted (from a magazine article) to teach myself the steps of the Castle Walk.

So, still in my travelling clothes, I crept out of the room, down the back stairs and into the front hall.

There were two doors opening into the long drawing room, one from the hall where I was standing, the other from the dining room. It would have been impossible for me to stand at either without being seen and no doubt shooed away, but I figured, on such a hot night, that the french windows—there were four of them connecting the drawing room to the trellised veranda beyond—

would certainly have been thrown open. I decided the best view would be from the bushes a few yards in front of the house. So, back through the servants' hall I crept, through the side door, through the flowerbeds all the way round the side of the house to the bushes by the driveway out front.

It was wonderful to be outside. I felt the cool evening darkness settle on my skin. The sound of music filled the air, and the great sky glittered with stars—the way it never did at home. Suddenly, as I scrambled through the last of the flowerbeds, struggling not to catch my clothes on invisible thorns, a sense of exultation at my new surroundings, at my new freedom—at being so far from England and the war—overtook me; a great explosion of joy, and it made me bolder than I might otherwise have been. I reached the bushes, which would have hidden me safely, and decided I wasn't close enough. I could get a better view if I climbed right up onto the veranda. So that was what I did. With my heart in my mouth, I tiptoed up the few steps, squeezed into the shadows by the nearest of the open french windows and peered in.

The hotchpotch of rugs had been rolled back, making the room appear even larger and less cared-for than before. Chairs and couches had been arranged in a row along the opposite length of the room, so that the guests were facing out, directly towards me. I was confronted by an array of expensive clothes and shiny, red faces—some of their owners more inebriated than others, of course, though all, I would hazard a guess, a little distance from their sharpest.

In any case it didn't matter which way they were

facing, since everyone's attention was focused not on me but on the end of the room, where the two professional dancers stood facing one another, waiting to begin.

The chubby duke and another man, waxy-faced and horribly thin, were slumped on one couch, leaning feebly one against the other, their eyes glazed with drink. A shoeless woman, wearing trousers, stood behind the waxy-faced gentleman, softly nuzzling his neck. He didn't seem to notice it. Neither did the duke, who appeared to be so far gone I don't suppose he would have blinked if a German Taube had flown across the room and dropped a bomb right there in his lap.

On another couch, pawing one another in languid fashion and both glistening with sweat, was the woman in vibrant yellow, who had earlier so distracted my father, and a dandy gentleman in some sort of military garb, with hair that matched her dress.

And there was another woman, too, alone and dishevelled, propped up in a high-backed rattan chair in the far corner. Her mouth was hanging open, and I think she was asleep. There was Mr Hademak, hovering nervously at the door. And various others, lithe and elegant bodies mostly, lounging this way and that. Finally there was Papa, already smitten—that much was too obvious, even without seeing his face. He perched awkwardly on his chair, his body turned entirely towards Mrs de Saulles, who was stretched out on a chaise-longue beside him, fanning herself. The silly dub had placed himself at such an extreme angle to be in her line of vision that it would be impossible for him to watch the dance. He was talking and

41

jabbering—bending his slim body towards her. But, though she nodded once in a while, she didn't look at him. Her wide—wired—eyes were fixated on the dancers.

Like a circus master, Mr de Saulles stood beside the Victrola, preparing to set the needle down. Finally, he allowed the music to begin. After that I think, judging by the stillness, everyone—except Papa, of course—forgot everyone else.

The two dancers seemed barely to touch as they glided through the empty space between us, not each other or even the floor. Miss Joan Sawyer had looked so ordinary before, but when she danced with Rudy they transformed, together, into a seamless, shimmering stream, so graceful as to seem barely human. The beauty of it, in such inebriated company, seemed to be especially incongruous. They took my breath away. I had been exposed to more of life than most girls of my age; bawdiness, beauty, wickedness and wit. But this—this was glamour! This was something entirely new.

Then the music stopped, and we were returned to earth. Mr de Saulles, with glassy-eyed determination, stepped forward to dance with Miss Sawyer; Mr Guglielmi melted away, ignored by everyone, except Mrs de Saulles, who didn't take her eyes from him—and even before her husband and Miss Sawyer had reached the centre of the room Mr Hademak was at the Victrola, setting the needle to the start again.

Before long most of them were dancing—at least, in a manner of speaking. The chubby duke stood swaying, all alone, his glazed eyes roaming over Miss Sawyer; the waxy man and the trouser girl were clasping each other tight, rocking one way and another in a grim effort to respond to the beat or perhaps simply to stay upright. And then the yellow couple joined them, and a few others, until, of all the guests who remained awake, only Mrs de Saulles and my father remained seated. He was leaning towards her, imploring her; she gazed steadfastly at Rudy. My father leaned closer, imploring harder still. She barely bothered to shake her head. Poor Papa. Women adored him, usually, at least at first. It was painful to see, and I looked away.

*　　*　　*

Rudy—Mr Guglielmi—stood slightly apart, in the corner of the room closest to where I was. I watched him watching them; he looked thoughtful, I remember—perhaps even a little melancholy. And then suddenly he spun away from them all, and the next thing I knew he was walking directly towards me.

I jumped, flattened myself further into the frame of the house. As he stepped out through the french windows and onto the veranda I could feel the breeze of it on my face—I could smell his cologne. He passed me, crossed to the edge of the porch, leaned a shoulder against the trellises and, looking out over the moonlit garden, pulled out a cigarette.

I could hear my own heart beating. The sound of my shallow, panicky breath was half deafening to me. It seemed inexplicable that he couldn't hear it, but he gave no indication. So, trapped between wall and open french window, and horribly conscious of the moonlight shining on my pale dress, I could do nothing but stand and watch.

I watched him pull the cigarette lighter from his pocket. Watched the flare as he put flame to cigarette, watched as he inhaled and exhaled and the smoke floated out into the night. I watched him and wondered how such a very simple act could be so imbued with grace that it became quite mesmerising. He was mesmerising.

He sighed, and it was all I could do not to burst from the shadow right there and throw my arms around him. Actually I might have done—he looked so horribly melancholy, standing there, except I heard footsteps.

A woman's footsteps, light and hurried, coming from the side of the house whence I had crept what felt like such an age before. I could do nothing but squeeze myself closer to the wall and pray— something I rarely did, even then.

I guess I needn't have bothered, so fixed was she on her goal. It was clear to me from the instant Mrs de Saulles appeared that I might have been an almighty elephant and she wouldn't have noticed it. She tripped up the steps onto the porch, full of purpose, and from the expression on her face she seemed a different woman. Still beautiful— without doubt. Nothing could ever change that. But all the wistfulness, all that hollow helplessness, the languid, aristocratic boredom, was gone. She looked angry. She burned with it.

She paused just before she reached him. She stood behind him, directly between the two of us, with her back to me, and seemed to compose herself for a moment; she unclenched her little fists and emitted one of her own little feather-light sighs.

'Rudy?' It sounded tentative.

'Aha!' he said, without quite turning to her. 'So—after all—you are still speaking to me? I didn't imagine you ever would again. Not after last time.'

She took a tiny step closer to him, put a small white hand onto the shoulder of his black evening coat. 'Oh, don't be mean to me, Rudy darling. Please.'

He didn't say anything.

'Only I was wondering . . .' there was a break in her voice '. . . I was wondering if you had reconsidered.'

A long pause. He took a deep pull on his cigarette and tossed it out into the darkness. 'I have considered and reconsidered. I have lost count of all the different views I have taken of the wretched thing,' he said at last. 'And you know it. Blanca . . .' he turned to look at her, finally '. . . I would love to help you but—'

'Oh, yes . . . *Always but.*'

'But what can I do? What can *I* do? In any case, the world knows it already. Look, now! The two of them are entwined like lovers and there is a roomful of guests to look on. Why—of all people—why do you ask me?'

'Because . . .' she said, edging further in '. . . because, Rudy, you are my only friend.' He looked at her, fondly, I think—and yet unconvinced. She was standing very close, so close they could feel each other's breath, I'm sure; so close he could have kissed her at any moment. He looked, I think, as if he wanted to.

I felt horribly jealous! Even then. And (I admit) entirely riveted, too. Part of me could hardly believe my good fortune to be walking in on such

45

intrigue—and my first night in a new place! The other half wished the world would swallow me. There was a long pause between them and I noticed his expression soften. He ran a fingertip along her bare arm—as if he'd done it many times before—and he smiled. 'Sweetheart,' he said, 'you have a new "friend" every fortnight so far as I can tell.'

'Don't be horrid.'

He didn't say anything.

Gently, she dropped her head onto his shoulder. 'You don't believe me,' she murmured, 'but, Rudy, you are my only true friend. In all the world,' and it sounded for a moment as if she might be about to cry.

'I am trying to believe you, Blanca,' he replied, briefly touching her dark hair. 'I should love to believe you. Or—no, I don't mean that. I mean to say—I should love to believe that we were even friends at all . . .' Gently, he stepped away from her, so she had no choice but to take back her head. 'Only I'm not even certain you understand what is meant by the word.'

'How can you say that?'

'In any case you have friends everywhere, Blanca. Lovers, friends . . . Wherever you are. People fall at your feet. The English gentleman this evening, the portrait painter, for a simple example. He can't take his eyes off you. And I know you will deny it but even your husband—he looks over to you even while he is dancing with Joan.'

She waved it aside. '*You* don't adore me, though,' she said.

He laughed aloud. 'Self-preservation, Blanca! I

46

know you well enough. In any case,' he added, 'I'm only the dance tutor. It's not my place to adore you.'

'One can adore a woman from any place. From her bed, in particular. I seem to remember.'

'Yes, perhaps.' He pulled out his cigarette box. She watched him tapping on it nervously. I watched him, too. 'I want to help you,' he said. 'Of course I want to help you. Except I'm convinced you only ask me as a sort of—test. A proof of your power, as a woman. Regardless of what the consequences to me may be.'

'Oh, Rudy, that's ridiculous.'

'Only because I won't fall at your feet, like all the other men.'

'You fell into my bed!'

'We fell into your bed together. And it was hardly—frankly—it was hardly as if I were the first. Or the second. Or the third . . .'

'But you were!'

'Ha! Which, Blanca?'

Her lip trembled. 'You are too revolting,' she whispered—and he seemed to relent a little. He stroked her hair again, with affection and tenderness, until she recovered.

'I am poor, and Italian, and an immigrant. Your husband, with half Tammany Hall behind him—he would cause nothing but trouble for me. Have me thrown in jail. Have me returned to Italy. God knows . . .'

'Don't be absurd, Rudy,' she said carelessly. 'Of course not.'

'At very least,' he said, 'I will lose my job. You know it.'

'Does our friendship mean so little to you, then?

47

That you wouldn't even sacrifice that?'

'I would sacrifice it and much more—and for any friend—if I believed it was truly necessary. But it is not. There are so many others, with nothing to lose, who would be perfectly willing—Ruth, for example. She would do it for you! She adores you! And she's richer than Croesus. Your husband couldn't harm her. He wouldn't want to and he wouldn't dare. Why don't you go and ask her—now? Right now, while your husband is still dancing?'

'I don't *want*—' she started angrily, but stopped herself. Sighed a small sigh, light as little feather. 'Rudy, darling Rudy, you are mistaken. Ruth is not a friend! I despise her! I despise them all! *You*, Rudy, are my only friend. Whether you are willing to acknowledge it or not. Tell me—truly—who else can I ask?'

'We go over it again,' he sighed, 'but you don't listen. I said to you last time I could write a list of ten or more names. And I will even ask them for you. They would be willing to give evidence for you . . . People who have nothing to lose by it, who would be more than happy to help.'

She continued in the same pitiful voice as if he hadn't spoken. 'I am alone, Rudy, far away from my family . . . far away from everyone I love . . . And I know you know what it is to be alone. You have told me so. You *know* what it is like to yearn for home . . .'

'I do.' He sounded weary.

'And you have seen me crying my heart out . . .'

'I have.'

'And yet still you refuse me? Even though you understand my torment . . . and the others don't

. . . Oh, I long for my home, Rudy. I am sick for it. You don't have children. You can't imagine . . . how a mother feels.'

He gave a burst of laughter. 'What on earth does that have to do with it?'

'All I ask is that you attest to something in a courtroom which you know to be true . . . Is it so much to ask?'

Her small white hand was back on his shoulder. She was edged so close to him, and in the long, warm silence that followed, I swear they might have kissed. But just then a loud voice came from the drawing room: 'Blanquita? . . . Blanca, darling? . . . Anyone seen my wife?'

'She's on the loggia with the wop,' we heard His Grace declare, 'having a smoki-poo or some such . . . Wish I could persuade her to have a smoki-poo with *me* . . .'

A moment later, in time for Rudy and Mrs de Saulles to step apart, her husband was at the french windows. 'Sweetheart,' he said, ignoring Rudy and not noticing me, still flattened between window and wall, barely two foot away from him, 'why don't you come dance, sweetie? I should so love to dance with you.'

'I'm very tired,' she said.

'Just a quick dance?' he said, stumbling slightly, as he stepped towards her. 'Please? With your admiring husband . . . who so entirely admires and adores you?' He was very drunk.

She turned away. 'I'm not certain I can imagine anything I should like to do less,' she said. 'Besides, I can see Joan over there, looking awfully hopeful. I'm convinced she's longing to dance with you again . . .'

49

And with that she hurried away, leaving my employer and his not-quite-guest in uncomfortable silence. They looked at one another, Rudy with some dislike, I think, Mr de Saulles with something much closer to anger. He hesitated, as if on the point of saying something, but then seemed to think better of it. Without another word he spun around and followed his wife's path back into the house.

And still I stood there. Rudy turned back to the position he'd taken before Mrs de Saulles had interrupted him, and snapped open his cigarette box. It glinted in the moonlight . . . I watched again as flame and cigarette connected, as the light of the flame played on his face, and the smoke rose from his lips. I watched him gaze out into the darkness, deep in thought. And once again I was amazed by him—his elegance and grace.

After what felt an unendurably long pause, during which I'm quite certain I neither moved nor breathed, he suddenly said, 'It's all right, by the way—you can come out now. It's quite safe.'

I didn't. I clung to my wall, and to the forlorn hope that he might perhaps have been talking to someone else. But then he turned and looked directly at me. 'I'll step away from this spot, shall I,' he said, 'to a spot over here, where we can't be seen? Come out and tell me why you've been standing there all this time.' He smiled at me. '*Spying* on us . . .'

'I wasn't spying.'

'What else could you call it?'

'I was stuck.'

'Ah.'

By then he had travelled to the far end of the

50

veranda, out of view of the french windows. He turned and beckoned for me to join him there so, with some reluctance, I edged from my hiding place to be beside him . . . And we stood in silence, quite close to one another, with the music from the Victrola seeping out through the warm night air, and with me wondering at nothing, in spite of all I had just witnessed, but the richness of his voice . . .

He seemed to be waiting for further explanation and I felt an irresistible urge to fill the delicious silence with some of my habitual babble.

So I told him the truth—something I always do when I'm nervous (I still do it today, despite quite strenuous efforts to break the habit). I explained how I'd come down from my room because I had wanted to watch the dancing . . . and I might easily have finished it there, except I didn't. I told him everything about how mad I was for the new type of dancing—and about how I'd read a little of Miss Sawyer while I was still in England, and about how I had always longed to see a real tango, danced by the professionals, and about how I thought he and Miss Sawyer were the most fabulous, most magical dancers I had ever set eyes on. 'I was going to watch you from the garden,' I said to him, 'but then I realised the windows were open and I could get a better view from the porch, and—I'm so sorry, truly—very sorry, Mr Guglielmi. I didn't hear a word you and Mrs de Saulles were saying. Not a word.'

He smiled. 'Your hearing is damaged?'

'By which I mean, that is, not a word that made the slightest bit of sense to me . . . In any case, it has nothing to do with me. I am sorry, but there

51

was nothing I could do. First *you* came out and then *she* came out. And then *he* came out . . . And I was utterly trapped . . .'

He asked me my name after that and I told him. Jennifer. Jennifer Doyle from London. 'My father is the portrait painter in there. The one who can't remove his eyes from Mrs de Saulles.'

'No one ever can,' he said grimly.

I wasn't sure what to make of that. 'It drives her quite mad if we aren't all head over heels in love with her,' he said.

'Well,' I replied carefully, 'then I suppose my father is keeping her happy.'

He glanced at me. 'It's hard for her. To be here. So far from family . . .'

'I'm sure it is.'

'But tell me—never mind that—tell me something more about yourself. What are you doing, here at this house?'

'Well—I am—his daughter. And he is an excellent painter. And I'm here to teach the boy to speak good English, I think. Though I don't quite understand that because his mother seems to speak perfectly good English herself.'

'Of course, because she was educated in England.'

'She was? . . . Well. Well, then, I'm not certain. I'm also meant to keep company with Mrs de Saulles, apparently. Due to her being so far away from home, my father said. But she doesn't much seem to want that and—apart from just now—I've not really even met her yet . . . I asked Mr Hademak several times this afternoon what my job here was meant to be—and all he can say is, I'm supposed to make them "giggle", which isn't something I've ever been particularly good at. But. Anyway, I have no idea what I'm doing here really, Mr Guglielmi. I wish I did . . . I'm a not-quite-guest,' I added, 'a bit like you'—and immediately regretted it. 'Only even more so, because they don't seem to want me to do anything . . . Except stay out of sight.'

He laughed aloud at that. A wonderful laugh, it was—it still is: heartfelt, so warm, and so magically infectious. I heard myself laughing with him . . . And then, from the drawing room, the music reached us . . . just a silly ditty, it was. So silly.

You made me love you . . .
I didn't want to do it
. . .You made me want you . . .
And all the time you knew it
. . . I guess you always knew it
. . . I guess you always knew it . . .

I think I fell silent. He said, 'You look worried.' But I wasn't worried! I was listening to the music, and the night creatures, and feeling the warm air on my skin. I could feel nothing but the music, the warm air—and his voice—and I longed for him to ask me to dance, and in my head the longing obscured everything. I was frightened he might ask me to dance and yet even more frightened that he would not, and that this moment would end without his arms around me, and he said, 'It's beautiful music, isn't it?'

And it was!

You made me love you. . .
I didn't want to do it

53

. . .You made me want you . . .
And all the time you knew it. . .

'Do you like to dance, Jenny?'

I told him I loved to dance. And whatever else it may have been, it was bold of me, I think, to dare to dance with him, after I had seen him dance with Miss Sawyer.

For once, I resisted the urge to babble. I was silent. Without any more words, he turned to me— and we danced. There on the veranda, by the light of the moon . . . I swear I never danced so well. I think, in his arms, it would have been impossible to dance badly—as if his grace were like his laughter: irresistibly, magically infectious . . . the most generous dancer, the most generous lover; the most generous man in the world.

. . . Did I write that I hadn't fallen in love with him that night? Did I write that?

How absurd!

And now I simply have to sleep.

HOTEL CONTINENTAL

NEW YORK

Saturday, 14 August 1926

Not so sure what to do with myself. Don't want to sit, in case the dress creases. But it's only seven o'clock. I have two hours to kill and—oh, hell, maybe I should change back into my chemise, just for a short while. But then I shall want to shower again, in this heat, and it was a long enough wait to get a turn in there the first time, and then suppose they ran out of water? Besides, it so happens I look just about as good at this particular instant as I have in my entire life.

The party's too far to walk. Maybe I'll take a taxicab, which means leaving at—what time? I mustn't arrive before Rudy. They may not even let me in! But if I arrive too long after he does he may think I'm not coming at all.

I'm so goddamn nervous. I could have dined with him at the Colony tonight, and gone on with him to see the show. Why didn't I? He said he'd come by and pick me up, and I know he wanted to.

He said, I can't contemplate a whole evening without you . . . Only I couldn't contemplate an evening of sharing him, I suppose; of dining with him and all the others whom I know he is obliged to be dining with tonight. I couldn't have done it—

as his date? I think not! As his newly engaged scenario writer? Perhaps . . . Except then I would have to sit there in my off-the-peg beautiful, beautiful dress, and my off-the-peg beautiful satin slippers, and smile sweetly, which isn't my style, and they would all bawl at one another across the table about this and that, and whether Rudy and Pola intend to be here or there . . . I couldn't quite have done it. I would have half shrunk into the floorboards, and that's no way to keep a man's interest, when he's recently been voted the most desirable movie star in history . . .

The party tonight is in his honour, as parties he attends are prone to be, these days. I should have preferred not to go to that either, and to wait to see him tomorrow, when we can be alone again, but he wouldn't hear of it. He said he would send his driver to fetch me. I said I didn't know where I would be, and he said he would order his driver to search every corner of the city until he found me.

So I've said to the nice fat guy—the room clerk—at the front desk that when a driver and a big car arrives for me he is to send them right away again. The fat guy was dreadfully curious, needless to say, but I wouldn't give him any more details.

I shall make my own way. When I'm good and calm and ready. That's what I'll do. Call a taxicab. Or something . . . Oh, God . . .

A cigarette!

And a cold shower.

The trouble with this new-fangled, fancy-pants typewriter, which I adore more than anything I ever had, except the dress—no, *including* the dress—the trouble with this beautiful machine is you can get the words out so fast that you wind up scribbling down any amount of hogwash. So. A little self-control is what I seem to be lacking. (Nothing new there, I guess.)

Two hours to kill until I see him, or slightly less now, and not enough running water in the joint for me to be sure of another cold shower. I wish I could sit still. I wish I could stop remembering his hands on me, his eyes on me, his tongue, his fingers, his kiss, his . . . Oh, I shall go crazy any minute. I shall go stark raving round the twist.

*   *   *

A long, deep breath . . . A slurp of magic, rancid moonshine from my little flask . . .
Much better.

> This Is What I Did Today
> On the Second Best Day of My Life
> By Lola Nightingale
> a.k.a. Jennifer Doyle
> a.k.a. Mrs Rudolph Valent— I'm getting ahead of myself.

*   *   *

So I slept for six hours straight and I swear I've not done that since God knows when. First, I didn't sleep until the day was already begun and I could hear the autos honking and grinding outside, and my skin was already beginning to prickle with the morning heat. And then, finally, when I woke, half the day was already gone. I heard a bang and a crash outside, and somebody knocking at my door. I staggered out of my cot with every intention of being vile to whomever I found on the other side.

Fortunately for them, by the time I opened the door there was no one out there—not a soul. Just the biggest, sweetest-smelling mountain of pink lilies that I ever laid eyes on, and in the middle of it all this typewriter! With a great ribbon tied around it. Not just any typewriter either . . . Rudy left a card tucked in. I have it here:

Ha ha ha! That's what he wrote.
Cara Mia, thank you!
And by the way, if you are wondering what the long wire is for . . . you have to plug this machine into an electrical point before it can record your wonderful words.
  You are brilliant as well as beautiful.
XXXXXX

Imagine that. Brilliant as well as beautiful.

I don't suppose even Frances Marion has an electrical typewriting machine she can call her own. She probably doesn't know they exist. I certainly did not until this morning. I don't think they have even heard of them at the studio, because Mr Silverman, the old tyrant, is very proud of his modern approach with gadgets so I'm certain if *he* knew there was such a machine he would have acquired one by now so all the people passing through the outer office could admire it, and think what a fine, modern fellow he is. God only knows where Rudy must have found it—or when—between last night and today . . .

But here it is. And, come what may, just as soon as I am the slightest bit cooler—in body and mind—I intend to use it religiously, to write hundreds of photoplays. Some of them for Phoebe and Lorna, of course, because I promised I would, and I must. And then all the rest of them—for not a soul but Rudy. If that's what he would like.

Well—except the one I must write for Miss Davies, I suppose. If Miss Marion says I should.

* * *

I was meant to watch that wretched Marion Davies movie this morning. I had been meaning to watch it in time to meet Frances Marion for luncheon, but then she left a message saying she couldn't make our appointment after all. And what a stroke of luck *that* was, considering by the time I got the message I had already slept right through it anyway.

It frightens me, though, to have been so careless. It frightens me even more to notice just how little I can bring myself to care.

One hour and forty minutes . . . Oh, but it's so humid tonight! Perhaps if I type with my elbows out . . . *like this* . . . and I have a jug of coolish water by the bed perhaps I can dab it on my forehead . . . carefully. . . else my hair will go into a frizz . . .

Tomorrow, if Rudy has nothing better to do, he might come with me back to the Strand, and we can watch the movie together. If he kept his hat on, or he wore the silly disguise I just bought him . . . and if we sat at the back, and we stayed as quiet as possible and he made a great effort to look entirely innocuous—might he still be spotted? He tells me he goes regularly to the movies back in Hollywood, despite having a screening room of his own at home. But then, I suppose, Hollywood is Hollywood. There are stars about wherever you care to look. Take a walk down Sunset and you'll generally spot one or another driving by . . . Only last week, in fact, Pola Negri almost ran me down in her Pierce Arrow. Her turquoise-and-gold Pierce Arrow. If you please. Ha! If she'd known whom she was steering towards, she might have tried a little harder. The point is, in Hollywood even a star as big as Rudy is let alone to go about his business without being constantly mobbed.

Trouble is, this isn't Hollywood, and in New York people get a little crazy. You'd think mobbing the stars was some kind of a city sport, the way they behave. It's as if they read something in the paper and the next thing they can't leave it alone. They've just got to be a part of the story.

*   *   *

I did ask Rudy about Pola. Eventually. I think it was before we got into that beautiful Chinese bed, but maybe it was after. She seemed irrelevant. She did, and she still does, but I had to ask him because it's been in the papers for months. Every article they write, they ask him about it, and he always answers the same. He says, *You must ask the lady.* It's his stock reply. He won't say yes, and he won't say no. Whereas when they interview *Pola,* she won't shut up

60

about it . . .

So, I asked him if he was engaged to be married to her and I do believe if he'd told me to *ask the lady* I would have done—what? He didn't say it, of course. He simply laughed.

He said, 'Oh, Lord, Jennifer, is that a serious question?'

I said it was.

He said, 'You ask me that? Now? When I look at you like this, and you look at me as you do, you can ask me that?'

'I just did, didn't I?'

And he sighed. 'Well, now . . .' he began carefully '. . . Pola . . . is a sweet girl.'

'Oh! Sweet!' I interrupted. '*Is that right?*' Because there are plenty of adjectives that spring to mind when describing that attention-seeking little *sex*-crazy minx. But *sweet* for sure ain't one of 'em!

He smiled. 'Oh. Well—perhaps that's not entirely right,' he said. 'No, I suppose, not entirely. But . . . I am fond of her. She has some remarkable aspects . . .' For a moment he looked on the point of laughter, but he pulled himself back. 'Really, Jennifer, I am no more engaged to be married to Pola than I am engaged to William Randolph Hearst. How could you possibly imagine, after all we have said and done—'

'Because she keeps on saying it,' I said. 'And nobody ever seems to contradict her.'

'It wouldn't be terribly chivalrous . . .'

There was a pause between us then. I wasn't so sure how to fill it. Until suddenly he shuddered and then, rather sheepishly, he added, 'Jennifer, if you want to know, she is a nightmare. A crazy

61

woman!'

'A crazy woman—whom you formed an attachment to?'

'Well, I admit that I did form a *sort of* attachment to her, briefly . . . after the divorce . . . I was dreadfully low. But she's like a dog with a bone! By that I mean to say,' he added quickly, 'she's a very sweet girl in her own way . . . An extraordinary girl—and I am full of admiration . . . But if anyone could advise me on how to shake her . . .'

I must admit, I felt rather better after that. I didn't mention her name again. And I'm not thinking too much about her. Not so much. If I do—if I allow myself to dwell on Pola, not to mention all the others—I shall soon be even madder than she is, and furthermore without an eighth of her beauty, wealth or fame. In any case I am delighted she's not in New York at the moment. She's back in Los Angeles, shooting a movie about a wicked count and an adorable servant girl . . . And good luck to her, I guess.

I went shopping again this afternoon. I had to. I came to New York with just two evening dresses—three, I guess, if you count the other one, which was only ever meant as a spare. I tried it on in front of the glass and I knew at once it was all wrong. It looked cheap, even to my not-so-terribly-expensive eye . . . And Rudy isn't like a lot of men: he certainly notices these things. He appreciates beauty, elegance and all that. So I was standing there in front of the glass, seeing the wretched dress as I imagined he would see it, and just knowing I would have to go and buy another, and thinking about all the other things I had meant to do today—watch the Marion Davies movie, visit Papa's grave, which I've not done, not even once, not since . . . and then I realised that, more than anything else, more than a new dress, even, I needed to get a gift for Rudy.

I wandered up and down Fifth Avenue in a ferment of indecision. A mah-jong set? A cigarette case? Something terribly clever? I went to some lengths to discover what was the most recent offering from Sigmund Freud . . . *Inhibitions, Symptoms and Anxiety* . . . Well, I flicked through *that* pretty briefly, and thought I would probably die from all the symptoms of every anxiety under the sun, if I ever laid eyes on the thing again . . . Finally, I was on the point of buying a live parrot (green and yellow and quite stunning—Rudy adores animals) when I had the most wonderful brainwave.

I headed to Altman's and bought him the disguise. There is a Homburg hat and some spectacles, and a wig made from the hair of some poor German, I suppose. Or Swede. It's quite blond—actually it reminded me of Justin Hademak. I don't suppose Rudy will much want to wear it, my funny wig—but he might. He doesn't complain but I see how it gnaws at him to be constantly recognised and fawned over. I think in some ways he is horrified by what he has done—the crazy whirlwind he has created. But perhaps it won't last for ever. Perhaps one day he will be forgotten again, and we will be free to wander about, with our children around us, like any ordinary couple in love. Perhaps we could live in Italy. And he could build his cars and breed his horses, and I could write . . .

By the time I'd collected all the parts for his disguise it was late, the shops were about to close for the evening, so I had no choice but to stay at Altman's—which was not quite the place I had in mind when I set out to buy the perfect evening dress. (I should be astonished if Pola Negri had ever crossed its threshold. Ditto for the last Mrs Valentino.)

But then *there it was*! Just crying out to me . . . the most beautiful dress I had ever laid eyes on and, by the way, at seventy-five dollars, the most expensive dress I have bought in my entire life.

It's of pale blue, made from the sheerest, sleekest satin, with a hemline a little lower at the back but to the knee at the front. And there are flowers embroidered at the back—which scoops very low—and at the hip-band there are flowers too, only slightly larger ones.

And then, of course, I had to buy a set of beads to bring out the blue of the flowers, and slippers to match the beads—if only I'd stopped there. I was about to. But on my way out, when already I was feeling quite sick about the money I'd spent—I saw the stole. It was of rabbit skin—like the stole Papa gave me, and which I gave to Madeleine in the midst of all my angry grief when I simply couldn't bear to look at the thing again. It was the same colour. That's all. How many hundreds of rabbit skins have I seen in the intervening years and thought nothing about them? But this one stopped me, on this hot August day. There I was on my way out of the store, and I simply couldn't move away from it. Exhaustion, I suppose, mental and physical. I stood in the middle of Altman's, my fingers running through the fur and the maddest tears streaming down my face: tears for my father, tears I haven't wept in many years, and they wouldn't stop.

I felt quite a prize fool. And I'm sure Mr Sigmund *Inhibitions-and-Anxieties* Freud would have plenty to say on the matter. Too bad. Only it's true that just then, at that particular moment, I felt my papa very close.

Buck up, my silly friend, I could hear him saying. He would have been horribly embarrassed. And pleased, perhaps, and even surprised—as surprised as I was—to discover that I miss him still, and that I am still so very, very fond of him. I felt his arms around me. Truly, I did. How silly is that? I could hear him teasing me; and it made me smile. And I picked up the wretched rabbit fur—all fifty-eight dollars of it, if you please—and I gave it to the shopgirl, who wrapped it up in tissue. I have it here, lying on the bed, still wrapped in tissue. It's far too hot for tonight. Too hot for Hollywood. Heaven only knows what I shall do with it.

1916–17

LONG ISLAND

The plan, so far as I understood it, had been for Papa to go back to the city with Mr de Saulles first thing the following morning. Mr de Saulles had, until that point, taken quite a shine to Papa, of course, and I think he'd been intending for the pair of them to have a lot of fun together. He would

65

show my father round town a bit, and help him to drum up work among his rich friends.

But I guess Mr de Saulles's friendly and helpful intentions were just too advantageous for Papa not to feel driven to sabotage them. I often wondered if Mrs de Saulles hadn't played some part in it too—if she and Papa hadn't cooked up something together the previous evening. It doesn't matter anyway. The point is, Papa had fallen madly in love with her and was, as always, unwilling to fight or even to hide it. His budding friendship with her husband, which promised to be so helpful to his career, rather withered on the branch as a result. It didn't survive beyond breakfast, in actual fact.

Papa informed everyone in the dining room that morning (young Jack Junior and myself included) that he had decided not to travel to Manhattan with his host but to stay behind at The Box.

'Would you mind awfully, Jack?' Papa said, pulling a long face. 'Only it's so frightfully hot in the city. And my lungs . . .' He gave a series of feeble little coughs. 'It would be far better for me if I stayed here a while. Until it cools down. I could set to work at once . . . Perhaps begin with a painting of your delightful son . . . Or perhaps Mrs de Saulles . . . if she will permit it?'

A silence fell. An awkward clattering of knives and forks. My father's intentions were obvious and I think, even in that brazen crowd, everyone was slightly embarrassed.

Mr de Saulles didn't bother to look up from his plate. After a while, his mouth still full of griddled waffle, he said, 'Your lungs are perfectly fine, old sport. And I've made all sorts of plans for you. Come back to town with me.'

66

My father coughed a bit louder.

'Oh, do stop,' Mr de Saulles said.

'I wish I *could* stop, Jack. Sincerely. I do.' (Cough cough.) 'I really think I should call a doctor.'

Mr de Saulles just kept shovelling in more of the griddled waffle, and nobody spoke.

'I must say,' the duke finally piped up, 'you seemed perfectly fine last night. It's rather boring of you to—suddenly decide you're ill. Just like that.'

'I couldn't agree with you more. And I can't tell you how sorry I am.' Cough cough cough. 'But last night is one thing. This morning, I hardly need to point out to you, Your Grace, is entirely another.'

Silence again. This time it was Mrs de Saulles who broke it. Looking not at her husband or at my father but at Rudy, she said, 'Well, if you're utterly determined that Marcus should paint me, Jack . . . Although honestly I can't see why you would be . . .'

'Because, sweetest, you are my wife. And I should like to have a painting of you.'

'Well, then, he might as well paint me now as later. I intend to be home in Santiago by the end of next month in any case.'

Clearly, it was the first he had heard of it. He looked at his wife—they all looked at her, the duke, the thin man with the waxy face, Miss Sawyer, my father—all of them looked at her, except the one whose attention she sought: Rudy, I think, made a point of looking anywhere else. He caught my eye, briefly, sent me the smallest flicker of a smile, and I felt myself blushing.

* * *

67

So, the meal ended on what might be called a sour note. Papa got what he wanted. As, of course, did Mrs de Saulles, even if her motivation was less immediately obvious. After breakfast Mr de Saulles climbed into his car, Miss Sawyer at his side and a black cloud over his head. He drove off without addressing a word to anyone, except his son. There was a moment, as the boy clung to his father's leg, when it seemed he might even have taken the child with him, simply scooped him up and dropped him in the back of the auto. But then he glanced at his wife, seemed to wince slightly at the look she gave him, and apparently thought better of it.

'I shall come and fetch you in a day or two,' he said instead. 'Don't cry, little fellow. Crying is for girls. Instead, Jack, as soon as I get into the car you must start counting. All right? And I promise you, before you have reached a hundred hours, I shall be here again! Understand? Start counting, Jack. I shall be back before you know it . . . And with a whole carful of toys!'

There was a grim, subdued flurry as the guests said their goodbyes. Nobody quite knew how to deal with my father, who stood before the front of the house, waving them off as if the house were his already. I think that was the first time I wondered if Papa was altogether—*all there*. It looks a bit rotten, seeing it on paper like that, but there was a hint of something unhinged about the utterly determined, quite shameless fashion of his standing there. I remember feeling embarrassed— worse: I felt ashamed.

68

Before getting into the waiting auto Rudy crossed the gravel to say goodbye to them both. He reached out for Mrs de Saulles's languid little hand.

'Mr Hademak will call you when I am ready for more dance classes,' I heard her saying. 'Perhaps in a day or two . . .'

'I shall look forward to it,' he said. But he didn't smile, and neither did she, and then she glanced at my father, so attentive to her—and even before the cars drove off, the two of them had started their slow wander back into the house.

Rudy said goodbye to me last. He sought me out, took my hand with both of his and, in a low voice that only I could hear, told me how he hoped we should meet again soon. 'I enjoyed our dance together very much,' he said.

And then he was gone, and we at The Box were left alone: Papa, Mrs de Saulles, young Jack, his Jane Eyre and the rest of the servants. The place felt very still.

I looked across at the little boy, who was trying hard not to cry. God knows how I broke the ice—I wasn't accustomed to children—but somehow I persuaded him to take my hand, and before long he and I were chattering happily and he was taking me to visit his nursery.

I remember he hesitated just as we were about to open the door. He looked up at me with those big brown eyes. 'You know, after this, you probably shan't like me terribly much,' he said. 'I mean to say when you see all my toys. You shall probably think I'm dreadfully spoiled.'

I don't know what I answered—something soothing and untrue about having a nursery of my own back home in London, so full of toys I couldn't open the door. 'In any case, I've already seen your nursery, and so far I like you very much.' And suddenly, inexplicably, he simply melted into giggles.

It's nothing. Just a stupid thing. But something about the way he laughed—far from dislike him—I loved him right away. He was the sweetest, warmest, frankest, most humorous, most entirely adorable little boy I ever met . . . But I am getting maudlin. I miss him. That's all. And I wonder whatever became of him.

*   *   *

Papa was a slow worker. He always pretended not to care about his work, presumably because he had failed to make much of a mark with it, but I know he did care, passionately. Not just from the look of concentration that came over his face as soon as he had pencil in hand, but from his stubborn unwillingness ever to accept that a piece of work was finished. Perhaps if he had cared a little less he might have done a little better. Probably. It doesn't matter now, in any case. Either way, when the time came for him to leave The Box he had little to show for all the hours he'd spent closeted away with his muse: a canvas that was almost blank— and a collection of small sketches. But they were wonderful sketches. Some of the best of his I ever saw. In spite of his ardour—or perhaps because of it—he had uncovered something in her that most people never saw: the harshness in her elfin face; and in those big doe eyes, an unmistakable gleam of ruthlessness. If only he could have heeded it as

70

sharply as he drew it. But taking heed was not in his nature. By the end of that first day, he and Mrs de Saulles had retired to her bedroom, and for the next few weeks we saw very little of them.

In the meantime Mr de Saulles barely appeared at The Box. When he did, it was with a large group of friends in tow, and Papa would usually start up with his coughing again and stay in bed. But young Jack was not forgotten. He often travelled back and forth to visit his father in the city. And each time, when he returned (with a nursery-maid, sadly never with me—I don't think Mr de Saulles much wanted to be reminded of anything related to my father's existence) he looked exhausted. I used to tell him about the long nights I spent with my own father and his friends back home in London. 'The trick,' I said, 'is to learn to sleep while still at the table, in a position that looks as though you're awake. Then they won't disturb you, and you won't disturb them.'

We used to practise it together, with the two elbows in front and a hand covering each cheek, carefully obscuring the eyes. Finally, after we agreed he had perfected the position, he lifted his face from his chubby young hands, and he said, with that sweet formality of his, 'And now I shall never be able to forget you, Jennifer, even after you leave, because I shall think of you every time I fall asleep.'

Oh . . . but damn it! Now the tears are welling again, and I shall ruin everything . . .

Jack and I would spend hours together up in that overcrowded nursery. We would lie on the floor side by side, dismantling that wretched steam engine, and I would tell him stories about an

71

imaginary England, a magical England, full of kings and queens and knights—oh, and of loving, living mothers and so forth—and nothing of the brutal, dowdy wartime England that I had left behind and barely missed at all.

When Jack was away with his father I used to feel quite bereft. I would mope about the house hoping for a chance to catch Papa alone, which I never did, and mostly feeling rather sorry for myself.

But he was not my only friend, of course. Madeleine and I enjoyed each other's company. We used to reminisce about Europe—though her memories of Ireland and mine of London had very little in common. And we used to spend enjoyable stolen minutes, swapping tales of outrage about our dreadful employer. For the most part, though, Mrs de Saulles was so demanding, sending poor Madeleine this way and that, and winding her up to a point of such terrible tension, she rarely had the mind or the time to chatter. It wasn't until later that we became close friends.

Mr Hademak, too, would occasionally pause from his nervous activity, and we would sit in the kitchen and discuss the 'flickers', as he still insisted on calling them. There was plenty for us to talk about, since—though back then I had only the faintest idea of what it might involve—I was already determined to forge some sort of career as a writer of movies. I told Mr Hademak so, and he was quite encouraging. He found an unwanted typewriter, which belonged to Mr de Saulles, and he arranged for me to have use of it, though only, he said, when Mrs de Saulles was out of the house, for fear the noise disturb her. We talked about that—my unformed dreams of the future. Mostly, though, it would be Mr Hademak doing the talking, telling me how much improved every film on earth would be if only the director had had the foresight to make Mary Pickford its star. He adored Mary Pickford to such a degree that I wondered sometimes where it left his beloved Mrs de Saulles.

*   *   *

The highlight of my life, of course, was when Rudy came by. And as her affair with my father continued (at some volume, I might add, especially when she knew Rudy was near) Mrs de Saulles began to summon him more and more, until there came a point when he would be at The Box almost daily. She told Hademak she was keen to have as many dance lessons as possible before her return to Chile—but the truth was, there was no return to Chile booked, and though Rudy came, day after day, Mrs de Saulles only rarely bothered to come down from her little tower, even to speak to him.

Rudy didn't seem to mind. He seemed to know what game she was playing—and since she paid him well for his time I have to presume he was grateful for the money. He would sit on the veranda gazing out over that garden, smoking one cigarette after another, with the cries of his employer's lovemaking echoing overhead.

At first, when he came from the city, I would hide away, too shy to let him see me. But then one day Jack and I were in the garden when Rudy's car pulled up.

Jack began to dance about—he adored Rudy, as

I imagined all children would. In any case I snapped at him to be still and he stopped dancing at once. He looked at me consideringly—long and hard. He said, 'Are you in love with Mr Guglielmi?'

'What? Don't be ridiculous!'

'All the girls are. My papa said. So I don't see why you wouldn't be.'

'For Heaven's sake!'

Jack ignored my plea to stay quiet, and bounded over the garden to greet him. I hung back, watching with some jealousy, I suppose, as Rudy's face lit up. He threw down his cigarette, caught the boy in his open arms, with that peculiar grace of his, and tossed him high in the air. You could hear their laughter through the garden—over the grunts and groans oozing from other quarters . . . Oh, I'm exaggerating, of course. But the truth is, it was wonderful to watch them together: an unexpected blast of joy in that miserable, complicated household.

I had planned to slip quietly away, but Rudy saw me before I got a chance. 'Aha! Jennifer!' he cried. 'I was hoping I would see you! But where are you going?'

'I'm going . . .' Where was I going? 'Well, I'm going to the house, of course. But I shall be back in a minute,' I said. 'I have to fetch something from the nursery.'

I saw Jack mumbling something into his ear, then Rudy nodding solemnly, smiling slightly, glancing back at me.

'That's all it is.' Jack whispered loudly. 'You see?'

'Oh, absolutely,' Rudy said—loud enough for me to hear it. 'How extremely fortunate for me.'

At which point I'm almost certain I broke into a

run.

Madeleine was in the hall—at a loose end for once. 'Wait up!' she said, delighted to find someone to gossip with. 'Have you seen who's here again, Jennifer?'

'I have,' I said.

'Surprised you're not out there. Batting your eyelids.'

'Oh, be quiet.'

'He's handsome.'

'I know it.'

'And so does *she.*' She indicated the tower boudoir. 'Crazy bitch,' she added, because she always did.

*   *   *

Madeleine followed me into the nursery and I suppose half an hour passed while she filled me in with details, some of which I could have survived without, regarding the conversation she had only that morning overheard between Mrs de Saulles and my father.

'Though it wasn't really a conversation, to be honest with you, Jennifer,' she was saying. 'More a series of grunts.'

'I don't believe you.'

'Yes, you do. And with me in the room, too! Good God, to look at them both—him an old man and her fragile as feather—on the *outside*. The crazy bitch. You wouldn't believe they had it in them.'

'Yes—well. The racket they make, I should think the whole of Long Island knows it by now,' I said.

'And there was me thinking, after a certain

75

number of years, the mechanism stopped working. Didn't you? A man as old as your father . . .'

'He's not *that* old . . .'

'But the mechanism—'

'Anything! Please! Can we talk of *anything* but my filthy papa and his ancient mechanism!'

We were laughing loudly, both of us, sprawled out lazily on the nursery floor. I looked up and there, standing side by side, were Rudy and Jack.

Madeleine gave a silly shriek.

'Sounds like I missed an excellent beginning,' Rudy said.

'Not at all,' I said, scrambling to sit up. 'Actually Madeleine was being disgusting.'

'I didn't mean to interrupt.'

'No, no,' said I. 'No no no.'

Madeleine guffawed.

'Only Jack told me,' Rudy said, 'there was a steam engine up here, not working as well as it once did?'

'Quite the opposite, Mr Guglielmi,' gurgled Madeleine. 'On the contrary. Ask Jennifer's papa!'

How I longed to knock her out! Rudy looked for a moment as if he might be about to laugh himself—but then I suppose he saw the mortification on my face and thought better of it. He said, 'Jack said he had a toy train that was broken. I thought perhaps I could fix it.'

'And Jack is absolutely right,' I said. 'Madeleine—' I looked at her, and almost—very nearly—started giggling myself. 'How clever of Jack to remember. He and I have spent *days* trying to put the wretched thing back together. I'm not sure it can be fixed. Nothing we try seems to work . . .'

'Well, perhaps I could—ah!' He spotted the components, strewn across the table, and right away settled himself before them.

And so the four of us wiled away a little time, with Madeleine and me on the floor, Jack on my lap, and Rudy at the table, with his back to us, bent intently over his work. We talked of this and of that—of nothing, really. I don't remember a word of it. But I do remember Madeleine, as Rudy worked away, slotting together small pieces of metal—I can see Madeleine now, pulling a face at me, rolling her eyes and pretending to swoon.

Jack said, 'Mr Guglielmi, poor Madeleine is coming down with something pretty serious.'

He didn't look up. He said, 'Oh, I don't really think so, Jack . . .'

Rudy moves like a cat. You don't hear him when he approaches. And he sees things when he doesn't seem to be looking. Hardly reasons to fall in love with a man, I know. Nevertheless, when he said that, as cool as anything, and without even turning around, I remember even Madeleine blushed. Afterwards she always pretended she disliked him.

The steam train was put back together in no time. Too quickly. I believe that short half-hour, with none of us saying anything much, was the happiest half-hour I could remember. His voice, the faint smell of his cologne, his quiet concentration, the warmth of his presence—they softened the edges of the world for me. I could have stayed there for ever, with the boy on my lap, and Madeleine sulking, and Rudy, so very much there with us and yet so peacefully abstracted. I was in Heaven.

The weeks passed, and then the months. Christmas came and Christmas went. Rudy was at the house a great deal. Sometimes he would come by train, and Mr Hademak would pick him up from the station. Sometimes, though, much to Jack's delight, he would arrive in his very own auto, and the two of them would spend happy hours playing with it. In any case, however he came, he would always seek us out.

It wasn't entirely simple, however. Mr Hademak said he didn't approve of Rudy 'as a man' (so he told me over tea one afternoon, though God knows quite what he meant by that). He was certainly very jealous of Mrs de Saulles's affection for him.

On the other hand, Mr Hademak was undoubtedly fond of young Jack, and knowing how cheerfully he and Rudy played together, I am certain he would have been willing to overlook his disapproval. The problem (once again) was with his mistress. She, who never troubled to entertain the boy herself, who expected Rudy to sit indefinitely and wait, day after day, until she emerged from her sex-den to receive him, who barely acknowledged that I lived under the same roof with her, had ordered Hademak to ensure that the three of us be kept well apart: not simply Jack and Rudy, mind, but Rudy and me too.

'She is worried what influence Mr Guglielmi might have,' Mr Hademak told me, without quite looking at me. 'Not just on the Little Man but on you, too, Miss Doyle. She has your best interests at heart.' I remember laughing aloud when he said it. Mr Hademak chose not to react.

Her ruling meant that when the three of us were together, our meetings were always a little intense, and always conducted in whispers or at far corners of the garden, out of earshot of the house. Neither Jack nor Rudy nor I ever referred to the illicit nature of our lovely secret get-togethers. Needless to say, it only cemented our friendship further.

Not that Rudy and I were ever alone. In fact, since that first magical night on the terrace, we had not touched. We had barely spoken without young Jack being present. And yet there was a connection between us. Not simply—not only—of desire, but of tenderness, too. Oh, it seems so absurd and vain, seeing it written down here. Anybody who read these words would laugh and remind me that the very essence of Rudy is his magnetism. It is who he is; a man who has made half the world fall in love with him. And yet I know it was not imagined. I know it, because for all the long years when he was lost to me, it was this—this powerful, unspoken tenderness between us—that I could not give up on, that would never release its hold.

*   *   *

One evening, my father sought me out. He came to my room—something he had never done before. When I let him in, he sat himself morosely on the edge of my bed and gazed silently out of the window. I noticed he had lost weight—and heard myself asking if he was happy.

'What?' he said. 'Happy? What an inane question, darling girl. Am I *"happy"*? Is that what you asked?'

'I mean to say . . . are you miserable, Papa? You

look quite miserable to me.'

'Never been happier, Lola, my love! What about you? Do you like it in your new home? How do you find America?'

I told him I liked it very much, which was almost true, and his shoulders seemed to droop a little.

'Excellent,' he said. 'Excellent. Yes, it is. Rather splendid. Isn't it?'

I agreed that it was, and then we fell silent.

'She's terribly lovely, you know,' he said.

I sighed. 'Oh, Papa . . .'

'I know you probably think she's—' he began.

'No, I don't. I don't think anything, Papa.'

'Don't you?' He seemed disappointed. He looked at me and smiled. 'Nonsense. Tell me, Lola. What do you think?'

I hesitated. But not for terribly long because, of course, I was itching to tell him. 'Well, Papa,' I said, 'if you're sure you want to hear. Since you have asked me, I will tell you. Actually I think she is—'

'Oh, God!' He ran both hands through his hair, and kept them there—half humorous, half not so humorous. Half desperate, I think. 'Actually. Second thoughts, old girl. Don't tell me! Don't want to hear! Shouldn't have asked.'

But by then it was too late. I couldn't stay silent. 'Papa, I see you getting thinner,' I persisted. 'You have lost weight. Have you noticed it? You have lost weight, and you look so wretched half the time—'

'I can see you're not taken with her. But the thing is—'

'The thing *is*, Papa—'

'I am absolutely head over heels in love with her.'

80

'No, that isn't it. The thing *is*, Papa—'

'Don't want to hear it. Don't want to hear!'

'Why? Because you know it already! You know quite well what I'm going to say!'

'Know what? I know nothing of the kind.'

'She is exploiting you, Papa. She is using you for her own ends.'

'Using me? Using *me!*' He laughed aloud. 'But I am perfectly useless!'

'Because—Papa, you can't be completely unaware of—I mean to say, for reasons of her own, Papa, you are not uppermost—by which I mean Rudy—that is, Mr Guglielmi . . .'

'Rudy? *Rudy?* Ha!'

'Mr Guglielmi . . .'

'I see I should have been keeping a better eye on you, my friend . . .'

'She has him hanging about the house, while the two of you are— Oh, God! She wants him to go to the divorce court for her, so she can take Jack with her back to Chile, and Mr de Saulles, who loves the child so much better than she—he will never see the poor boy again.'

'Yes! And I have said I would do it for her!'

It silenced me. Silenced us both.

My dear, darling father had the grace to look at least a little shamefaced. 'I thought we might all go to Chile together,' he muttered. 'Don't you think, Lola? Sweetheart? Jack and his mother, and you and me? You seem to get on so well with the boy. Don't you think? It might be rather fun.'

I said nothing.

'In any case,' he said at last, 'she has refused it.'

'Of course she has refused it. Because she doesn't love you, Papa. She doesn't love anyone

81

but herself. Or if she loves anyone but herself, she loves Mr Guglielmi. But the truth is, she loves no one but herself. She is a horrid, *horrid* woman.'

He stood up. Full of silly, wounded dignity. 'Well, Lola, sweetest, I'm very sorry you feel that way.'

'I only wish you could see it. The thing is, I believe you can.'

'I should never have called on you.'

'Oh, Papa,' I cried, 'yes, you should! I wish you would call on me more often. You have no idea how happy I am you have come—don't walk out now! I'm sorry. I shouldn't have said—only you asked me, and I worry for you—and then you mentioned going to Chile, as if that were a sensible idea, with that dreadful, selfish, wicked woman, and I'm sorry I couldn't stop myself . . . Papa?'

'Darling,' he said, 'it doesn't matter.' He stopped at the door and turned back to look at me. 'I forgive you.'

'For what?' I cried.

But he was gone.

*　　　*　　　*

I had lain awake all that night, worrying for him. And then morning had come and, with it, the arrival of Rudy and all the appalling noises from her tower boudoir . . . Rudy and I had wandered into the house—it was too cold to stay out—and were in the nursery with Jack, more careless together than usual, because Mr Hademak had taken the auto on some errand for his mistress.

Mrs de Saulles had crept in as Rudy and I were lying side by side on the floor, with the miniature toy circus in front of us. We were deep in conversation. Jack, it so happened, was sitting quite absorbed in his story book, in the nursery's furthest corner, and Rudy and I were laughing. He had a hand on my forearm, and he was telling me something lovely. He was telling me . . .

He was telling me he thought I was beautiful. There. I have written it. He had never said it before, and I was laughing because it was such a wonderful thing for him to say. And he was laughing because I was laughing.

That was when Mrs de Saulles wandered in. The one and only time I ever saw her in the nursery. She didn't say anything, and Rudy only slowly removed his hand. He looked up at her as she stood there, still as stone.

'Mrs de Saulles,' he said, with the smallest smile. 'You are ready to dance?'

'To dance?' she said, her voice low and expressionless. 'I shouldn't think so. I wasn't aware that you were here, Mr Guglielmi.'

'No?' He sounded unconvinced. 'But you sent for me only this morning. I have been here since noon!'

'Oh, I shouldn't think so,' she said again. 'In any case my head aches dreadfully, so you might as well go home.' She turned away from him to her small boy, who hadn't yet looked up from his book. 'Jack—darling,' she snapped at him, and he jumped. 'My baby, come here and say hello to your mama. I've been looking all over for you.'

She wandered away soon afterwards, ignoring me, just as she always did, with the boy following dutifully behind her.

Rudy sighed. He reached across, held my cheek in his hand, and looked at me with a sort of wistfulness I didn't fully comprehend. We were alone, side by side on the carpet, our elbows resting on the floor. He kissed me.

'Only promise me,' he said, pulling away, 'promise you'll keep in touch?'

But the kiss was still working its magic. My mind wasn't there. I laughed at him. 'Keep in touch?' I repeated. 'Rudy, I'm not going anywhere. What can you mean?'

It was then he took the pin from his collar, a small gold pin. He gave it to me. 'Look after it, will you?' he said. 'I brought it all the way from Italy.' I have it still, of course. I have looked after it ever since.

* * *

Retaliation came curving back before we'd even plucked ourselves up from the floor. Mrs de Saulles sent a message to the nursery barely half a minute later, via Madeleine, who arrived looking as if she'd been through a hurricane. She tapped on the door, saw us seated there, closer than we might have been, his hand on my bare arm, but she didn't even snigger. Rudy was to go to the hall and wait there, alone, she told us, until Hademak returned from his errands. As soon as he returned, he would be leaving at once to drive them both— Mrs de Saulles and Rudy—to the train station.

I never saw Rudy at The Box again.

* * *

Later that afternoon, after she had reached New York, Mrs de Saulles sent a message via Hademak,

84

ordering my father to pack up his belongings. She said she wanted him out of the house by nightfall.

Poor Papa. Poor, stupid man. We overheard him—the entire household overheard him—bawling at Hademak, the pair of them as lovestruck and as broken as each other. And yet he bawled as if his exile were all Mr Hademak's fault.

'You think I don't know your game?' Papa was roaring, and upstairs, alone in my bedroom, I'm sorry to say I winced for him. 'You think I don't see you wheedling away, gazing at your mistress like a Goddamn puppy dog? You think she and I don't laugh at you? We laugh every time you have left the room! And now, the moment her back is turned, you try to oust me—but you can't win! You can't win, you filthy Swedish wheedler . . .' Why, he suddenly declared, *only that morning* he and Mrs de Saulles had been contemplating running away together to Chile. Or Uruguay. Or London . . . 'You can't stamp on a love like ours with your filthy Swedish wheedling. Eh? Ha! Get out of here! Get out of my sight before I have you fired. Get out!'

Hademak came knocking at my door. He stood there, his head stooped to fit beneath the frame, a great giant of a man, and he was shaking like a leaf. 'Your father doesn't listen,' he said to me. 'He thinks I am guilty with some terrible plan. But he has to leave immediately. At once. This afternoon . . . Mrs de Saulles won't tolerate to have him in the house.'

'But why? Why him? Why not me? What has he done?'

'She has complained to Mr de Saulles that—he has performed inappropriate and, er, unwelcome approaches towards her, and, er . . .' he couldn't

85

bring himself to look at me '. . . Mr de Saulles iss
. . . enthusiastic to telephone the sheriff.'

'*What?*'

He shrugged—a tiny little shrug, for such
enormous shoulders. 'Madame is . . . most
unhappy. Your father has to leave us at once, or I
have been ordered to telephone Sheriff Withers.'

'But to leave for where? Where is he to go?'

'I am to give him two hundred dollars for his art
and then I must drive him to the train station . . .
Your papa iss insisted on taking his art with him.
But I have been told to order him . . . that the
money is only when he leaves the art behind.' Mr
Hademak's English seemed to deteriorate, the
more distressed he became. 'He must leave it all
behind, and go out at once. Can you explain to
him? . . . I am ssorry, Jennifer . . . I can direct him
with an excellent boarding-house in the city . . . It
is cheap . . .'

There was little choice. Father could leave for
the city with two hundred dollars or he could be
arrested and leave without a cent for Mineola jail.
Either way, we all knew there was no possibility of
Mrs de Saulles relenting. He had to go at once.

Sadly, I agreed I would go to talk to him. I told
Mr Hademak that I would pack up my own things
first, to give my father a few moments to collect
himself.

'Absolutely not!' Mr Hademak cried. 'Under no
account. You are under the orders to stay here
with the Little Man. In fact, in the telephone call
to me, Mrs de Saulles made it quite clearly—the
money I will give to your father is only depending
on three things: first one, he leaves in this moment;
second one, that he leaves all his workings and

86

sketches behind; and third one, that *you* remain here at The Box, with the Little Man. You understand, Mrs de Saulles,' he added shyly, 'is well aware of his very strong fondness for you. She is determined about hating to break that little heart of his.'

'It has nothing to do with it!' I retorted—for I was never in any doubt. 'She wants me here to keep me apart from Rudy!'

'Not at all.' He didn't look at me. 'Not at all.'

'But I can't stay, Mr Hademak! Not without Papa!'

'You must.'

'Perhaps I could look after the boy in New York, when he's with his father. I should love to do that. Couldn't I do that?'

'Not,' said Mr Hademak, shaking his head. I knew it in any case.

'But I could at least meet him there. Often.'

'Not,' said Mr Hademak again. 'It is forbidden. The moment you are leaving here you not be seeing the Little Man again.'

'But, Mr Hademak—*my father*! He can't survive on his own. Not in New York! What will he do?'

'Without money, you shall neither one nor two of you manage in surviving here or in New York or anywhere in this big country . . . I am sso ssorry, Jennifer. But there it is the story . . . He must leave, and you must sstay, and that is for your best survival, father and daughter both.'

And so it was. An hour later, Hademak drove Papa through the cold winter rain to the train station. I came along too, but only to wave him goodbye. Papa didn't speak the entire journey. He sat silently, submissively, crestfallen and quite

87

bewildered, his hands shaking—an old man and a disgraced schoolboy at once. He looked terrified.

'You'll be all right,' I said to him as we waited on the station platform together. (Mr Hademak had tactfully stayed in the car.) 'Mr Guglielmi will help you, I'm certain of it. Mr Hademak has given you his address, hasn't he? And you know where it is? Don't forget—you have it in your wallet. Promise me you will contact him as soon as you arrive. Promise me!'

Papa promised, but I didn't believe him. He climbed onto the train.

'And you have the address of the boarding-house?' I called after him. 'And Mr Hademak says you can walk to it from the station. From Pennsylvania station. It's very easy, he says . . . Or you can take a taxicab . . . You have cash for a cab?' I was crying by then, couldn't stop myself. There were tears on my cheeks, and he turned back and looked at them, then up at me; and with an effort that was truly painful to see, he stretched his mouth into a form of smile.

'Don't you worry!' he cried, with not even a trace of light; a parody of his old self. 'I shall be *absolutely fine*! . . . Looking forward *enormously* to a spell in the big city. Isn't life a grand adventure? And Mr Guglielmi shall show me the way! No, it will be quite marvellous. Jolly good fun! No doubt about it at all!'

He blew me a kiss, and I watched him stumbling away to his seat, and I think I knew then that he was done. Finished. Gone. The charm was gone. The fight had gone. As the train rolled out of the station, I was weeping so profusely I couldn't see or hear when it finally departed.

*   *   *

After that I don't know what happened, or how, or why, but it was written in the paper a few days later that Mr and Mrs de Saulles were to divorce, and that a hearing had been set a month or so hence.

Mrs de Saulles and Jack, Mr Hademak, Madeleine and one or two others, myself included, moved from The Box to a smaller cottage in the village of Roslyn, just a few miles down the road. I wanted to take the typewriter with me, but Mr Hademak forbade it. He said the noise, in a smaller house, would upset his mistress. But he was a kind man. He used to take me to the train station early each Sunday morning so I could spend the day with my father in the city. And other than that, life continued pretty much as it had before. Except there was no Rudy. And each week there were the Sundays. I spent most of the week worrying what would become of my father while I was away from him, but I'm afraid I used to dread those Sundays.

*   *   *

Somehow, some half-remembered instinct for his own survival had guided my father on the journey from Penn Station to the boarding-house Mr Hademak had recommended. But after that, which I suppose must have been a gargantuan effort, he was clearly exhausted. It was three days before I was first able to visit him, and when I arrived he was still in the clothes he had been wearing when he had left The Box. From the greyness of his skin, and the dreadful hollows beneath his eyes and cheekbones, it was obvious that my once handsome, talented papa had neither slept nor eaten.

His room was small and grubby, on the fifth floor of a gloomy dilapidated building on East 39th. It had a gas stove in the corner, which he never learned to use, but which I did—to cook him food he never ate—and a single bed. On the first floor there was a small washroom, shared by forty or so residents, with water that ran only intermittently. And that was it. Papa's home.

His materials lay stacked against one corner, by the door, where I suppose he had dropped them on the day he arrived, and beside them his suitcase, which, without me, would have remained packed for ever.

He lived there for about four months in all—and did nothing. He sat on that bed beside the window, gazed out onto the street, and he drank. First he drank through the money given him by the de Saulles, and then he drank through the money I delivered to him from my wages each week. Poor wretched man.

*   *   *

That twenty-minute walk across midtown to Papa's boarding-house was, for some time, all I managed to see of the great city of New York. And in truth I used to walk it with feet that pulled me in any direction but the one I was meant to go. I would zigzag the blocks, sucking in the magical, frenetic activity, awestruck by those long, wide, endless avenues, the shameless gleam of the new buildings,

90

the glorious chaos of the building sites, and the crowded ramshackle stores; the foreign voices, the steaming food stands, and the autos, and the horses, the newspaper boys and the boot boys— the heaving, exhilarating mass of striving, shouting humankind. I still adore it, even now, in this August heat. Back then, when it was so new to me, so unlike the greyness of war-bowed London, or the neurotic silence of Roslyn, it made my spirits soar. I would draw out that short journey for as long as I dared, before guilt at the pleasure I was taking and worry for my poor father overcame me.

I did abscond, just once, with Madeleine's encouragement (though she couldn't come herself: even on her day off, Mrs de Saulles would never allow her to stray beyond Westbury). We planned it together, my little escape.

It was only for an hour. I walked across town, as I always did—gazing this way and that, as I always did—as far as East 39th, and then continued another three blocks to the Rialto on 42nd. Rudy had described it to me in detail, and I had read about it, too. It had only been open a few months. The papers—and Rudy, too—insisted it was the grandest, largest, most fabulous, movie theatre in all the world.

I had watched movies before, of course; any number of unmemorable five-reelers in dismal little halls back in Chelsea. Three or four times Madeleine and I had visited the picture house in Westbury, too. But this was like entering another world. *Intolerance* was playing—what good fortune was that? To see the most extravagant film in the history of film-making in the most extravagant movie theatre in the history of movie theatres! I watched it—the first half—and I was spellbound. As we all are, of course, when first we see it. I would have liked to stay to the end and watch it again, and again, and possibly spend the rest of my life in there, staring at that cinema screen. But after a while the image, though I tried to banish it, of my papa gazing listlessly out of his window, all alone, burned through even D. W. Griffith's most extravagant depictions, and I had to go.

I ran all the way to his boarding house—arrived at his door breathless, full of excitement. And before his melancholy overcame us both, I tried to pass on a little of the magic: I described to him, before even I had sat down, the Rialto's vaulted golden ceiling, and the row upon row of gilt and velvet chairs. I told him about the spotlights that danced in time to the music on either side of the enormous cinema screen, and of the golden organ sound which filled every corner of that massive space. I told him of the phenomenal, unimaginable tricks of Mr Griffith's camera—the 'close-ups' on actors' faces, magnified so as to fill the entire screen, allowing the audience to read every flicker of their smallest emotion. I told him about the ghostly superimposing of one image upon another, the different-coloured tints—sepia, blue, amber— all the tricks which Mr Griffith used to tell his story; and of the live elephants in his Babylon, and of the thousands upon thousands of extras and of the sheer, extraordinary scale of the film, and the theatre, and the wonderful, beautiful world just waiting to be discovered outside his window . . . I tried my best. I did. I tried to lure him back to the Rialto to watch the film with me.

God knows what miracle I had been hoping for. Of course he wouldn't come. He wouldn't have done so before, when he was still well. Papa belonged to the generation who believed that movies were designed for the degenerate masses, not for him—and most certainly not for his daughter.

*   *   *

By then, in any case, Papa never left his room—except, I suppose, to stock up on liquor, since he seemed never to run out. Often, when I came to see him, he wouldn't talk to me. When he did, when he volunteered any comment at all, it was almost only in relation to Mrs de Saulles.

Was she well?

No.

Did she speak of him?

No.

Had she sent a message?

Of course not.

Whole hours would pass and he wouldn't speak a word. I would tidy the room, cook for him, chatter about this and that—anything that came into my head: England, mostly; memories of happier times. I would tell him my feeble gossip—that Madeleine was seeing a car mechanic in Westbury; that Mr Hademak had written again to Mary Pickford—but my father rarely responded. I told him the typewriter lent to me by Mr de Saulles was broken.

'What d'you want it for anyway?' he asked suddenly. His voice made me jump.

'For my writing,' I reminded him. 'I am still writing stories and—scenarios and things . . .'

'Ah, yes . . . Like your mother. Always scribbling . . .'

I hadn't known it. I had no memory. I asked him to tell me more—scribbling what? Did he possess anything, still, which she had written? But he wouldn't be drawn. Wouldn't speak.

I had lost the art of coaxing him from his melancholy.

Endlessly, clumsily, stubbornly, I would ask him about his 'future plans', though of course I knew he had none. He would pretend not to hear me.

Once, when I was feeling very brave, I asked if he had yet been in contact with Mr Guglielmi. 'I'm sure he'd be quite a friend to you . . .' I said.

With a flicker of the old spirit, he replied, 'I would be most awfully grateful, Lola, if you didn't mention that repulsive little gigolo to me by name or implication. Ever again.'

'Papa, do you still have an address or a telephone number for him?' I persevered. 'I could telephone him myself, if you prefer?'

He gave a mirthless, unkind little snort. 'You shall do no such thing.'

*   *   *

Often he would ignore me altogether, and simply drink, and gaze out of that window onto the noisy, lively street below. I would sit with him—and try very hard to remember the years he had looked after me; all the warmth and humour and joy he had shared with me, in his own particular way. And I would look at him, so wrapped in his defeat, and try to remind myself of the times when he had been a different man, whom I could still easily love—but

94

I did. I did still love him.

Our hours together seemed to crawl. Through the stillness, and our silence, and the window he insisted on keeping shut tight, the sounds of the city would seep in; the sounds of a whole world, still fighting at life, not yet despairing . . . I am sorry to say there were times, on those long afternoons, when I yearned to be out there, and away from him, and free of him. I wished for it so intensely it was almost as if I wished he were dead.

I don't believe my presence helped him much. There were times, I'm sure of it, when he longed for me to leave him as much as I longed to be gone—mostly, I think, he wanted nothing any more but to be left in peace. I explain all this to myself and maybe one day—who knows?—I might even believe it.

Papa would wince when he saw me sometimes. There I would stand, bright and early each Sunday morning, fresh and young and bursting with life, and smiling, carrying groceries—as if I believed he might one day eat something. And I would watch, and try not to wince, as he slowly absorbed the disappointment—that it was only me standing at his door. Not Mrs de Saulles. Or my mother. Or any of the others. Just his daughter, whom he used to love. I would see the weariness return to his face, and the sorrow—because he *did* still love me. Enough to try his best not to hurt me. I would watch him struggling with the impulse to close the door in my face; and then the monumental effort it took for him to summon some spark of warmth, and to reassure me that he was so terribly delighted I had come . . .

I heard nothing from Rudy. The days passed and I longed for him—I'm afraid I thought more of him than of my father's suffering. I thought of him all day and all night.

Mr Hademak saw me moping about one morning, squinting over his shoulder as he arranged Mrs de Saulles's post on her breakfast tray. He said, with his great shoulders still turned to me, but the back of his neck glowing beetroot red, 'You do it effry morning, Jennifer.'

'Do what?'

'And if you're waiting for correspondences from *any one person or gentleman in particular*,' he said, 'you must understand that any . . . person . . . in particular . . . won't be so rude to write it to you here. He can't. It would be a very unhappy idea. To keep our little ship steady. And so *I have said to him* it might be better if he is writing in the care of a certain boarding-house. And that is I am sure what he is doing . . .'

So, the next time I visited Papa, and the next and then the time after that, I asked him if there were any letters for me. But he always said no.

*   *   *

It must have been very close to the time America joined the war. I don't remember on which side of the declaration it actually fell but there was war in the air, war on everybody's lips.

More immediately, at least for our little household, the de Saulles divorce hearing had taken place the previous day. Little Jack was

96

staying with his father, and so I had nothing to do. A message came down, very early, via Hademak, that Mrs de Saulles was not feeling well.

The hearing had not gone as she had hoped, Mr Hademak reported, though he refused to be drawn on the details. Mrs de Saulles wanted 'isolation for her peace', so she could reconcile herself to her new situation. She didn't care what we did or where we went, but there were to be no servants in her eyesight until nightfall.

It was bitterly cold outside. Unseasonably cold. There was snow on the ground and what looked like the promise of more to come, but I had a free day. I contemplated spending it with Madeleine, at the movies—only she was busy with the car mechanic in Westbury, whose wife, Madeleine said . . .

Oh, Madeleine!

'Oh, I know it!' she cried.

You never mentioned a wife!

'How could I?' The only times I ever saw her weep, it was about the married car mechanic in Westbury. She adored him.

Mr Hademak offered to drive me to the station so I could spend the unexpected holiday with my father. Moved more by duty than enthusiasm, I accepted the offer. I had nothing better to do.

As I travelled into the city I searched the newspaper for details of the divorce hearing and was horrified to read that Rudy had played his part in it, after all. He had given his testimony, stood as a witness to Mr de Saulles's adultery, and the reporter had gone to some lengths to mock him for it—mocked his dark appearance, his foreign accent, his profession, his decision to appear at all . . . It was painful to read.

I was mulling on all that, worrying for him, missing him, resenting him, dragging my feet through the busy crowd, that magnificent space at Penn Station, and feeling, for once, quite unmoved by it, when suddenly—I heard his voice! Was it possible? Was I dreaming? There were hundreds of people between us, rushing this way and that. And yet there he was, beneath the soaring arches, the giant columns, between all those hundreds and thousands of people—*there he was*. And in a few graceful, invisible steps, he was beside me, with his two arms wrapped around me.

'Jennifer! . . . It is! It is you! I must be the luckiest man in New York! Where in heaven's name have you *been*?' He lifted me in the air, and he kissed me, one on each cheek, and it was so un-American; so careless—all I could do was to laugh. 1917, it still was; a lifetime ago. We had our hemlines still flapping just above our ankles! We were still so terribly correct! But Rudy's warmth overrode all that. I could feel the people's stares as they elbowed by. It couldn't have mattered less.

'Jennifer, wonderful Jennifer, where in God's name have you *been*?' he said again.

'I should dearly love to tell you differently. . .' I laughed '. . . only, Rudy, I think you know quite well where I've been!'

'But I have left you so many messages—and nothing! Not a word! I wondered if I had done something to offend you . . . and so I thought and I thought—and I thought and I thought . . . and I could think of nothing!'

'Nothing!' I repeated. Like a fool. 'Of course you've done nothing to offend me whatsoever . . .

but you left messages where? At Roslyn? At The Box? Mr Hademak said you might have left them with my father.'

I had missed him and longed for him. Until that moment, with his arms still wrapped around me, I'd not the slightest comprehension how very much. I felt a rush of—relief, I suppose, flooding through me, and the most crazy, wild happiness . . . and then a lump in my throat, and my eyeballs stinging . . .

I longed for nothing more than to sink my head onto his shoulder and never ever to lift it again. He put me down, and gave me a moment to collect myself.

'I went to call on your father. Five times. But he would never let me in.'

'You called on him?'

'Of course! When I didn't hear from you. What did you expect?'

'He never said so!'

'No? No. He doesn't like me very much . . .'

'But he never said so! Are you sure?'

He laughed. 'Quite sure, Jennifer. Yes. I left letters for you each time. The last time I took him an excellent bottle of Scotch and I made him promise me that, in exchange for it, he would pass the letters on to you . . .'

I tried to laugh, but I know it sounded bitter. 'Father and his promises,' I said. 'I suppose he took the Scotch?'

'But—sweet Jennifer—who cares?' he cried. 'What does it matter? Because, after all, here you are! At last I have found you! If you had any idea quite how much I have thought about you— Tell me, Jenny, what are you doing right now?'

'I am—I am . . .' Actually, I didn't want to remember what I was doing right then: I was on my way to Papa's, of course, where I would spend the day with him in his room while he gazed out at the street below . . . 'I read about you in the paper this morning, Rudy,' I said instead. Rather carefully. 'It was very . . . courageous, I suppose. What you did.'

'Not courageous. *Stupid!* Stupid of me. I should have stood firm . . . Joan Sawyer is refusing to dance with me ever again. She is furious with me— and I don't blame her. I am furious with myself. Only in the end . . . I simply couldn't see a way round it.'

I replied, still carefully, 'Mrs de Saulles can be . . . a hard woman to resist . . .'

He shook his head. 'She is a wretched, awful, terrible, *dreadful* woman! Determined to have her way, no matter what.'

'Well,' I said, trying to hide the swell of delight his words brought me; trying to pretend to be balanced and fair, 'I suppose she needed your help. For all her—for all *the way she is*, she's quite alone here. Like the rest of us. I suppose someone had to speak up for her.'

'Nonsense! She has the world eating out of her hand.' He shivered. He didn't tell me then. All these years he kept it to himself—only Mr Hademak told me, afterwards. But the reason he did it—went to court for her—it was for me: because she told him she would throw me out, and I would be homeless and jobless, with a father to take care of . . . He did it for me.

'She is very beautiful,' I said, God knows why.

'Not when you look more closely,' he said. 'Look closer and you'll see she's quite possibly the most hideous woman in the entire universe.'

I giggled, but he didn't. 'She's an awful woman, Jennifer. I swear to it. Unlike any other. Her egotism—it's like a mad woman. I swear she would do anything . . . But let's not think about it.' He shivered again, as if trying to shake off even the thought of her. 'What's to be gained? Nothing at all! And, Jennifer—of all the people in the world to bump into this morning, when I was feeling quite so low—I cannot believe my good fortune. Jennifer—*cara mia*—tell me, what are you doing right now? What are you doing today?'

'Well, I am on my way—'

'Oh, don't answer it! Tell me instead how you're on the way to spend your day with me! Why don't you? I have nothing planned, nothing at all—I have nothing to do except to mope about my stupid mistakes. And feel sore about all the rude things they said about me in the newspaper this morning. And I have . . .' with a flourish he emptied the pocket of his overcoat, pulled out a chaotic bundle of dollar bills '. . . I have all these dollars to spend! Won't you let me spend them on you? Please? We could have lunch! We could . . .'

It was snowing.

'We could catch the steam ferry to Coney Island and spend the day on the beach! And ride the roller-coaster at Luna Park. We could . . .'

I thought of my father, wincing at my arrival, and of the wasted day I would spend in his cold room. I thought, too, of how he had failed to pass on the messages from Rudy, even when I had directly asked if there had been any. I thought of all the days I had spent in the city, unable to explore, and I thought of riding that famous roller-

101

coaster at Luna Park. I thought of spending the day with Rudy.

I thought of myself.

So I left my father to his private wretchedness, to gaze out of that cold window undisturbed, and Rudy and I took the steam ferry to Coney Island.

*   *   *

I had glimpsed the minarets and towers and flashing lights of the island amusement parks as our ship had sailed into New York harbour and, in spite of what I had heard—that it was the most horribly crowded place on the universe, overflowing with every manner of unsavoury human specimen—I had been itching to visit the place ever since. It was, I imagined, the essence of everything my father despised about this country and, in a small way, the essence of everything I found inspiring.

We drank beer, on board the steam ship—at nine in the morning—and Rudy, who said he adored Coney Island better than any place in the world, told me about the dance halls and the sideshows, and the light shows and freak shows, all the wild amusements that were awaiting us: the levitating ladies and the fat ladies and the two-headed ladies and the midget ladies . . . and the fortune-tellers, the escape artists, tightropers and elephant trainers, the stilt walkers and knife throwers . . . I wanted to see and do it all.

'And for luncheon,' he said, 'we can go to somewhere ritzy on Manhattan Beach, and drink champagne and eat clams. Jennifer, a person hasn't lived until they've tasted Coney's clams . . .

And then, if you like, after that, we can enter a dance competition, which, of course, we shall win.'

'Except, don't forget, you'll be dancing with me!' I said. 'I mean—that is—I certainly hope you will . . .'

'We dance perfectly together—don't you remember?' He stopped. 'You haven't *forgotten*, have you?'

'No!' I laughed. 'I certainly haven't forgotten.'

'And with our winnings we can go—where? Where shall we go together, Jennifer? Paris? London? Perhaps when the war is over. Shall we go to Paris together?'

'Paris . . . why not? Or maybe—perhaps if our prize money isn't quite so much as all that—if we win today, I should love to see something on Broadway, perhaps. *The Miracle Man*. I read it was a sensation, Rudy. Have you seen it?'

'I have not seen it, no, Jennifer, and I should love to see it with you. I will take you there, and introduce you to everybody, and we shall have a wonderful night . . . And then in the morning . . .' I smiled. We both smiled. 'In the morning we will board the next ship to whatever place takes our fancy—to Peking! Have you been to Peking?'

'I have not.' I laughed.

'Jenny, neither have I . . . I can't tell you how wonderful it is to see you!'

*   *   *

Since I first glimpsed those flashing lights from the deck of the *Mauretania* all those months before I had longed to ride that roller-coaster at Luna Park. I said it to Rudy and so, the moment we docked, we began by heading there. Rudy insisted on buying me a 'hot dog' as we walked along the Concourse—which is broader and grander and, even under a blanket of snow, more full of life than the Mall on Coronation Day.

I would have liked to pause at every trinket stall, stop and stare at every show, but Rudy, who had frittered numerous days at Coney Island and considered himself quite an old hand when it came to getting the most out of it, insisted on chivvying us forward. 'Or you won't see anything, and we'll never make it as far as Luna Park and, Jenny, I will have failed.'

'Failed in what?'

'Failed,' he said, as if I were stupid, 'in getting to Luna Park!'

In Luna Park (he didn't fail) we sat together in our little metal roller-coaster carriage. As it began its slow, steady climb towards the sky, I felt suddenly very sick. 'I think,' I said to Rudy, 'that this may have been a mistake . . .'

He took my hand and squeezed it tight. 'It's going to be fine,' he said. 'You mustn't worry. You're supposed to feel like this. Horribly sick. It's an essential part of the experience . . . You have no idea how I loathe it.'

'The whole experience?'

He smiled at me. 'From beginning to end.'

Which made me laugh, and at that instant our little carriage tipped over the peak, and we plunged through the air towards the ground and I was never more certain that my life was about to end. I couldn't breathe or move, and we clung to each other; and I remember thinking, with Rudy's

104

wonderful laughter ringing in my ears, and my own too, and the electric lights flashing and the view of the snow-covered world at our feet, and the ocean stretched out before us, and the wind on my face, and Rudy with his arm around me, holding me, laughing with me, I remember thinking, *It wouldn't be such a bad way to end . . .*

Afterwards, with those dollar bills burning a hole in his pocket, he insisted on taking us up to the Manhattan Beach Hotel, the swankiest establishment on the island; and we ate clams and drank champagne—out of champagne glasses back then, not hidden in tea mugs as we must drink it today . . . And then, when we were quite drunk, we wandered out through the snow onto the long pier.

We stood side by side, looking out to sea. He lent me his coat and we leaned together against the wind. 'Imagine us,' he said, 'in ten years' time . . .'

'Impossible!' I said.

'Once the war is over . . .'

'Impossible!' I said again. 'Truthfully. I'm not sure I can remember what life was like before it began. I mean to say—I can't remember England without the war . . . And now here it is, caught up with us again.'

We talked about that—and the possibility of his being called to fight. He would offer his services, he said. Perhaps this time round, with so many men already killed, they might be prevailed upon to accept him. If not in Italy—whose army had already rejected him (he wouldn't tell me why; it was because of his eyes, I read in a magazine)—then here in America. He said he hoped the Americans would be more welcoming. I hoped not. But I didn't say so. In any case, we were on Coney

105

Island. It was our day together, and even if the war hung like a black cloud over all of us, over everyone, we didn't want to dwell on it for long.

So we talked about the future—our hopes and dreams—as if the war was already over. 'What would you like to do, Jenny?' he asked me. 'If you could do anything. Anything at all?'

Just then he was standing rather close to me, and I caught a hint of his scent, and of the warmth of his body—the warmth and strength that seemed to radiate from him—and the answer that first sprang to my mind made me look away. He laughed softly—I could feel his eyes upon me; I knew he was thinking the same. And yet he didn't move any closer: he stayed just where he was, with his warm eyes gazing on me, and his hands in his pockets. It was very distracting.

'What do you want, Jennifer?' he asked again.

'I want . . .' I said—I remember feeling quite bashful. It struck me, at the time, as such a terribly peculiar question. Looking back, I suppose it is extraordinary how much has changed—not just about me, my circumstances, but the world. Today, I suppose, for better or worse, I am a Californian, and a woman. I was an English girl back then—and it was 1917. What did I want? A husband and children. Of course . . . But I wanted so much more than that. What did I *want?* I didn't quite know how to put it into words. I didn't know where to begin. 'Well, I should like to get out of Roslyn and come to New York . . . I should certainly love to do that . . .'

'And then? *And then what?*'

'Well—I should love more than anything to set up on my own. As a secretary, I suppose. There

106

aren't many things a girl can do.'

'But you can do anything! Anything you want. Jennifer, you are young and beautiful and intelligent—and this is America!'

Behind Rudy, waddling up the pier, I saw a young couple—married, and fat as butter, both. The man reminded of the great Fatty Arbuckle, who started life as an unloved little porter boy, orphaned, rejected, and who was now the most highly paid actor in America. Reminded me of Charlie Chaplin, who spent half his childhood in a pauper's workhouse. Reminded me that anything was possible in America; and most especially in the thrilling, new-fangled world of film making. I said, 'Well, of course, what I should really like is to write photoplays . . . That is what I would truly love to do.'

He leaped on it. 'I knew it!' he cried triumphantly. 'Jennifer, I knew it! From the way you talk about the films. You see? Ha ha! I know you well! Better than you think!'

I laughed. 'But what do you want, Rudy? What do you want?'

'There are books that show you how to break in, Jenny, I'm certain of it. Have you seen them? I shall get you some. And there are magazines, too—trade magazines—and they can direct you about where to send your scenarios, once you have written them, and they can tell you what sort of subject matters the studios are looking for, so you don't need to waste your time writing stories nobody is interested in . . . I'm sorry . . . I imagine you know all this already, do you? Of course you do . . .'

'Of course I do . . .' I lied. I knew nothing. I

hadn't the faintest idea.

'Of course . . .'

An awkward silence. I didn't look at him.

Suddenly he burst out laughing. 'Never mind! I shall find them for you . . . and I shall send them to you—or I shall give them to you next time you are in New York!'

*   *   *

Rudy knew what he wanted. And he wanted nothing less than the world. He wanted to design and build automobiles and to breed and train horses . . . He wanted to own his own private zoo . . . 'And to pay for it all—for you know I want only the best and most beautiful things in life . . .' He was smiling, and so was I. It all seemed so absurdly ambitious, just like our plan to go to Peking, but I realise now he was serious. '. . . I have thought that perhaps I shall go into the movies too . . . As an actor, Jennifer. I am certainly no writer. In any case—we can't have two writers in the same family . . .'

I smiled. Pretended not to. Blushed, I'm quite certain. And told him at some length about the modern type of apartments for single working ladies, which I had read about in magazines. They had their own little kitchens with sinks, and their own private washrooms with their very own bathtubs. . . I had spent many hours, in my bedroom in Roslyn, imagining how I might arrange my own: a looking-glass here, a pot of flowers there . . . I was burbling about that, burbling about the writing I would do at the table by the window, which would look out over . . . and then I felt him turn towards me, or maybe turn me towards him, so that I could feel the warmth of his breath on my cheek—

In any case, he kissed me. Under the orange electric light bulbs . . . And for ten years I held on to that kiss; and sometimes, just once in a while, when I was in the arms of other men and it was all quite ordinary, I used to wonder if my memory was playing tricks—if a kiss could ever be as that kiss had been.

And it can.

*   *   *

We won the foxtrot contest and with it a thirty-five-dollar prize, which was quite a fortune to me back then; almost double what I earned in a week.

We took the train back to the city, because it was faster than the steam ship—and it was still early, barely six o'clock. I might have gone to see Papa then. He was only a few blocks away. But I didn't.

'We could eat dinner at the Colony!' Rudy suggested. 'I never have. Have you?'

I laughed. Of course not!

'Or better still, Jenny, I know the chef at Rectors. I'll bet he would send us something by the back, if we asked him. We could buy ourselves a feast, and make a picnic and eat it in Central Park.' I wasn't hungry. But nor did I want our day to end.

'I think,' he said, 'perhaps we should go to the movies first.'

And afterwards, I said, before the last train home, I should visit my father . . .

Rudy said he would come with me. Whether my father liked it or not. He said I needn't worry about trains—he would drive me all the way to Roslyn.

And so we went to the Strand Theater.

That's right.

As magnificent as the Rialto, or very nearly. And we watched Miss Mary Pickford, starring in *Pollyanna* . . .

We let the movie flow right over us. A gentleman in the row behind us tapped Rudy on the shoulder, said he'd have the pair of us thrown out . . . We couldn't stop laughing. Oh, we laughed until there were tears rolling down our cheeks. And meanwhile Papa waited quietly.

We stopped at Rectors and, by the back door, he sent out three freshly boiled lobsters and a small tureen of Hollandaise; and some asparagus and two bottles of chilled champagne.

'Do you suppose,' said Rudy, leaning back in the taxicab as if the entire world belonged to him, and he to it, 'that anyone in the entire city has spent a day as perfect as ours?'

'I don't see how they could have done,' I replied.

And we took our booty by taxicab to Papa's. If lobster and champagne didn't warm him to Rudy's presence, then nothing would. So we said to one another.

'Do you suppose,' Rudy said again, this time as we paused in the dirty hallway outside Papa's door, hesitating one final moment before breaking the spell, ending our day together, 'do you suppose he will at least pretend to be pleased to see me?'

'Not for a moment,' I said. 'And nor to see me, either. He'll be thoroughly fed up at the sight of both of us . . . I should think we'll be quite lucky if he lets us in.' It made us laugh.

Oh, God.

Finally, I took a deep breath, raised my fist—I always had to knock hard to raise him, though the chair where he sat was only a few feet away—and I banged on the door.

But he didn't answer.

I knocked again. Nothing. Of course.

And then again.

'Perhaps,' said Rudy, but I could tell he didn't believe it, any more than I did, 'perhaps your father is feeling much better suddenly. Perhaps he's gone out for a walk!'

'Perhaps,' I said.

Rudy returned to the ground-floor desk to seek out the caretaker, in case by chance he might perhaps have glimpsed my papa shuffling out. It would explain the silence . . .

And I sat in that cold and miserable hallway, my back against his door. I sat there for half a lifetime or longer, listening for signs of movement on the other side. But I already knew. Somehow. God knows how. I knew it.

The caretaker—he was a skinny guy, peculiarly, uncomfortably skinny—arrived, bunch of keys clinking, bones knocking together, the caretaker coughing his guts out. Scowling. Nobody had seen my father for a couple of days, he said.

He put the key in the latch and I *knew*. I said— stop. Stop. Wait. Stop.

Stop.

*   *   *

111

Damn, it's so hot tonight. I should have taken another shower. Perhaps I can. I still have time. What time is it? It isn't even nine o'clock and yet I feel I've been writing all night. And now my dress is crumpled up and half ruined—and I'm tired. I'm so tired ... Oh, I wish Rudy were here. I wish I didn't have to go this dreadful, party. I wish—

Stop.

Damn if that skinny guy didn't open the door anyway. And in a rush I lunged for him and pushed him back into the hallway, out of the way. I think he swore at me. I don't remember. I told them both, him and Rudy, to wait right there, in that vile hallway, not to come in until I called—and I think Rudy maybe pulled the guy back, I don't know, but I heard him behind me, growling and coughing, clinking and swearing ...

My father was lying on the bed. Like a wax doll, stiff as board, spoiled in the sun: his skin was speckled with dark spots, his right arm jutted out, and his naked foot was half hanging over the floor. Like the room where it lay, his body was cold and still, and there was a streak of something—vomit, I suppose—dried up, from the edge of his lips to the pillow. He was dead.

They didn't come in. I forgot about them. I saw the empty Scotch bottle—finest Scotch, his old favourite—lying on its side next to the bed, and actually that made me smile: he'd made the choice, at least, to go out with a pleasant taste in his mouth. Next to the Scotch was the poison—what was left of it. Not much.

It comes in pretty box. One I had seen before— often. There was a pack identical to it in the kitchen at The Box. And another in Roslyn. And another in almost every kitchen in New York. Wherever there might be rats, there will always be a box of Rough on Rats. Fifteen cents per packet.

Rough on Rats, it says, in big writing across the top.

I'll say.

Clears out rats, mice, bed bugs, flies, roaches . . . And my papa.

There is an illustration of a Chinaman with a long ponytail on the front, and beneath him, a picture of large rat lying on its back with its toes in the air. No trickle of vomit on that rat's chin. No black arsenic specks on his glossy black fur. No.

I took the whisky bottle and placed it upright on the table by the window. I wiped away what had spilled of the poisonous powder, took the packet and threw it in the trash basket—overflowing—by the bed. And then—I was going to close Papa's eyes. But I couldn't. Close his mouth. I couldn't. I put the sheet up over his face, and I climbed over his body, over the sheet, and lay beside him, between the wall and him—between the wall and the thin sheet that covered him—and I tried to feel . . . something. I tried to feel as he had felt, lying there, his fear, his loneliness, his despair, his body melting away. I couldn't do it.

Not that I knew it then. But it's a painful affair, dying of arsenic poisoning. Excruciating. A patient, a victim—what do you call someone who has administered it to himself? My papa would have been in terrible, unimaginable pain—and delirious most of the time. Agony and madness, both together. To die of arsenic poisoning and despair must be painful indeed.

113

I fell asleep.

*　　　*　　　*

When I woke it was dark, and the street outside was almost quiet. It seems silly, having lain there all that time, but suddenly I was frightened. The man beneath the sheet, whom I'd slept beside that night, and a thousand times when I was a child, was no longer my father. I climbed over him again, recoiling when my arm accidentally brushed against his. Didn't even switch on the light. I picked up my bag and left, without looking back.

Rudy was outside in the lighted corridor, flat on his back, arms behind his head, sleeping. I had forgotten about him. When he heard the door, he opened his eyes, climbed slowly to his feet and put his arms around me. I didn't cry. Couldn't. I've no idea what time it was or how long we stood there. Finally he said he would drive me home. Was there anything I would like to take from the room, he asked, and I said no. Nothing at all.

'You are certain?' he asked.

I couldn't wait to get away from the place. He asked me again—didn't I want to take one last look, say one final goodbye? I shook my head. No. Nothing. Never. Never again.

'The caretaker went down about an hour ago to call the undertaker . . . but we could leave, if you prefer. I can come back in the morning. '

'I don't have any money.' I laughed. 'Perhaps if we returned the lobsters?'

'Oh, I've taken care of it,' Rudy said, waving it aside. 'Don't worry about that. It's all done. But,

114

really, you know what I think, *cara mia*?' he said. 'I think you and I should go some place—not too cold, if possible. My auto, perhaps . . .' He smiled. 'Or I could take you to my favourite bench in Central Park, if you like. Where I used to sleep, for a very short while, when I first arrived in America. And we can eat the lobster, and drink the champagne, and you can talk all you like, if you like, or not at all if you prefer, about your wonderful, extraordinary, charming, elegant and slightly wicked papa . . . Decidedly wicked papa. And I think we should eat and drink until there's not a scrap of anything left, and then perhaps try to celebrate something about the fact that we are alive . . .' He smiled again. 'If you agree with me about that? At least we are young and still alive.'

Sunday, 15 August 1926

Not feeling so hot this morning. Didn't get to bed until after two and then I couldn't sleep, not a wink. About six o'clock I gave up trying—I took my aching head across town to St Raymond's Cemetery to see if I could visit Papa's grave. But I was too early. The cemetery keeper wasn't about. And the truth is, I couldn't quite remember where I'd left him.

I tried to picture the day of the funeral . . . Mr Hademak and Mr de Saulles and me, standing side by side in the rain . . . and then Mr de Saulles and Mr Hademak waiting for me in the auto, and only me standing alone in the rain . . . But all I could remember for a landmark was a tree somewhere, and the raindrops splashing onto my hat, and, before that, Mr de Saulles sneaking a look at his pocket-watch as they lowered the coffin—and me always wondering where Rudy was—and Mr Hademak, sombre and still, the only one of us with his mind on the matter.

Papa doesn't have a gravestone, because I never gave him one, or any marking whatsoever to remind me where he lies. There was really no way of knowing. So I never found it. Not this time.

But I will organise a stone for him. Before I go back to Hollywood. And next time, I shall go to that cemetery when the cemetery keeper is about, and he will be able to show me. And maybe then I'll be able to stand at Papa's grave, and grieve.

*   *   *

Last night.

I was blasted. That's what. It was because I was nervous. Boy, was I nervous. I should have held back on the juice—at least before I left for the party. It's too bad. In any case it was a beautiful evening—mostly. He still loves me. And I love him.

Last night.

I was so busy writing I lost track of the time. The bellhop came up, despite my asking not to be disturbed. But he could hear me clattering away on the typewriter, I suppose, so he simply wouldn't leave until I came to the door.

Sure enough, he said there was a driver downstairs. The bellhop was pretty impressed. I'll guess it's not many guests at the Hotel Continental who get such a driver, in such a hat, coming to take them away. The bellhop said the driver had been told by his boss to wait, and to go nowhere, until I came downstairs. 'Who's the boss?' the bellhop asked. 'Must be rich. You should get down there.'

Which I thought was a little bit fresh, so I ignored him.

'What's the party?' he asked.

I told him to tell the driver I would be down in a minute.

Trouble was, I'd been sucking back on that flask, and by then I was so caught up, writing about Papa, I couldn't snap out of it at once. Still can't, quite. Something's stirred everything up, and I can't get any of it out of my head.

Papa must have gone out of his room at some point with the *intention* to buy that poison. He must have shuffled around and found his coat, and been sure he had the money with him, and crossed the street and said to the guy in the drugstore—gone right up to the till, looked the guy in the eye, and said—*I'm looking for some poison.*

Did the guy know? The guy knew. And as he said it, did Papa mean, I'm looking for some poison *for now*, or did he mean he wanted it *for some time in the future*? Did he put the packet away in his bedside cupboard—and did he look at it from time to time and think, *Maybe not today. Maybe tomorrow*?

Papa must have bought a few hundred bottles of Scotch from that same drugstore in those few months. Would the guy at the counter have recognised him? Would he have cared what some old sot of an Englishman was purchasing or for what purpose? And if he'd known the answers, would he have sold the damn stuff to him anyway? I suppose so. Does a man like my father go into drugstores to buy anything other than alcohol, unless he's trying to kill himself? I don't think so. No.

To kill the rats.

Maybe that's what he said. Maybe the guy behind the counter gave him a funny look. So, from the depths of his death wish, Papa summoned the energy to set the guy's mind at peace. *Would you mind awfully, old man? Only I want something that's Rough on Rats . . .*

So, there I was in my beautiful dress, ready to spend the night with the man of my dreams, all togged up to continue with my fairytale. But I couldn't shift the images.

Of Papa in the drugstore. Laying down his fifteen cents. Sitting on the edge of his bed. With the glass and the Scotch and that packet of poison . . . And meanwhile Rudy and me eating clams on Coney Island, telling each other our dreams, and *dancing . . .* And Papa tearing open that packet—thinking of me, perhaps. Maybe he looked at the sketch, that beautiful sketch he never showed me, and he thought, *Lola will be all right. She will understand. She can look after herself.* Or maybe he didn't think that. Maybe all he thought was, *How do I get into this damn pack?* Maybe he'd done all his thinking by then, and it was just a process. He probably spilled a bit, because his hands were shaking. He spilled the powder—because I saw it there on the side table. Spilled the Scotch as he poured it into the glass. Watched them in the glass together, the powder slowly dissolving . . .

So there I was in my beautiful dress, and that was where my mind was. When the bellhop came to tell me about the car, and the chauffeur in his hat, I told him to go away, and I went back to the typewriter, even though I could hardly see the keys by then because of the tears. I suppose I went on typing until the flask was empty.

Finally I laid the typewriter down by the bed, tiptoed up the corridor to the washroom and tried to make myself pretty again. But I guess my eyes were a bit blurry. When I got down to the lobby,

119

the driver was right there, still waiting for me. He looked at me in some surprise, I think, as if to say, *You mean* this *is the broad I've been waiting for*?

I knew what he was thinking, and I looked right back at him and laughed. 'That's right, mister,' I said to him. 'And how's your fairytale coming along?' I must have been blitzed, mustn't I? What a stupid thing to say!

He said, 'Very nicely, miss.'

I still can't work out what he meant by it.

I followed him through the lobby, with the bellhop and the fat guy at the desk both goggling. He opened the door to the car and I settled myself in the back, like a lamb to the slaughter.

As soon as we pulled out I was seized by the most dreadful panic. I called out to the driver to stop, but maybe he didn't hear me. He drove on, in any case. So I couldn't do much, at that point, except sit back and wait to black out, or for the edges of my brain to reappear.

I should have eaten something, only in all the madness it's not easy. Because I try to eat—but then I think about Rudy—his hands, his tongue, his arms, the scent of his neck, the warmth of his body, the feel of him inside me. I can't possibly eat a thing.

But I have to eat. Definitely I shall eat plenty today. Rudy is taking me to lunch. He's taking me to Coney Island again, and I suppose in this heat it won't be easy. We're going to eat Coney clams. That's what he promised. We're going to eat Coney clams, and drink French champagne, only this time out of tea mugs—and we're going to ride that roller-coaster again . . .

So. Last night. There I was, gliding through Manhattan in an enormous limousine. The next thing, the driver was holding open the car door for me, and I was standing on Park Avenue, right outside Mr Warburton's apartment block. I was standing on the sidewalk, kind of holding up the traffic in such a way that the driver couldn't close the car door, doing anything I could to hold off the moment when I would be on my own, with nothing left to do but to go in.

He said, 'You got a bit of lipstick . . . you might want to do something about . . .' And then, when I'd dealt with it and still I hesitated, he said, 'Get on up there, lady. How long you going to keep the guy waiting? You got nothing to be afraid of. You look a billion dollars next to the rest of them.'

I don't know why he said it, because we both knew it wasn't true. But it was kind of him. I kissed him on the cheek, which embarrassed us both, and then he more or less pushed me into the building.

*   *   *

Barclay Warburton's apartment was on the top floor—I was shown in by a butler, not so kind as the chauffeur. He seemed to take one look at my crumpled department-store dress, and the look of terror on my unpolished face—and, like Mr Hademak, like every well-trained servant—he saw me at once for what I was: only a not-quite-guest, after all. Not rich enough or quite beautiful enough to fit in, just an out-of-her-depth office-girl, slightly fuzzed on her own home-brewed gin, in a dress she'd bought from Altman's. And eyes

121

all puffed up with tears. In any case, he ushered me in and then left me stranded. It gave me a moment to survey the surroundings.

The room was enormous, arranged more like a super-deluxe mobsters' speako than a normal person's drawing room. There must have been forty or so guests present, stunning young things, lounging this way and that—on giant cushions, mostly, and low leather couches, which were scattered at elegant angles around the place, between silk carpets and polar-bear skins . . . Someone was at the piano, strumming something cool and jazzy. The lights were low, beneath clouds of smoke, and the air was sweet with the smell of hashish. And yet, in spite of so much beauty and elegance and splendour and perfection, there was an uncomfortable edge to the party. Partly it was the cocaine, of course (tiny paper wraps of it, piled high in a bowl beside the door). But mostly, I think, it was the presence of Rudy. Even here, in Barclay Warburton's Park Avenue drawing room, among some of the most glamorous and fortunate human beings in America, Rudy's excessive fame seemed to put the room out of kilter.

I spotted Rudy at once, of course, standing unobtrusively in a far corner, surrounded by beautiful women, lacquered and lean, and elegant men, laughing too loudly. He was inclining against a wall, arms folded, his face fixed in well-mannered attention. The people beside him wouldn't leave him alone. It wasn't that they addressed him directly, only that each time they spoke to one another, they glanced at him, to reassure themselves he was listening. I watched him, nodding kindly, laughing politely—and then—

Well, he spotted *me*!

I grinned at him, and laughed aloud. It was all I could do. When someone you love looks at you like that—with all the love you have for them returned—there is nothing to compare with it in the world.

He apologised to the group, and their shoulders sagged. He manoeuvred through them with perfect grace and intent, then across that great big room—with people waving and beckoning and calling his name—and he never once took his eyes from me. And then, in front of them all, he swept me up in his arms and kissed me. '*But you are so late!*' he cried.

I could feel the scrutiny of every person in the room, and I knew quite well what they were thinking.

'Oh, gosh,' I whispered. 'Rudy—you'd better let me go. I think they want to kill me. Let me go! I should probably leave right away . . .'

'What's that, *cara mia*?'

'Look around!'

'My darling—are you cracked?'

'*Look around!*'

He looked around, saw the banks of beautiful, unfriendly, curious eyes peering surreptitiously at us, looked back at me and simply chuckled. 'Oh, gosh, Jenny, darling. Never mind that! Don't care about *them*. They certainly don't care about you.'

'It's not what it feels like.'

'We could probably sit here all night and I don't suppose a single one of them would acknowledge you in the morning. Unless I stood up, right now, and announced at the top of my voice, "Ladies and gentleman, your attention please. This beautiful woman is the only woman I have ever really loved! I loved her when I was nothing but a gardener's boy."'

'It's not true!'

'Almost, it is. In any case, they're not to know. "I loved her when I was nothing but a gardener's boy. Her name is Miss Jennifer Doyle." '

'Lola Nightingale'

'Whatever. Her name is . . . Miss Lola Nightingale. And I adore her . . . More than my life.'

'They wish I wasn't here . . .'

'And we wish they weren't here,' he said. 'At least, I know I do . . . Let me find you a drink, Jenny—but quickly, sweetheart. We don't have much time. A minute, if we're lucky, and then we'll be surrounded, and we shan't get a chance to exchange another word . . . I've been waiting for you all night, Jenny—I thought you would never come!'

'I was always going to come—of course I was . . . Only I got caught up . . . I'll tell you about it later. Honestly, Rudy, these people . . . Must we absolutely stay here? I can feel their eyes on me and I *know* it's stupid to bother what they might think—'

'Well, we both know it, then. Tell me— Jennifer darling, gosh, I have missed you, more than I thought possible. Please. Tell me everything! Did they send you that ridiculous typewriting machine this morning? Did it arrive? Was it any use? If it's no good let's send it back!'

'They did—you did, Rudy! Where did you find

it? And please don't send it back. I adore it! In fact it's the reason—'

An arm cut between us, slender, bronzed and bare, but for a heavy diamond bracelet; the hand rested on Rudy's shoulder, '*Rrrrrruuuudy, darling, I haven't seen you since Juan-les-Pins!*' The woman was beautiful, of course, her dark brown hair in an Eton crop, her angular body draped in perfectly sleek scarlet satin. I paused a second to absorb her, this apparition. And immediately, without even a sideways glance in my direction, she bent her mouth to his ear and began whispering to him in French.

Rudy speaks French as well as he speaks English—as well as he speaks Spanish and Italian, for that matter. He answered her politely enough, but in English, and turned back to me. But by then the next one had arrived. And the next. And then a lanky gentleman in spats, with dribbles of sweat at his temples, chewing on his jaw and talking nonsense . . .

They came from every angle, until we were surrounded—and it felt almost as if they were working together, simply to keep us apart, because except for the instant when Rudy introduced me, and they were forced to shake my hand, not one of them addressed a word to me. So I stood there. A couple of times, Rudy made a point of turning himself away from them and talking only to me. But it was no use. And the funny thing is, even though I'd been so afraid beforehand, their rudeness didn't upset me. Because I knew who Rudy truly wanted to be with. I knew I was loved.

I wandered off. Since nobody but Rudy was

likely to miss me, and since he was trapped, I decided to take a little tour of the apartment. I pulled a face at Rudy. And—I am what I am, for better or worse—when I passed that bowl of cocaine wraps I couldn't quite resist. Just a little one. It had been a long time. And then I just slipped away.

Barclay Warburton is heir to the Wannamaker department-store fortune. He's a very rich man indeed, as became increasingly obvious with every new room I entered. There was a dining room with a mahogany table long enough to seat thirty (where I snorted my cocaine). It was so heavily laden with silver and gold ornamentation I couldn't imagine where the servants were meant to place the dishes. There were another couple of sitting rooms, and a study lined wall to wall and floor to ceiling with matching leatherbound books, designed to be looked at, I imagined, more than read.

I should have turned back, but then I found Barclay Warburton's bedroom and it was just too magnificent for me not to inspect it more closely. There was a pair of Matisse on the black-painted walls, and aquamarine silk drapes at the windows; and in the middle of the room, some distance from what must have been the biggest bed I ever laid eyes on, a low, square table that seemed to be made of solid gold . . . I travelled through the room, peering at this, picking up that, until I reached the two doors on the other side. One led to his dressing room (and more suits than a man could ever need in a lifetime) and the other—finally—to Mr Warburton's bathroom.

No hooch-brewing paraphernalia in here! Far

from it. Instead a bath of pure white marble set into the floor, with platinum taps, and the walls lined in black-and-silver watered silk. I caught a glimpse of myself in the glass above the bathtub, and it was quite a shock to see the image that gazed back. Rudy could make me feel so wonderful, the most beautiful woman in the world, even in a party like that, but the vision that met me in the glass quickly brought me down to earth again.

Not a great beauty. Just another N-one from N-where little flapper girl, not so young as she once was, not so fresh, just another prettyish secretary bird from Hollywood, hair bobbed like every other prettyish secretary in America; lipstick smudged; dress—which had seemed to fit the fairytale so perfectly when the evening began—suddenly so crumpled and drab. With the drink—and all the weeping, and the heat, and the lack of anything to eat—I suppose it's not surprising I looked a wreck.

I rummaged about in the cupboards, looking for something—anything—that might help put my appearance back together again. They were crammed with all sorts of ointments and trinkets . . . I emptied one, too wired to be careful, piling everything into the basin: cold cream, if I could only find it, might take the red out of my face. Or even a comb might help.

Funny thing, fate, I guess. There was no cold cream. No comb. But a familiar pack of rat poison.

I saw it, felt an icy hand on my heart, and—it sounds silly now, I don't care—it was as if Papa were there in the room with me again, as if he

127

were trying to tell me something, though what, I couldn't possibly say.

I took it out. Set it on the surface by the marble basin, set my champagne glass down beside it, and continued exactly where I suppose all my thoughts had been leading, not just this afternoon and yesterday, but since the night I'd found him.

I didn't want to drink the stuff—of course not, on such a happy day, in the middle of my fairytale. But my head was buzzing with cocaine. I wanted to watch while the powder dropped into the glass—I wanted to see it dissolve. I wanted to feel what my papa had felt as he swirled the liquid round the glass, as he peered at it to see if the residue dissolved or simply sank to the bottom, and I wanted to taste . . . I simply wanted to . . . *understand*.

I spilled some in the basin to add to the chaos in there. My hands were shaking as I mixed it in, and I made a careless attempt to rinse it away. I watched the powder. It dissolved quite easily. No need to swirl. Papa hadn't needed to swirl. First I tipped in just a little, then I tipped in just a little more. Finally I tipped in the lot. Left the packet where it fell, lifted the glass . . .

No smell. Didn't smell. But I knew that. No taste. No smell. It's why arsenic is so popular in murder stories.

Well. I was standing there, the glass at my lips, staring into it as if somehow it held all the answers . . .

Looking back this morning, with a clearer head, I can see that I wasn't quite myself. I hadn't eaten all day. I was—drunk and wired . . . and

128

worn out, I guess. And I felt the cold sweat on me, and the edges of the old brainbox going black all over again. I grasped hold of the washbasin, because the room was swimming, and then I heard Rudy's voice on the other side of the door

Jennifer?

I wasn't sure if I was dreaming. His voice seemed to grow louder and then softer and then louder again. And my own voice I couldn't seem to find at all. But I knew I needed him. I needed someone. I needed help.

Jennifer? Are you in there?

He tried the door. Fortunately I must have forgotten to lock it. I suppose he saw me swaying, with the glass at my lips—because all at once he was holding me and the glass was gone. He had taken it from me and my head had flopped onto his shoulder.

Then everything went black. I came round on the floor of the bathroom, with my back against the wall and Rudy crouched over me, looking at me with a face of such tender, sweet concern.

I don't really know what happened after that. I remember saying I needed terribly to eat. He said he would take me somewhere, and then back to my hotel. He organised it all—fetched our coats, reordered the bathroom, said goodbye to our host and—It is a magical thing to be taken care of.

And then somehow, shortly afterwards, there was I sitting across the street from my flophouse once again, in the same café as the night previous, swallowing cake and coffee as if my life depended on it—only this time I wasn't alone. Mr

Rudolph Valentino was sitting opposite, looking out for me, taking care of me.

It was late, I know. And the place was virtually empty. And it was hardly the sort of establishment you'd expect to bump into the Most Adored Man in the Universe . . . but nobody recognised him.

'I have a present for you,' I said. 'I forgot to bring it with me. It's a disguise.'

He said he couldn't imagine anything he wanted more, and he laughed. He promised me he would wear it—wig and all—when we go to Coney Island today.

I swallowed the cake, and then he took me back to my hotel. He seemed a little distracted. He wanted to come up with me but he was looking a little green himself, not that he would admit it, and what with one thing and another it had been a messy night. My cheap little room was in no state to welcome anyone . . .

In any case, we have time. There is no rush . . . we have plenty of time ahead of us.

He kissed me, in the lobby there, with the bellboy and the friendly fat guy behind the desk and a couple of others goggling at us, but I didn't care.

'You're going to be OK, aren't you?' he said. 'And tomorrow, I don't care what you say, I'm sending my driver to move your things to the Ambassador.'

'I'm all right here. I prefer it here.'

'Nonsense. We can get a separate room for you . . . so you can work. But it's impossible. You can't stay here . . .'

'It doesn't matter to me, Rudy.'

'But it matters to me . . .' He fell silent, took my face in his hands—and he looked at me with more tenderness than I ever saw in anyone's eyes, or was ever looked at, or ever dreamed of, or ever knew was possible. 'We have so much to look forward to . . .' he muttered, and he kissed me again, and then he was gone.

*   *   *

And now it's just a few minutes before he comes by to pick me up and here I am, ready as I'll ever be. Got a good dress. And a belly full of breakfast, for once.

What time is it?

I telephoned Frances Marion at her hotel earlier. She sounded lovely, so warm—I am exceptionally lucky. She is taking me to lunch at the Algonquin! We have a date for Wednesday, and she says she has someone who wants to meet me. 'I shan't tell you who it is,' she said, 'because it's not absolutely certain she'll be in town. And I don't want you getting your hopes up . . .'

So it's a she. My mind is running through the possibilities—because Frances Marion knows everyone . . . I certainly hope, by the way, that Frances Marion really does mean to do business with me or, the rate I'm spending my cash, I shall pretty soon find myself in jail.

What time is it, by now? Rudy should be here. Any minute, he should be here. But that's all right. I'm more than ready. Maybe while I'm waiting I should think about arrangements for Papa's gravestone.

Not so sure about this dress suddenly. Maybe it's too formal for a day trip to Coney Island. Maybe I'll just quickly try on the other . . .

The yellow one was better.

The yellow dress is lovely. I'm fussing . . . but where is he? He's late. Perhaps I should go down. Maybe he's left a message . . . On the other hand he's hardly very late. Twenty minutes. After last night I don't want to make any fuss. I just want to be calm and wait . . .

Where is he?

Forty minutes. Perhaps I should go downstairs and make a call to his hotel. Except how would the Ambassador operator know that it was me, as opposed to some crazy fan? How could I explain to them? 'But this is Lola. I am the One. I make him happy, he said so. Like none of the others. And he makes me happy. Like none of the others. He loves me, operator. And I love him. So will you please be sweet and connect me through . . .?'

Perhaps I should go down to the lobby and just ask at the desk if he hasn't left a message . . .

*   *   *

No message. And a goofy new guy at the desk, thank goodness. So no comments about my gentleman caller last night.

Half past two. He's an hour and a half late. Or maybe it's only an hour. Maybe he said he'd come by at one thirty. I bet he did. I'm certain he did . . . Oh, God, what can have happened?

I've decided the yellow dress won't be quite right, after all. Not for tea. And I guess we won't

132

make lunch now, and I guess it's too late for Coney Island. No matter. It would have been too hot and too crowded in August in any case. Maybe my white one, which I wore when he came to the studio? Except I guess he's seen it. Oh, God, *where is he*?

Why doesn't he call?

Three o'clock . . . He's probably forgotten the name of the hotel. He's forgotten where to find me. He couldn't remember it last night. He thought it was called—What did he think it was called? It doesn't matter. He was meant to be here two hours ago. That's later than simply 'late'. Even for a movie star. Something must have happened. Or maybe my stupid, horrible behaviour last night . . . Maybe he never meant to keep our lunch date. Maybe, when he said we'd go to Coney Island together, he was only trying to be kind, trying to get shot of me the kindest way he knew. Except it's not very kind, is it? To keep a girl all togged up in her yellow dress, and then her green one, and then the yellow one again, and now the white one, when you never have any intention of meeting up with her in a single one of them, ever again. Oh, God, I hope he's all right. *Where is he?*

What if there's been a message waiting for me all this time? Ever since he left me yesterday night—and downstairs they've all been laughing at me, watching me, dashing in and out, singing to myself, beaming like a Cheshire cat, looking so Goddamn happy? And meanwhile they've been in possession of the very message from him, and they've not had the heart to pass it on: *Take you to lunch? Don't be funny! I'd rather swing from the top of the Woolworth building by my own braces ...*

Except I know he loves me.

But why doesn't he call?

Maybe something's happened. He was looking pretty ropey last night. Even so—he might have called. Or maybe asked for one of his people to telephone me at least . . . What's happened to him? Has he forgotten me? Already? Is it possible for a man to look so tender one minute and to forget about you the next?

I'm going downstairs. I'm going to ask again. Only first I'm going to change my clothes. I don't want to look like I'm all togged up, ready to go— and then only to get the message, in front of them all, that Rudolph Valentino can't make lunch with me today because he has just run off to Mexico to be married to Miss Pola Negri.

Damn it, why do I do this? I'm going downstairs.

*   *   *

The fat guy—Larry—he was back behind the desk. He was the one who told me. He said, *Surprised to see you here.*

But he didn't say it unkindly.

. . .There's a big crazy crowd by the hospital. It's in the late papers. Weeping and everything. They think he's —

They took him in an ambulance early this morning. And now they say he is unconscious. He is unconscious. And nobody knows—Nobody seems to know what is wrong.

1917

LONG ISLAND

That night, after leaving Papa in the room, we didn't speak of him again. There was nothing to say. Rudy and I spent the hours until dawn getting smashed, lying on Rudy's coat, spread out over the snow-covered grass by that bench in Central Park, drinking champagne and eating lobster—and that was when he told me for the first time that he loved me, although, of course, I knew it already. We talked about a future together. We talked about driving to Europe when the war was over; to Italy, to visit his family; and to England, to visit— my old home. We talked about the photoplays I would write and the movies he would star in; and— of course—once the second bottle of champagne was inside us, we talked of the children we would have together. And the splendid house we would build, and all the lobsters we would eat, and all the champagne we would drink—every night. Not just tonight but every night of our lives.

'Do you suppose, Jennifer,' he said, as if it were the most important question ever to be asked, 'that there is a finer drink in all the world? Is there any drink so sweet, so helpful, so gentle on our wretched spirits than a bottle of the finest, crispest, coldest champagne?'

And we laughed about that—very hard—without needing to explain why. It was because of the solemn tone he used, when until that point we had been so busy denying the awful solemnity of

135

everything. We laughed until I began to shake—
and then he held me for a long time without saying
a word.

He drove me all the way back to Roslyn, and I sat
in silence beside him, his warm presence keeping
the pain at bay. A little way up from the cottage,
out of its sight, he stopped the auto.

'She won't allow me to write to you here.'

'I know.'

'She's told Mr Hademak to destroy my letters.
No messages will ever get through to you . . .'

'How will you reach me, then?'

He kissed me. 'I will think of something,' he said.
'One way or another . . . Don't give up on me,
Jennifer. Never give up on me. Promise me.
Promise me you will never give up.'

I promised him.

*　　　*　　　*

We were all miserable at Roslyn. Papa died in early
April, just as America went to war. But apart from
the constant hum of aeroplanes from the Mineola
airfield, and the interminable house callers
insisting we invest in Liberty Bonds, we at the
cottage might hardly have registered the war was
even happening. Our dreadful mistress, with her
endless headaches and occasional wild tantrums,
demanded every ounce of everyone's attention.
Madeleine, Mr Hademak, little Jack and I—we
were all quite terrified of her.

She existed in a permanent state of barely
controlled rage; any small incident could trigger
her tantrums. But at the base of them all, as well
we knew, was one thing: her husband's victory in

136

the divorce court. It had given him shared custody of Jack. And that was all she talked about: the injustice of it; the evil of it; the monstrous absurdity of it. It made not the slightest difference to her that her son adored his father or even (God forbid) that the adoration was mutual. She hated her husband to such a degree that you could see it sometimes, even as she sat there doing nothing, gazing at the wall. The hatred would be burning away behind those big, mad eyes. It was all she seemed to think about.

Occasionally I managed to escape the awful black mood at the cottage, and go with little Jack to visit his father at The Box. In fact, after Papa died, Mr de Saulles seemed to take quite a kindly interest in me. On one occasion he called me into his study and, with terrible awkwardness, while I stood before his desk, thanked me for staying with his son. He did it without quite acknowledging the awfulness of—everything; without quite looking at me, either. He said, 'I want you to know . . . What a great comfort it is to Jack—and to me too—to know that he can depend on you as a friend. It is . . . probably rather difficult for him. And for you, too, of course. In any case, the poor boy is terribly fond of you.' Then he opened his wallet and handed me twenty dollars. 'There will be more,' he said. 'I will make it worth your while, for as long as you can bear to stay with us, Miss Doyle . . . Only perhaps it would better if you didn't mention it to . . . other members of the household.' He kept his word, too. Not each time, but often, when I saw him, he would slip me a handful of dollar bills, without a word passing between us.

I had no plans to leave in any case. The extra

money was welcome but it didn't alter much. I loved young Jack as much as he loved me: we were a comfort to each other in that terrible time, and the notion of abandoning him to the dreadful, neurotic solitude of life at his mother's cottage was too awful to contemplate. Apart from which—honestly—where else could I go? I had no qualifications to mention, I knew no one in America, except Rudy, of course. And he had his own troubles. In any case I had no idea where to find him. Since the death of my father, I had not heard a word.

Weeks turned into months . . . and I heard nothing at all.

Even so, of course there were moments of lightness. I got the typewriter back. Briefly. My little friend Jack confided to his father my dream to write scenarios, and his father had his chauffeur deliver the typewriter to the cottage the next day. I was delighted. Touched, too, that he should have bothered. Mr Hademak, so protective of his mistress, could hardly refuse it for me under the circumstances.

I was careful not to use it when Mrs de Saulles was about—but some time very shortly afterwards, she returned from one of her outings a little earlier than expected and I suppose she overheard me tap-tapping away. She complained at once (via Mr Hademak) that the sound made her head ache, and though I promised I would never again use the machine while she was in or even near the house, she forced me to send it back again.

Poor Mr de Saulles! What a fatal mistake he had made in marrying such a woman. He was a good

138

father. A better father by far than his ex-wife was a mother. And he was *never* as wicked as they said he was afterwards. When the whole wretched country turned on him. Never. He had a good, kind side, in spite of everything.

*   *   *

Mrs de Saulles's single contribution towards the great American war effort, and the fervour of patriotism that was sweeping the land, was to instruct Hademak (or so Hademak claimed) to fire the Hun who looked after the cottage garden.

But it occurs to me suddenly that perhaps Mr Hademak took the law into his own hands and fired the wretched Hun of his own accord, as a peace offering for the village. Because I find it quite hard to believe, with all the festering hatred which possessed her, that she had even registered there was a war going on—except in the single way it inconvenienced her—let alone that she had a Hun for a gardener. Her refusal to buy Liberty Bonds, or to knit the soldiers' socks, or to do anything generally deemed worthwhile towards the effort, had been noted in the village and—combined with her aloofness and her foreignness—was causing a certain amount of bad feeling. Given America's feverish mood just then, the poor German gardener had probably already been fired from every other gardening job in the district—it would have been an easy way for Hademak to let it be known that, in spite of appearances, Mrs de Saulles was supporting the right side.

Oh, who cares, anyway? What does it matter?

Somebody did or didn't get rid of the gardener; the rest of the world was or it wasn't at war—The fact is she was very angry because the courts had forbidden her, while travel by sea was dangerous, to take her son with her back to Chile—and that was all she could think about: that international events had conspired to keep her trapped, with her staff of eight, in her pretty cottage on Long Island's Gold Coast. And we were all made to pay for that. Some of us to pay rather more than others.

*　　　*　　　*

In the mean time, not surprisingly, I was more unhappy than I had ever been. My mind seesawed between raw, bewildered thoughts of my father, who had abandoned me; and an obsession with Rudy. Rudy, who had promised he would find a way to communicate, and yet, as hours turned into days turned into weeks turned into months, had failed to do so.

I imagined every possibility—that he'd persuaded the United States Army to sign him, despite his damaged eyesight and that he had already been sent out to the trenches. I considered it endlessly. Then, of course, there was the other possibility: that our day together, and our promises to one another, simply hadn't meant so much to him as they had to me, and that he had forgotten me. Sometimes late at night, when the shock of Papa's final disloyalty clawed at my every thought and feeling, I could almost believe the worst of Rudy, too. But I had promised him I would never give up on him. And the truth is, in spite of the long silence, I never did.

*   *   *

It was terribly hot. Unspeakably hot. And so it had been for days. That afternoon the airplanes were humming incessantly overhead, and there had been a workers' march in Westbury, which held up the traffic and prevented the Bond Collecting Ladies from collecting their bonds. It had also, we understood, prevented Mr de Saulles from making the journey to Roslyn from The Box to return young Jack to his mother. Mrs de Saulles claimed her ex-husband had telephoned, very early, and that she had taken the call—which in itself was curious, because she never answered her own telephone. In any case, she said he had called, explaining about the workers' march and the consequent delay . . . Mrs de Saulles was convinced that her husband had promised to return little Jack in time for luncheon.

On that occasion I had not been asked to accompany Jack to The Box so I was skulking about, along with the rest of her staff, trying my best to stay out of sight. Mrs de Saulles, her thin, pinched face glistening in the damp heat, spent the morning pacing the cottage, upstairs then down, up and down, muttering to herself—we could all hear it: she was burning up with anger.

How dare he? . . . How dare he imagine? . . . Was she a fool? Did he think she was a fool? . . . She was not a fool! How dare he mock her with a 'workers' march'—a workers' march? Was that an excuse to keep a mother from her son? . . .

She was always angry when Jack was with his

141

father, but on those occasions when Mr de Saulles failed to deliver him back at the appointed time it was frightening to watch her.

I suppose she was fond of little Jack in her own very limited way—otherwise she could simply have left him behind and returned home to Chile without him. It would have been better for everyone if she had. But I never once believed that her anger, on those occasions when little Jack was returned late, had the slightest connection with her limited affection for him. When he was with her she hardly seemed to draw much pleasure from him, after all. She would sit him at the end of whichever couch she was reclining on and lament to him the wretchedness of her unique position.

Poor Mama, he would mutter, stroking her feet, her forehead, her arm—whichever part of her elegant body she proffered him . . .

. . . until he was dismissed again.

It was painful to witness. I felt for the boy—and sometimes, once in a while, when I saw on her face a glimmer of understanding at her own inadequacy as his mother, I would feel for her too.

But on that day—3 August 1917—I did not feel for her. She was at her worst. She threw her coffee at Madeleine in the morning. Madeleine came down to the kitchen drenched in it, and we took that as a warning.

Lunchtime came and went, and still there was no sign of Jack. Mr Hademak was ordered to telephone The Box, but—so we understood—there had been no reply. By four o'clock, still the little boy had not been returned. The mood in the house was blacker, more suffocating than ever I had known it.

142

We'd not heard from Mrs de Saulles for an hour at least, which was most unusual—as Madeleine and I commented, sitting at the kitchen table with Mr Hademak. She'd not called for Madeleine, without whom she was normally unable to function for longer than two or three minutes at a time. We'd heard no objects being sent crashing to the floor. No shouts of anger from behind her bedroom door. Only her dainty footsteps going back and forth, back and forth . . .

'D'you think she's finally lost her mind?' Madeleine whispered. 'What's she doing up there?'

'She is resting,' Mr Hademak said. 'And I will thank you, Madeleine, to display some respect for your mistress. At a time like this.'

Madeleine rolled her eyes. 'Time like *what*?' she muttered.

'She suffers from the heat,' Mr Hademak said. As if we all didn't.

Finally we heard the bell. Madeleine tripped upstairs, and returned, moments later, with the message that Mr Hademak was to prepare the motor-car.

'She says,' Mr Hademak said, looking uncomfortable, 'that we are to go to The Box ourselves and take the Little Man home with us . . . I have reminded her about the workers' march, which may well have been delayed—but she doesn't seem to agree . . . In any case, Miss Doyle, she wants you to come too.'

'Me?'

143

'She thinks,' he said unhappily, 'that the Little Man might be rather upset.'

I remember, so clearly, as she and I climbed into that car together, the way she patted her little purse, and checked it, checked it again. She had bright spots burning on either cheek, and her beautiful, innocent dark-brown eyes had a gloss over them, like a perfect varnish. It made them more beautiful than ever. She didn't look at me, or acknowledge me in any way, though we sat side by side. She patted her bag, and looked out of the window, and threw angry instructions to Mr Hademak behind the wheel.

'You're driving too fast,' she said—more than once. 'Slow down. Or I shall be ill. Why can't you slow when I tell you to?' And then, 'Why, I could walk there in half the time! Can't you drive any faster? What's the matter with you today, Hademak? Do you not *want* my little boy to see his poor mother today?'

And then, 'You see? Where are the workers? There are no workers . . .'

'It certainly seems,' Mr Hademak said, 'that the march has been and gone . . . I hope we don't pass Mr de Saulles with the Little Man, on his way to see us at Roslyn . . .'

'Why would the workers come out on such a hot day, in any case? Of course they wouldn't . . . He invented it. He invented the whole thing . . .'

When we reached The Box, she ordered Mr Hademak to stop at the top of the drive and she climbed out, mouth set—that beautiful little face a picture of quiet malignance. I can see it now. I shall never forget it. Just as I can see her patting

144

that little bag. Did I have an inkling of what she had in her bag?

But how could I? It did not even cross my mind. Only I suppose, afterwards, something about it was never a total surprise . . . In any case she insisted we both come with her on the long walk down the drive.

'It is a little hot,' observed Mr Hademak. 'Might Madame perhaps find it more comfortable if we were to drive directly to the house? In this terrible heat I worry . . .'

But she was already on her way, and Mr Hademak knew as well as any of us the mistake of requiring Mrs de Saulles ever to issue the same order twice. He clambered quickly out of that motor-car into sweltering heat, and so did I. She was walking very fast, and we had to run a few steps to catch up with her.

Nobody said anything after that. In that dull, damp heat we could hear the voices on the front porch—where Rudy and I had danced only a year before. There was music playing. And father and son were singing along, and laughing. They sounded happy.

Several moments passed, until we were close enough to hear every word that was spoken: Mr Hademak and I hung back, embarrassed, but Mrs de Saulles strode on until she was only a yard or so from where they were sitting. There were several people present on the porch that afternoon: Mr de Saulles, with his son playing at his feet, and beside him a stern-looking couple I recognised as Mr de Saulles's elderly parents—and another couple, too, whom I had never seen before, but I learned later were the Degeners, Mr de Saulles's sister and brother-in-law.

It was Mr de Saulles who noticed her first. He was saying something to the little boy. He looked—well, now, I see it all so clearly but I wonder how much is distorted by what happened next. From my memory it seems to me that his face registered much in the few seconds before he found the presence to speak: there was surprise, I think, quickly followed by something that might almost have been pleasure—quickly clouded by uncertainty . . . and then, I'm almost certain, by fear.

She had her hand in her bag. Did she? God, I can't remember. Or had she already taken out the gun? Did she give him a chance or was she already decided? Did she know that, *whatever happened*, she would only leave him dead?

I can't remember!

Because—afterwards—what did she imagine would happen? Did she really imagine that, with his father shot dead in front of us all, she could simply take the child and sail away to the U.S. and live with him happily ever after? Without having to face the consequences? Is that what she thought?

How funny.

*　　　*　　　*

She said, with or without the gun already pointed, 'I've come for the child.'

No—not that. First Mr de Saulles stood up from his chair and said, *Blanquita, what are you doing here? What a pleasure . . . Jack, say hello to your mother. Say hello, Little Man . . .*

146

Jack was muttering to himself. Playing with his train on the floor. He didn't seem to register what his father said. He turned away a little.

Mrs de Saulles said, *Baby?*

But he didn't reply. And then she turned back to Mr de Saulles. *That* was when she said: 'I have come for the boy.'

And Mr de Saulles laughed. 'But the boy is with me. We have already agreed. Mother and Father are here. They have come to see their grandson. You are taking him tomorrow.'

She must have forgotten. I believe she had forgotten. But by then the gun was out of her purse for sure, and it was pointed at her husband. Ex-husband, I mean. And maybe it was the shock of that—of remembering that she was in the wrong—what with the heat and the madness and her husband's laughter and the cold expressions on his parents' faces, and the muttering of her boy, who turned away from her, and that intolerable heat, and perhaps even the presence of Mr Hademak and myself, just standing by and gazing. In any case, something caused her to pull the trigger, and she shot him—not just once, but five times. Hit him in the chest with every bullet.

Blood and screaming—I can't remember anything, except so much blood and noise. The blood was gushing from him and spilling onto the wood of the terrace, and spilling across the terrace where Rudy and I had danced, and spilling out onto the steps. I ran up the same steps—there was blood on my shoes afterwards—and I tried to—stupidly, I suppose, it wasn't my place—I tried to take hold of little Jack, to shelter him from what was happening. But then somebody had already done it. I'm not certain who, but by the time I reached the terrace, he was gone and Mr de Saulles was trying to say something. There was blood everywhere. His father was bent over his body . . . Somebody shouted at me to get back off the terrace . . .

She had, I think, put the gun back in her purse by the time her husband fell silent. After that, she didn't seem to show much interest in what happened—not to him, or to her son, or even to herself. She went to sit on a bench somewhere on the edge of that big garden and she waited.

She was arrested, of course. The local sheriff carted her off to the Mineola jail soon after the ambulance carried away the body of her ex-husband.

*   *   *

Mrs de Saulles stayed in jail for five months before her case came to court. Her mother (who was, indeed, the sister of a former president of Chile— my father's information had been quite right) did what all former presidents' sisters would do, I suppose, when their daughters shoot dead their estranged husbands in front of seven or so witnesses: she engaged the most distinguished defence attorney in New York. Thanks to him—Mr Uterhart, he was called—there wasn't a day of those five months when the newspapers didn't present the world with some sympathetic story about his client—usually on the front page. Mrs de Saulles, in all her languid, wasted beauty, needed to do nothing but sit in her cell and receive visitors,

148

though—from what I understood—not many came.

We read about how slim she had become, and pale, and lifeless (as if she wasn't all those things already). We read about how she had ordered a Thanksgiving feast to be prepared and delivered to her fellow prisoners at Mineola jail (but even Mr Hademak admitted it couldn't feasibly have been her idea). Most of all, we read about how she suffered maternal deprivation between the short visits from her small son. But never—not once— did we read a word about regret.

By the time the case came to court every man in America was in love with her. Not only that, so many foul stories had been circulated about the husband she had slain—his drinking and philandering—there was barely an adult in America who didn't at least half believe he had deserved to die.

*   *   *

Mr Hademak and I—and Madeleine, too, since she'd been with Mrs de Saulles all that morning— were each required to stay nearby to give evidence at the trial and it was decided, by the powers who decided such things, that in the meantime we should continue to live at the cottage at Roslyn. Mr Hademak, still on a full salary, was often busy running errands for the de Saulles estate, but Madeleine and I, who had had our salaries cut by two-thirds, had nothing much to do but wait.

We used to go to the movies a couple of times a week, sometimes even more. I had some money left over from Mr de Saulles's generosity, and we spent our way through that—but the time hung heavy, for both of us.

Perhaps it was the relief from tension, after so many months under the yoke of Mrs de Saulles's foul mood swings. Perhaps it was the solitude of her situation, far from home and family, at the centre of a tragedy she could not control . . . but Madeleine seemed to find the change in our situation very hard to take. Above all, though, the source of her greatest unhappiness was the man she adored—a married man and a father of two—who did not return her adoration. She couldn't and wouldn't accept it.

The two of us sat together, night after night, at the kitchen table, churning over the same ground: her love—and mine.

She didn't understand my passion for Rudy. And I suppose, if I am honest, I did not entirely approve of her passion for the married man. But we listened to each other all the same, and comforted, and reassured as best as we could. I should have attended to her more closely. How different things might have been if only I had.

We weren't allowed to see little Jack. He was whisked away immediately after it happened, first by the parents of his slain father, and later—in what was quite a public coup for Mr Uterhart—by his Errazuriz grandmother, who had rented a large house a mile or so from Mineola.

I missed him terribly. Sometimes, on the days he was due to visit his mother (he came, as Mr Uterhart had so obligingly informed America's press, at noon, on Tuesdays and Thursdays of every week), Mr Hademak and I used to stand

150

outside the jailhouse simply to catch a glimpse of him—and to let him catch a glimpse of us, too. I wanted him to know that we were thinking of him, that we had not abandoned him—even if we were forbidden to meet.

There would be reporters lying in wait, and a crowd of onlookers, and then Grandmother Errazuriz and her other daughter, a coarser version of the sister behind bars, would roll up in a great limousine, and between them, dwarfed by all the activity around him, would walk little Jack, clutching the hand of his grandmother—as hard-looking a woman as any I set eyes on. The reporters would shout and the crowd would shout; and Mr Hademak and I would shout until our voices were hoarse.

He saw us once. I'm sure of it. His solemn little face lit up. He stopped—turned towards us—and then, just as we were about to reach him, his hatchet-faced grandmother tugged angrily on his sleeve and he had to walk on, sandwiched between the two women, with the cameras popping on either side of them, and the sheriff standing at the top of the steps, shaking their hands as if they were royalty arriving at a film première, not two spoilt women come to visit their murderous kin in a jail cell.

*   *   *

Rudy's letter arrived with me at Roslyn almost seven weeks after the story of the slaying first hit news-stands across America. Mr Hademak arrived from The Box, where he had spent most of his days since the police cleared out. The de Saulles family

151

had employed him to help with closing up the house. He handed the letter to me with a flourish and a blush. He said, 'This one is for you, Jennifer! Perhaps a little happiness for you in this black days . . .'

I took it. Simply—stared at it. Too shocked, too full of hope to be able to speak. After all, who else would be writing to me? I knew no one—no one but him.

'It sseems from the envelope that Mr Guglielmi posted it some time ago—Six weeks ago—do you see? To The Box, I'm not sure why. Perhaps he imagined . . . In any case—look! He has moved himself to California! You won't mind me taking note?'

I laughed aloud. Mind him taking note? I minded nothing! Nothing . . . I examined the envelope—a little confused. Having never received a letter from him, I did not know Rudy's handwriting then. And there was nothing on the outside to tell Mr Hademak from whom the letter had come. I wondered . . .

'But—'

Mr Hademak seemed to realise his mistake before I did. If he hadn't blushed before, he blushed then. 'I only guess,' he said quickly. But it was too late. In any case the poor man was so ashamed I think he longed to confess. I learned then that Rudy had written to me before this—at the cottage. It was immediately after my father died, even though he had told me he would not. And, sure enough, the letter had been intercepted. Not by Mr Hademak, he explained hastily, but by Mrs de Saulles herself. Mr Hademak had found her bent over it, standing in the hall in her night clothes. Rather than attempt to disguise her actions she had passed the letter to him and ordered him to read the rest of it to her aloud.

'I am sso ssorry . . .' he said.

'What did it say?' I asked.

'Oh, gosh. I don't remember . . . The usually things . . . I don't remember. It was very— affectionate. It was very affectionate . . .' he said again. 'I am sso ssorry . . . I tried to prevent it but Madame was . . . she was not herself, and I see now I should have stopped her. She took it and she ripped it into pieces. I should have stopped her.'

'It doesn't matter.'

'It matters, yess. And I am truly sorry . . .'

'It doesn't matter,' I said again. With this new letter in my hand, nothing mattered . . . In any case, I knew what it was to go against Mrs de Saulles—I had witnessed, with my own eyes, what happened to those foolhardy enough to try . . . And Mr Hademak was in love with her, the poor dub. We all knew it. How could I not feel for him? 'But tell me Mr Hademak—was it the only letter? Has he written to me since?'

'Not since then. He has not. He dared not. After he wrote the last time, Mrs de Saulles . . .' For a moment, Mr Hademak looked as if he might burst into tears. 'Mrs de Saulles . . .' he tried again. 'After he wrote the last time, I'm sorry to say Mrs de Saulles—she told him if he wrote again, she would turn you outside of the house.'

'She said that?'

'She said it before that—if you ever wondered. Before that—she threatened him with you, and it's why he agreed to make the appearance in the courtroom for her divorce.' He paused, then

153

seemed to decide something, and continued, 'Mr de Saulles—I don't like to speak unkindly of the dead man, but as a result of it he set a type of trap for Mr Guglielmi. He organised some documents . . . making it appear that Mr Guglielmi was mixed up in all sorts of criminalities, with unsavoury peoples, and bribery and so on, and they had him arrested . . . Mr Guglielmi was treated very roughly—by Mr and Mrs de Saulles. I must admit to it.'

I stared at him. 'You knew all that? And you didn't tell me?'

He didn't look at me. 'Finally I don't know what happened. But he was let go again, because even with the documents it couldn't appear that he had done so much wrong—and I don't think the case of his criminality went to the court . . .'

'But Mr de Saulles was so kind to me and he came to Papa's funeral. And then—But how could he?'

Mr Hademak shrugged. He didn't understand any better than I did, the depths to which the educated and privileged will stoop to protect their position. 'It's about the time you know it all,' was all he could say. 'And I am truly sorry for the role I have played in it. I knew it was wrong. They were wrong and I was wrong and it was all wrong.'

'It was very wrong.'

A long silence—and then, suddenly, I couldn't wait to be rid of him. What did any of it matter now, in any case? Rudy had written to me, and he was alive.

With hands that shook, I opened the envelope. It was a long letter, and on the paper was the faintest hint of his scent. I breathed it in, felt for a brief

154

moment as if he were there with me in the room, his arms around me . . . From between the sheets dropped a handful of dollar bills. He had sent me money.

Dearest, Darling Jennifer

(I have the letter still, thumbed and torn, and with a hole worn in the paper at the corner where the page is folded. I know it by heart, every line of it. Its image is as familiar to me as my own face.)

I have just now read the shocking news—how could I miss it? It is everywhere. And I admit my first thought was not of sorrow for Mr de Saulles— I will come back to that. It was this—that with Blanca de Saulles locked up in a jail cell, where I have long since wished her, my letters will finally be allowed to reach you. I hope I am right.

When we were together last you promised you would never despair of me. Do you remember? I have clung to it. Have you kept your promise, in spite of these months of silence? I can only pray that you have. If not, I pray that at least you will be generous enough to read this letter to the end . . .

And now I'm not even certain where to begin. With an explanation for my long silence? Or a declaration of my continued love for you, which has never once dimmed, not once in the four long months since you climbed out of the auto, that unforgettable night, and I watched you return along that lane, so bold and brave and dreadfully alone . . . You have been with me, in my thoughts and my heart, every moment of every day since . . .

He explained about the arrest. The charges had indeed been dropped but within hours of being released he had received a letter, anonymous, but on Tammany Hall writing paper even so, threatening further charges, and the inevitable deportation back home to Italy. Mr de Saulles had personal and business connections through to the very top of the Democratic Party—all the way to President Wilson himself. That was well known. Rudy had hightailed it out of town that same day— the day of Papa's funeral. He took a job with a travelling theatre and wound up in California where for the last few months, it was clear he had been struggling to scrape a living, working as an extra for the studios. But he had not forgotten me. He had been saving money to return to New York and fetch me.

As it is [he wrote], *I have enough money now for one person's passage from New York to Los Angeles. In a few months I would have enough for both of us but it occurs to me, now that you are free to receive my letters, why would I wait? Instead I am sending you all the money I have so far saved . . .*

In that way, Jennifer, there is no need for either of us to wait a moment longer than necessary, and the choice to come, or not to come, is yours completely. If you have missed me a quarter as much as I have missed you, I know you will not hesitate. You will take the money and buy a train ticket to California, and you will come and live with me here, and I will build my cars and act, and you will write your scenarios and make me laugh,

156

*as only you can, and be beautiful as only you are—
and you will become my wife . . .*

*Will you come to Hollywood? It is wonderful
here: the orange groves, the warm sun, the hot, dry
landscape—they remind me of my home . . . And
yet, with all its hope and peculiar vigour, and with
so much changing, so much that is new here every
day, this little town—which grows bigger by the
hour—possesses everything that is most
exhilarating about America! You would agree with
me, I'm sure of it. Jennifer, I swear you would love
it here. Will you come?*

*I have enclosed an address for you to reach me
in Hollywood. I will not pretend it is a palace—not
quite yet. It is a small grey room, in a small grey
boarding-house, where women are not even
permitted . . . But if you come, we will find a new
place together, and in no time we shall be building
our own palace together. We can do that, can't we,
Jennifer?*

*I shall wait, and pray . . . Jenny, darling, please
come! I cannot think of a person on this great
planet of ours I should be happier to see. I have
missed you—your beautiful face, your courage,
your humour, your spirit. I have missed you,
darling, more than I can ever express. Sometimes it
is so intense that I look out from my window onto
the sun-baked street and imagine I can see you
appearing as a mirage through the dust. It was
always an impossible dream before and yet when I
looked out I could still believe it. Now that you
know where to find me—perhaps, one day, when I
look out, it will really be you . . .*

*In any case—if you have read this far—please
know it for ever, cara mia, that I love you, and*

157

wherever I go, whatever I do, there will always be a place in my heart which waits for you . . .

Hopefully and for ever yours, darling Jennifer your
Rodolfo

HOTEL CONTINENTAL

NEW YORK

Monday, 16 August 1926

He is at the Polyclinic Hospital on West 50th. In the 'lucky suite', it says in the paper, because a few years back Mary Pickford was in the same room and made some kind of miraculous recovery. I'm praying it might be so lucky for him.

They told me on the telephone he was in the operating theatre. That was yesterday. I went directly to the hospital as soon as I finished on the telephone and of course they ordered me right away again. I told them my name—I suppose I hoped it might have registered. There might even have been a message for me. But, of course, how could there have been when by all accounts poor Rudy has been unconscious since he arrived?

Today everything is much worse. There are reports on all the front pages that he is gravely ill, having been operated on for a 'perforated ulcer'. But what does that mean? How does a man, perfectly healthy one day, suddenly have a perforated ulcer the next? Is a 'perforated ulcer' something people die from? Apparently, it says in the paper, if it's bad enough, yes, they can. Or if something goes wrong, yes, they can. Yes. Except it's impossible. I cannot imagine a universe without Rudy.

I have already been to the hospital again this morning, but now there is such a crowd out there they have barricaded the entrance and they aren't letting anyone in. This morning I couldn't reach the desk to discover what news there was—let alone to give them my name again. He might have asked for me.

And now I have returned to my hotel because that way at least I can telephone the hospital from the lobby. But I have tried fifty times already and the line is always busy. I have telephoned the Ambassador Hotel too. Not surprisingly, they sounded thoroughly fed up when I told them my reason for calling, and spent almost our entire conversation listing reasons why they were too busy to help—time they could easily have spent checking he hadn't left me a message, or at least allowing me to leave a message for him.

But the hotel is flooded with calls, since nobody can get through to the hospital, and now they are simply refusing to help anyone at all. God forbid Mr Charlie Chaplin should call for news of his friend. Or President Coolidge. Or me. Because we shall none of us receive it in any case. The hospital won't answer the telephone. The Ambassador won't even receive messages.

'All enquiries regarding Mr Valentino should be directed to the Polyclinic Hospital on West 50th,' the operator said, the instant I uttered his name. I got a little choked up trying to explain, which didn't help. I could hear my voice rising, however hard I tried to stop it—because I could tell that any minute she was going to cut me off, and then it would be another half an hour or an hour before I could get through to talk to them again.

'But I was *there*!' I cried. As if she cared. 'I was *with him*. We were supposed to be lunching together!'

'I'm sorry to hear that, ma'am,' the operator said.

'*But don't you get it? I simply have to speak to him*!' She thought I was nuts. I didn't care.

'I understand, ma'am,' she said, with the exaggerated patience that can drive you crazy sometimes, when you just know they couldn't understand, couldn't possibly. 'It so happens there are a lot of people out there wanting to speak with Mr Valentino. I'm sorry I can't help you. All enquiries regarding Mr Valentino should be directed to the Polyclinic Hospital on West 50th. If you like I can give you their number.'

'But I can't get through to the hospital! The telephone line is always busy. I'm sure, if you would only check—I'm certain he might have left me a message.'

'I don't know what newspaper you've been reading, ma'am, but from what I've been reading, Mr Valentino is in no state to be leaving messages for anyone.'

'Or perhaps Mr Ullman has left me something. Perhaps Rudy asked Mr Ullman . . .'

'I really can't help you, ma'am.'

'But won't you please—couldn't you just quickly have the smallest little look for me? It's Lola Nightingale. My name is Lola Nightingale. And I know you probably think I'm cracked but I was there with him all Friday. All Thursday night and all Friday, and if you don't believe me, why, I could describe his room to you if you'd only give me half a chance. There is the Chinese

161

lacquered chest right by the—in the . . .'

'I'm sure you were, ma'am. I guess he must have been mighty busy because I've had fifty ladies calling this morning saying just the same thing. I'm sorry. I can't help you. *All enquiries regarding Mr Valentino should be directed to the Polyclinic Hospital on West 50th .'*

And then she cut me off.

*   *   *

The newspapers say he's gravely ill— unconscious or in terrible pain. They talk about perforated ulcers—but nobody explains why: I keep asking—but how can a young man, perfectly healthy one day, be unconscious and close to dying from a perforated ulcer the next? How can that be?

I will go back to the hospital. God knows why. I know I shan't be allowed in. But I can't sit here doing nothing. I can't bear to sit here and wait.

*   *   *

The rumour ripped through the crowd while I was standing in the midst of it, and as it spread—from what source, who knows?—there rose the dreadful sound of gasps and wails, until within a minute the air was echoing to the din of their sobbing.

It is almost all women outside the hospital, of course: a great host of Lola Nightingales. N-bodies from N-where. And every one of them convinced they possess a little part of him. Except *they don't*. I watched them all, weeping

162

and wailing, and I wanted to take hold of every one of them and shake them until their teeth fell out.

Because what did they have to wail for? Had they known him when he was a no one, too? Had he helped them as he helped me, when my father lay dead; had he kissed them as he kissed me? Had they lain in his arms and talked of the children they would one day have together? Had they waited for him, as I had, and longed for him, as I had, and believed in him, as I had? Had they—had the girl over there, with the tears streaming down her face as if her own child had been wrenched from her—had she felt him so deep inside her there could be no certainty where he ended and she began? *Had he loved her as he loved me?*

The ladies' wailing got so bad, maybe he heard it in his hospital suite up there on the eighth floor. Maybe it raised him to consciousness for the briefest moment. In any case there I was, right in the thick of it all, jostled by the wailers, too numb to move, and then the front doors to the hospital were pushed open and Mr Ullman appeared. The reporters went crazy, pushing and shoving, their cameras popping . . .

'Tell us, Mr Ullman! Mr Ullman, over here! Is Mr Valentino dead? Could you tell us, please—is Mr Valentino dead?'

Mr Ullman seemed to look from one reporter to the next, from one big, bawling mouth to next, as if uncertain where to start. His brash face was pinched with strain, and the sight of him standing there, so bamboozled when he ought to have been in his element, made me realise suddenly how bad things had to be. On Thursday Mr Ullman had been a picture of vulgar health. He was a different man today, his skin grey, with dark rings under his eyes and a face shrunken with lack of sleep. Seeing the change in him made me wonder—was it possible—was it possible what they were suggesting?

He began to speak—but over the noise he couldn't be heard. He tried again, three or four times. The crowd grew quite angry, instructing itself to be silent. Finally there was quiet.

His hands were shaking when he brought out his sheet of paper. He didn't say much, and what he said was said too quietly. In spite of the silence, we had to strain to hear.

'Mr Valentino,' he read aloud, with that paper shaking in his hands, 'has rallied from a brief relapse earlier in the day. But the danger has not yet passed. He remains unconscious . . .'

IS HE DEAD? yelled the reporters.

Mr Ullman lowered the shaking sheet. 'He is not dead,' he said. 'No.'

A murmur of relief tinged with disappointment, I think, from those ladies enjoying the drama; and then the newsies sparked up again with another hundred more questions.

What exactly was it that ailed him?
Was there any suggestion of foul play?
Would he pull through?
Was Pola Negri with him?

Pola Negri was not with him. Pola Negri was being kept informed of his progress but remained in California.

Was Pola Negri going to come to New York to see him?

164

'At the moment,' Mr Ullman said, 'Mr Valentino is not in sufficiently good health to be receiving any visitors at all.'

He announced to the crowd that several extra telephone operators had been brought into the hospital to deal with enquiries, and that there was now a 'Valentino Information Desk' inside the building, from where a statement regarding the patient's progress would be given out 'every few hours or so'.

In the mean time, he said, Rudy had been sent so many flowers by well-wishers they were now being distributed throughout the hospital. 'He has also received many thousands of telegrams. We have decided that these . . . will remain unopened until the patient himself is in a condition to appreciate them . . .' He seemed to struggle for a moment. There was a pause. Finally, he said, 'I should thank you all, on his behalf, for your kind concern.' And with that he turned hurriedly away, beneath a barrage of further questions, all of which he ignored.

And I could not get to him. The crowd was so thick I couldn't reach him or even catch his eye. Would he have recognised me, if I had? Perhaps not. But if he had seen me, and if I had reminded him and if, perhaps, I had found a chance to tell him my name . . .

But even then, even if he'd realised it was I who had been with Rudy all Thursday night and all Friday, when he was tapping on the suite door, would he have known—how could he ever have known?—what we mean to one another, Rudy and I, how much those hours together mattered to us both?

And now what? I am here again. Waiting. Going crazy with the waiting. Perhaps now, with the new operators and the 'information desk', I shall be able to get a message to him. Perhaps. Except the hysteria, along with the crowd, seems to be growing every moment, and he only grows weaker . . . I sent him a telegram—which lies somewhere unopened. I sent him flowers, which lie beside some stranger's bed. With a message from me . . . I wonder, would they have removed it?

*   *   *

Afterwards—after Mr Ullman disappeared back into the hospital—I walked across town to the Ambassador and waited in the lobby as unobtrusively as I could. I sat at a small table and scribbled a long letter to Rudy, which I intended to hand to Mr Ullman the moment he came by, or possibly to the girl, Rudy's assistant, who had shown me up to the suite when I had first arrived, what seems now like a lifetime ago.

But then, after an hour of my sitting there, maybe a little longer, somebody in uniform, with tassels on his shoulders, came over to ask me what I was doing. I pretended I was waiting to meet someone. Unfortunately I'm a lousy liar and I didn't remember to cover up all the papers in front of me. Too late, I saw him peering down at the top of my letter.

Darling Rudy . . .

When I failed to offer an explanation that

satisfied him, either for my presence in the hotel lobby or for the letter I was writing, he ordered me to leave.

I asked him if he would let me take the letter—still unfinished—and hand it to the girl at the desk, so that she might give it to Mr Ullman. He was kind enough to let me do that at least. But then the girl at the desk refused to take it. She looked at me with utter disdain and told me Mr Ullman had organised a bed for himself at the hospital.

'You had better take the letter there,' she said. 'He won't receive it if you leave it here.'

I'm not sure whether to believe her. But, for the moment, I am out of ideas. I can do nothing, it seems, but read each fresh edition of every newspaper for more bulletins, and call the 'Valentino Information Desk', and stand outside the hospital. And return to my room. And wait.

Thank God, at least I have my typewriter. I should work on one of the photoplays. I know I should. Except I don't want to.

I want to write this.

LONG ISLAND–HOLLYWOOD

I suppose there's no point in writing any of it if I end up putting down lies or half-truths or, at any rate, not properly explaining things. I am ashamed to remind myself how I came to be on that train heading west, in my smart new clothes, and with a job lined up, and enough cash in my purse to set myself up in Hollywood quite comfortably for a couple of months at least. It wasn't Rudy's money that took me there. I had already spent it.

*   *   *

Madeleine—darling, brave Madeleine—embraced me when I showed her Rudy's letter. She danced around the kitchen, laughing aloud and clapping with glee.

'You've had a rotten time of it, Jenny,' she said, hugging me. 'Of course *I* can't see what you see in the man, not me.' She smiled. She knew I found it impossible to believe. 'But there's no hiding *you* think the world of him. And after these past few months, with your papa and all, on top of everything, I swear you deserve every piece of good fortune that ever comes your way.' And then, quite suddenly, she burst into tears.

It pierced through my own exuberance, of course it did. Poor wretched Madeleine. I apologised for my tactlessness, and Madeleine apologised profusely for her tears. She wiped her eyes on her sleeve, muttered something about feeling under the weather. I didn't believe her, of course. But I didn't argue either. We both knew that my dreams had come true and hers, with her good-for-nothing lover, had not; and we both knew it was quite unfair. Because— It's so terribly easy to be moralistic. But it's a matter of luck, isn't it? You can't really help who you fall in love with.

I tried to persuade her to come with me to Hollywood. She had no family here and a lover who didn't love her, with a family of his own. Added to which—as I said to her—she had the look of a movie star already. And she did, too. Madeleine was beautiful. With her golden russet hair and those slanting grey cat's eyes, she was stunning. Anyway, she laughed when I suggested it—and simultaneously started crying all over again. She had no interest in Hollywood, or in becoming a movie star, or in anything else. She was in love. It was all she cared about: how best to make Mr Jeremy Leahy love her back.

*   *   *

A few days later Mr Hademak and I returned from a shopping trip in Westbury, which was meant to have taken all afternoon. We came home several hours earlier than expected, however, due to my having left my purse at the cottage.

I found Madeleine lying in the bathtub of Mrs de Saulles's private bathroom, the water lapping at her nostrils. She was out cold. In her limp hand, half submerged, was an empty liquor bottle—gin. By her head, there was the residue of some foul-smelling tea and, beside it—not even a knitting needle: a kitchen skewer, rusty and red. The bath water was coloured with her blood.

I pulled her from the tub—her skinny white body with the tell-tale streaks of blood, and just a small bump where the baby was. Later she told me she guessed she'd been three months gone already and yet she had never said a word. And I had never asked, or ever noticed. All the nights we had gossiped and confided, and she had been carrying the secret . . .

I covered her with a towel and yelled for Mr Hademak, who appeared at the door; a blond, awkward giant. But he took one look at the scene and seemed to understand at once, better than I did, what was required.

'She's pregnant,' I said.

'Of courses . . . Poor girl.'

'I think she's been trying to get rid of the baby,' I explained unnecessarily. I was kneeling beside her, sitting her up, patting her face.

'You knew?' Mr Hademak asked me.

'I didn't. No. I didn't know . . .'

He shook his head. 'She needs a doctor. But not perhaps simply any doctor, Jennifer . . .'

'No. Mr Hademak—and I have no idea where to begin to look. Do you know of one?'

He nodded. 'It iss difficult. A difficult situation . . . I can call someone. He is in the city, but he will come at once, if I call . . . He—helped the mistress in a similar . . .' I didn't need to look: I could feel his discomfort burning up the room. My half-brother or sister, perhaps? Probably not. It was not a moment to be considering it. No moment was. 'Any cases,' Mr Hademak continued, 'he was a very good doctor. Excellent. Kind. Very discreet. But the trouble, he is expensive . . . I have a little money saved. But . . .'

I didn't think about it. 'Never mind the money,' I said. 'I have the money. Please—just call. I will pay.'

Madeleine came round while the doctor was on his way. She protested as well as she could. She said she knew of a woman who would 'finish the job' and charge a quarter the price. But, in my mind, that was out of the question. Not considering the state she was already in; not after the damage she had already done to herself. Mr Hademak agreed with me, and—really—she was not in any position to fight. The doctor arrived a few hours later. Madeleine spent the next two days in bed.

* * *

It's a funny thing, the turn of fate, because if Madeleine had waited just a day or two more, God knows what might have happened to her, but I, most probably, would already have been on the way to Hollywood.

Once I had received Rudy's letter I had no interest in sticking around for the trial. I knew I was meant to, of course. But I couldn't see the point. The deed was done. The man was buried. His blood had long since been washed away. With or without my evidence the verdict could hardly have been in doubt. It's what I thought. And meanwhile Rudy was waiting for me. My life was waiting to begin.

I had already written him a letter telling him I

was on my way. It had been lying on my bedside table for four long days by the time I discovered Madeleine in the bathtub. The only reason I hadn't posted it was because each time I reread the previous draft it seemed imperfect in some way, and I felt an irresistible urge to reword some small part of it.

And then, once I had given the money—his money to Madeleine, I couldn't post it. Worse than that—I discovered I simply couldn't write anything to him at all.

How could I write to him that I was on my way to him when I no longer had the means to get myself there? On the other hand, if I told him I was *not* on my way, he would want an explanation as to why, since he had sent me the money to make the journey. And how could I write to him, after all this time, only to tell him I had spent the money he had so lovingly saved, and in such a way—and without even consulting him? Rudy, I knew well, was intelligent, liberal, kind. Not a fool. But, still, he was a man. What man on earth would understand it?

I couldn't do it. I tried—but I couldn't find the words.

So . . . I said nothing. Day followed night, followed day . . . the war raged on. American soldiers left for Europe in their thousands and died in Europe in their thousands . . . Mr Uterhart filled the papers with ever more heart rending stories of Mrs de Saulles in her Mineola jail cell. Madeleine returned to health, and to her dreadful, unloving lover. But she was mortified at having, she felt, ruined my hopes, and she couldn't stay silent about it—and no matter what I said, no matter how I

172

reassured her, she could not forgive herself for it. And, truth be told, in my heart of hearts, though I knew—*I knew*—it wasn't her fault that I had spent the money on her, I couldn't entirely forgive her, either . . . We swore eternal friendship. But really, after a while, it became easier for us to avoid each other's company altogether.

And all I thought about was Rudy. I could feel my silence wounding him: six weeks had already passed before the letter reached me, and now another six weeks had passed—I could feel him slipping away from me . . . Day followed night, followed day . . .

It makes my skin crawl to remember it, but in my desperation to raise the money I had spent, I attempted to make advances on a young soldier. He was sitting on a bench outside the train station, minding his own business. It was dusk, and I had put on lipstick—my first time. The look of incredulity on his face as I stumbled through my proposition will stay with me for ever. To his credit, perhaps—to my eternal chagrin—he laughed aloud when I had finished. He told me to get home at once, or he would telephone my mother.

And then, just days before the trial began, I was made an offer of five hundred dollars. I don't want to dwell on the details. In any case the individual never told me his name. He said that what he was suggesting was not illegal. Ha! That he was 'under no circumstances' suggesting I should lie, only that I try to be 'generous' when it came for my turn in the witness box.

*　　　*　　　*

I didn't lie. But, then, I didn't entirely tell the truth either.

All right, I did lie.

I said she was a good employer. And a loving mother.

I didn't mention how many times she patted her purse on that awful journey from Roslyn to The Box. And I didn't mention her liaison with my father or the peculiar meeting she had on the terrace with Rudy, that first night I arrived. I didn't mention her vile temper; her jealousy; her inability to spend more than twenty minutes with little Jack before sending him away again. I didn't mention how she used to pace the cottage, muttering to herself, half mad with hatred for her husband, whenever he had custody of the child. Oh, God— does it matter? By then the deed was done. The man was dead. The blood was washed away.

I told the court instead about the evening I arrived on Long Island, when Mr de Saulles danced with Joan Sawyer and Mrs de Saulles looked on.

'How did Mrs de Saulles appear to you, as her husband cavorted and danced with Miss Sawyer before his own wife?' Mr Uterhart asked me.

I knew the question was coming. Of course. I was well prepared. So I said— I took a deep breath. I swallowed and glanced about me, at the crowded court room, at the public gallery, where there was not an inch of space unused. I burned under all the eyeballs that were directed on me, waiting expectantly for my dishonest reply . . . And I thought of my train ticket to California, and of

Rudy, his arms outstretched to hold me, and of his arms wrapped around me, and of how happy we could both be as soon as all of this was over . . . I thought of my new life with the man I loved, and I said: *You ask me what did she look like, Mr Uterhart? I would say she looked just terribly sad. Terribly wounded. And lost. And alone. She looked just terribly, terribly lonely.*

'And would you kindly tell the court—on that tragic afternoon when Mrs de Saulles arrived at The Box to reclaim her son, who had been kept from her by her husband, despite his having promised to deliver the boy to her earlier that day—what did she say to him exactly?'

She said (I told the court), 'Hello, Jack. I have come to fetch the boy.'

'And what did Mr de Saulles reply?'

'He laughed at her.'

'And was his laughter unkind, to you, knowing the dreadful psychic strain being suffered at that time by Mrs de Saulles?'

I said his laughter was unkind. And when Mr Uterhart pushed, I agreed with him that I thought it sounded very cruel.

So. There. I have said it. Mr Hademak gave similar evidence, from what I read—and I have no idea if he received money for it. He didn't see her tapping that little purse, as I had. He didn't see her as the rest of the household saw her, as anyone who knew her saw her. Like most of America, he was in love with her.

Mrs de Saulles was found not guilty. When the verdict came, so enslaved by her listless beauty was the public gallery, it erupted as one into cheers. Indeed, I heard they unfurled a banner in Times

Square in New York that afternoon, and the same thing happened. Crowds cheered with delight that the killer had been freed. She left America soon afterwards—within days. She took her son with her, and I have never seen or heard from either one of them since.

I don't know or care what became of her. She was in Paris once, not long ago, at the same time as Rudy—he told me. He sent a message suggesting they meet, but she didn't reply. And I read somewhere she was married again, to a rich Chilean businessman. Well, he had better watch out.

*   *   *

On the day before I finally left for California, I insisted on taking Madeleine and Mr Hademak to lunch at Sherry's, the place where Mr de Saulles and Papa had eaten together on the day he and I arrived in New York.

It was a stupid attempt to make things tidy that could never be tidy; and to remember Papa, I suppose, and to say farewell to him now that I was leaving him behind in New York; and also to acknowledge something of what Mr de Saulles had done for us both by bringing us here to America in the first place—Oh, God, I don't know—and to apologise to him, in some hopeless, stupid way, for what I had said in court.

In any case, whatever I was attempting to achieve by going there, it wasn't achieved. I felt miserable all through lunch. It was a magnificent dining room—closed now, of course—but we were all a little overwhelmed by our surroundings.

176

Mr Hademak could hardly stay in his place; I think he hated to be seated before so many important fellow diners, some of whom (though I didn't recognise any) he said he had waited on himself at The Box.

And Madeleine, forever uncomfortable around me now, was horribly tetchy about the prices, despite the fact that I was paying. In the end I ignored them both—and tried instead to imagine where Papa and Mr de Saulles might have sat on that day, and what they might have said to one another, and how they might have made each other laugh, and of how cheerful they would both have been, to be reunited for the first time since London—and of how little they realised what few and painful days lay ahead.

*   *   *

Mr Hademak came with me to Grand Central Station. It was sweet of him. I shall never forget him standing there, so large and so lost in the crowd, waving at me, wishing me luck . . .

Poor man. I wonder what became of him. He had no plans when I left him there. I think he was waiting for a summons from Mrs de Saulles, so he could continue his service with her at home in Santiago. I think that's all he wanted. I wonder if the summons ever came. I hope so, for his sake— but I doubt it.

The first train took me as far as Chicago, and then there was another, which took me on to Los Angeles, and I don't believe I spoke more than ten words to anyone during the whole long, broken

177

journey. For five days, I sat and gazed out of my window and watched the scenery go by—the infinite, unending scenery. It was beautiful. Staggering. The sheer scale of it, after small grey England—it took my breath away: those wide open, endless plains, and the vast canyons . . . on and on . . . until the plains turned to desert, and on and on . . . through the dry heat and the rocky, barren land, and on and on . . . to the orange groves and pepper trees of California . . . I drank. I remember I drank a lot on that journey, more than I ever had—because it calmed the turmoil inside. And the further west I travelled and the more I drank, the further I seemed to leave that awful war behind—and so much else too: so many unhappy memories. It was in those five days, those empty, befuddled hours, that I first began to love this country better than I ever loved my own. Long before I had arrived there, drunk or sober, I knew in my heart that California would be my home.

But it was a long and lonely journey. I took care not to catch the eye of anyone for fear they might engage me in conversation, and I don't know what human-repelling vapour I must have been releasing, but in any case, nobody bothered me much. I sat in the dining carriage and drank and ate alone. I retired to my cabin and slept alone. And I wrote, of course, to keep myself company: the first half of another photoplay. It was about a lonesome English girl who heads west on a train from New York to start a new life with her lover in California . . . Oh dear! I remember taking one last look at it as the train drew into the station at Los Angeles, and leaving it there on the cot. Maybe somebody picked it up. I do hope not.

But it kept me occupied and, combined with liquor, it helped in my chief objective, which was to avoid having to reflect . . . about Papa, and the courtroom and, worst of all, of course, about the possibility that I might be coming all the way to California to be reunited with Rudy at last, only to find him gone.

I had written to him the moment my evidence was given and the lucre was in my dirty hands. I had intended to wait in Roslyn for his reply but, in the end, how could I? Close to five months had passed since he had written to me, and it was close to five months before that since I had seen him last. With the court case finished and the money to travel in my purse, I simply couldn't force myself to wait any longer. It meant, as I travelled to join him, there could be no way of knowing even if he had received my letter, let alone, after so many months, if he had the slightest interest in seeing me again.

Whenever the fear of what lay ahead became too overwhelming I would bring his letter out to remind myself—for, after all, how could a man write such a letter one day, then so quickly forget about it the next? If he had missed me even an eighth as much as I had missed him, he would still be waiting. I was sure of it.

*　　*　　*

When I reached Los Angeles the sun was shining, as it does in Los Angeles, and the autos were honking, as they do in New York. Only in Los Angeles, beneath the sunshine, they were bigger cars and they honked louder. Or so it seemed. The air smelled of gasoline, and orange groves, and

179

mimosa. And possibility and enterprise and fantasy and hope . . . Oh, I don't know—maybe that's nothing but hogwash. Maybe we Californians begin to believe our own propaganda. Nevertheless I swear I felt it that morning. There is something about the place—even there at the train station— something magical, some kind of gold dust in the air. It is everywhere—it glimmers in the hot, dry sunshine, luring us to a sort of madness; a sort of fever of greed for life.

Back then the movie magazines were already warning young people against coming to Hollywood. There used to be long articles about the thousands of girls who arrived, full of big, innocent dreams, only to wind up destitute, living on the streets, sleeping around, whatnot . . . And how right those magazines were. It's just a matter of fact that some of us prefer to find these things out for ourselves.

I had read one article claiming that so many hopeful young women came flooding into Los Angeles train station each day, there were missionaries lying in wait for them on the platform. The poor girls were being stopped as they came off their trains by zealous California matrons, who blocked their paths and tried to dissuade them from travelling any further before it was too late and the corrupting forces of Hollywood ruined them for ever.

I wonder if a single missionary lady ever succeeded in persuading a single girl to turn back. I doubt it. In fact, now I think about it, I wonder if there ever were any missionaries there at all, or if it was simply nonsense invented by reporters to fill up their nonsensical magazines. Certainly, on the day I arrived, my new suitcase bulging with the wardrobe I had bought with my ill-gotten gains, there was not a missionary matron in sight.

Even if there had been, my defence was already prepared. I had my letter of introduction from Mr Uterhart in my jacket pocket, ready to present to them . . . I also had, thanks to Mr Uterhart, a job as an office clerk awaiting me at a legal office on Vine Street, Hollywood.

Above all, of course—though this I intended to keep to myself—I had Rudy.

*   *   *

After keeping him waiting so long, I realised I needed to be careful how I first presented myself to him. Only imagine if he saw me (I worried) and at the sight of me was aghast that he had bothered to wait for me so long.

I was determined not to arrive at his door helpless and needy, with clothes all wrong and hair in mess. My plan—inasmuch as I had formulated any—was first to find myself someplace to stay, then to fix my hair and clean myself up; next to present myself at that legal office with the letter from Mr Uterhart and assure myself that I did indeed have safe employment there. It would take a day or two, and would be quite excruciating, I imagined, to force myself to it; but I was willing to wait. It seemed vital to me that I presented myself in a good light.

*   *   *

My future employer had provided me with the

address of a respectable rooming-house for ladies, situated close to the offices, but the taxicab I took from the train station refused to drive me all the way there. He said he had business back in Los Angeles and I was too overwhelmed, at that point, to put up a fight. He dropped me a couple of blocks away, on the corner of Vine and Sunset: the heart of Hollywood.

I stood there that very first morning, squinting in the dry, busy, dusty sunlight, feeling the heat on my back, and the sweat trickling beneath my New York clothes. I hadn't yet taken a step. Not a step! I glanced up the noisy street, and between the roaring traffic, the hamburger stands, the bootboys and, up and down the dusty sidewalk, the realtors shouting out their prices, I spied a herd of twenty or more cowboys approaching! Nobody around me seemed to think much of it. I stared at them: was I dreaming? As they drew closer I noticed the thick white screen paint on their faces. Ha!

The sight of them riding by, in the midst of the noise of the city, it made me suddenly laugh aloud—for I knew I was in Hollywood then. I might have been standing in the middle of a film set, or at the centre of the universe—or both: sometimes I do believe they are one and the same. In any case at that instant I was overcome by a rush of elation, just as I had been that first night at The Box. I had made it! I had arrived! All the horrors of the last year were behind me. A life with Rudy, and all the glamour and excitement of this new world stood in front.

*　　　*　　　*

The Vine Street offices of Wormholt and Simmons brought me down to earth again quickly enough.

Mr Simmons (an uncle, by marriage, of Henry Uterhart's wife) ran a small, dull legal partnership on Vine Street. It was staffed by himself and another dull old man, named Mr Wormholt—and both, in my opinion, were well overdue for retirement. They appeared to have no business at all. I think they only kept the office of Wormholt and Simmons as a place to be away from their spouses. And I can only imagine that they agreed to employ me (I hardly flatter myself) partly as a favour to their glamorous nephew-in-law, whose name, thanks to Mrs de Saulles, had recently been all over the newspapers, and partly because they liked to have some fresh flesh about the place.

I am being unkind. Only people who work in the film colony say such dreadful things about the gentlemen, and I'm hardly likely to defend them, but really those two respectable old duffers, their heads all dusted up with legalities, their weekends arranged round Anti-Saloon League tea parties, they were quite the most uninhibited pair of lechers I ever came across.

Nevertheless, in that town, with so many young women looking for work, I was fortunate. I didn't complain.

I joined them on a Friday, which was fortunate. First thing Saturday morning, having not slept a wink, I took myself to a hair salon on Hollywood Boulevard, recommended by one of the girls in the rooming-house.

The beautician persuaded me to get a bob. I watched as great clumps of my beloved brown hair tumbled to the floor—and by then I was in such a ferment, such a state of terror about what lay ahead, I am ashamed to say I wept.

'Don't you worry,' she said, chop-chopping away. 'All the girls cry the first time. When I'm finished you'll wonder what you were fussing about!'

She was quite right. Afterwards, as she and I gazed back at my new light-headed reflection, I felt marvellous. Like a new woman! Like the sort of modern girl other girls were, but not me.

'Congratulations!' she said. As if I'd joined some kind of club. Which I suppose in a way I had. Not many girls had gone for the big chop back then.

I only wondered what Rudy would think.

I returned to my room to change; settled, after a frenzy of indecision, on a dress of flat crêpe, sky blue, with new pumps to match. It wasn't the dress I had intended, of course—the dress Madeleine and I had shopped for with so much care, that day in Manhattan. That one looked quite wrong, in the way dresses only can look utterly wrong when it's absolutely vital they look utterly right. And I'd spent some money on face paint, too, which I had never worn before, but which all the girls seemed to wear in Hollywood.

I looked back at my slick new reflection one final time before heading out. I wondered briefly if Rudy would even recognise me . . . I laughed. *Of course*, I thought. *Of course he will!*

*   *   *

Rudy's boarding-house was only a few blocks away, easily walkable—or so it seemed by the street map. But the blocks are so big in Hollywood! By the time I reached his address, way up on Sunset

Boulevard, the California sun was high in the sky. My beautiful blue dress of flat crêpe looked flatter than ever, my feet were swollen inside their beautiful new pumps, and my new short hair was sodden between hat and head.

I found a pepper tree not far from the building—just a wood-fronted, beaten-up old boarding-house. My knees were shaking so badly I couldn't quite dare to present myself before it—just yet. I was hot and thirsty and—having taken to smoking on the train journey from New York—I was longing for a cigarette. I lit one then, under the shade of that pepper tree, and tried to collect myself.

*   *   *

A hundred images skipped across my mind—of him and me and little Jack in the nursery at The Box, and then of Rudy, simply, his head thrown back in laughter, and then again, as he had looked that night, the first time he told me he loved me . . . I remembered him on the terrace at The Box, before the blood was spilled—how we had danced that first night, and how we had kissed on the pier at Luna Park; and then again at the movie theatre, until the gentleman beside us had said he'd have us thrown out if we didn't stop. And I remembered how tender he was that night, and natural, when I lay with my father, and he lay asleep in the passageway outside; and of how he organised and paid for Papa's funeral without ever saying a word; and of how he took me to his bench in Central Park, and we opened the champagne and as he passed it me, to drink from the bottle, he said,

185

Gulp it back, cara mia, gulp it back! Because tonight, my darling, more than any night, we are celebrating Life!

I glanced up at the battered old boarding-house. Would he be in there? Really? Was this all a dream? And if he wasn't—what then? I had not the faintest idea . . .

What in God's name had I done?

Ten long months since last we'd spoken. Five long months since he'd written to me, asking me to come . . .

I took deep drags on that cigarette, so deep I began to feel the blood draining from my head, and I pulled out his letter again . . .

. . . I look out from my window onto the sun-baked street and imagine I can see you appearing as a mirage through the dust . . . before, in my heart, I always knew it was an impossible dream and yet, when I looked out, I could still believe it. Now that you know where to find me—perhaps, one day, when I look out, it really will be you . . .

The door to the boarding-house was hanging open. I called hello, but nobody replied, so I stepped inside. It was just a bare room, not very welcoming, whitewashed and windowless, with an odour of frying in the dark air. There was an empty kiosk by the stairs and a sign in front of it:

No Jews. No Actors.
No Women. No Vacancies

There was a bell, too. I rang it. For ages, nobody came. When the man finally emerged—from the depths of God knew where—the stink of him half knocked me sideways. He gave me a look, and he said, 'No women.'

I told him I was looking for a gentleman named Guglielmi. Rodolfo Guglielmi.

He didn't reply. Chewed on his lip and glared at me.

'Guglielmi,' I said. 'Mr Guglielmi. He's staying in room . . .' I waved the letter, pretended to check, as if the number weren't scorched on my memory '. . . room number twenty-three.'

He stared at me.

'Mr Guglielmi.'

He stared.

'With dark hair? He's a young gentleman . . . Very handsome. You couldn't miss him.'

He stared.

'I mean to say he's—Italian. He's got dark hair . . . ?'

A long silence.

'Is something the matter?' I ventured at last.

'I said no women.'

'Oh. But I'm looking for—'

'Never heard of the guy.'

'But he's staying here. He's a dancer. You couldn't miss him.'

'No dancers here.'

'But he was staying here. I have his letter. He's—he was staying here.'

'Never stayed here. Never had no Guglielmi

187

staying here. What is he—a Yid? No Yids allowed.'

'He's not a Yid! What's the matter with you? I just told you. He's Italian. He's living here. He's written to me his address. And he's a dancer—from Italy.'

'*Italy!*' And at that—he spat. 'No wops here. No dancers here. No Jews. And no women.'

'I've only come to—'

'No women.'

'No, but I—'

'You deaf, lady? I said no women. Get outta here. Before I call the cops.'

*   *   *

I sat under the pepper tree all afternoon. And every time I saw somebody walking into the building, I would stop them and ask, Did they know of a Rodolfo Guglielmi? A dancer. Very good-looking. He lived in room twenty-three . . .

Nobody did. It began to grow dark. And then it was dark, and finally I was making the long walk back to my room on Carlos Avenue. Some guy pulled up and offered me a lift home. Or maybe to his place. Or maybe we stopped for dinner first. Maybe we did that. Maybe he was a really nice guy. Hell, I don't remember any more. But of course I do. I remember very clearly.

He wasn't Rudy. So what does it matter anyway?

HOTEL CONTINENTAL

NEW YORK

Tuesday, 17 August 1926

4 p.m.
It is gruesome out there—part summer fair, part death watch, part funeral wake. They have people selling hamburgers and roasted corn, people selling picture postcards of Rudy. They have every reporter in America, or so it seems, jostling to get a view of the hospital door (never mind a whole bunch of others, the ones with privileged passes, filing their articles from a special room somewhere on the first floor). There are the newspaper boys selling special 'Valentino' extras, and the women, hundreds of them, sometimes many more, chattering and laughing—only pausing to gasp when each new rumour of death reaches them, before starting up with the chattering again.

And up above it all, up there in his 'lucky' suite on the eighth floor, slipping in and out of consciousness, lies my darling Rudy—so far from his home and family, in so much pain, and it kills me to think of him, alone amid all this madness, when I could be there with him, if only they would allow me. I could be comforting him.

I detest it out by the hospital. And yet I can't seem to keep away. What else can I do? I am only waiting for news of him. I suppose if Frances

189

Marion were to call, and we were to discuss our work over the telephone, it might at least keep me occupied. I wish she would. If I could for one minute concentrate on the work that brought me to New York in the first place I think it would help. It might give me something other than Rudy to fret about.

The *Evening Graphic* put out an extra with a big front-page headline this afternoon:

RUDY DEAD

And a picture of him, if you can believe it, a picture of him superimposed, 'as he might look' in Heaven. Oh, it seems utterly absurd, so absurd I have kept it for him, because I am sure the sight of it will make him laugh when he is better. But the mood is so fraught—and any official news comes so irregularly. In any case the crowd went so crazy when they saw *The Graphic* somebody had to come out of the hospital and issue a statement to the contrary . . .

'At present Mr Valentino's temperature is 100.8,' the man deadpanned, amid all the wails and catcalls. 'His respiration is 20, and pulse 86. His condition remains favourable. Unless unforeseen conditions develop, recovery is considered possible.'

And that was it.

Recovery is considered possible.

No questions. No answers. He turned around and strutted back inside again.

* * *

Suddenly I couldn't bear it any longer, not the reporters' undisguised disappointment at the lack of more dramatic developments or the women with their crocodile tears and hamburger-grease chins. I hated them all. I left them to it and headed back to my hotel.

I was passing by a place, a little speak off Broadway, right by the hotel. Out front it was a tobacconist. I've been passing it however many times since I got here . . . only I didn't have the password. This time I wanted a drink badly so I waited a few minutes outside; watched a lady and gentlemen turning in; and then a gentleman, and then another. Finally I struck up the courage (amazing what a thirst can do!). When the next gentleman turned in I asked if I couldn't travel on his coat tails. He was a little surprised, I think, but happy to oblige. In any case I wanted a drink so badly . . .

And now it's only four o'clock, or five o'clock or something, and I'm back in my room at the Continental, and I'm smashed again. Like father, like daughter.

The room clerk at the desk called out as I was going through the lobby earlier. It was the same guy who'd been at the desk the other night, when Rudy was with me. 'Hey! Where you been all day?'

I pretended not to hear him.

'Had a reporter down here looking for you,' he shouted after me.

That made me stop. 'You did?'

'He was mighty interested.' He paused. 'I hope you don't object to that.'

191

'Do I?' I said. 'I don't know . . . Depends. What did you tell him?'

'Don't want to intrude on your feelings, lady,' he said. 'It's the last thing I want. Only by the way you two were gazing at each other the other night, I'm guessing this whole circus is pretty hard on you.'

It was kind of him to say that. Thoughtful. Not what you expect from a room clerk in a lousy, oversized hotel in the middle of Manhattan on a steaming hot August afternoon. And it's little comments like that, after a hard day—if you're not careful they can send you right over the edge. He's called Larry, the room clerk, and he's a fat guy. I mean *really* fat. Maybe twenty-five years old. It's seems silly when I write it down, but it was just the most wonderful feeling to know that Larry had seen us together, Rudy and me. It meant that Rudy really had been there with me. It wasn't something I'd dreamed up in my own crazy imagination.

I smiled at him. 'That's very sweet of you to say that,' I said. 'So . . . what did you tell him? How did he know?'

'It was a job to get him down here.'

'Oh! You called him?'

'Of course. How else? And then I told him— you don't mind, do you? I told him what I saw— that Mr Rudolph Valentino was right here, in our lobby, *right here* in the lobby of the Hotel Continental, and that from what I could tell, he was here with his sweetheart . . . He didn't believe me, though . . . little creep. He gave me ten bucks and then, once he knew you weren't here, he tried to take it back again.'

'Well, I hope you didn't give it to him,' I said.

I reckoned we were friends after that—or friendly enough. I leaned across the counter, slipped him a few dollars and asked if he could maybe arrange for a bottle of something to be sent up to my room.

So, I have a friend in the city at last! And I have my typewriter and now, since he sent it up, I have a bottle of gin. What more does a girl need for a night on her lonesome, here in beautiful New York City?

Oh, maybe I'm too smashed to write any more right now . . . I'm so tired. I wish I could sleep! I can't sleep. It's no use. Doesn't matter what I drink or where I sit or how I lie or what the hell I do . . . I haven't slept since Sunday night.

What time is it?

Maybe another walk.

*   *   *

6.30 p.m.

Barclay Warburton's been denying there was ever a party that night. He's told the newspapers that he and Rudy dined at the Colony with a couple of friends and then everyone retired to an early bed. But of course he's going to say that. Because all the reports were of the wild party he threw, up there in that fancy-pants apartment of his—and with all the bootleg I'll bet he has stashed somewhere, not to mention the dope, the last thing he wants is for the police to go poking around. Nobody believes him, of course. On the other hand, no one's coming out and saying any different. He's got reporters camping on the sidewalk on Park Avenue . . .

Not only that, there's a girl called Marion Benda saying she spent the night with Rudy down at Texas Guinan's. I've never heard of her, but the papers tell me she's often been seen out with him. Nobody at Texas Guinan's will say a word—obviously—and I can only assume that Miss Benda's receiving payment from Mr Warburton to provide them all (us all, I should say) with some kind of alibi. That's what I believe . . .

On the other hand she's saying she didn't get to Texas Guinan's until one in the morning—which was after he left me, I'm sure of it. So maybe that's what he did, after he left me. Maybe that's why he didn't telephone.

Larry the room clerk called me over again, when I came back from my walk. I don't think he takes many breaks. Poor man. I wonder if he has a family somewhere, or a life of his own. The hours he spends here, I don't see how it's possible.

He had a copy of the *Evening Post*, fresh off the press. 'Look at that!' he said, before I'd even reached the desk. He threw down the paper so it skidded across the counter towards me. He was grinning like a Cheshire cat. 'It's open on the page. There!' he said, prodding it with his fat finger, 'There! Read it! Go on. In the middle there. I drew a circle round it. Read it!'

I have a copy here: it's just a couple of paragraphs in the middle of a much longer essay about Rudy.

. . . Meanwhile, as the Great Lover lies ailing, the mystery deepens as to how he dispensed with those final few hours before falling ill. Today 'friends', all claiming to have spent some part of Saturday evening with Mr Valentino, came to present themselves thick and fast . . . the latest, an unknown English 'script girl', resident in California, name of Lola Nightingale. In a far from swish hostelry in a not-so-salubrious corner of town, a telephone call was made early this morning. From Miss Nightingale herself, the call did not come. It came from the hotel concierge, Larry Lewenstein. He is determined that Mr Valentino was in the lobby of his establishment around midnight Sunday night, bidding goodnight to his English sweetheart, before leaving the establishment on his own.

What, then, of Barclay Warburton's party? And what of Marion Benda, a friend of Mr Valentino for some time, who vouches that she and the star spent that latter half of the evening at Texas Guinan together? Mr Lewenstein, along with bellboy Casey Richards, both insist that, as he left the building, Mr Valentino was clutching his middle as if in great pain . . . However, when our reporter called at the hostel this afternoon there was no sign of Miss Nightingale, if exist she truly does. Perhaps Messrs Lewenstein and Richards are simply two more illustrations of the concern, verging on hysteria, which appears to have overtaken every corner of our fair city . . . Verily, Mr Valentino has us Sheik-en to our very core!

'Hmm . . . Seems nice . . .' I said carefully.

'Nah!' Larry laughed. 'I told you he didn't believe it!'

Larry didn't care. He advised me to get out and buy myself a copy of the paper before it sold out—'Oh, hell, why don't you keep this one?' he said. 'I got five in any case. You take this one. Go on now . . .' And then he peered down at me, at my miserable face. 'And don't you worry, you hear me?' he said gently. 'Your friend Mr Valentino's going to be just fine.'

I wanted to embrace him for his kindness! I managed to restrain myself, just about. Just about managed to get across the lobby to the elevator without bursting into tears.

So, here I am, back in my room.

There was a message from Frances Marion slipped under my door. She has changed our date, and now we're to lunch together on the day after tomorrow, instead. She wants to talk first about *Malicious Intent*—which scenario, in spite of her encouragement, I hardly rate any more. I itch to rewrite it entirely, but I suppose there's no point until I hear what she has to say.

And she has asked me to bring a copy of *Idol Dreams*—which I had forgotten I ever showed to her but I suppose I must at some point. Or some version of it. Considering how long I've been working on the wretched thing, and for how long I've been sending her my efforts, I suppose I shouldn't be surprised.

The fact is, *Idol Dreams*, as I have it written, *still* isn't quite right, and when it finally is right, I want to show it directly to Rudy, since I always

196

wrote it with him in mind . . . I shall have to tell her. She is a writer herself. I hope she will understand. I'm sure I can explain it to her, without needing to explain about Rudy and me. She is friends with him herself. But she will be rather surprised, I think—

Oh, good God.

How did I not think of it before?

HOTEL CONTINENTAL

NEW YORK

9 p.m.

I glimpsed her, elegant and svelte and self-contained as ever, tripping down the steps of the Algonquin with a woman friend, small and slim and light-footed as she, as dark as she was blonde, as confident as each other.

In my excitement I ran most of the way. But then, just before turning into the street I stumbled, over nothing, over my own silly feet, and it crossed my mind that—for the task in hand—I was not quite as sober as I ought to be. A long way from it, in fact. I was on the very point of turning back. It was late, in any case—seven o'clock, I suppose, by then: even if she had wanted to help it would have been too late for her to do anything tonight.

I paused, the utter stupidity of my actions slowly dawning—to have raced half way across town, still drunk, to broach a subject of such delicacy to an individual who had the power to alter my entire life. For the first time in many days, I remembered the long and lonely hours I had spent crouched over one photoplay or another; and of all the photoplays I had sent to all the studios for their consideration; and of all the photoplays that been returned to me with polite and not-so-polite rejections; and I thought, coolly, for once, of exactly how, thanks to this one woman whom I was on the point of drunkenly accosting, all that work was finally going to pay off. If I offended Frances Marion, or gave her cause to think her faith in me was misplaced, it could be the end of everything. Without her, and without Rudy, I would be at the beginning again.

I pulled back.

...All my life I have been waiting for you ...

I pictured Rudy in his hospital bed, so far from anyone he loved, still waiting for me . . . The words came out—came bawling out—before I could stop them. 'MISS MARION!'

She looked faintly startled. I was only a few yards away. She glimpsed me and her sharp, pretty face broke into a warm smile. 'Lola!' as if I were her oldest friend in the world. 'What a wonderful surprise! Gosh, I was only this minute discussing you! Wasn't I, Anita? I was telling Anita how very much I was looking forward to our luncheon on Thursday!'

'Why—yes . . .' I said.

She looked at me expectantly. 'Lola? . . . Sweetie, are you all right?'

'Am I all right? Why—yes. I'm very well. Thank you. Except I think maybe I'm . . .' I was going to say, 'a little soused,' but thought better of it.

A silence fell, and then she laughed.

'Goodness, what on earth have you done? You look as guilty as—'

'Blanca de Saulles?' I burst out.

She blinked in surprise. 'Blanca de Saulles?' she repeated politely. 'Well, yes—I suppose. How funny . . . Except wasn't she the one . . .' Miss Marion turned to her companion—pretty, I suppose, beneath her absurd purple turban; with quick, dark, frantic eyes, and eyebrows that arched like little semicircles. 'Nita, darling—you'll remember . . . it was so long ago . . . Wasn't the de Saulles woman found innocent in the end?'

Purple Turban took a deep pull from the end of long cigarette holder, glanced sullenly at me, turned immediately back to Miss Marion. 'She killed her husband in front of half of Long Island. Don't you remember? The butcher, the baker, the candlestick maker . . . And they let her go. Specifically because she looked so damned innocent . . .Your young friend here,' she said, tilting her turban toward me, 'wouldn't get off so lightly.'

Miss Marion laughed. 'Well, darling, you should look carefully at my "young friend" here before you pack her off to Sing Sing. I told you—she's a very talented young scenarioist.'

Purple Turban raised one of her arched eyebrows, rather gloomily, I thought. 'You did?'

'She has an ear and eye at least as sharp as yours, darling. And beneath it all, I suspect, double the passion of the two of us together . . . Lola, this is Anita Loos. Anita, this is—'

'Anita Loos!' I burst out.

It was Anita Loos!

'Why, *Anita Loos*!' I said it again. I looked from

one to the other, from Miss Loos, to Miss Marion, to Miss Loos again: the two most successful scenarioists in Hollywood—and there they stood before me! I couldn't hide what a thrill it was. 'Miss Loos, I'm such an admirer of your movies,' I cried. (Wish I hadn't.) 'I mean *all* of them! And I read your book. I have read all your books—I mean I read your other book, on how to write a photoplay. And I think *Gentlemen Prefer Blondes* is quite the funniest novel I ever read. Ever. I must say it's quite an honour . . .'

Anita Loos pulled on her cigarette long and hard. 'Isn't that wonderful?' she drawled. And I don't care if I was half soused and talking much too much, it was dreadfully rude.

Miss Marion, I think, was embarrassed. 'So, Lola darling,' she said, 'how exceptionally lovely to see you. Where are you headed, in such a rush?'

'Where am I headed?' I repeated.

'Anita and I are on our way to dinner . . . I would ask you to join us, but we're meeting our husbands . . .'

'Husbands!'

'. . . and we've not seen each other in quite a while. But I am looking forward to our Thursday luncheon enormously . . .'

'Oh, *gosh*, no!' I cried. 'That is, I'm longing for our luncheon too . . .'

Silence. Both women eyed me uncertainly. I was aware, dimly, that I was blocking their onward path, yet somehow I simply couldn't bring myself to step aside.

'Well . . . Lola . . .' Miss Marion tried again, with her usual tact, to bring our meeting to some sort

200

of conclusion. If only she had succeeded! But I interrupted her before she had a chance to finish.

'I was only just passing,' I began. 'That is to say, I wasn't. Simply passing. That's not quite how it is. I was passing because I was hoping I might bump into you, Miss Marion. Only—I'm so sorry to trouble you with this. When you're seeing your husbands and everything . . . But truly I'm at my wit's end. I wanted to ask for your help . . .'

Anita Loos heaved a long, weary sigh. She turned away, as if in danger of collapsing with *ennui* right there on the sidewalk. 'Well, then,' she said, 'I'm going to find us a taxicab, Frances darling. I shall wait for you on the corner there. Good to meet you,' she said to me. Which was funny, really. Because she made it sound like it had been the most ghastly experience in the world.

'Miss Marion, forgive me. I am so sorry . . . You probably think it's about the photoplay . . .'

'Well, I—'

'Actually, it's *not* about the photoplay. Though I'm going to bring that to you on Thursday and I'm truly more excited than I can say about it . . . In fact I believe when you read this latest version, which I intend to finish today and tomorrow, in time for our luncheon, you'll think it so good you'll want to throw everything else of mine you ever read into the rubbish heap!'

She waited—but I saw her expression freeze. My words were coming out fuzzy. I could hear it. She must have caught the alcohol on my breath. She said, 'Well, Lola dear, I'm in quite a hurry, as you can see—I don't want to keep everyone waiting. Are you quite certain whatever it is can't wait until Thursday?'

It couldn't wait, I said, 'For he might be dead by Thursday.' And then, in a great rush of panic and nonsense, as if the faster I spoke the more likely she would be to believe me and the less likely I would burst into tears, I told her how Rudy and I had known each other and had lost each other and about how—thanks to her—we had been reunited only this week, the week he fell ill, and that I could never thank her enough for the part she had played—

Her face grew colder still.

—and that he and I were meant to have had lunch only the day before yesterday, except that of course by then he was already at the hospital. And then, because I was utterly desperate, and her face was so cold and so full of disbelief and because I knew—I know—how absurd it must have sounded, I told her about how he had said to me, as we were together, lying side by side in his suite, about how he told me, *all my life I have been waiting for you*—'Don't you see?' I cried. 'And now he is waiting for me again!'

And then, because I could see that something—everything—about me, my whole demeanour, the reek of gin on my breath—was repelling her . . . I showed the newspaper with Larry's bit in it.

She held it between finger and thumb as if it had just then been pulled out from a drain, barely cast an eye over it—and quickly handed it back. 'Lola,' she said quietly, '*ssssh . . .*'

There was a long pause. I looked at the ground, and the tears began to spill from my eyes. I watched in shame, as they slowly splashed onto the dry pavement between us. 'I'm so sorry. I am so sorry. I am so sorry . . .'

She put a hand on my arm. 'You need to calm yourself . . .' she said.

'Only I can't get to him. No matter what, they won't let me through. Not even a message. And I feel so certain I could help. Does that sound too absurd? If he could only hear from me, I know—because I know how he loves me—I know it would soothe him, if I could just be with him . . .'

She said: 'From what I have heard, Rudy, our dear friend, is gravely ill, Lola. Perhaps you would be better to wait . . . as we all must, however painful we may find it . . . until he is feeling stronger . . .'

'But I could help him!'

'I dare say . . . But, as you know, Rudy has many, many friends . . .'

'Oh, I *know* that!'

'And if you are the friend to him you say you are, you had better grow used to it . . . There will always be a whole waiting room of people, standing in line for their turn. To soothe him.'

'Oh, I *know* it!'

'You are not the only one to be kept from his bedside.'

'Of course. Because Mr Ullman is keeping Rudy all to himself!'

'He is very, very ill.'

'I know it! You hardly need to tell me! It's all I think about. I think of him lying there, in pain, so far away from all the people who love him—his family, his country . . . *me*. I know how ill he is! Only the telephone operators at the hospital won't pass on any message. And there are so many of these crazy fans trying to reach him, and then the stars, too, as if they truly cared—all trying to get in on the action. No one will see that I am his closest, most loving friend, who cares for him more than I care for my own life—'

'Calm down, Lola.'

'Oh, please! Don't you see? They arrested a girl for trying to take her live monkey into his sick room! Why can't anyone see? How can I persuade them that he and I are different? How? And now they have security guards outside his suite! And there are security guards at the hospital gates, and they won't take a message for him at the Ambassador, and *nothing I do* reaches him and I am utterly, utterly wretched and utterly desperate . . . But *you*, you who have always been so kind to me, such a kind supporter—you, who have so many connections, Miss Marion—you could help me! I know he holds you in high regard. All of Hollywood holds you in high regard. *I* hold you in the highest regard of—Miss Marion, you must know, I hold you in the highest regard of anyone. Please . . . Please . . . I beg you to help me . . .'

And then finally, I suppose, I simply ran out of steam. I had presented my case—perhaps as badly as I ever could have presented it. And I had only one thing to add. But by then I knew it was hopeless. 'I thought, perhaps, you might be able to . . . make a call to Mr Ullman . . . Maybe . . .'

She is, truthfully, as fine a woman as any I ever met, and if ever I could become half the woman she is I would be proud. She was not unkind, exactly. But she was not moved. She did not

204

believe me.

She said, 'Lola, you're soused. Go back to your hotel and sleep it off. I can't help you. Nor would I, given your current state. If Rudy is the friend you say he is, then I have no doubt he will send you a message the first minute he can. In the mean time—you forget, Lola: I was in the room with the two of you before now . . .So you see . . .'

I did forget. I had forgotten.

What could I say? Nothing. She had silenced me.

'It is a difficult time for everyone who loves him,' she said, after a long, humiliating pause. 'And, Lola, rest assured, *there are plenty of people who do*. He makes us all feel special . . . Lola—you are not the only one.'

I said nothing. Like a schoolgirl, though in fact I am several inches taller than she, I kept my eyes to the ground.

She squeezed my arm. Kindly again. 'Go back to your hotel. Sleep it off.'

'I apologise,' I said stiffly. 'I know you don't believe me.'

'We have a lunch date, day after tomorrow. Don't be a fool, Lola. You have a golden opportunity. I am giving you a golden opportunity—because you deserve it. I know you do. Please don't let me down.'

'Of course not . . .' I muttered.

'Sleep it off, whatever you have inside you. Sleep it off, and get back to that photoplay you have so much confidence in. Finish it.' She smiled at me then. One professional to another. One writer to another. 'It's the best way to keep from going crazy, isn't it? That's what I find. *Write it all down!'*

I think, at that, I managed to smile.

'And on Thursday I shall expect to see the fruit of all your labour. And, furthermore, I shall expect you to be sober.'

*   *   *

. . . And here I am back in my stinkpot hotel, in front of my beautiful typewriter—and not a drop of gin in the place . . .

And maybe Rudy hasn't called me yet. But I am here, with my typewriter, and his letters, and the feel of his kiss still very, very close.

When he bought me this typewriter he was thinking of me. He loved me then, and nobody, not Anita Loos, not Frances Marion, not *anyone*, can take that away. He loved me then. And, no matter what, I will always love him.

HOLLYWOOD

The gentleman who picked me up the night I lost Rudy might have been anyone. Really, given my reckless state, I was exceptionally fortunate and, for a short time after we met, I believed I had fallen on my feet.

Before I met him—before that night—I was still a girl, still decent enough to marry a decent boy, settle down and raise a whole bunch of decent children. And there may be plenty of things I regret these past years but, funnily enough, climbing into Perry Turnbull's old rustbucket of a motor-car, the night I lost Rudy, will never be one of them. And that's the truth.

It was ten o'clock, but the streets were deserted and not so well lit back then. Really, it's hard to remember how quickly Hollywood has changed. It was a little town back then, busy as hell during the day, and growing by the minute, but still just a country town.

I was on the corner of Sunset and Highland, heading back to my boarding-house, thinking of Rudy, thinking, What next? What in the hell next? One minute, I was numb—and then, quite suddenly, there it came, out of the darkness, the absolute, awful aloneness of my place under that big black sky.

Rudy had gone. He was gone. For the first time since the night we had danced together, I understood what it felt to be in a world without him. For the first time I was existing under that great big sky without the knowledge that he loved me. Wherever he was, wherever I was, that knowledge had always been there for me, protecting me, silently pushing me forward . . . And now—now it was gone. He had not waited. He had not loved me as I believed he had.

I stopped still. My knees buckled. I couldn't prevent it. I had folded onto the sidewalk, into the dry dust and the darkness. I laid my head to the ground, which was still warm from the sun. And I didn't weep, because I couldn't. I crouched there, my forehead to the warm earth. I have no idea for how long.

The car stopped right behind me, and my heart told me it was Rudy. I *knew* it was Rudy. From the sound of the engine; from the feel of the air. When he asked me if I needed a ride somewhere, I gazed back at him

He was a handsome man (they often are in Hollywood), with dark hair slicked back—like Rudy; and big, dark eyes—like Rudy; and white teeth—like Rudy—which shone under the dim street light. And there were deep laughter lines at the corners of his eyes. I always liked those lines. Say what you like about Perry—and I could say plenty—he always had nice laughter lines.

He shouted out of the window at me, through the darkness, something loud and inordinately cheerful: '*Hey, hey, HEY, pretty lady! You OK out there? Can I give you a ride somewhere?*'

I looked at him, and he looked at me, but I didn't reply.

He said, 'You know, it's not really safe round here, this time of night. Come on, hop in! Where are you headed? I'll drive you wherever you want to go.'

Then he considered me, still kneeling on the ground, dirt smeared across my forehead—and he laughed. That must have been when I first saw those laughter lines. Such a warm laugh, it was. Like Rudy's. And, gosh, I was in need of a little warmth that night. 'No need to be afraid of *me*, little lady,' he said, his nice white teeth flashing. 'Only I hate to see a pretty girl on her lonesome. Dark night like this. Could never forgive myself if something happened to you. Why don't you just look on me as a set of wheels? A knight in shining armour. I'll drive you anywhere you like!'

He seemed like a nice man. And, honestly, I was so Goddamn lonely. And the laugh was so warm it sounded like music. It reminded me of Rudy.

So I considered it for a while. Maybe 'consider' is putting it too strongly: I mean it washed around inside me, all the laughter and warmth he seemed to offer, and finally, after a long while, when I was still crouched in the dirt, I said to him, 'You know what I would really appreciate? Much more than a set of wheels?'

He looked a little surprised. 'Tell me what you'd really appreciate, sweetheart,' he said, and it sounded just a little bit kind, along with everything else. I believed so. 'Tell me, honey. I'd surely love to know.'

'Due to the fact I have just suffered a setback,' I said, 'quite an unfortunate setback . . . I would greatly appreciate a strong drink. And perhaps—if it's not too much to ask—maybe a little conversation. Is that a terrible thing to ask? Is it very forward of me? Would you take me

209

somewhere? For a stiff drink?'

He laughed again, that lovely big laugh of his. Threw his head back, and I could see those straight teeth glinting. 'Sounds good to me,' he said. 'Sounds like you're my kind of girl.'

*   *   *

We drove all the way back to Los Angeles. I didn't ask where we were going. Didn't say much at all, in fact. We stopped at a bar and talked, but not about anything much—and then he took me back to his rooms at the Pico, and we got smashed on a bottle of rye. Like father, like daughter . . . I would like to say it was Perry who introduced me to the advantages of being so horribly, entirely smashed that nothing hurts any more. But to some degree, I'd discovered it for myself, on the train journey. And sometimes you just have to ask yourself, What does it matter what the consequences are, so long as it helps numb the pain? That night, I needed it

Pico House is horribly run down, these days. It was pretty run down then too—in spite of what a fine building it must once have been. But Perry claimed he liked it. 'Feels like home,' he said. But I don't think he knew what home felt like, any more than I did.

That night we didn't tell each other much. I told him Papa was dead—everyone was dead: Mama, Papa, Benedict. And I told him about Rudy . . . I told him I was in love with Rudy. I told him I had come to California probably to be Rudy's wife . . .

It didn't seem to deter him. Actually, nor was it meant to. I was only telling him because it seemed the natural thing to do. Perry listened and it was all

210

I needed that night.

Of course it was clear from early on exactly where things were headed. We were seated on a couch by the window—not so far from his big mahogany bed. It was a large room, with views out on the plaza—and it was exceptionally messy. He had his clothes piled up high in a big dirty heap in one corner. There were a couple of empty rye bottles by the washbasin, and another on a side table by the couch, and overflowing ashtrays dotted about pretty much everywhere, between bottles of cologne and hair grease and brushes and combs, and tubs of screen pancake covered in dust, and pens and bits of paper with illegible jottings on them, a lipstick, left over from some other woman, dirty glasses, and books . . . popular novels, mostly. By his bedside was the novel *The Four Horsemen of the Apocalypse*. He said he was negotiating to buy the rights, because he was convinced it would make a great movie . . . And how right he was. Not that he ever had anything to do with it.

So we sat there, drinking, until finally I had nothing more to tell him. '. . . and that,' I said to him at last, 'is about when you drove up and found me there on the sidewalk . . .'

'Making me . . . very possibly. . .' he murmured, leaning over towards me '. . . the luckiest man in southern California.'

And maybe I could smell the rye on his breath. Maybe I could smell that he hadn't washed in a little while, and that his clothes weren't as fresh as they might have been—but, honestly, I didn't care. He put an arm around me and it felt so strong and warm, and just to be touched was such a comfort . . . such a pleasure . . . so I welcomed his embrace.

Because even if he wasn't Rudy, he was a man. And I could say all sorts of things: that I only acted as I did . . . because I was so damn lonely . . . so damn drunk . . . Or I could pretend, like Mrs de Saulles, that I was under so much mental strain I was out of my senses at the time. But that night, when Perry ran his fingers through my newly cropped dark hair, I welcomed it. When he undid the buttons of my sky blue, flat crêpe dress, which I had not chosen for him, I admit I closed my eyes and I thought of Rudy . . . But Perry was generous and imaginative and thoughtful in bed, if nowhere else. Our first night together left me wanting more. When we fucked, I lost myself. Thought of no one and nothing. And what could be better than that?

*   *   *

Perry called himself an actor—and a producer and a writer and a director, too—but as for the details, he was never very forthcoming. That night he told me he'd come from Chicago but really he could have told me anywhere. Within a few weeks of knowing him, I learned never to believe a word he spoke.

He had arrived in California, however many years ago, with a handsome face. He still had that, even if it was a little creased, and maybe a little hard around the edges. He had arrived with the face—and, he claimed, a photoplay he'd written, though he never let me read it. He told me he was thirty-three years old.

For a while, in spite of everything, I have to say it was OK. Perry was good to me. He showed me round town and introduced me to his friends, and he kept me tanked up with rye, and, to be blunt, we fucked a lot. From night until morning, when he wasn't too high. And it was all I wanted, more or less.

When I woke each morning my first thought wasn't of Papa, cold and hard, with vomit on his chin. It wasn't of Jack de Saulles, with the bullets punching his chest. It wasn't the expression of perfect entitlement on his killer's beautiful face, as the head juror read out his verdict . . . And sometimes, just once in a while, it wasn't even of Rudy. I would open my eyes and see Perry, asleep with his laughter lines, and I would think, maybe, with compromises, life needn't always be so unremittingly lonesome after all. And maybe, one day, I would find Rudy again, and he would explain.

Perry had a lot of friends. Low-lifes and dreamers, most of them. They called themselves writers, actors, producers—but they were just a collection of bums. Some of them worked as extras down at the studios, or they did odd jobs here and there, or they fixed people's cars, or they sold wonder drugs and hair lotions to the stars . . . For the most part it was difficult to understand exactly where their money came from.

We used to get smashed most nights, often in Perry's rooms, and they would take it in turns to hear about each other's little triumphs. A guy called Russell boasted of spending a passionate night with Mabel Normand. We whooped as if he'd discovered a cure for the influenza. He said Mabel had agreed to fix him up with a character part in her next movie.

I remember we celebrated that for a couple of evenings on the trot. But then the days passed, and he didn't hear a word from her or her people, until finally he turned up at the Keystone studios. He kicked up such a scene that eventually the guys at security called her off set to deal with him. She looked at Russell, long and hard, and she said: 'Never seen the guy in my life.' And they threw him straight out onto sidewalk. He wound up with scratches and bruises all over his face.

If it wasn't Russell and Mabel Normand, it was Perry bidding for rights to *The Four Horsemen*; or William befriending a man who was friendly with Cecil Beaton; or Poppy having dinner with a casting director at Famous Players-Lasky; or Teddy posting his photoplay through the window of a car he was convinced belonged to D. W. Griffith.

There was always someone in the group riding high, on the cusp of everything. And almost always nothing would ever come of any of it. So we drank to celebrate, and we drank to commiserate. We drank a lot.

*   *   *

Of all of the people I met during that period only the twins, Phoebe and Lorna, seemed to have their feet on the ground. Like everyone else, they had come to California to be in the movies, but they were different. The way they talked about the work, the way they got themselves out of bed to find it—and the methodical way that, between them, they seduced every studio casting director and every worthwhile casting agent in town—it set them apart. Somehow, there was never any doubt the twins were going to succeed.

Phoebe's hair was dyed white blonde and she always dressed in black, while Lorna's was jet black and she always dressed in white. But, really, they were identical. They were beautiful and funny, too, and daring: a couple of baby jazz goddesses, admired—and enjoyed—by every horny producer in the colony. Enjoyed by Perry, too, I'm almost certain.

We were friendly, in any case. When Perry was busy they used to come round, and the three of us would go to the pictures together. And afterwards, we used to sit around and analyse the movies we'd seen like a trio of professional film reviewers.

Our friendship was cemented when I let them move into my room back in Hollywood. They were flat broke at the time and it was nothing to me— the room was lying empty while I spent every night with Perry, and I would have been paying for it in any case, but they were so grateful. When I think of the infinite number of ways they have helped me since, it seems absurd.

Meanwhile, not for very long, I succeeded in holding down my job at Wormholt and Simmons. Their office, in contrast to the noisy, drunken nights, was an oasis of tranquillity. And of boredom, frankly, but I was grateful for it. Grateful for the money—and the escape it provided from the demands of living with Perry. I would have kept it, too—put up with any amount of boredom—but then, about a few months in, Mr Simmons, who was always standing much too close, he took it into his head to make a lunge for me. While I was sitting demurely at my stenograph, he dived at me from behind—pushed his nose into the nape of my neck.

And, honestly, I would have put up with that, would have found a way to shrug it off—there were enough young women in Hollywood without any work at all—but for all his lunging, he was a churchgoer and a Temperance man. At the time, Prohibition was still a few months off, and I think it was all that interested him. He and his wife used to give tea parties for the Anti-Saloon League, and when he buried his nose in my neck, the silly dub got a lungful of old alcohol fumes. He smelled alcohol on my skin, and he was so entirely outraged by it, he fired me.

It was always a battle to get out of Perry's bed, a drawn-out negotiation with him—partly pleasurable, partly infuriating. He used to make me feel guilty for going to work at all. So he was most amused, even a little delighted, when I finally got the boot. He laughed like a hyena when I explained to him why, and then he told me to pack up my stuff from the rooming-house, and move lock-stock into the Pico with him.

'It's OK, sweetie pie,' he said, with his laughter lines. And he leaned across the couch and ran a hand along my leg, and then, with the other hand, began in his unhurried way, to undo a few of the buttons on my shirtwaist. 'I haven't got a cent either! But something'll come up. It always does. And the girls'll look after you. Beautiful girl like you—never had any trouble in Hollywood before. You'll be just fine . . .'

I laughed. '*That's* a joke.'

But Perry wasn't joking. His idea of trouble was on a grander scale than mine, I suppose. 'We'll get

Russell on to it,' he said. 'He's nice with the people at Metro, I think. I'll bet he can get you work as an extra girl . . . much more fun . . . and you won't have to put up with those awful men in that awful office . . . And you won't have to race across town for that awful trolley car . . . We'll be just fine . . . Come here, baby . . . And if we starve, well, hell! We can starve together!'

* * *

Perry didn't like me to talk about Rudy. Understandably. And I didn't, not after that first night—but, more and more often, Perry would mention him instead. He would make some snide remark, especially when he was drunk. Perry was the most flirtatious man I ever met—worse than Papa, even. Sometimes he used to disappear for days on end without the slightest explanation. Not for one second did I imagine he was faithful to me. Nevertheless, he was a jealous lover.

'Oh, *Perry*. Are you still thinking about him, after all this time?' I would laugh. 'After all that's happened since? I have forgotten him entirely! If only you would!'

It was a lie. There was never a moment that we were out—in bars and dance halls, simply walking along the street—when I wasn't searching for him. Sometimes Perry would catch me, my eyes scouring. It would send him crazy.

And then it was Prohibition night—31 January 1920, the last night before the terrible Volstead Act became law and, like most of America, we were ready to see it in with style. To party as never before.

We drove out to the Vernon Country Club (along with half of California, so it felt). All of Perry's cronies were there. Phoebe and Lorna were there, of course. Hell, *everyone* was there! The whole of Hollywood! We were dancing and drinking—everyone was. It was a crazy night: everyone was feeling wild—and then through the crowd, out there in the middle of the dance floor, I glimpsed him—I was sure of it. Yes, I was boiled. Maybe I couldn't see straight. But so what? Nobody in the world dances as Rudy does—and before I could stop myself I was halfway across the floor. I had an arm out to touch his shoulder—that's how close I was when I felt a sharp tug. Perry turned me round by the hair.

I couldn't get free, and by the time I did—just enough to turn my head again—Rudy was gone.

We left at once, on our own, and I wept all the way back home. It was partly with misery at having missed him, but more, it was with happiness that, after all, he might still be alive—and not just alive, but alive, right here in Hollywood.

That was the first time I missed him. Almost six years ago. It was also the first time I saw Perry truly angry. We had a terrible fight. Back at the hotel he got so mad he lashed out—and, I have to say, so did I. Only he was stronger and taller, and come the third round I hit the floor. Blood in my hair, out of my nose. It shocked him. It shocked us both. He apologised. I said it was OK—but it's funny, every time I see blood, even now, I see Mr de Saulles lying on that terrace, the terrace where Rudy and I danced, with the blood seeping through the floorboards. It makes me shake: sort of freezes me up. So—by the time I came round, so to speak,

I was hearing the door bang shut behind him, and he was gone. He didn't come back for a week.

It probably sounds all wrong, I know. I was in love with somebody else, and Perry had just knocked me to the floor, abandoned me in a pool of my own blood. But when he left, I was wretched.

I missed him horribly. And yet I longed for Rudy. I went back out to that dance hall six times—every night while Perry was gone—but there was never any sign of Rudy. When I asked, not a soul recognised his name.

Perry finally returned, exactly a week later. He sauntered in as if he'd only popped out for a pack of cigarettes. Only along with the cigarettes he had a pocket bulging with cash.

*   *   *

So that got to be a pattern. We'd fight, always about Rudy. He'd storm out, often without leaving a penny, and I would have to go to Lorna or Phoebe and beg them for a loan. Days would pass and he would reappear, always sunny, always with a new supply of cash. I didn't ask where it came from. There didn't seem much point . . . In any case, while the cash lasted, life went well. But the cash never lasted. And then we'd be back where we started, with both of us fighting again . . .

Meanwhile, between searching for work that might actually pay me something, I wrote a handful of scenarios and showed them to Perry. I don't believe he ever really read them. Nevertheless he would take them away with him and come back later, declaring I was a 'genius', and insisting on

219

celebrating by taking me to bed. 'What you need to do,' he would say, 'is send them to William. William knows a guy at Universal. He's always looking for new stories.'

But William didn't know anything or anyone, any more than any of Perry's friends did. I wasn't relying on them. I took the trade magazines, where there were advertisements sometimes from the studios, asking for scenario submissions. I would submit them something, and wait, and never hear a word again . . . And, when Perry allowed it (he really didn't want me to have a regular job), I would approach the offices down town and try to find work as a typist. But there were so many young girls out of work in Hollywood, and thousands more pouring in every day. It wasn't easy.

'The twins'll help you,' Perry used to say. 'Ask them.'

The twins did help me. Thanks to Phoebe and Lorna putting a good word in, I managed to get a few days on set as an extra girl, here and there. Horrible, hard days they were too, sweltering under those damn mercury lights, forbidden to speak or even to move without express permission. As anybody knows, extras in Hollywood are treated considerably less well than cattle (due to the fact a farmer tends to have at least a passing interest in the future welfare of his animals). Extra girls (and boys) are hired by the day. If, from one day's shooting to the next, they happen to drop dead—from exhaustion, underpay, mercury-light blindness—who's going to care? Not a soul. Because just outside the studio gates, more than happy to step over the corpses, there'll always be a long line of hungry faces, who all believed, once, that they could be stars, and who would count themselves lucky to get a day's work on set with lunch included.

Life wasn't perfect but it wasn't so bad either. It was exciting, full of wild nights. We fought, but in bed we always made up.

Until the day in Santa Monica. We were on the pier. My mind filled with memories of Rudy and me at Coney Island and, as hard as I tried, I couldn't shake them. And God knows how it happened—but, by mistake, I called him Rudy.

He went crazy. He threw me out of the car and left me there to make my own way back to Los Angeles. When I finally got back to the Pico, several hours later, I found a notice on the room door: *Due to lack of Payment . . .*

We were locked out. All my belongings—my scenarios, my clothes, the gold pin Rudy gave to me at The Box, the letter he wrote—everything I owned and cared about was locked in that room, and I had not a penny, and Perry was nowhere to be seen.

*   *   *

The room clerk—fifty years old, wearing the same brown cotton shirt he'd worn since the day I first laid eyes on him, grey with grime around his paunch and with two buttons missing round the belly button—dangled the key in front of my nose.

'Couldn't you give it to me? Please?' I said. 'Only until Mr Turnbull returns, and sorts everything out . . .'

'Mr Turnbull's gone, lady. Upped and gone to Reno.'

'Gone to Reno?'

'So he said.'

'But—why?'

'How should I know?' He smiled. For the first time, perhaps because I'd never before paused to look at him properly, I noticed his top row of teeth were missing, all but one. 'Mr Turnbull said to me, he said *you*'d sort it out . . .'

I could have walked away, I suppose. It was my choice. I considered it, too—I looked at him. And I tried to imagine a life with nothing—walking back out into that hot dry city with nothing: no trace of my past to accompany me, nothing of Rudy. Nothing, nothing, nothing. It was unimaginable. I made the choice at once, though at the time it hardly felt like one at all. Sometimes, to stay alive, you just have to do things. I looked away and didn't look at him again. Not once. But I nodded.

And that was how I got my stuff back. He took me round the back, into one of the kitchen pantries—it didn't last long. He pressed himself up against my stomach, undid his buttons and set to work—and I remember the sharp edge of the shelf against my shoulder, and the back of my head knocking against the bone of a big joint of ham, half covered with a tea-towel to keep the flies off. He smelled of cooking grease, and he called me Baby. And that was it. Then it was over. He reached up for that tea-towel, very carefully, meticulously, wiped himself clean. He tossed the cloth at me, asked if I needed it. A moment of thoughtfulness, I guess. He buttoned himself back up.

I followed him silently out of the larder, up the stairs to Perry's room. He unlocked the door and watched while I collected my things together.

He was still standing behind me as I pulled out the envelope, opened the letter with hands that shook. I was crying, my vision was blurred, but the words were so familiar, every shape of every word . . . and the sound of his shallow breathing, the pain and fear and revulsion I felt, it all faded, just for a little while . . .

. . .When we were together last you promised you would never despair of me. Do you remember? I have clung to it. Have you kept your promise, in spite of these months of silence? I can only pray that you have. . .

. . . Or perhaps you have long since despaired of me. If you have, I shall try to understand. I shall try to forgive you. In any case—if you have read this far—please know it for ever, cara mia, that I love you, and wherever I go, whatever I do, there will always be a place in my heart which waits for you . . .
Hopefully and for ever yours, darling Jennifer
your
Rodolfo

The next day I waited for Perry to come back for me—but he never did. He didn't come back for years.

HOTEL CONTINENTAL

NEW YORK

Wednesday, 18 August 1926

I have called the hospital and the operator has given me the doctors' latest statement, which she delivered exactly as if she were reading a grocery list. Not that it matters. I read in the papers that calls enquiring after his health come in at almost a hundred per minute, and I suppose it must be dull to have to keep saying the same thing over again, even if it is mostly good news.

> Mr Valentino passed a relatively comfortable night. His temp is 100.5; respiration, 21; pulse 87. Unless unforeseen complications develop . . .

I'm not certain what to make of the respiration figures—not entirely sure, if I'm entirely honest, what to make of any of the rest of it, either. I tried to ask the girl on the telephone but she hadn't the foggiest idea, and I think she was quite offended that I even asked. The important thing is, his temperature has dropped, which I know to be a good thing, and somehow or other I shall find out from someone about the rest . . . It only matters that he is improving, and not weakening. He passed a relatively comfortable night. He's going to be well very soon. I feel it. He's going to be just fine.

Nevertheless, nothing appears to encourage Mr Ullman. He is quite the lioness with his superstar cub. He turns everyone away. Yesterday he turned away Joseph Schenk, who is only the head of United Artists, and Rudy's boss, and with him was his movie-star wife Norma Talmadge, who, everybody knows, is one of Rudy's dearest friends. I can only imagine that all the attention and drama of Rudy's illness, and of his being Rudy's one and only gatekeeper and all—must have gone halfway to Mr Ullman's head. It must be quite something to be such an ordinary man, and to be at the centre of so much attention.

I'm being horrid. Only I can't help seeing him as the enemy—the great big insurmountable barrier that prevents Rudy and me being together . . . and I lay awake last night, with Mr Ullman's stupid square face blocking out all other thoughts or visions.

To be fair to the wretched man, he looks terrible, as if the mental stress of these past few days were wearing at his very core. When he emerged from the hospital again yesterday to give his statement, he looked as if he hadn't slept or eaten in a month. And I suppose he cares for Rudy. Of course he does. It's impossible not to.

*   *   *

As for myself, I feel a good deal clearer than I have in a long time, and I am determined never again to behave as I did in front of Frances Marion yesterday evening. Never again.

I have a busy day ahead. After all that

happened yesterday, I lay awake feeling terrible for most of the night—until finally, about three a.m., my thoughts turned to *Idol Dreams*—and at long last I had the brainwave about the finale I have been searching for all this time. All these years, and I have found it! And, once again, I suppose it's Miss Marion I have to thank for it. She really is quite a model for us girls. I admire her enormously.

It's the ending that's all wrong, of course. It's the ending that makes the whole thing so damn ordinary . . . Because why *should* he rescue the girl from her hopeless, inert little life when the silly girl can't even be bothered to rescue herself? It's what's been troubling me all this time. What has she ever done to deserve his attention—let alone his love, let alone her happy ending? Of what value is the love she offers, when the value she puts on her own survival is none? In fact, I am tempted to go further: how dare she ask to be loved when she can't even have the courage to love herself? When I, her creator, can't love her either.

So—that was what I realised, at three a.m. last night. And I realised that before I handed the completed photoplay to Miss Marion tomorrow I would have to rewrite the entire final act, making Louisa a heroine who deserves her end: who understands that if she loves him as she believes she does, she must first become her own saviour and transform herself. Gosh—it seems so terribly obvious, and yet all these years the answer eluded me.

I felt the most tremendous rush, such as I haven't felt about my writing in a long time, and I leaped out of bed right then. I pulled out the typewriter—which I suppose may have been a little thoughtless, considering the wretched din it makes, but nobody complained. I comforted myself that it was no match for the frightful snoring and grunting I've been enduring all these nights from the old gentleman next door, and which, by the way, I could still hear, even over the typing.

And then, when I suppose I had been hard at work for six or more hours without a break, I took myself to breakfast where last I'd been with Rudy. I ate as well as I could—but I've eaten so little recently I couldn't swallow much before my stomach began to ache. I drank five cups of strong black coffee, smoked half a pack of Chesterfield and thought of nothing but *Dreams*, and of all the small changes that would transform it, and wrote notes on some paper I begged from the little waiter, and returned to my writing table.

Another six hours or so tapping away, and I can hardly believe it is possible—I can hardly believe I am writing this—but the thing is finished! Truly. I have it at last! After four years of wrong turns and phoney endings, it is finally mine! I can honestly say that, of all the scenarios and photoplays I've ever written, of any word I ever put to paper, *Idol Dreams* is the pinnacle. And when I hand it to Miss Marion at luncheon tomorrow I shall do so without the slightest doubt in my mind. Because in truth I believe it is as close to perfect as anything can be.

Beverly of Graustark, the damned Marion Davies movie, which I was supposed to see and which I am growing to hate, is showing at the

Strand at eight o'clock, and I simply have to stay awake long enough to see it. After the dismal show I made yesterday I might just as well take my *Idol Dreams* and set a match to it than turn up to my luncheon tomorrow having missed the wretched thing. Tomorrow I shall not put a foot wrong. I swear to it.

In the mean time I know I should sleep. I have four hours until the picture begins, but I'm terrified if I close my eyes I shall never wake up again. So I shall stay awake. I don't care much, anyway, because even though I ought to be exhausted, I'm not. I'm just on a terrific high, because now that *Dreams* is right, and Rudy is improving, everything seems to fall into place.

*   *   *

Last night I returned to my room after the dreadful scene with Miss Marion, and I wrote first about those early days at the Pico, and it was difficult, raking through all that dreadfulness.

Afterwards I tried to work on the scenario, but it was before the great epiphany so there I was, stuck, yet again, trying to resolve the puzzle. Before long there were pages spread all over the bed, and the floor, and the table by the window . . . and then somehow, the next thing I knew, my feet had led me downstairs, past fat Larry at the desk, out through the lobby, and I was back in front of that damned hospital again.

By then I guess it was about ten o'clock, still warm and airless. There was a small, dismal crowd congregated by the Polyclinic entrance, and as I arrived a light was switched on at his window. Everyone was distracted, nobody noticed me—and I suppose I was still a little soused—so I didn't stop. I continued to walk right on past them, past the barrier that was meant to keep the fans at bay . . .

'Look out, guys,' one of the reporters shouted. 'Body approaching . . .'

I didn't glance to left or to right, but proceeded as if my right to pass through those big wooden doors had been written in the Constitution. In any case, it should have been . . .

My hand reached out—nobody stopped me. For a moment, indeed, it seemed possible that I would simply brazen right through. But then—

'*Hey!*' The same reporter again, quite angry this time. 'Guards! You, Baldie! What's the matter with you, didn't you hear me? I said look out!' A camera flashed and, from the other side of me, a security guard emerged from the shadows, swooped down from a great height and grasped me tight by the wrists.

I looked up at him . . . There wasn't a hair left on his head. Eyebrows and eyelashes too. All gone. But I recognised him at once.

'*Jennifer Doyle?*' he said.

'Mr Hademak!'

God knows what those reporters made of it; I remember hearing them distantly, shouting something about stitch-ups, though what or whom they supposed either of us to be stitching, I couldn't say. In any case, I guess we were both so stunned at the sight of one another that our emotions overcame us. The next thing, he had released my wrists and—it seems absurd—but we fell on each other! Embraced one another like long-lost brother and sister. And I declare there were tears in both our eyes.

*   *   *

It has been a good many years, of course, and the horrible events that parted us had left their scars on us both. Looking at Mr Hademak last night, I would say they had left a harsher mark on him. He was impossibly thin—so thin that his pale eyes seemed to be lost in their deep grey sockets—and of course all his hair was gone, and he looked, with those long gaunt cheeks, and that vast, hairless head—there is no kind way to put it—he looked like something out of a child's nightmare. Like a ghoul. And when he smiled his crooked smile at me, first one corner, then the other, the lower lip dropping into a gum-baring grimace, it seemed as if he didn't quite remember how to do it. As if he hadn't smiled in some time. His two front teeth were missing.

'Jennifer?' he cried again. 'Jennifer!' And he put his thin long arms around me and squeezed so hard that, for a moment, I couldn't breathe. What a lonely pair we must have been, all these years, to greet each other so warmly! I don't know which of us cleaved harder to the other, but we must have looked quite absurd.

Finally, while we were both still too upset to speak, Mr Hademak's colleague, in similar security-guard black—but as swarthy as my friend was luminously white—tapped Mr Hademak on the shoulder. 'You need to put the lady down, Ghoul,' he murmured, 'and stand away from the door.'

Mr Hademak released me, blushing. Of course. 'Sssteffen,' he said, and I laughed aloud to hear it, his peculiar semi-lisp always more prominent when he was in an emotional state. 'Sso ssorry—but I don't ssuppose you would object. My friend here . . . I haven't seen her in many years . . . Could I—'

'Spare me the life story,' Steffen said, waving him away. 'Get outta here. You're showing us up. Just make sure you're back in half an hour . . .'

We walked a few blocks in silence, adjusting to one another's company, embarrassed, I think, by the effusiveness of our meeting. He broke the silence eventually, with that peculiar titter of his. 'Miss Doyle—Jennifer,' he said. 'You probably notice I haf lost all my hair.'

'I admit . . . I did notice that . . .'

'It was as a result of the great mental shock.'

The mental shock, I presumed, of watching his employer shoot someone dead before his eyes. But he said not. He said, 'Oh. Not sso much that . . . I woke up one morning, and all my golden hair was there on the pillow beside me, and it wasn't any longer attached to my head.'

'How awful,' I said, thinking (and wishing I wouldn't) of the silly golden wig I had bought for Rudy but never given to him.

'You know when it was?' he said, peering at me, as we paced along. 'You would like to know what event preceded the discovery of hair unattached on the pillow? It iss quite a thing, you know, to wake up and your hair is on your pillow.'

'I would imagine . . .'

'It was the day the mistress set sail for Santiago. I knew only because I read it in the

231

newspaper. For some time she was in Hawaii. You knew that. Of course, we thought she would return to New York, with little Jack. And then out of the blue—she set sail for Santiago . . . It was just a week or so after you left for California. Did you know?'

'I am so sorry,' I said.

'She broke my heart.'

'Yes. I suppose . . . I think, Mr Hademak, she made quite a speciality of that.'

'She broke her husband's heart.'

'Perhaps,' I said. 'She certainly made a few holes in it.' I regretted it at once . . .

He winced. 'She broke your father's heart,' he said.

'It had been broken long since.'

'You think so?' He sounded surprised. But not terribly interested. He didn't wait for me to reply. He sighed instead, a long, deep sigh. He said, 'Between you and myself, Jennifer, it has been a difficult few years.' And then, suddenly, 'Have you heard any word from her?'

'From?'

'Of courses. From Mrs de Saulles. She was fond of you, you know.'

I managed not to smile. 'I have not heard from her, no,' I said. 'But I wouldn't have expected it, Mr Hademak. In any case, she wouldn't know where to find me.'

'I read in the paper she was married again.'

'Is she? . . . Pity the husband.'

Again he winced. Again, I regretted it.

'She is married to a wealthy businessman,' he continued. 'From Santiago . . . But I have not heard from her myself. I wrote her at her mother's house at Valparaiso, to congratulate her, but perhaps she never received my letter.'

'Perhaps not.'

'I wrote once before, asking if she might kindly provide me with a reference. Unfortunately, when she left, she had so much on her mind, she quite forgot to do it. And, you know, that can be very hard in this ssort of work . . . To be a butler or a valet requires for so much trust, and with no references, how can there be trust?'

'She never wrote back?'

He raised his hollow head. Poor, darling man. 'She did not.'

A pause between us. We had found a coffee house with its lights on, and had drawn up beside it. The place looked welcoming enough. I wondered what it might take to get a little something added to the coffee. I wondered if I could find a way of asking without Mr Hademak being aware, since I remembered he didn't drink. My head was beginning to ache.

'Shall we go in?' I suggested.

'Of course it is possible the letters never reached her,' he continued. 'With the war . . . and everything . . .'

'Very possible. I'm so sorry, Mr Hademak . . .'

I pushed open the door and he followed me in.

'But it was hopeless from the beginning,' he said. 'Of courses. Or courses it was.' He looked embarrassed. 'I mean to say I would never dream to imply . . . But that'ss just the thing, isn't it, Miss Doyle? Unfortunately we cannot control our silly hearts, can we? No. We cannot. Of courses.'

We settled ourselves, one opposite the other, while a waiter plonked down our coffee—when it

233

came to the moment of asking him to slip in a little extra flavour, I lost my nerve in front of my old boss. Couldn't do it. I needn't have bothered in any case. As soon as the waiter left, Mr Hademak produced a hip flask of his own and, without consulting me, splashed its contents into both of our cups.

'I never knew you drank, Mr Hademak.'

He said, 'Oh! Well. We all drink now. Don't we Miss Doyle? . . . I suppose you have come on account of poor Mr Guglielmi.'

I nodded.

'It seems the entire world has fallen in love with him.'

'It's too extraordinary, isn't it? Could you ever have imagined how things might turn out?'

He offered up the ghost of a smile. 'I remember your face—do you remember? On that afternoon, when you arrived, and you were so lost without your papa. I felt terribly for you—you were quite a brave little thing. And I was talking all the time, so as to keep you from—' he waved a long hand in front of his face '—falling all over the place in awful sobbings . . . Do you remember?'

'Yes, I remember. I hadn't realised . . .'

'Well, and I was a little foolish, because I was sso terribly *jealous* of him . . . Mr Guglielmi. Because, of course, Mrs de Saulles had quite a soft spot for him. And I explained to you his status at the house. You were terribly shocked, I think. That I should have been so particular about it. Not at all democratic! And you an English girl!'

'Not so English now.'

'Yes. I see it. You even walk like an American girl nowadays, Miss Doyle. It is quite different.

And your accent is almost gone. You are transformed.'

'For the better, I hope? . . . Oh, don't answer that.'

He shrugged. 'I suppose,' he said. 'So thin, like all the flappers. And with the bob and the rouge and all . . . Quite the chic young lady. Quite a beauty you have turned into, Jennifer Doyle.'

I blushed. I think we both did. Lucky it was such poor light. 'By the way,' I said, 'I changed my name.'

'You did?'

'Everyone changes their name in Hollywood. It's part of the . . . everything. We re-create ourselves in the City of Dreams!'

'You make it sound awfully appealing . . .'

'Oh, it is.'

'I bet.'

'I'm called Lola Nightingale now. Lola because it's what Papa used to call me, when he was feeling affectionate . . . And Nightingale—because it isn't Irish.' I laughed. 'Nobody wants to be mistaken for a Paddy in the new world. Isn't that right? Or a wop . . . Unless, of course, you're Rudolph Valentino. It suits him very well, don't you think?'

'You are still in love with him, then?'

The question made me choke.

'He was so fond of you, too, I remember,' he continued calmly. 'The pair of you, with the little master, we could hear you talking and laughing all over the house . . . It used to make the mistress quite livid . . .'

'Yes,—'

'Oh!' And from the depth of their craters, those

235

sad dark eyes shone with fondness. 'The mistress could be quite the Jealous Miss! Don't you remember? If she sensed there was a man about who didn't adore her . . .' He chuckled. 'No, no, no. She didn't like that one bit. But you knew it, didn't you? Of course you did! Your friendship with Mr Guglielmi . . .' He shook his head. 'It used to make her desperate.' He sighed. 'It was all such a long time ago, wasn't it? And now Mr Guglielmi is the big star . . . He was a good man, though, in spite of it all. He looked after you, Miss Doyle . . . He took care of you. You would have been out, you know, if he hadn't gone to that courtroom for you . . . He took care of you . . .'

'Y-yes . . .' I said. 'Yes. I know he did.'

'I am assuming it, from your efforts to break into the hospital, that you may have lost contact with him, since he joined the . . . Immortals?'

'For a long while, yes . . . Or that is to say . . .' But I fell silent. Suddenly memories of our time at The Box were filling my head again, and along with them, creeping up on me before I could stop it, came this terrible rage. 'They were dreadful, you know,' I burst out. 'Both of them. Mr de Saulles too. What he did to Rudy—'

'Ohhh.' Mr Hademak waved it aside. 'No, really. You have to see it from his angle, Miss Doyle. Really, it was nothing.'

'They caused nothing but misery.'

'Nonsense! Why, if it weren't for Mr de Saulles you would never have come to America. If it weren't for Mrs—'

'She—'

'Please, Miss Doyle—'

But hearing him defending her—I thought I

236

might explode. 'I *hate her*, Mr Hademak. I hated her then. I still hate her. I hate her.'

'It's difficult for you, I know it . . .' he said. 'But you mustn't forget it, that Mrs de Saulles was handicapped by an awfully poor temperament. She was easily upset.'

I laughed aloud. 'Mr Hademak—I do not forget that! Actually, like you, I should think that, one way or another, I remember it every single day of my life.'

'Yes . . . Yes. Well . . .' He shuffled in his seat, another silence fell and I knew I had pushed too far.

'I'm sorry,' I said. 'I apologise. Forgive me.'

He tipped his bald head in acknowledgement. His cheeks were burning. I had offended him horribly.

'I am so sorry,' I said again.

'I am pleased for Mr Guglielmi. That things have worked out so well. He was a decent man. For all he was a—not quite a gentleman . . .'

I smiled.

'I see Madeleine,' he said, 'from time to time. I'm sure she'll be delighted when I tell her I have encountered you. She said she'd written you, via one of the film studios . . . I don't suppose you have ever received the letter.'

I didn't reply. 'How is she?' I asked instead.

'Very well. Married, of course. To a butcher in Brooklyn. Quite well-to-do, I can see. She hass five, maybe six children. I lose the count. Faring better than any of us, I should think. She was always the strong one.' He chortled again. 'It would take quite some sledgehammer to break that little Irish heart. Not like yours and mine. She

237

can forget the hopeless ones, and march on like the little soldier.'

I laughed. I didn't like Rudy being placed in the same category with anyone; certainly not the faithless car mechanic, or with Mrs de Saulles, either. 'Nobody's broken my heart just yet. Rudy and I—just before he fell ill—Rudy and I . . .' I felt his sad eyes on me—curious but not unkind; not yet disbelieving. I felt myself blushing again. And then the most peculiar thing happened. Suddenly, without a moment's warning, I began to cry. I couldn't stop.

I told him our history. He listened carefully, kindly. Finally, when I had finished, he leaned forward, looking at me, and his long, gaunt frame seemed suddenly to shimmer with energy and life.

'Well, then, Miss Doyle, of course I must help you. You and he were made for one another all those years ago. I have always known it. Madeleine knew it. Even Mrs de Saulles . . . Ten years is a long time . . . but if what you say is true—and of course it is—and you have found one another at last, we must do whatever we can to bring you together before it is too late. After all, he is very sick. He has rallied a little today, but from what I hear there is still a chance he will never—'

'*Please, don't say it.*'

'I beg your pardon.' He paused a moment. 'You say he loves you as much as you love him. And why shouldn't he?' He puckered his long face, considering. 'It is more than possible . . . And while he still lives—there is still hope for you both. We mustn't waste a moment. Come back with me now, Miss Doyle. And then we must wait until Steffen takes his break and I shall let you in through the door. But you need to change your appearance or the reporters will make a great fuss and you shall be turned away at once.'

'You would do that for me?' I asked him. 'But why?'

He looked at me quizzically, as if I were a complete fool. '*Why?*'

'I mean to say . . . Because if they catch us, Mr Hademak, there's no doubt that you'll be fired.'

He brushed it aside. 'Oh, it's just a little job,' he said, 'until I can get myself back into service . . . Besides, employment such as this—really, it is not sso hard to find.' He smiled. 'Not when you are a giant, as me. So *hurry*. Hurry, our half an hour is finished, and Steffen will be angry, wanting to take his break.'

In a rush of excitement, we agreed that no change of clothes on my part would put the wretched reporters off the scent, and that the time it would take me to return to my hotel, throw on a different frock and come back again might lead to missing our opportunity altogether, since by then Steffen would have returned from his break. So the plan was for Mr Hademak to go to his position first and that I should simply linger out of sight until Steffen came off duty. At which point I would edge towards the door once again, wait until the reporters—there were only two—were engaged in talking to one another and then, simply, while Mr Hademak looked the other way, slip smoothly through the hospital's front door.

'Mr Guglielmi is on the eighth floor,' he told me. 'The same room as Mary Pickford.'

I smiled. 'Oh, I know.'

'If you go to the end of the hall, you will find an elevator. But I think you will do better to take the stairs—there are two sets of stairs from the hall, as far as I am aware, and I would make a guess, since it's from those stairs that the manager Mr Ullman, and also all Mr Guglielmi's doctors appear when they come to give their statements, I would suggest you ascend the stairs on your left . . . And after that, Miss Doyle,' he said, 'it is up to you. You are on your own . . . Let me know, won't you, how it happens? Now I really have to go.'

By then we had left the coffee shop, and were standing on the corner of 49th Street. He was itching to leave, all his jittery nerves returned, and he looked such an odd fellow, standing there, such a lonely, bedraggled giant ghoul, I wanted to embrace him farewell but this time, his diffidence all recovered, he stepped away from me. 'Good luck, my friend,' he said awkwardly. 'Old friend . . .' he said, and he looked lonelier than I could stand.

I caught his arm, just as he was turning to leave. 'Where will I find you? I mean, if it all goes wrong?'

'Find me?' He laughed. '*Find* me? I am staying at—' He stopped. 'It doesn't matter.'

I guessed it at once. 'You are staying at Papa's boarding-house? Which you recommended.'

'I am always in contact with Madeleine, you know. She has become quite a friend to me . . . And I have an address for her. Would you like it?'

As he wrote it out, by the light of the street lamp, I reached up and kissed him on the shoulder. It was an absurd thing to do, and I wish

240

I hadn't. He pretended not to notice.

*　　　*　　　*

So I waited for Steffen to leave. I waited for the reporters to look away. And I slipped right past them, under the barrier, past Mr Hademak, through that big wooden door . . . but before I could even inhale the smell of the disinfectant, even as the door was closing behind me, I heard that same Goddamn reporter's voice, booming out from behind me: 'Hey, Baldie! Your flapper friend just walked right in through those doors! What the hell? You going to pretend you don't know? What do you take us for?'

I broke into a run, raced through the hall, past the elevator, turned left and began to climb, first one flight, then another. There was no one behind me. No one. No voices. No footsteps.

Perhaps, I thought, *perhaps* . . .

As I climbed, I began to imagine how it would be: knocking softly (would I knock?) . . .

Would the door to his suite be guarded?

Would I find him alone?

I pictured the large mahogany bed—the same bed from which Mary Pickford had made her miraculous recovery only a year or so before . . . I allowed myself to imagine the moment of his opening his eyes, and the expression on his face when he saw it was me, as I tiptoed across the room, as I reached out for his hand, his shoulder, his forehead . . . as I kissed him lightly, tenderly . . . as I whispered his name . . .

I felt a pair of rough hands on my neck. Next thing I had been thrown to the ground, and my

241

right arm was being twisted up between my shoulder-blades—and, oh, the pain!

I never got a look at his face—my assailant. It might have been anyone—he was tall, though not as tall as Mr Hademak, and he was rough. He dragged me down those stairs, back through the hall, out through those double doors, and tossed me right onto the sidewalk. In all the time it took, and I suppose it wasn't long, he said only three words: *You crazy bitch!*

They rattled in my head as he flung me to the ground, the words and the reporters' laughter, and the cheerful gasps from the small crowd.

You crazy bitch!

A photographer's flash illuminated the moment of my landing, with my cheek banging into the ground and my skirt flung up over my rolled stockings. When finally I raised my head, all I could see were those vile reporters, laughing at me: 'She's a-Sheikin' like a leaf, ha ha ha!'

'The nutso Sheba's all a-shiverin' and a-Sheikin' now!'

'Mr Valentino didn't want to see you, huh? You crazy bitch!'

I stood up with what dignity I could muster, which really wasn't so much. I looked about for Mr Hademak. 'Excuse me. Where is—'

'And if you're looking for the ghoul,' one of them shouted, 'he's been sent packing. All because of you . . .'

'Did he leave a message for me? Did he say where he was going?'

'Not to us he didn't.'

'He just left?'

'They sent him packing!'

I turned away.

'And I hope you feel pretty good about that, Nutso.'

1921

HOLLYWOOD

The twins were sharing a room at a girls-only boarding-house on Fountain Avenue back then. They weren't terribly surprised to see me.

'Gone again, has he?' Phoebe said, as soon as she opened the door.

'Gone for good,' I said.

'What makes you so sure?'

I told them Perry's belongings were missing. I was locked out.

'Probably got the law after him,' Lorna said, appearing behind her sister.

'He's an idiot,' Phoebe said.

Lorna nodded. 'Tell me something new . . .'

Phoebe stood there, looking at me thoughtfully. I waited, biting back tears, trying to hide my desperation, still with the touch of that foul man unwashed from my skin. It felt like an eternity passed, but finally, she smiled and pulled back the door. 'Come on in, Jennifer. Make yourself at home.'

It was a small room with nothing much inside it except the two beds, a stove, a small table and their clothes. Pile upon pile of the most beautiful clothes—and purses and stockings and shoes and hats and powders and combs and lotions and

243

paints. Somehow I found a space for my case and put it down. Then, before anything else, before I could try to be civil, or begin to explain, I asked if I could take a shower.

They looked at me, both of them—and, God knows, they'd been in this town longer than I had; perhaps it was as simple as that—but somehow they seemed to know. Lorna passed me soap and towel—gave my arm a squeeze. 'Forget about it,' she muttered. 'It never even happened.'

'Welcome to Hollywood, sweetheart,' Phoebe said.

And we never mentioned it again. When I returned from the washroom, skin raw from scrubbing, and in fresh clothes, they sat on the edge of their beds, waiting for me. Lorna handed me a big glass of her gin, though it was only breakfast time. 'C'mon,' she said. 'There's no work for us today. We're going to celebrate!'

Phoebe said, 'Gosh, Lorn, maybe she doesn't feel like celebrating.'

'Of course she does!' Lorna said. 'Anyway, never mind Perry. Perry is what he is. There's no changing him. We learned that long ago, didn't we, Phoebe? Love him or hate him—only for God's sake don't depend on him.'

Phoebe nodded. 'Honey, you got to trust us on that.'

'Oh, I believe you,' I said.

And then, right away, Lorna leaned forward. 'So let's talk about the other one—the Mystery Man, who Perry's always on about . . . Oh, *please*—please let's talk about him! You've no idea the control we've applied up till now, Phoebe and me. We've been longing to ask you, only it didn't feel quite right, did it, Phoeb?'

'It didn't seem fair on you—'

'—to put you on the spot like that.'

'Not while you were still in Perry's bed.'

'But if he's in the lock-up—'

'—which I just know he is . . .'

'He was in some sort of a jam, that's certain.'

'The way he and Willy were muttering the other night—'

'Anyhow, never mind *him*!' Lorna cried. 'Come on, for pity's sake! Let's talk about the man who brought you here in the first place . . . Tell us honestly, Jennifer—I know Perry believes it—are you still looking for him? And before you deny it, I know perfectly well that you are. We both do. We've watched you, haven't we, Phoebe? The moment we're out, your eyes are darting this way and that. You never stop. You can't blame Perry for feeling a teeny bit desperate.'

'No!' I cried, appalled. 'What can you be talking about? Of course I'm in love with Perry—absolutely!'

I glanced at Phoebe hoping for support. Instead she gave a little snort, and a poke to my ribs. 'Oh, come *on*,' she said. 'You can tell us . . . What's he like? You're still in love with him, aren't you?'

*   *   *

It was the same week I decided to change my name. Or the twins decided. In any case it was all part of the twins' Life After Perry celebration. 'Name me one single successful individual in this town with a Paddy surname,' Lorna had said. 'Name one.'

I couldn't.

'Because there aren't any. You want to be someone in this town? You don't want to be a Paddy. Nobody trusts a Paddy. Least of all the Yids.'

That was one reason I changed. The other, I can't explain. Or not so it makes any sense to me. I did it so Rudy could never find me. Should he ever happen to be looking.

Sometimes it is so intense that I look out from my window onto the sun-baked street, and imagine I can see you, appearing as a mirage through the dust. It was always an impossible dream before and yet when I looked out I could still believe it. Now that you know where to find me—perhaps, one day, when I look out, it really will be you . . .

They were his words, and I knew them better than any I had written myself. Every single day, a hundred times a day, I felt as he did—or as he had. Every single day, every single window . . . and each time I looked out and failed to find him, I turned back with the same unforgiving thump of rebuff, disappointment, longing . . . and I just wanted it to stop.

I changed my name, not so much so he could never find me but so I could stop hoping that he would.

The girls said they could get me more work as an extra girl—but I didn't want it. I longed for the quiet stability of a dull office job.

Thanks to the twins' patience and their financial support, I found one in the end. Having trawled from building to building, studio to studio, up and down Hollywood, Los Angeles, Culver City, Santa Monica, I was offered a job as receptionist at a quack practice, in a little house on Whitley Heights, only a half-hour walk from our boarding-house.

The quack was called Dr Leibowitz, though he wasn't really a doctor. He had invented a tonic, Dr Leibowitz's Amazing Slimming Beverage, which was a mixture of vitamins and a few other things—vegetable seeds or something, I have forgotten what. He sold it for twenty-five dollars a pop—the same as he was paying me each week to sit behind a white desk, in a white room that always smelled of baking (due to the yeast he put in his slimming beverage). My job was to smile pleasantly, and be slim, and reassure the purchaser, as I took their cash, that they couldn't be spending it more wisely.

Dr Leibowitz was a great salesman. I never believed his wonder tonic did anyone the slightest good since, in the year or so I worked there, the same ladies used to return week after week, never an ounce slimmer than the week before. Nevertheless, they swore by him. He used to sell five or ten of those Amazing Slimming Beverages every day. By the time I left, it was closer to twenty.

It was a very pleasant job. Dr Leibowitz had a wife, and a daughter about my age, whom I liked well enough. They were in another part of the house and for that reason, if not for any other, Dr Leibowitz left me alone. He was always polite, and his wife too—and because his practice was popular, there were always people coming and going, sometimes even stars.

As soon as I had an income I moved out of the twins' crowded room and rented a room of my own in the same building. It was a lovely thing to have them nearby and yet not to be sleeping on their floor. I spent as much time with them as I could, but their evenings tended to be far busier than mine.

After the traumas of Perry, on top of everything that had come before, I wanted only to live quietly for a while, lick my wounds, write my scenarios. And that was what I did. I spent my days at the surgery, and my evenings doing nothing much, dreaming of Rudy—dreams that were becoming increasingly fuzzy. Occasionally, in my mind, his face would merge with Perry's and I would forget quite what he looked like. But then I would remember his kiss, his voice, the way we danced . . . and then, before I had even noticed I was doing it, his letter would be unfolded in front of me, and I would be gazing out of my window, searching yet again.

I spent most of my spare cash going to the movies, sometimes with the twins but often alone. I wrote endless scenarios. I wrote them and rewrote them and rewrote them again. When I went to the movies, I took paper and pen and I used to make notes. I read books on how to write photoplays, swotted over the trade magazines for hints on how to break through. Nothing seemed to help—not the books, not the magazines, nothing. I sent my scenarios to the studios. Sometimes I even delivered them in person. Nothing. And somehow the more rejections I received, the more determined I became. Somehow I just couldn't seem to bring myself to stop.

*   *   *

A year or so went by. Phoebe, Lorna and I moved from our boarding-house into one of the bungalows. It was on Citrus Avenue, below Melrose, and it cost us twenty-five dollars a week, furnished. Oh, and how we loved it! There were two bedrooms—we took it in turns to take the smaller bedroom on our own. The lounge we made our project. We painted it ourselves—a pale yellow to reflect the California sunshine; we bought cushions and lamps, and a new dining table large enough to invite our friends round. Not that I had many. But the twins did. Plenty of them.

Finally, perhaps most importantly, we bought ourselves a still as a house-warmer, and set ourselves up with a little gin factory in the bathroom.

Most weekends the twins would go dancing. Sometimes I accompanied them, but generally I preferred to stay at home. I was still licking my wounds, I suppose—and I dreaded getting back in with Perry's crowd. Or with any crowd, actually. I dreaded getting in with anything or anyone that might set my pulse racing ever again.

From time to time the twins would nag me enough, and I would agree to go on a date with one of their friends. And sometimes, I have to say, though I always went unwillingly, I would have a lot of fun—and would be reminded, faintly, of what it was to be wicked and young and alive.

But those long, heavy nights such as I had enjoyed with Perry were a thing of the past. And, in truth, I didn't miss them. I didn't miss him. I didn't miss his wild friends. Most of all, I didn't

249

miss that encounter in the pantry at the Pico.

Which is why, apart from my fruitless trips to the studios to deliver my unwanted scenarios, I kept away from the film colony. I played safe. I put money aside. And maybe, maybe, memories of Rudy began to fade, just a little.

The twins complained I had given up taking any care with my appearance. 'One day,' they used to say, 'you'll wake up and you'll be old and ugly, and you'll want to do something about it and it'll just be too late.'

I didn't care. I spent nothing on clothes. I left the wonderful bob to grow long again. But it was all right. Everything was bearable. My quietness—and plainness—may have irritated my glamorous roommates, but I could still make them laugh. The three of us were quite happy in our little apartment. It was—nice.

*   *   *

There came a hot afternoon in August. I was sitting quietly behind my clean white reception desk, arranging bottles of the Amazing Slimming Beverage into an enticing pyramid. Peace and order reigned. And then the door burst open, and Campbell Hays staggered in.

He was a youngish man, not much older than I was, handsome, brawny—but, above all, in great pain. His face was twisted with it. As he drew nearer, leaning his weight against a poorly dressed Chinaman, I could see the problem centred on his left leg: there was blood gushing down over his shoes and onto the clean white tiled floor, and it looked very much like a shin bone was jutting right

250

through his torn pants. The Chinaman brought his bleeding friend to my reception desk, deposited him there and waited politely for his tip.

I felt terribly sick.

'*Thank you kindly*,' gasped the wounded man. 'I can't quite get to my wallet, but if you would take my weight for a second . . .' After a moment's struggle, a dollar note was produced and offered to the Chinaman, who took it and bowed and wandered away.

Which left me, and the man, and the blood.

'Mr Leibowitz has just gone out,' I said, feeling the room begin to spin, wishing above everything that Campbell Hays and his gushing blood would take themselves elsewhere. 'But I should tell you he's not a qualified doctor, or not for the purposes I should think you want. He is actually an expert in dietary matters—so I don't know how well he can help you . . . He'll be back in two minutes,' I gabbled. 'But, really, it looks to me as if you'd be better off at the hospital.'

Somehow he managed to smile. 'If I can just get it bandaged up . . . There's no hurry . . . only maybe a chair . . .'

'Oh! I'm so sorry!' I hurried to fetch him one, and a glass of water. I handed him a towel to catch the blood, and looked away. 'I'm so sorry,' I said again. 'Dr Leibowitz'll be here any minute. I am so terribly sorry. Only I was there once, when a man was shot . . . and there was so much blood . . .'

'That's OK,' he said. 'You just look away.' He sat and wrapped the towel around himself. A few moments later, he said, 'Want to tell me about the shooting?'

I said not. Did he want to tell me about the

251

accident?

He said he did. He'd been run off the road right outside our door.

'Beautiful car she was driving . . .' he said, through gritted teeth. 'Piers Arrow. Movie star for sure.'

'Oh, really? Which one?'

He laughed aloud at that, because his comment had stirred me to spin round and look at him. He had turned quite white, and there were slow driblets of sweat at either temple. 'I'm sorry to say I couldn't be sure,' he said. 'Don't know much about which movie star is which. But she sure looked familiar . . .'

He was nice-looking; nicely dressed, if a little old-fashioned. A well-to-do farmer, I imagined. Nothing to do with the film colony, that was certain.

There was a silence between us. He glanced at me. He said, with something that was meant to be a smile, except it was more a grimace, due to the discomfort he was in, 'I can see you're disappointed, miss, but maybe if I describe her to you, you might recognise her. Are you a fan of the movies?'

'Oh, I adore them,' I said. 'I'm quite obsessed. But never mind that . . . Perhaps—are you all right? Perhaps you might be better lying down.'

'Well now,' he said, ignoring my question, 'she was certainly petite. Small as a child. In fact, she could barely see over the bonnet to drive . . . I think maybe that was partly the trouble.'

'Mary Pickford?'

'Miss, I wish I could, and I know I should, but I'm afraid I couldn't say. Is Mary Pickford blonde

252

or dark?'

It seemed extraordinary that anyone could exist in Hollywood—anyone could exist in America—who needed to ask such a question. Nevertheless I managed not to gasp. 'Oh, she's blonde,' I said. 'Was the lady blonde?'

'Well, now . . . I would say she was dark. But under the hat it was a little hard to tell.'

'What kind of a hat was it?'

He cupped both hands—big hands—and put them above his head in some effort to imitate something approximating some kind of hat and then, realising how absurd it was, shrugged his great big shoulders. We both laughed. 'Well, miss, I'm not quite sure,' he said. 'I think maybe it was black. Or—or maybe she had on a scarf . . . Now I think of it— ' He stopped short suddenly, took a sharp intake of breath. 'Well, gosh,' he said. 'This leg is getting sore. I wonder if . . .' He fell silent. His eyes rolled back, and then, with a final gasp, he slumped forward and fell with a great thud onto the floor in front of him. He was out cold.

I was attempting, without success, to disregard the blood, and to drag his great big body back up onto that chair, when—thank God—Dr Leibowitz arrived. He had bandages in his room, it so happened, along with the wonder tonic, so he wrapped up the leg as best he could and I called an ambulance.

And, truthfully, as Campbell Hays was carried out on his stretcher, I assumed that would be the last I ever saw of him.

*   *   *

But then, three weeks later, he appeared in the practice once again, all scrubbed up this time, in a collar and tie. And with the free arm—the one without the crutch—he was carrying a bunch of flowers. He looked quite awkward as he presented it to me. As a decent boy would, when approaching a decent girl.

'Hello there,' he said, smiling.

'Hello! Good to see you back on your feet! How's the leg?'

'The leg? . . . Oh! The leg's just fine. Thank you. By the way, I worked out who that star was . . . the one who ran me over . . . Remember?'

'You did?'

'Well, she was very dark, with long dark hair all braided this way and that, and she smoked a long cigarette. And her face was quite white, except for the red-painted lips . . . and she had evil, glaring eyes . . . and it was Thelma Bara!'

'Theda Bara?'

'That's the one!'

'Theda Bara . . . But I thought you said—last time I'm sure you said she was wearing some kind of a hat.'

'So she was . . . but underneath it . . .'

'How could you see?'

'Well. Of course I only got the smallest glimpse but she was looking just like a vampire. Thelma Bara.'

'Theda.'

'That's the one.'

I burst out laughing. 'I don't believe you have the faintest idea . . . I think you're just saying Theda Bara—Thelma Bara—to keep me cheerful. I don't believe you have the faintest idea which movie star

254

ran you off the road!'

For a moment he looked ready to deny it, but he thought better of it, and offered me a grin instead. 'Might have helped if I got her name right,' he said. 'She sure looked like a Thelma to me . . . Anyway I came by to thank you for taking care of me the other week.'

'Hardly,' I said. 'Gosh—I'm embarrassed to think. There I was complaining about the blood, grilling you about which movie star, and the next thing you were passed out. I should be apologising.'

'But you made me laugh. Really, that was quite something . . .' Then, in an awkward movement, he handed me the flowers: a glorious big bunch of roses. Must have cost him a fortune. I thanked him, and then, to avoid awkwardness, quickly busied myself in the cupboard beneath the desk where the vase was kept, and while I was down there, he leaned over the counter. 'Also I was wondering . . . if you might let me take you to the movies one night. Maybe we could see something with my friend Thelma, and I could reassure myself I'm accusing the right movie star . . .'

'I would love to go to the movies with you,' I said. And I meant it.

*   *   *

Campbell Hays told me he had inherited his father's grain store down in Culver City when he was just eighteen. By the time he staggered into my life, blood pouring over his shoe, he already owned a couple of grain stores and was just beginning to invest in real estate. He was smart: a local

California boy who could see the direction things were going. He got in early, bought up tracts of land all around Hollywood just as the prices were going completely crazy. It so happens he's one of the richest people in California today. Clever guy. But back then, he was only just beginning.

Our weekly outings to the pictures became, very quickly, a regular date. Each week he would take me to a different movie, and each week he would sit patiently beside me until the end. He tried to enjoy them as much as I did—I know he did—but the truth was, though he lived in the movie capital of the world, films simply did not interest him. Fantasy and make believe were a foreign language to him, and I knew, even while he sat beside me and I was enrapt in the story unfolding, that he was only waiting patiently until the end. And at the end he would give a wry, good-natured grimace, say something like 'Well, well. Another heiress falls in love!' or 'Another rotten scoundrel gets his just deserts!' and I would smile—because, of course, he had a point. The stories were absurd. All stories, by their nature, are absurd. And in some strange way I admired it, his complete inability to set aside his rational mind, the sense of clarity he had, which meant he could never be entirely swept away . . . It was so completely the opposite of me—everything about him was the opposite of me; and I loved that. He made me feel safe.

*   *   *

'Lola,' he said, after about a month, on the night he first kissed me, 'you looked especially lovely this evening. I love the way you keep your hair like

256

that. Like a lady. Not cut short, like all the other girls. I love the way you don't fuss about the way you dress. You're beautiful just as you are, Lola . . .'

He kissed me in the car, across the street from the apartment on Citrus Avenue, that Saturday night and each Saturday night for many weeks after. Sometimes, as a surprise, he would turn up at the surgery in Whitley Heights and take me for lunch at a sandwich bar on Franklin. He and Mr Leibowitz befriended one another, and before long the two of them were engaged in real-estate deals together. (Mr Leibowitz was delighted with me, he often said, for having introduced him to such an astute businessman.)

Campbell told me about his businesses. He told me about his parents, first one then the other, slain by the Spanish flu three years previously; he told me about his younger sister who lived with a pastor and five kids in San Francisco. And I told him about my scenario writing, and about England, and about my father—I told him how Papa died, and even something about Mr and Mrs de Saulles. He was wise and kind and always interested. Nevertheless I had learned from my mistakes: I never mentioned Rudy. Never. Nor even Perry. Nor— In any case, there was plenty I kept back— not because I didn't trust him: I did. But because there seemed nothing to be gained from telling him things that could only cause upset and unhappiness. I grew increasingly fond of him.

*   *   *

He smelled good. He felt strong. He was kind and

257

polite and intelligent and thoughtful—and he made me laugh. Through and through he was a gentleman. And the truth is I had been living like a nun for too long. Even his somewhat chaste and gentlemanly kisses turned my stomach in circles.

Somehow, God knows how, he had snuck up on me by surprise, stolen through my defences and reawoken the fire that, all this time, I'd been so very careful not to fuel. And some nights, after his kisses led yet again to nowhere, I would lie awake unable to sleep with the frustration.

How, I wondered, did decent girls get the message across, without shocking their gentlemanly partners? How could I tell him that—decency aside—I was also flesh and blood?

Late one Saturday evening, as we were sitting in his auto outside Citrus Avenue and he was about to kiss me—it simply burst from me before I could quite prevent it. 'Campbell. You know, you can kiss me right here. Or you can come into the apartment and kiss me properly. If you like. Why don't you come in? The twins are out. I'll give you a glass of our home-brewed gin, which is just about drinkable—if you mix it—and we can be just as friendly as we want, as friendly as you would like to be . . .'

A horrible silence fell. Oh, it seemed to last for minutes! Had I shocked him? Certainly. Had I angered him? Horrified him? Repelled him? I couldn't tell. 'Forgive me,' I said at last.

'Don't be silly! I'm sorry—I mean to say I'm delighted . . . delighted . . .' But he couldn't look at me, and in the moonlight I am certain I saw him redden. 'I suppose I'm just a little surprised.'

'I'm so sorry,' I said again.

Finally, he looked at me and grinned, that boyish grin. 'Well, Lola—for sure *I*'m not! I should love a glass of that gin . . .'

'Wonderful!' I moved to climb down from the motor-car, but he stayed where he was. I could feel his eyes still on me.

'Lola . . .' he said, suddenly serious.

'Yes, Campbell? . . . What is it? I am so sorry if I offended you.'

He shook his head, and seemed, for a moment, to be searching for the right words. Finally, he took a deep breath, gently grasped both my hands in his. 'Since we're . . . moving forward . . . in the way I believe we are . . .' he gave a wry smile '. . . and since . . . The fact is, Lola, I've been wanting to say it since the first day, the very first day I met you. There has never been a doubt in my mind. Only I held back, for fear of alarming you.' He took a deep breath. 'But, honestly, since we're—really—at this wonderful point in our friendship, I might just as well say it out loud . . .'

I knew, of course.

'Sweetheart,' he said. 'We haven't known each other so long—I know that. And I hope it doesn't sound too completely dumb. But the fact is, since the moment I walked into your surgery and we fell into conversation, it felt—to me—as if we'd known each other all our lives. And I just knew it. I knew you were the girl for me. I think you're amazing, Lola Nightingale. And I know there's a lot I don't know about you. And I know there's a lot you choose to keep back. But I also know that I love you . . . Lola—this evening, the gin—and all the rest—putting all that aside . . . I swear I would be the happiest man alive—if you would agree—if you would do me the honour of becoming . . .'

So.

I thought of Rudy, fleetingly; of that kiss under the electric light bulbs. I thought of him, his head on his hands, asleep in the corridor, the night my father died. I thought of him the first evening I saw him, gazing out over the garden at The Box, smoke curling from his lips, so melancholy, so breathtakingly handsome . . . so very, very, very much the man I knew I loved . . . I thought of glimpsing him, as if in a mirage, appearing through the California dust . . . But he never had appeared. He never had.

I closed my eyes tight and, in that moment, swore never to think of him again. And when I opened them and looked up into Campbell's kind, handsome, intelligent face, I knew I could love him. If not quite so well, then very well, at least. I wanted to make him happy, and I knew I could, and I knew that making him happy would make me happy. I knew all that. So when I replied, there was not a doubt in my mind.

'Why, Campbell,' I said, and I smiled—and my heart was filled with love for him. 'I should love to marry you! I should love it more than anything else in the world!'

*　　　*　　　*

Campbell and I were engaged to be married, and had been for several weeks, the first time I encountered Frances Marion. We were at the Piggly Wiggly grocery store in West Hollywood. It was a Saturday, and the twins and I were in there buying—oh, hell, it doesn't matter what: our

260

weekly groceries, of course. In any case the three of us were all together, as was often the case. I was carrying in my bag a couple of scripts—one, I remember, called *Snow Queen* and the other called *Catnip*. It was a comedy about a man so irresistible to women that . . . All sorts of situations ensue.

And now I think of it, I wonder if, with a little work, it couldn't still be rather good? Perhaps even with dialogue . . . Gosh—I had quite forgotten it—but what a thrilling idea . . . I shall discuss it at my luncheon with Miss Marion. Wonder what she will think on the matter—if it's worth it, to invest any time in the new talkies, or if it's just a silly thing. Just a gimmick. I read in the trade magazines that it's certainly what Mr Charles Chaplin thinks.

In any case, *Snow Queen* (best forgotten) and *Catnip* were in my bag, because I was intending to deliver them to some guy who'd come into Mr Leibowitz's surgery the previous week, who said he knew somebody who knew somebody . . .

The girls and I walked to the Piggly Wiggly on Melrose to do our weekly grocery shop every Saturday. It had become quite a ritual. On that occasion, just as we were turning in, a flashy motor-car pulled up in front of us.

Out hopped a small, well-dressed woman, blonde and good-looking, about thirty—at least ten years older than we were. I didn't recognise her. She was not a movie star. And yet even in the way she stepped from that car there was an aura of elegant authority about her—the sort of aura I dream of possessing one day.

Lorna, Phoebe and I were instantly intrigued. We fell silent, all three of us, and peered first at her, then, necks twisting, into the automobile she had exited. Phoebe gave me a violent poke in the ribs. For sitting right there inside, upright as Queen Victoria, and so small as to be barely visible behind the steering-wheel was, not Thelma or even Theda Bara, so much as America's one and only Sweetheart. It was none other than little Miss $20,000-a-week Mary Pickford!

You absolutely are not supposed to gawk in Hollywood. Only the tourists and the new arrivals do that. The rest of us make it a studied art to appear unimpressed by stardom in whatever form it presents itself. But—as my good friend Mr Hademak himself would vouch—Mary Pickford was, and is, something else entirely. She is America's Sweetheart! Possibly—probably—the most beloved woman in the entire world!

The three of us stood on the sidewalk barely a couple of feet from her, whispering and giggling like horrible schoolgirls, staring at the poor woman, until eventually she could ignore us no longer. She turned a stiff pair of shoulders towards us, looked the three of us coolly in the eye—as if to say, *Shame on you*—and nodded: a thoroughly royal little nod. It took the pep out of us in an instant. We stopped giggling and continued on our way.

We pushed through the turnstile in silence, rather shamefaced—and then all of a sudden Phoebe, the rib poker, let out a squeal and did it again!

'*Phoebe, will you stop!*' I cried.

'Oh, my Lord!' she said, grabbing a hold of my

arm. 'You realise who that other girl was, don't you? The one who came into the store ahead of us?'

'You're pinching me,' I said irritably. 'Would you let me go?'

'Pinch yourself, little sister!' she said. 'It was only the Most Powerful Woman in All Hollywood! That's who it was. Only the Most Successful Scenarioist in the Entire World. Why, it was only *Frances Marion*!'

'I know perfectly well who it was!'

'Of course you do. Only a shame you didn't recognise her. And only your good fortune *I did*. Lola, she's in the store. Right now! She's in the store, *right now*!'

I felt a lurch of something not too positive in the pit of my stomach. Phoebe and Lorna both knew I was carrying the scripts. If it was Frances Marion—and it was well known she and Mary Pickford were the closest of friends since, apart from anything else, it was Frances Marion who wrote most of her films for her—I knew just what was coming next . . .

'What in hell are you waiting for, Lola?'

'Nothing. . . Anyone else feel like ravioli tonight?'

Phoebe looked at Lorna, who looked back at Phoebe. Lorna said, 'If you don't get over there, right this minute, and put that damned script into Miss Marion's sweaty little paw, I swear to you, Miss Lola Nightingale . . . you're not coming home with us. You understand? We're locking you out . . .'

'Don't be ridiculous. You can't do that. Anyway, I can't . . . What would Campbell say?'

'Campbell?'

'I don't think he'd like it.'

'Don't be feeble,' Lorna said. 'In any case, he wouldn't give two hoots, and if he did, then he shouldn't.'

'And anyway he isn't here.'

'It's not the point,' I said, sounding pathetic, even to myself. 'I'm going to be his wife. I can't go around . . . accosting people in grocery stores.'

'Then perhaps you should think twice about marrying him,' Lorna said. 'If he doesn't want you to succeed in life . . .'

'He does!'

'As a wife and mother, yes, I'm sure.'

'Please,' I said wearily. 'Let's leave him out of it.'

They never could, though. I had confided in them too much. And despite the fact they had nagged and bullied all the months and years I wasn't dating and, by their own admission, could perfectly appreciate what a fine man Campbell was, they were distraught—they were *livid*—when I broke it to them that he and I were to marry.

'I'll leave Campbell out of it if you go over there and talk to her,' Phoebe said.

I didn't move.

'And, by the way, she means it,' Phoebe continued. 'About locking you out. And so do I. And, furthermore, if you don't "accost" that damn woman in this damn grocery store—right this instant—I swear I'll tell Campbell you can't marry him after all.'

'Because you've got syphilis,' Lorna said.

'That's not funny.'

They thought it was. 'And you're pregnant. By a Catholic priest,' Phoebe continued. 'And you're a

Bolshevik . . .' They both began to giggle.

'And in any case,' Lorna couldn't resist adding, 'you're in love with another man.'

'That's not funny,' I said. 'That's not funny.'

'Oh, we know it's not.'

We fell silent, while the awkwardness—and their unkindness—subsided a little, and we could perhaps pretend the words hadn't been said. Then, suddenly, with a little grunt of exasperation, Lorna gave me a violent shove. 'Do it!' she ordered.

And I suppose that's what friends are meant to do, isn't it?

'Do it, or I'll go right over there and do it for you,' she said.

*   *   *

The most powerful woman in Hollywood was reaching for a pack of macaroni when I stopped her. I had the script already pulled out of my bag, and I was so nervous that when I first began to speak, and she turned to me, macaroni in hand, with those cool, clear, intelligent eyes gazing up at me, I felt a lump at the back of my throat as if I was about to be sick. She had to wait while I pretended to have a coughing fit, just to stop myself throwing up all over her patent tan-and-white Mary-Janes. (Perfect, they were. I can picture them still!)

She was wonderful. I will never forget. It is the unwritten law of life in Hollywood (and I can't emphasise it enough) that one should never, under any circumstances, accost an industry professional in a public place.

It's what I did. Frances Marion wouldn't have

265

strayed from the rules of decency if she'd told me there and then to take a hike, but she didn't. She waited for me to stop coughing and gagging, and listened politely while I stumbled out my unprepared introductory speech . . .

'Miss Marion? I'm so sorry. I hope you will forgive me . . . Miss Marion . . . My name is Jennifer—I mean, no, it isn't. Actually it's Lola Nightingale. And I have been—gosh—just like everyone else, I have been such a great admirer of your work. I so much admired— Where do I start? I can't think of a film of yours that I haven't admired. But I suppose my favourite—it would be either *Pollyanna*, of course . . . And then perhaps *The Flapper*—I wished I could have written that one myself, and then, well, *The Restless Sex* made me laugh aloud and weep all at the same time . . . And then *Poor Little Rich Girl* . . .'

She laughed. 'I'm very flattered,' she said. 'I fear you may have to go through my entire catalogue before I stop you, because this is all too enjoyable. But, sadly, I have a friend waiting outside . . . and, as I imagine you know, I have written quite a number of films. How can I help you, Lola Nightingale?' She looked at the script I was holding out to her. It was still addressed to the friend of the friend of the friend of the person who . . .

'Would you like me to deliver it to him?' she asked me. 'I believe I recognise the name.'

'No!' I laughed. 'Gosh, no! That is to say—yes, of course I should . . . If you could persuade him to read it . . . But in truth I should much prefer it if by some chance you had a small moment to glimpse at the pages yourself. It's—I've written quite a number of these things over the years, and I confess I've not got anywhere with any of them . . . to date . . . But I'm convinced that I'm improving. I know it. And if only I could persuade a person like yourself—if only I could persuade you to take the smallest look . . .'

She held out a dainty hand and—perhaps it was only to silence me so she could politely move away—she took the script.

'Thank you! Thank you! I can't begin—'

'And if it's to my liking,' she interrupted (with a smile), 'where in the world might I track you down, Miss Nightingale? To tell you that I intend to help you with it?'

I stared at her stupidly. Then: 'Oh! OH! *Oh!*' I began to rummage desperately in the bottom of my bag for a pencil, but she had already found one of her own. 'Where do you work, Lola?'

'I work . . .' But I didn't want to tell her I was working for a miracle-beverage peddler on Whitley Heights. It had the wrong ring to it. 'I work all over the place, Miss Marion. Here and there. Actually I'm just on my way home . . .'

She smiled, sensing my embarrassment. 'Maybe you should tell me your home address, then. But don't go waiting by the postbox each morning, will you? It won't be at once, mind. I have a horrible amount of work stacked up but I promise you I shall look at it when I can. It may be several months—if you can wait that long?'

I could wait, I said, for ever. And she laughed.

By the time I was back beside my friends—spying on me from behind the high shelves—my knees were shaking so badly I needed to lean on them to stay up. They put their arms around me, laughed,

267

congratulated me on my courage . . .

'I never would have dared!' Phoebe cried. 'But look at you! You did it! *Look at you!*'

'Oh, my gosh, Lola,' Lorna said. 'I swear it, you're on the way now!'

*   *   *

Campbell took me to Vincenzi's for an early dinner. He had tickets to see a movie at the Million Dollar Theater, downtown. (Campbell did everything properly.) Normally, since becoming engaged, we would go to the movies and he would take me to dinner afterwards. This time he said he couldn't wait that long. He had a gift.

I tried to stop myself, but as we followed the waiter to our booth my eyes slid instinctively, surreptitiously, along the other tables—just in case. There was no Rudy. There never was.

We sat down opposite one another, ate a happy, companionable dinner together, and at the end Campbell delved beneath our table and emerged with two teacups filled with Champagne, and a small, square leather box.

It was a beautiful ring—he'd had someone in San Francisco design it especially. It was surprisingly modern: a diamond, cut in a perfect square and as big as my thumbnail, with a plain platinum band holding it in place. It was beautiful, and it fitted perfectly. He said, 'Lola, sweetheart, don't you think it's about time we set a date?'

*   *   *

With the ring on my finger and a date set for

July—three months hence—we set off to the movie theatre.

As we walked together, my beautiful sharp ring pressing between our clasped hands, Campbell talked of the future. 'When we are married,' he said, 'as soon as we are married, Lola, I will buy us a little bungalow of our own in Hollywood. Would you like that? And you can do it however you like. I don't mind. You can paint the outside any colour you want, if you want to. They've got them all sorts of colours, haven't they? Purples and pinks. I shan't mind. And you can have as many children as you like, and you can have a little room where you can write your movie stories, if it's what you'd like—though I expect, with the kids, you might find you're a little busy for that . . . But it doesn't matter at all, if you do or if you don't—because whatever you do, Lola, I will love you, and I intend to make you the happiest girl in all California. In all America. In all the world . . .'

He had bought us tickets to see *The Four Horsemen of the Apocalypse*—from the novel, strangely enough, that Perry, in his feeble way, had been trying to turn into a movie when we'd first met. There had been enthusiastic reviews just about everywhere, most especially for its new star, and for numerous reasons I was excited to see it. The previous evening Dr Leibowitz's ordinarily quite sensible daughter had returned from a viewing, and had been so struck by this new, unheard-of star it had rendered her quite idiotic. 'I swear,' she said, 'I could hardly prevent myself from swooning right there in my seat! Thank goodness I only went with the girls—and all the girls were saying it, not

269

only me . . . He's dark, really quite dark, and he dances as if . . . he is the most—it is the most . . .'

*   *   *

He had changed his name. Of course he had. Everyone changes their name in Hollywood. And when I saw him up there on the big screen for the first time, with Campbell beside me and his custom-designed diamond engagement ring glistening on my finger, I gasped. I gasped, as if the whole world had stopped: for there, before me, and magnified a hundred times over, and as handsome as any man I had ever set eyes on, appearing through the dust, as if in a mirage, was the man I adored. The man who had kissed me under the electric lights at Coney Island . . .

Rodolfo Guglielmi.

My Rudy.

Rudolph Valentino.

I must have screamed. Because from the edge of my vision I noticed Campbell turn to me, full of anxiety.

'Sweetheart, are you all right?'

But he needed to ask me three or four times before I even registered it was his voice . . .

'Sweetest Lola. Darling. What's happened? Are you all right?'

'Lola, my love—what is the matter? Are you ill?'

I craned forward, to be closer to that vast screen. I felt him pulling at my shoulder.

'*Lola?*'

I stood up.

'*Lola!*'

I remember the brief moment of silence, the

music from that giant organ-player must have paused. It's such a big theatre, and ordinarily the music plays so loud I might have said anything and nobody would have heard. But there—just then—the camera lingered on Rudy's face, and in the silence I heard myself shouting out his name: 'RUDY!'

I looked back at Campbell, becoming aware of him for the first time. He looked bewildered. Shell-shocked. *'It's Rudy!'* I told him, as if the name might mean anything to him at all, when I had gone to such pains never to mention it. *'Campbell, don't you see?'*

'Sweetheart, sit down. Please. Calm down. You're making a show of yourself.'

'But don't you see?'

'See what? *Lola, I have told you to sit down. Do as I ask. Please. Sit down at once!'*

'But can't you realise?' I shouted, pointing at the screen. 'Campbell—don't you see that—that man there? It's why I came to Hollywood. It's why I wake up each morning and go to bed every night. Because of that man! *All this time I have been looking for him!* And now I have found him, and all you can think to say to me is, sit down!'

Thursday, 19 August 1926

9 a.m.

Rudy is improving. I knew it at once because when I went down to the hospital early this morning there was barely anyone there. The summer fair had upped sticks and departed, and all that remained was a statement from Rudy's doctors attached to the door.

'*Mr Valentino,*' it said, '*is making satisfactory progress and, having passed his most critical period, no further bulletins will be issued unless some unexpected development occurs.*' I wept when I read it—unobserved, thank heavens. The gawking, wailing crowds and those horrible pressmen have lost interest now. My darling Rudy is going to live. There is nothing to report.

Well, it is only nine o'clock and I have been up for hours, but he has not called for me yet. He will. He will. The morning stretches ahead. And he shall call for me, just as soon as he is strong enough. As soon as Mr Ullman allows him . . .

In any case, in all the dreadful happenings of the last few days he has no doubt forgotten the name of this stinkpot of a hotel I am staying in. And really, what with Larry the room clerk and his meaningful glances each time I pass this way or that, and the night-time wheezing and coughing from the johnnie in room 348, and the crazy couple on my other side alternately caterwauling

272

at one another or banging away so furiously even my own bed creaks, I should happily forget the name of this place myself.

And so I shall forget it, one fine day . . . when my scenario writing leads me to a bed of my own at the Algonquin. Oh, imagine that! And there will be Miss Dorothy Parker, inviting me to join her for luncheon, and poisonous Miss Anita Loos, sitting up and taking notice, shuffling up to make a space, and Miss Frances Marion, of course, and Miss Hedda Hopper, and Louella Parsons and Elinor Glyn and Mary Pickford . . . What a thing it would be to be a part of that crowd, and to feel as if I had every right to be among them! Not just this once, today, as a special charity case, but on any day I pleased. Gosh, I should die of it! I should die from pride.

Enough. I have a long way to go. So—I shall wait. Calmly. And with the utmost confidence. Rudy will call for me as soon as he is able.

They have a picture of me in this morning's *Graphic*. Unfortunately I am caught flying through the air, my legs up above my head, my face already flat against the sidewalk: ***GRIEFSTRUCK SHEBA EXPELLED FROM SHEIK'S BEDSIDE,*** it says. But it is a small article, a long way from the front page, and they didn't know my name. Or even, I'm pleased to see, that of Mr Hademak. I wonder if he will see it? Oh, my gosh—what if Rudy should see it? What would he think? Would he recognise me? Perhaps not. Almost certainly not. I've never worn that dress for him, and my face is quite hidden. I suppose, if it weren't me but somebody else, I might even think the picture quite funny. I look a sight.

273

But it is me. And it isn't funny. It is utterly appalling. And now I have a bruise across half my cheek, and a dreadful graze on my forehead, which no amount of face paint seems to cover. God knows how I shall explain it at luncheon today. Perhaps Miss Marion will be too polite to say anything, but after my last performance, it's hardly likely to inspire much confidence . . .

Far worse than any of that, I have lost Mr Hademak his job. And before I do anything, I must be sure to make amends for it. My intention is to repay the favour he did me. I have constructed something resembling a plan—and I intend to set the wheels in motion later on today. It's well known what a high demand there is for first-class east-coast servants out in Hollywood. The stars have so much money and not a clue what to do with it; liveried servants are all the rage. I intend to mention him today at my luncheon. Before I do anything, I shall tell Miss Marion what a wonderful man he is, and I shall ask her—quite forcefully, if necessary—to help me find him a job among her associates. She is bound to know someone, if I can persuade her to concentrate on the thing. And I shall. It's the absolute very least I can do. And if she can't help, I shall send a wire home to Mr Silverman and ask him, and if he can't help, I shall keep asking everyone I meet until I find someone who can. In the mean time, I have at least three hours to kill until luncheon. I could go to the cemetery again, find the warden, set the wheels in motion for that gravestone. Except I don't want to go out; not now I hear Rudy is conscious again. Because what if he telephoned?

HOLLYWOOD

I don't know what more I can say about Campbell. He was a good, kind man. A fine man—and I was ashamed of my cruelty as soon as I came to my senses. It was never intended—but that's hardly an excuse. After I shouted those terrible words he took a hold of my arm and half dragged me from the theatre. I didn't want to leave. He dragged me out, in a way that made it seem as if I were walking—I don't much remember, except the pressure of his large hand just above my elbow, which was painful; painful enough to keep me walking with him, not quite painful enough to make me cry out.

It doesn't matter. The expression on his face as we stood before each other just outside the theatre revealed to me that his pain was far greater. It was the pain in his face that brought me to my senses at last. I looked back at him until I was too ashamed to look any longer, and my gaze slid to the ground. I apologised. What else? What else could I do? What was done was done. The wound I had inflicted without thinking—it was done.

'I am so sorry,' I said again.

He said, 'So am I.'

I took off the ring.

He said, 'Oh, for God's sakes, Lola, never mind the ring.'

But it was burning my finger. So I slipped it into his jacket pocket, and he left it there. We stood for a little longer, with the traffic on Broadway roaring by, just behind, and I could feel his bewildered, unhappy eyes on me, but I couldn't bring myself to look up. Finally, he said, 'I'll drive you home.' And that was what he did.

We drove in silence.

'I am so sorry,' I said. But this time it was he who wouldn't look at me. Kept the engine running, kept his eyes on the road. I climbed out of the car. 'Forgive me,' I said. 'I thought I could forget him . . . But I love you, you know . . . I would have been a good wife to you . . .'

He nodded. I closed the car door. He drove away, and though I have read about him occasionally in the *Los Angeles Times*—he is one of Hollywood's foremost citizens today, owns great tracts of real estate around the city and is, in fact, one of our most generous philanthropists, and a husband, too, and a father of three—I have never laid eyes on him since that night. And I am very sorry for all of it. It's just too bad.

*   *   *

Mr Leibowitz, when he heard about Campbell and me, decided it would embarrassing for Campbell to have to encounter me at the Whitley Heights reception, should he happen to come by to discuss business. Apart from which, he said, he wanted to give the job to his daughter. So, shortly after Campbell and I broke our engagement, he sent me packing.

Fortunately (this time around) I had saved a little money, and Mr Leibowitz was very generous. He paid a month's salary in advance, which he needn't have done. It reduced the urgency to find work.

Meanwhile, of course, Rudy returned to my thoughts with a vengeance. When I ought to have been searching for a job, I was sitting in theatres around town watching *The Four Horsemen*—again, and then again. I was scouring the movie magazines and the trade papers for any new snippets of information about him. And they weren't hard to find. Actually they were hard to avoid. Suddenly his name was everywhere. Within a month of *The Four Horsemen* coming out (breaking records along the way: it was one of the first films in history to make more than a million dollars at the box office), he had another movie released, and then another, and each one launched with more of a fanfare than the last. And then, as if he weren't already adored enough by his female public, there came *The Sheik*. A phenomenal worldwide hit, it was the movie that elevated him to the status of a god, the man most hotly desired by women on the entire planet. Which is quite something, I think.

I watched the films religiously, obsessively. And I fell in love with him all over again—just as half America did.

Except I was different. Sometimes it was hard to remember why, or how, as I watched him in his sheik's clothing, galloping across the desert on that fine-looking stallion, or taking Agnes Ayres into his arms and locking her in a passionate embrace . . . I admit that I sighed as any fan would sigh, and I would forget . . . Sometimes it all seemed like such a long time ago. I wondered if I wasn't mad, if I hadn't perhaps imagined the whole thing.

I learned that he had been married—once already—and separated. It was painful enough—though actually the marriage had lasted less than a week. More painful: I learned he was living with another woman—a costume designer of mythical beauty, named Natacha Rambova.

Even so, I couldn't give up. Even so, there lived that small voice inside me, clear as a bell, and it would not be dimmed. *He still loved me.* Hadn't I been on the point of marrying another man myself? Hadn't I lived with Perry and dreamed of Rudy all the while? Perhaps, I thought, *perhaps* . . . If only he knew I was out here, waiting . . .

It was around then that I first started work on *Idol Dreams*. It has been my fantasy venture ever since, the one in which I write the story of my life as I would wish it to play out, with the Idol (of my Dreams) casting off his sheik's clothing, and whisking me away to . . . The wretched thing has gone through so many versions, just as my own ideas of a perfect ending shift and change . . . but in every one of its incarnations, of all the scenarios I have written, it is the one I care about most.

*   *   *

It was Lorna, one boozy night, not so long after I had broken up with Campbell, who suggested that if I really wanted to make contact with Rudy I should stop moping about the house and get myself an entry into the film world.

'Or if you don't want to do that,' she said, 'why in hell don't you simply send him a letter? I read someplace he gets nearly two thousand fan letters every week. And he replies to every one of them.

278

So I don't see what's preventing you from approaching him that way. In fact, Lola Nightingale, I don't really see why you haven't already thought of it. Unless it's because you only want to love him in a hopeless kind of a way.'

I laughed.

'Which is unlikely, knowing you. But I've come to the conclusion it's what a lot of girls prefer. All the girls back home, still holding candles for boys killed in the war. Sometimes spending a lifetime mourning for a dead man—or a man who is completely out of reach (not saying that he is) . . . It gives a girl an excuse to keep to herself. Is that what you're doing, Lola?'

I sighed. 'I can hardly be bothered to answer you, Lorna.'

'So? Why haven't you written to him?'

'But, you know, he *doesn't* reply to every one of the letters people send him,' I replied. 'It's simply a myth. It's just what they say in the magazines to keep us all writing. He doesn't even look at half the letters! They arrive at the studio, they're delivered to his dressing room along with a whole pile of picture portraits of himself, which he's supposed to sign, and they do it together, him and—*Natacha*. And sometimes it's just *Natacha* signing those pictures herself, because the signatures come back quite different.'

'They come back different? What can you mean?'

'And, by the way, it's *Natacha Rambova* who stuffs the pictures into envelopes and sends them off . . . I know it. I simply know it. So imagine if I wrote, and I got no reply, and it broke my heart, and I had no way of knowing it was only because that woman had intercepted the letter I wrote to him . . .'

'So—you haven't written?'

'Oh, Lorna, don't be so dim! Of course I've written!'

She looked at me. 'You have? So—'

'I've written about twenty times!' I left my floor cushion and wove a rather gin-drenched path to the chest beside my bed. Under the letter he sent me at Roslyn, under this and that—the ticket to the roller-coaster at Luna Park, the gold pin he bought and gave to me at The Box—I pulled out the portrait photographs: twenty-three of them, to be exact. They never came with anything else. No message. Nothing.

I took them back into the lounge and dropped them at her feet.

I think she was rather shocked. '*Honey,*' she said at last, taking a pull on her cigarette, giving the pictures a little nudge with one of her stockinged feet. 'I'm beginning to think you may be a little cracked.'

She stopped. Looked at me kindly. 'You know, Lola sweetheart . . . it's just possible . . . I mean to say—did you ever—did it ever occur to you that perhaps—that perhaps he received your letters, and . . . Lola, honey, you must have wondered if perhaps *he didn't want to get in touch.*'

I said, 'No. It has never occurred to me.' Which wasn't the case. 'I know very well, better than I know anything . . . I know that if he knew I was here, he would want to see me.'

It squatted there for a while, in our lovely yellow-painted sitting room: my stubborn assertion. Lorna smiled. She gave a small sigh. 'Well,' she said

280

finally, 'if Muhammad won't come to the mountain . . .'

*   *   *

Actually, there were plenty of reasons for me to approach the studios for work, and not only as a means (I was convinced) to get closer to Rudy. Rudy was reason number one.

My eternally rejected photoplays, which I couldn't seem to stop writing and rewriting, was reason number two.

Reason number three would seem absurd to anyone who's never lived in the place. But living in Hollywood, where the film colony is at the heart of everything, there's a sense that, so long as you remain outside it, all of life's action and passion is in some way passing you by. It's how I felt, certainly, living with Phoebe and Lorna, watching their careers progress.

And in any case, apart from all that, I needed a job. I needed money. Extra girls were paid five dollars a day back then—ten if they were required to do anything involving a close-up. Lorna assured me that with her and Phoebe's help it wouldn't be as harsh a life as it had been before, when I hated it so much. They were far better connected inside the colony now, and they would smooth the path for me. They would make it, if not easy (it was never easy), then endurable at least. I could make a decent living.

'But by the way,' Lorna said, 'I shan't do a thing for you—in fact I shall positively warn the casting boys *off* you, Lola Nightingale—and so will Phoebe if I ask her—unless you do something entirely radical about your Look. You have a lovely face. When we first met—don't you remember?—you had your hair in that fabulous bob and you looked quite wonderful and modern. Absolutely the thing . . .'

I giggled. 'The Thing? Really?'

'But you've given up! You look like a schoolmistress. An English schoolmistress, with all that hair piled up on your head, and your skirts flapping halfway to your ankles.'

The following day the three of us went on a spending spree: to a new beauty parlour on Melrose first, where the twins had their hair recoloured black and white-blonde, as before, and I had my hair bobbed all over again, and dyed with bleach-peroxide, for good measure. This time, as my unloved schoolmistress tendrils slopped to the floor (untouched by a pair of scissors, it so happens, since before that disgusting encounter with the hotel clerk at the Pico), I felt not the slightest inclination to sob. On the contrary. My head felt so light it was as if I were floating.

We bought clothes too. Three new dresses each—short enough to make a preacher's eyes water—and two cloche hats, and gloves, and silk stockings. At the end of it all Lorna and Phoebe declared they were proud to be seen with me—and I couldn't deny it. We made quite a striking trio. Even for Hollywood.

Fortunately—since after that little outing I had no money left—the twins were true to their word. They taught me how to fix my own screen makeup, and agreed to lend me their clothes until I could save enough to get my own. (An extra girl needs all sorts of outfits to keep herself in work: at least one

282

decent evening dress, and tea dresses, and sporting clothes, and mourning clothes . . .) Thanks to their introductions I was immediately integrated into a sort of extra-girl 'elite'. It was still tough but it was far better than before. At least I got a regular supply of work.

The days were long—twenty hours sometimes, with the overtime, and most of them spent sitting silently under the hot lights, waiting to be told what to do. I didn't mind. There was always plenty to look at—the stars coming and going, and the set musicians too, brought on (I couldn't understand it at first, since the camera couldn't hear them) to help the actors with their emotions when they were acting a scene. And then there were the giant sets that looked so real, and so permanently on the point of collapsing. Oh, it was fascinating. Added to which, of course, it was helpful for me to be able to see just how a written scene would eventually be shot.

I generally worked three or four days a week, and though, for such long hours, the pay wasn't brilliant, and though I never did get a chance to meet any script editors, and though I certainly never caught a glimpse of Mr Rudolph Valentino—it was exciting to be able to wander round the lots, and sometimes, once in a while, to spot some of the stars off duty.

I was sitting alone on a bench at Universal once, smoking a lonesome cigarette, and who should shuffle up and sit right beside me but poor, unfortunate Roscoe 'Fatty' Arbuckle. He wasn't so unfortunate back then, of course—probably the highest-paid performer in Hollywood. It could only have been a few months before the terrible tragedy happened—very early in my extra-girl career. In any case, he was awfully shy. He sat beside me, for no reason that I could see. The bench positively creaked under his weight, and he gave a funny sort of grimace about that. Then, after a moment or two, during which we neither of us spoke but looked straight in front of us, he simply stood up, smiled at me, lifted his hat, gave the tiniest little bow with his big ball of a head and waddled away again.

I can see him now. How little he knew what dark cloud loomed ahead! How little anyone knew! It was spring, I remember, because the orange blossom was smelling so sweet . . . By the end of the summer, Virginia Rappe was dead and Fatty Arbuckle was in jail for her rape and murder. (I met her a couple of times it so happens. Perry knew her. Crazy, she was, poor little thing. Everybody knew it. Had this thing about stripping. Every party she went to: first she'd strip, then she'd burst into tears. It was horrible. Nobody cared two pins about her, least of all herself. And *that*, by the way, is the real story. Virginia died, so I heard, not because of anything Fatty Arbuckle did to her but because the last abortion turned bad in her belly and the blood wouldn't stop.)

*   *   *

I was at home on Citrus Drive one evening about seven o'clock, having spent an unsatisfactory day in front of yet another scenario, doomed (it's how I felt that afternoon) to oblivion. I heard Phoebe and Lorna in the hall, back from a day on set, chattering and laughing in such a peppy manner that I guessed there had to be a gentleman in tow.

Phoebe called out to me to confirm it. 'Hey, Lola,' she shouted, 'lay down the pen, girl. We've got a surprise for you . . . Two surprises! Number one: you've got some real bona-fide fan mail, extra girl! Courtesy of kind Mr Hester over at Metro . . .'

'Fan mail?' I giggled. It seemed unlikely. I laid down the pen and hurried out to greet them. Having spent the day alone I was looking forward to the company.

'Surprise number two,' Phoebe shouted. 'Take a guess who we just found, sneaking around the Metro lot . . .'

Perry burst into the room ahead of either of them, and we slammed right into one another. *Bang*. With plenty of force. He smelled the same: not so fresh, but it was familiar—an unexpected, disconcerting reminder of the pleasure we had given to each other once; pleasure that, for me at least, had never quite been matched since. I stared at him. Quite forgot about the fan mail.

'*JENNIFER!*' he cried, with that irrepressible smile, those deep laughter lines. 'What a delight, what a wonder, what a *glorious thing* to see you again!' He spoke as if I had nothing to forgive him for! As if I could feel nothing but unreserved pleasure at being reunited with him again. And the truth is, I *was* pleased to see him. He had been a lousy friend to me but, nevertheless, he had been a friend of sorts. I led a rootless life—people came and people went. Sometimes, I felt, I had left so little impression on the world or on anyone in it that my very existence on the planet was open to question.

A lousy friend he may have been, but there was

285

something wonderful about feeling, at least, that we had a history.

Before I had time to say anything he had wrapped me in his arms, lifted me up and spun me round the sitting room. He planted a big, stubbly kiss on each cheek and then a third on my lips. 'What a sight for sore eyes! And look . . . My goodness, *look!*' He set me down, stood back. 'How entirely, utterly, mesmerisingly beautiful you have become!'

I tried not to be too pleased, but Perry can be very charming. I suppose I blushed. I always do.

'I told you she'd be pleased to see me!' he said.

'Well, I'm sure she is *now.*' Phoebe laughed. 'Who in hell wouldn't be, after a greeting like that?' She and Lorna had followed him in. Already, where my work had been, they had set out the cocktail jug, the wretched scenario brushed casually aside. 'But she'll have remembered what a downright scoundrel you were to her before the evening's through. And you'll be out on your ear in no time.'

'Oh . . .' he smiled at me '. . . I sincerely hope not.'

'You look thin, Perry,' I said at last. He did look thin. On the other hand he had clearly taken more care than he used to with his apparel. He looked even more the dissipated lounge lizard than I remembered. His dark hair had grown longer. It was slicked back and oiled, with one thick lock escaped and falling over one eye. He was dressed in white: a white linen jacket, white waistcoat, white shirt, tan-and-white spats, and a pale blue necktie. He looked as handsome as ever. And unmistakably seedy. 'Where on earth have you

286

been?' I asked him. 'Last I remember, you were popping out to get cigarettes.'

'Was I?'

'That was over two years ago, Perry.'

'Ah! Cigarette store was closed.'

I looked at him. 'Not so funny,' I said.

'Oh, I thought it was a *little* funny.' He shrugged. 'Hell, maybe not. In any case, I've bought us a large bottle of Scotch. Genuine article. Real McCoy. Cost me forty dollars, if you please, so it certainly better be. I think we should drink it as fast as we can and then head out to the Boulevard. What do you say? I have my auto parked right outside the door.'

'You still have your car?'

'An even better one! The girls will testify to it!'

'But you still haven't said. Where have you been?'

'Honey, he's been in the clink,' said Lorna, setting down glasses in a businesslike manner. 'Where in the hell do you think he's been?'

'Lorna!' cried Perry. 'You're such a spoilsport.'

'In the clink for what?' I asked. It occurred to me at that moment that it could have been for pretty much anything.

'In all honesty, I no longer remember. In any case I was framed. Whatever it was they got me on, I didn't do it. And the point is, I'm not in the clink now.'

'So I see.'

'Jennifer sweetheart, the girls tell me you've changed your name. Excellent. Excellent idea. Only they told me, but I can't for the hell of me recall what I'm supposed to call you these days.'

'Lola,' I said.

'Lola!'

'Nightingale. Lola Nightingale.'

'Perfect! English . . . and refined. And yet still somehow . . .' he left a long pause, as if giving the matter his most forceful consideration '. . . *snazzy*.'

It made me laugh, and I suppose that took the edge off things. It was obvious he didn't much want to talk about the past—whenever had he? He claimed only to have been released from jail a fortnight previously, and there was no particular reason to disbelieve him. He said he was sleeping on the couch at Teddy's place, until he made 'preferable arrangements'. (I should have thrown him out right there.)

He was flush—curiously so, perhaps, for a man two weeks fresh from jail. He took the three of us to dinner and then afterwards he drove us out to the Sunset Inn for more drinks and dancing. There, needless to say, we met up with numerous of Perry's old chums—most of whom I'd not laid eyes on since he'd gone away. They greeted me as if they'd been searching for me all this time, as if nothing on earth made them more joyous than our reunion. I suppose I played along. Perry had a way of insisting on it: of everyone around him being deliriously happy all the time. Something about him meant we tended to fall into line.

*   *   *

He made it pretty obvious from the beginning that, out of all of us, he had eyes only for me. So we danced. There's only one man who can dance better than Perry and he—Well. He was somewhere beyond my reach and maybe, that

288

night, reunited with my scoundrel fresh-from-the-clink lover, I was at last becoming reconciled to the fact. Rudy was a great star, perhaps the biggest in America, and I was an extra girl. I had known him when he was a dance teacher, and I was a child's nurse, and we were both nobodies; lonely and unhappy. Now things were different. Rather, I was still a nobody, and I was still a little lonely. But dancing with Perry that night, with the jazz band playing and the familiar smell of his body stirring more dangerous memories as the evening wore on, I was by no means unhappy . . . I admit that Rudy seemed a long distance away. Perry was—is—many terrible things. He is a terrible man. But his ability to turn every situation into a perfect celebration—a shindig to top all shindigs—is utterly infectious. I just wonder how he'd managed it in jail.

About two a.m. the twins were exhausted. They had been working since dawn, unlike me (I had lain in bed until almost ten), and they wanted to go home. Perry let his eyes slide from me to the twins and back to me . . .

'Very well,' he said. 'I'll drive you girls home. But only if I can sleep on the couch . . .'

'On the couch?' Lorna and Phoebe looked at one another and smirked. 'Perry, old boy,' Lorna said, 'something happen to you in the clink? You must be losing your touch.'

They both giggled drunkenly.

Perry turned from them. Pointedly, he put an arm round my shoulders. 'Worry not *un petit peu*,' he murmured into my hair. 'Your friends have filthy minds, but so do I. My intentions, I assure you, are entirely one hundred per cent disgraceful.'

'Well, they had better not be,' I said feebly.

'Because, if so, you shall only be horribly disappointed.'

'Of course . . .' he said.

* * *

The twins went directly to bed. Perry made a half-hearted attempt to persuade them to stay up for more merrymaking but he knew—we all knew—they wouldn't. I should have followed them.

Lorna turned to me as she was leaving the room. 'Now don't be a bunny, sweetheart, will you?' she said. 'Remember, you have a casting tomorrow. We'll be leaving six o'clock sharp.'

'I know,' I said.

She was at the door to the room she and Phoebe were sharing (as luck would have it—or not—it happened to be my month for having the second bedroom on my own). She turned back, quite sombre suddenly. 'Remember, Jenny, remember how he left you the last time . . .'

'Oh, I do,' I said.

'The guy's a stinkpot. Nothing better than a charming stinkpot . . . Maybe we shouldn't have brought him back. Only remember—for your own sake, honey, he sleeps on the couch!'

'Oh! Do, please, keep to your own affairs,' Perry snapped.

I should have heeded it, that little glimpse of ill-temper. Unfortunately, by then, my rational mind was not quite in control of matters.

What can I say? It had been a long time.

He sat himself down on the couch, patted the space beside him—as if it were his house, his couch and for him to invite me to sit down on it. In any

290

case, I did. He put an arm around the back of the seat and with his free hand produced, first, a hip flask and then a small, folded paper package, the size of my thumbnail.

'Care for some?' he said. I knew what it was. I had seen it but never taken it.

I said no.

He laughed. Tipped some of the white powder onto the shiny dark surface of my lampstand. 'Don't be a silly girl,' he said. 'Have you ever tried it?'

'I don't want to.'

'Oh, *Lola* . . .'

*   *   *

Well, he knew me too well, perhaps, thrill seeker that I am. My father's daughter and all that. I thought fleetingly of those God-fearing matrons who were meant to have been standing at the train station, waiting to save wretches such as myself from wretches such as him. And smiled. I was beyond saving in any case.

We were on the couch, and he was talking, or I was talking, or we were talking both at once, informing each other—and ourselves—and all the air around us of quite how desperately we had missed one another in the passing months and years, and before long his lips were tracing an irresistible path from my neck to my earlobe, to my neck and to my mouth . . . His caressing fingers reached the buttons of my dress. I looked down at his hand, working so expertly at getting each one undone— and suddenly, in a cold flash, I was reminded of

291

when last we had done this, and of the mess he'd left me in, and of the room clerk in the meat larder, with my head banging up against that joint of ham, and my desire for him vanished. I pushed him away.

'Don't. Perry. Don't. I'm not interested.'

He leaned back. Momentarily. Not in the least discomfited. Casually, he reached for his little package and tipped out another small heap of powder. I watched him doing it.

'I don't want it, Perry. I need to go to bed. I have work tomorrow. They won't use me if I don't look fresh . . .'

He said nothing for a moment, continued with his ministrations, his back turned a little towards from me.

'I met your movie-star friend last week . . . Childhood friend. Did I mention it?'

'What friend?'

'He's done well.'

'Who?'

Perry looked at me, his handsome, wired face watchful. 'You didn't tell me he'd changed his name.'

'I don't know who—'

He smiled—half smiled. It was something between a smile and something much more menacing. 'Don't be silly,' he said gently. 'Of course you do . . . You should have told me he'd changed his name. I might have been able to help you.'

'What? How? But, Perry, I didn't know!' I burst out. 'How could I tell you when I didn't know? And what do you mean you saw him? When? Where? Did you mention me? Did you tell him I was here?'

He laughed—not his usual, warm laugh. 'But, Lola, I didn't know if you were still in Hollywood. I didn't know where you were! How could I tell him when I didn't know?'

'But you know now!'

He bent over the lampstand and, with a silver straw produced from his watch-pocket, he snorted up one line of the white powder. He glanced at me. 'You sure you don't want any more?'

My heart was beating so fast I could hardly breathe. But—He smiled, another not-so-nice smile, passed the straw to me for a second time.

'Actually, the funny thing is,' he said, 'I've known him for an age. Not terribly well, I admit. But well enough. It's more of a business relationship now, of course.'

'You knew him—when we were living together?'

'Well, Lola dearest, you'll no doubt be relieved to hear I didn't meet him in jail.'

'Perry, how is he? How did you—how was he? Is he well? Did he strike you as . . . in good health? May I see him too? When will you meet him next? May I come with you?' The cocaine, in combination with the shock, was making my head rush, making the back of my throat throb so hard I felt that if I stopped speaking I might empty the contents of my empty stomach onto our laps. 'Is he well?' I asked again. 'Did he seem happy to you? Did he mention my name?'

'Which name, my sweetest?'

'Which . . . ?'

'I'm teasing. Of course he didn't mention your name! Not one of your names or the other. Why would he? Poppet, it breaks my heart to think you

still hold a candle for the man. You must know—
everyone knows—one can hardly open a
newspaper without reading how deliriously happy
he is, ensconced in a sweet little bungalow off
Sunset, about to move into a magnificent house in
Whitley Heights, and as good as married, sweetest,
to one of the most poisonous women I have ever
had the misfortune to meet. They have a lion cub,
and three dogs, and Christ knows what else.
Everything bar the children . . . Lola, I shall surely
mention you to him next time I see him. If it's what
you would like. But don't you think . . .' He leaned
towards me again, at just the moment when I felt
certain I should disintegrate into tears. He brushed
a fingertip across my cheek, let it rest on my—
trembling—lower lip, and looked at me with
something I suppose I mistook for tenderness.
Because I am a fool.

I felt the tears spilling over my lashes, and he
watched them fall, with what I mistook for
tenderness, and as they splashed onto his finger, he
lifted my chin and kissed me. In my confusion I
imagined he was Rudy. I think. I believe I did. And
I sobbed like a child into his shoulder. And he
spent the night in my bed.

*　　　*　　　*

The twins were pretty sore when they discovered
he had stayed—not only that, but that I had
decided (*he* had decided) I wouldn't be going with
them to the casting that morning.

'Well, you're a fool,' Phoebe said, her head
round the bedroom door just as she and Lorna
were leaving. It was five thirty a.m., and Perry and

I had barely fallen asleep. 'And don't come begging to us when you have no money for the rent.'

'Phoebe dearest,' Perry drawled, with his arm around me, his head on my pillow, my head on his chest, 'I shall pay Lola's rent from now on. She has nothing to worry about.'

'You'll pay her rent for how long? Until you're back in the clink?' She turned to me. 'Lola, you needn't come begging to us when all the casting directors have forgotten you existed . . . People,' she added meaningfully, 'have short memories in this town.'

I remember sitting up—trying to sit up—trying to apologise and explain, maybe even to ask for her help, but Perry must have felt me tense. When I tried to raise myself, I felt his hold on me tighten: gently, but unmistakably, he held me back. I could have moved, I suppose, with a struggle. But somehow a struggle didn't seem—it would have seemed all wrong. How do I explain it? All I know is, the pressure of his arm around me, and my own befuddled head, prevented me doing what I had previously at least halfway intended.

'Phoebe,' he snapped, 'what's happened to you since I've been away? You and your sister have transformed into a couple of blue noses of the highest order! What's the matter with you? Are you not getting any action of your own that you feel such a need—'

She didn't stick around to listen to the rest. She slammed the door, and I didn't blame her.

'That was uncalled for,' I said. 'Actually, she has a very nice boyfriend. He's a—'

Perry said, 'I'm happy for her . . . Now then, my sweetest . . . where were we?'

Dear God. Writing it down doesn't give me too much of a thrill. Until now I had always told myself it was the connection with Rudy that persuaded me to put up with Perry all that time, but writing it down now, as I remember it, I don't know how well I can continue to believe that. Would I have slept with him that night if he hadn't dangled that carrot before me, just at the perfect moment?

Well. Maybe I wouldn't. And maybe I would. Maybe, after all, it's not just my love for Rudy that has led me astray so often. Maybe—ha! and *this* is for my eyes only—it's just that I have an affection, a weakness for S-E-X. More like a man's appetite than a woman's. Or something. Oh, who cares, in any case? One way or another the pair of them—S-E-X and R-U-D-Y—have succeeded in making me more wretched than just about anything else, and I am still utterly addicted to both.

*   *   *

So Perry and I spent that day in bed. Except, I think, when he encouraged me to go to the kitchen briefly to fix us something to eat. That was when I found the envelope sitting on the table. The fan mail! I had quite forgotten about it. It was addressed to 'Jennifer Doyle, Extra Girl (Crying, in Feather Hat) *Treasures Unsurpassed* c/o Metro Studios. PLEASE FORWARD'.

Given everything, that I was only an extra and I had changed my name, it was nothing short of a miracle that it ever reached me, and only thanks to

Lorna's friendship with Mr Hester, who manages all the background actors.

The letter was from Madeleine:

Hello Stranger!

(That's how it began.)

Hello Stranger!
Remember me? Your fair-weather friend from Long Island . . . whom you helped in her darkest hour, and who has never yet had a chance to repay you? I often think about you, Jenny, and those awful, crazy, terrible days at The Box. There's probably not a week that's passed that I haven't wondered what became of you. Especially now, with our old friend Mr Guglielmi quite the most famous—

'Lola?'

Even then, I suppose, I was a little afraid of him. The sound of his voice made me jump. I put the letter away—tucked it behind the pot where we kept our coffee grounds—returned to our bed carrying the sandwiches my lover had ordered, and didn't think about it again.

Later I told him I needed to get out of bed to check the mail. Just in case there was a letter . . .

'From Frances Marion?' he cried, when I explained to him. 'Good Lord! And how long have you been waiting?'

A long time.

'Ah, well! Never mind. But what a fabulous story! In the Piggly Wiggly? You accosted her in the Piggly Wiggly? Darling, what a brave girl you are! I must say I've never encountered her. I don't suppose she frequents the same sort of parties as your old chum Mr Valentino and the rest of them. She's probably far too serious. Not like Mr Valentino. He and—mostly his friends, actually. He likes to dabble, but some of them, they can hardly get enough . . .'

Perry was a dope-dealer, of course. He didn't tell me in so many words, but neither, when I asked him—when I finally put the pieces together—did he bother to deny it. I don't know the details, what he dealt and what he didn't deal—he didn't tell me, and I didn't ask—but I suppose he cut the right sort of debonair figure to be able to slip in and out of the high circles without ever being too obvious.

What can I say? Nothing I'm proud of, that's for certain.

Somehow, from there, everything drifted. Perry stayed in my bed. At different times both Phoebe and Lorna—and then both of them together—took me aside. Tried to talk sense into me. Trouble was, they told me what I knew already—that everything was drifting. I was staying up through the night with Perry, snorting cocaine and drinking. It was just like the old days, only worse, I think. Gradually, I stopped working on the photoplays. I stopped making it out to the movie theatres. I stopped going to castings. And Perry took over my life—just about exactly where he'd left off, only this time he had cash, plenty of it. And he paid for everything.

Relations between Perry and the twins worsened until it came to the point where they ignored him entirely, except to ask him when he would find a place of his own. But there was no budging him . . . I think we were all a little frightened of him.

Finally, a month or so in, the twins gave me an ultimatum. Either I got Perry out or I would have to leave myself. We quarrelled horribly.

I suppose the problem, when deep down you know yourself to be absolutely in the wrong but don't want to acknowledge it, and when you're drinking and consorting with a dope fiend and—frankly—not so far off being a dope fiend yourself, and when you're full of self-disappointment, and guilt at being such a rotten friend to the two girls who were, and still are, your closest, kindest friends in the world . . . the problem with all that is it can make you into an utterly vile and unreasonable person.

So when they tried to tell me what a mess I was making of everything, when they told me I had to get rid of Perry, not only for their good but for my own, I wouldn't listen. Instead, I pointed out how well Perry paid his way—more than paid his way—not just my share of the rent but most of theirs, too. Which was certainly true—because Perry (I've said it before) in spite of his sins, was always very generous. He kept us all in liquor—and not just moonshine, but real liquor, imported from Europe, in bottles, with original labels stuck on. He kept us in cocaine, too—though I suppose the twins were never quite so fond of it as we two were. And—until the resentment made it impossible—he used to take the three of us out to dinner to some of the swankiest places in town, sometimes two or three times a week. I pointed it all out to them, and a lot more: said a lot of things I didn't mean, horrible things that Perry had said about them—until Lorna stopped me, her big blue eyes looking at me in a state of shock, and she said, 'Lola—*what has become of you*?'

And she burst into tears.

*   *   *

I am fortunate they still speak to me. They didn't for a while.

After the ultimatum, something happened, and I don't know what—Lorna and Phoebe will never tell me. But I can only imagine Perry terrified them in some way or another. And God knows how, because the twins are as tough as any girls I know. But I suppose he had something on them. The next thing—it must have been within a week or even sooner—the twins moved out of the apartment without a word.

Perry had insisted, that same morning, that we take a picnic on the beach. I should have known something was up. It wasn't much in character for him to suggest leaving the house at all during daylight hours. But I didn't ask. I didn't think. And when we came home they were gone. Their clothes, their stuff—everything: the cushions we had bought together and the fancy glasses I had bought them last Christmas, all gone. Without them, our beloved home felt dead.

Perry acted as if he was surprised, but I knew he wasn't. He said he had no idea where they might have gone. And when I wept because I felt terrible—terrible for my friends and maybe even a little frightened for myself—Perry's hands wandered down my dress, and he kissed me, and it occurs to me now that he loved it when I cried.

300

His clever hands wandered over my breasts, my hips, under my dress, and he whispered to me that the night before last, when he had been out and about, delivering his bounty to the deserving, he had mentioned my name to a certain gentleman . . .

I am pathetic. I detest myself. I can hardly stand to remember it. I hate to remember what a fool, what a weak and stupid person I have been. My confusion, my lust, my fear—and then the glimmer of a promise he gave to me—the reawakening of that wretched, hopeless dream . . .

And still no letter came from Miss Marion. Almost a year since I saw her in that store and nothing. Not a word from her. I was lost, off-course, and I knew it. In Perry's arms, his bed, his house, I had rarely felt so alone.

Thursday, 19 August 1926

Noon
Well. Time to prepare, I suppose. That is to say, I am prepared already—of course. I have been prepared for hours! But it is time to accept the dreaded moment has arrived when I must take leave of this room, this stinkpot of a safe haven, and head out into the noisy world again. I have butterflies in my stomach, but no gin.

I have survived Marion Davies in *Beverly of Graustark*, which was truly the most abysmal film. But at least I can say I have seen it.

I have my final version of *Idol Dreams*, all typed up with Rudy's typewriter, and ready for delivery.

I have my new frock, freshly ironed, and I have clean hair . . . and for once it is not unbearably hot. All I must do now is to rouge my sober, sensible face. And put some lipstick on.

Thursday, 19 August 1926

5 p.m.
I needn't have bothered. Not with that silly movie. Nobody mentioned it throughout the whole of luncheon. I wonder what Frances Marion had in mind when she suggested I look at the wretched thing in the first place, when nobody went to the trouble of mentioning it all through lunch. Oh, who cares? Who the hell cares?

In five hours it has all been turned on its head again, and Rudy's temperature is rising, and I have been by the hospital on my way back from the luncheon and—like vultures—the crowds are back. I tried again to walk through those doors, but I barely got within twenty yards before those two reporters from yesterday started yelling about it.

Hey-ho, people, we got the crazy girl back again . . . This broad just can't take no for an answer!

I didn't care. That is, I wouldn't have cared— except that the swarthy security man from yesterday, Steffen, the one who looks like a rat, and who called my good, kind friend 'ghoul', he spotted me, and came at me, with a glint in his eye, as if he believed one knockout punch would

303

cure all the ills of his entire disappointing life. He had his fist clenched, I swear to it, and his arm drawn back, and I could see it coming and I still couldn't quite believe—

Would he really? Lay that big fat fist on me, right here on West 50th, in front of everyone, in broad daylight?

It occurred to me very clearly that indeed he would. And most likely be cheered for it, too, such was the mood down there.

It is febrile, angry—everyone is tired—and there are the rumours flying around like bats, swooping on the crowd, swooping on all of us . . . awful, terrible rumours . . . But first— No, I shall come back to that because, for all the triumphs of my day today, it is at the hospital, of course, where everything begins and ends since nothing is worth anything without Rudy. And if the rumours are true then, of course, I am responsible. I am responsible for everything . . .

I saw that man's fist making its way towards me, and I ran. He yelled at me, a roar of pure rage. I had moved too quickly for him. I kept moving—ran most of the way back to the hotel, and I am dripping with sweat. I am sodden. And there is nothing I can do but wait—and wait and wait and wait.

But first—

I wish I knew where to start. So much has happened.

First, then. The good news.

I believe I have found employment for Mr Hademak. He is to be interviewed by my luncheon date. I have sent him a message. I sent the boy round with a letter, telling him to contact me here at the hotel, right away. I might have telephoned him directly, I suppose. Only I couldn't quite bring myself to call the boarding-house and hear that familiar *wheeze clink wheeze* of the concierge. Never again.

Mr Hademak is to be interviewed by my friend. Is that what she is? My new friend? Good God! This is barely above gibberish—I need to calm down or I shall achieve nothing.

*   *   *

First.

I arrived at my luncheon date very early—too early even to announce myself. But instead of taking a walk around the block, as I certainly should have done, I decided to wait in the Algonquin lobby, thereby encouraging my nervous energy to gather such a head of steam that I began to feel quite faint. So, after a while, I settled myself in a small leather chair in a far corner of the room. It was tucked a little behind the front door, and I surreptitiously tucked it a little further. I sat, watching the great and the good sweep this way and that as if—as if *life were easy.*

I watched the beautiful Nita Naldi gliding in—hatless, if you please! She was coming from the hospital, perhaps, since she and Rudy have long since been friends. It was all I could do not to call out to her and beg for her assistance in speaking to him—I didn't. I did not. Aside from anything, I am not even certain if the two were once lovers. In which case I sincerely did not want to complicate matters. Though I understand she is currently linked with the wonderful H. L. Mencken. The three of them, she, Mr Mencken and Rudy, had dinner together here, in her suite, only a few weeks back. Ha! See the top-notch circles I am almost moving in now!

But that's not the point.

I watched her as if, I suppose, she were a specimen from some other planet: that magical place in the galaxy where everyone already knows you to be friends with Rudolph Valentino and therefore allows you some private access to his life, his well being, his affections . . . I must try to order my thoughts. Otherwise, what point to write them all down? I might just as easily glide to the nearest speak and drink myself to oblivion. It would be better. It might be better. Except—what if he calls? What then? Somehow I have to make it through this interminable wait with my mind in place . . .

Well, I sat in the lobby of that hotel, and I listened to the brittle sounds of clever people in the room beyond, laughing lightly at one another's wit—and the longer I sat, the more nervous I became, until the time passed when Miss Marion and I were meant to meet, and still I sat. I noticed little damp patches on the paper where I was holding my finished photoplay, and I wished more than I ever wished anything, almost, that I'd at least had the foresight to bring my hip flask.

It reached a point, and looking back, I don't understand, can't imagine quite how, but hearing the laughter, witnessing so much personal confidence sweeping this way and that, and then, remembering the state I had been in when last I saw Miss Marion, I discovered that I simply couldn't pull myself out of that chair. I wondered if I would sit there for ever, with the sweat from my hands slowly obscuring every careful word of my *Idol Dreams*, and I would simply sit and watch as this one golden opportunity slipped slowly from my fingertips . . .

I might have done it too. I was bent over my hands, eyes shut tight and only a second from sobbing, when I heard her voice beside me: 'Lola? Are you sick?'

A long pause. I didn't know what to do. I did nothing. Said nothing. Didn't even move.

'You know,' she said gently, 'we have a table in the dining room, and we've been waiting for you. Wouldn't you like to join us?'

I forced myself to look up. And I swear, if ever I could have loved a woman, I would have fallen for Miss Frances Marion at that moment; she was looking down at me with so much kindness and intelligence and humour and beauty (for she is very beautiful, even though she is quite old now—at least ten years older than I am, not so far off forty, I should think). She smiled.

She said, 'My two friends are longing to meet you. They have read *Malicious Intent*, you know. I hope you won't mind that I gave it to them. And they are as excited as I am. Even more so, perhaps. Anita is feeling positively jittery. She hates it when there is competition.'

'Anita?'

'Loos. You met her the other day.'

'Oh, gosh. Oh . . . gosh. Oh, gosh.'

'You absolutely mustn't be intimidated. I love her dearly, and she's a fine writer. But she is a very silly woman. She wants to meet you because she sees that you are brilliant and—as she says herself—it has always been her philosophy to keep brilliant people close . . .'

'Brilliant!' I laughed—spluttered, actually. I sent a spray of spittle into the air, some of which, I noticed in horror, caught the light as it flew and landed on Miss Marion's hand. She stepped back a smidgen, and—very subtly—wiped the back of her hand upon her coat.

'You have written a terrific scenario.'

'No—but I have another one here . . . I'm convinced you'll think the last one is perfectly rotten as soon as you see this one. I wish you would look at this one instead.'

I am an idiot.

She laughed. 'Of course I should love to see it. But don't dismiss the last too quickly. You have a fan club for it, and, Lola, they're waiting for you at the table. Anita is complaining she's famished.'

I stood up, very slowly—worried that I might faint.

'There is nothing for you to be intimidated by,' she said again. 'In fact I should think Anita might do better to feel a little intimidated by you . . .' I laughed at that—without the spray of spittle, this time. I was beginning to collect myself. And Miss Marion smiled again. 'Well, that's better,' she said, standing back. 'You look stunning, by the way. What a wonderful dress. Come on, then . . . Are you coming or aren't you?'

'But first, if you wouldn't mind, Miss Marion—I wanted to apologise. It was dreadful, unforgivable, the way I accosted you on Tuesday. And after all you have done to help me. I am so terribly sorry.'

'Oh, never mind that!' She swept it aside. 'As Anita always says, because she thinks it gives her absolute licence to behave in any way she likes, "We creative folk sometimes act a little crazy . . ." And, Lola, I couldn't care in the least. What matters to me . . .' she paused, looked back at me in deep seriousness for an instant, then broke into a giant grin '. . . is that I was right! I *love* to be right! And I knew you were good, from that very first screenplay you gave to me—when you accosted me the *first* time. At the grocery store . . . Do you remember?'

'Do I remember? Oh, gosh—you probably think it's some dreadful habit, all this accosting, but I assure you—'

She interrupted with a delicate, dismissive wave, exchanging nods, as she did so, with a familiar-looking woman who was just then strutting across the lobby. 'I knew you were good from the first reading of that very first scenario. And you have turned out even better than I imagined! *Malicious Intent* is truly the freshest piece of writing for screen I've laid eyes on in five years or more. And I'm longing to hear what Rudy plans for *Wicked Pleasures*. Did he say? Or did that ghastly little Ullman put his great boot in the way of things? He generally likes to.'

'He—'

'Tell us all over luncheon. Would you? I want to hear everything. Only we should get a move on. I want you to meet Anita—properly, this time. And I want you to meet my dearest, closest friend, Mary. Are you ready? I hope so. Because I believe, if I have my way, this luncheon is about

309

to change your life.'

Was I dreaming?

'And that, by the way,' she indicated the retreating figure, still strutting, 'in case you were wondering . . .'

'Well, yes I was . . .'

'Yes. It showed. That was the wonderful Miss Dorothy Parker.'

*   *   *

So it was the four of us. Anita, Frances, Mary *et moi*. I mean to say, of course: Miss Anita Loos, Miss Frances Marion, Miss Mary Pickford *et* Miss Lola Nightingale. Just the four of us. Miss Loos kept her silly hat on. Looked at me from beneath it with the same languid dislike as previously, but I wonder if it's only a way she has, since I declare she looked similarly towards Miss Mary Pickford, and there is *nothing* about Miss Mary Pickford to make a person feel languid, even aside from her being the most adored woman on the planet.

She is (and I am trying my hardest to be moderate) not in the least as she appears on the screen. She is womanly, first and foremost, not some silly, simpering little thing,; she is thoughtful and tactful and gentle and so full of amusing stories!

Anita Loos was seated on the banquette. She and Mary Pickford were deep in conversation as Miss Marion and I approached. Anita Loos looked me up and down with that horrid look of hers—but then, after that, I know it sounds absurd—but the thing is—she saw me, and she shuffled up!

'I found her in the lobby,' Miss Marion said. 'Lola, this is Anita Loos, whom you met only the other day. And this—of course—is Mary Pickford. Who adores your *Intent*, don't you, Mary? She wants to discuss—well, perhaps I should let her tell you . . . And this . . .' she looked at me, standing before them all on one leg, like some dreadful schoolgirl '. . . *this*,' she said, 'is Lola Nightingale!'

'Well, Lola,' drawled Anita (as she shuffled up), 'we have all read *Malicious Intent*, and we all agree that you are quite brilliant. So you might as well sit down.' As I took the space beside her she muttered something about keeping the competition close, and we all laughed—though at the time I was still too befuddled to be certain what she meant by it.

Miss Pickford—*Mary* (it feels too odd to write it!)—leaned across the table and patted my damp, sweaty hand. 'I thought it was quite magical, Lola,' she said. 'May I call you Lola?'

'Yes—and thank you. I mean to say, *thank you*. I'm quite—actually I'm tempted to burst into the most hopeless tears, which is absurd, I know, but to be praised by—and—' I looked stupidly from one woman to the next. They waited politely for me to finish but, really, I had nothing to add. Anything I said would have been pointless in any case since, really, it was quite obvious how a girl in my position would be feeling in these circumstances . . . and after so many years of scribbling away. 'Yes, of course you may,' I said finally. 'Call me Lola. Please.'

'Excellent. And you must call me Mary.'

Mary.

Mary didn't drink. But the rest of us did. A bottle of vintage champagne first, followed, as it happens, by a bottle of Château Haut-Brion. Out of teacups, of course. Anita smuggled the drink inside her briefcase, and—I am happy to say—knocked back the lion's share of it herself, since I was utterly determined not to disgrace myself again.

I thought of my father. After six years of stewing my innards on nothing much but home-stilled gin, good wine, in or out of china teacups, is thoroughly wasted on me. But Papa would have appreciated it. He would have been proud of me, perhaps, too. I think so. Though he might have been the only man on the planet who had never heard of Miss Mary Pickford. Nevertheless, I wished he could have seen me—me and my scenarios, after all these years—drinking Haut-Brion out of teacups in the Algonquin, with three of the most successful women in America.

I believe, between them, my lunching companions earn something close to forty thousand dollars a week ($40,046, if you included my salary, of course). We ate fresh caviar, served up in tiny individual dishes carved of solid ice. And afterwards a salad from the heart of palms, and with it lobster, grilled, with sauce Hollandaise . . .

We talked first of my photoplay, *Malicious Intent*. I was quite uncomfortable, listening to them pour forth so many compliments; but the fact is—*the fact is*—Anita and Frances wanted to discuss elements of the continuity. They both offered suggestions to improve upon it, all of which seemed to be entirely brilliant, so far as I

312

could see.

And Mary Pickford . . . *Mary* . . . Mary Pickford wants to buy it! She wants not only to star in it, but to produce the movie herself.

I said, 'Miss Pickford—'

'Mary.'

'Mary, I swear to it, if you would truly like to star in my picture, I will give it to you! You needn't part with a single cent!'

To which all three women reacted with such irritation I very much regretted having spoken. Frances said she would negotiate a price for me herself—or, if I preferred, she could put me in contact with an agent, who might not do it quite so well, and who would cream off a hefty percentage for the honour . . . I didn't care one way or the other. Well, of course I did, but I mean to say, the money is secondary to my excitement at the thought that my photoplay might actually, finally, be turned into a real film. I can hardly bring myself to imagine it—hardly dare to believe it could be true: that I might visit the set—my set!—and see the actors—my actors!—and all of them in their makeup, and then the crew and the extras—my friends, the extras! And the lights and the music and all the fuss . . . and all as a result of something I wrote at my writing table, hardly believing . . . still not believing . . . My mind spins, only thinking about it.

And then, *on top of that*, there is the money!

I suppose that is what I meant to say.

Frances insists that even at the beginning, with my first produced work, I might be able to command as much as five hundred dollars for rights to the completed photoplay, and that with

313

each successful photoplay I produce thereafter, I can command more—a thousand dollars, two thousand, three thousand . . . Miss Marion can turn out a completed photoplay, with continuity all in place, in as little as a fortnight, and she is paid twenty thousand for each one—but she has been at it for years, and there is no one, man or woman in Hollywood, including Anita, who begins to be quite so successful as she.

The important thing, about the money at least, is that with money of my own Rudy would never have any doubt—not that he ever could, since he knows how long I have loved him. But it will help him to know it, I suppose. And the wonderful thing about writing is that I shall still be able to stay at home and have any number of babies—*hundreds* of babies! Rudy and I can— I'm getting ahead. In any case I would buy a place up in the hills, perhaps. I would buy a place close to his, so he would see me every day as he rode out on his Arab horses, and I would buy horses myself, and learn to ride, and we would find each other, early in the morning, as the sun was coming up . . . The head spins. My head spins.

I don't know if he will ever be well enough. So why do I dream like this?

But he will. I know it. And we shall set up our lives together, Rudy and I, and I shall spend the days writing, and he shall spend the days doing whatever he likes, of course, wherever he likes, with whomsoever he likes. It's true—I don't care! He is free, and I am free to love him, if I choose, and on any terms I choose. And my terms are, simply, that he is happy. That I make him the happiest man on this planet. And that he loves

314

me. And that, no matter what else, I am home. I am his. And he will always come home to me in the end.

But my head *spins*. I don't know for sure if he will ever be strong enough. Perhaps he will never recover. I can't—I will not—

Miss Pickford—Mary—oh, what does it matter? Mary Pickford is due to return to Hollywood later next week, and is enthusiastic, she says, to begin work on *Malicious Intent* as soon as possible, with the hope of shooting it on the lot at United Studios, some time in December . . .

I put the words down, and I gaze at them, and they gaze back at me—and I know them to be true, since I have only just returned from our luncheon, and she assures me she is true to her word. In fact, in Hollywood, I have read, she is well known for it. She is true to her word. And yet I find it impossible to believe that this could be happening to me.

So it was settled. And I gave Frances my one and only copy of *Idol Dreams*, which she was adamant I withhold from Mary until we have signed a deal with *Malicious Intent*. 'Otherwise, if it's as good as you say it is, Lola, she will promptly drop the one for the other and then, if you're not careful, you shall only ever get half the money!'

Mary Pickford laughed at that, but she did not deny it. She and Frances and Anita—they are women of business. It is quite extraordinary. It was a lesson for me, too. So wrapped up in my writing all these years, I never once thought of the business side. I suppose because there wasn't one! Not until today.

After that, and what with the champagne and the wine and so many compliments and promises, I was almost relaxed in their company. And that was when our conversation turned to more general matters. Mary and Anita competed with one another, I think, maybe just a little, to hold the table; but Mary was full of news. She was fresh from shooting a movie, I don't remember its name, whose action is set round an alligator swamp . . .

'How perfectly absurd of you not to have called me,' drawled Anita. 'You know my dear friend Alec, English Alec, Lord something Alec—you must know him. Doug'll know him, for sure. He went down to Florida to build a golfing hotel . . . But then it all went dreadfully wrong and the land turned out to be on some ghastly swamp, so instead of a golfing hotel he opened an alligator farm. Did nobody mention it? You might have shot the entire movie down in Florida, and saved the poor codge from bankruptcy. I believe he *has* gone bankrupt now . . .' She took an elegant pull on her cigarette—it was attached to a holder so long that it wobbled as she placed it between her lips. 'You could have saved him.'

'Except we didn't want to shoot in Florida,' Mary Pickford said patiently, in her quiet, sweet voice. 'We had all the alligators we needed in California. I told that rat Beaudine, as long as I have any say in the matter no one at United Artists shall ever work with him again . . .'

A hush. I think even for those two women, her old friends, it must sometimes be a little hard to reconcile that tiny voice with the extraordinary

316

power it wields in Hollywood.

'Why? Whatever did he do?' asked Frances.

'I heard you terrorised the poor man so badly half his face was paralysed. And then he walked off the set.'

'Well,' Mary replied, 'he deserved it. I told him we should use a doll when we were shooting in the alligator swamp and he insisted on using a real baby. A live baby! Imagine—one *snap* from those great big teeth and the thing would have been dead!'

'Was there a baby eaten?' asked Anita. 'I'm certain we would have heard if there had been.'

'There was not. Of course not, Anita, you're just being silly. That's not the point.'

I saw Frances looking wearily from one to the other. She took a breath, I think, to say something—but I had Mr Hademak on my mind and I knew that, unless I spoke at that instant, my chance would be lost. So I told them of my tall friend Mr Hademak, once a butler, now (I chose not to mention that he had been fired) working as a security guard, trying to control the crowds outside the Polyclinic Hospital.

'Yes, it sounds crazy down there . . . Poor Rudy . . . Mr Ullman turned away Norma Talmadge yesterday. And Joe Schenk! Did you hear? God knows what Rudy will say when he discovers.' Frances stopped suddenly, only then remembering. She turned to me. 'But I understand Rudy is doing much better today,' she said awkwardly. 'You must be very relieved, Lola.'

I could feel sweat prickling but I didn't have a chance to respond, because mention of Rudy had brought Anita springing back to life again.

'I suppose you've heard the latest rumour?' she said, leaning forward. 'That ghastly little man, Mr Ullman, told Gloria Swanson—whom, by the way, he also turned from the hospital yesterday. Can you *believe* that man? George Ullman let slip to Gloria there's a strong possibility poor darling Rudy has been poisoned. Why nobody thought of it before I can't imagine. Had you thought of it, Frances?'

'Not especially,' Frances said.

'Ullman says he's showing all the symptoms— mottled skin, intestinal agony, whatnot—and, you see, they're calling it a gastric ulcer, and that's all perfectly well, but these things have to be *set off* by something. Apparently. Healthy young men, at the peak of physical fitness, they don't suddenly get floored by gastric ulcers. Something has to set them off.'

'But why,' I heard myself asking, in a voice much fainter than my own, 'would anyone want to do that?'

'*Ha!*' Anita sat back in her seat, waved her cigarette holder at me in delight. 'Why? Lola, my dear, sweet girl, do you have *any idea* how much passion that man arouses in people? Do you?'

'I think I do,' I said, with a small smile—not daring to look at Frances.

But Anita was going full steam. I might have said anything. She wasn't listening. 'Good God, he must be the most adored, the most reviled man in the entire universe. Didn't you read that ferocious piece in the *Chicago Tribune*? They syndicated it halfway round the world. You *must have done*. There are people out there—men, of course, jealous men, and jealous women, I suppose—who utterly detest him. Somebody poisoned him at Barclay Warburton's party. That's the *on dit*. Mark my words. This time tomorrow it'll be all over the papers. Mary, had you heard it?'

Mary didn't reply. I looked across at her—she was looking at me very intently. 'Frances tells me you knew Rudy before any of us?' she said politely. 'Is that right?'

'Oh—I've known him since—since . . .' I beamed at her. It was so wonderful to be asked, to be given an opportunity to talk about him—and yet I had no idea where to begin. 'Why, I've known him since he was just a dancer, on a dancer's salary, and he and Mr Hademak and I were all working for—'

Anita Loos might have been quite intrigued if she'd allowed me to finish, but by then she was set on her course—the full significance of which I had yet to grasp—and she wouldn't allow it to drop. 'But isn't it dreadful,' she cut in. 'I just wish I'd been at Warburton's party myself. Who knows? I might even have saved him! And the wretched thing is, I might so *easily* have been there. I was *on the point of it*, but then I was with Max, and there was a cabaret little thingummy at Texas Guinan's and it was quite a scream, and it was so hot that evening, do you remember? So the thought of chugging off all the way to Park Avenue seemed quite an unimaginable drag— but if only I had realised . . . It's too annoying!'

'But he's going to be all right,' I interrupted. 'That's what the hospital said.'

Anita nodded. 'Apparently his skin is quite grey, and there are black spots and I'm not a doctor—'

'Really, Anita?' Frances said. 'You surprise me.'

319

Anita ignored her. 'But he has *absolutely* the look of a man who's taken—'

And then the penny dropped. I lost grip of my teacup, splattered our precious bootleg Haut-Brion right over the table. 'Rat poison,' I said.

'Arsenic,' said Anita. 'Absolutely. Arsenic.'

'*Arsenic*,' I said. 'He has black marks on his skin? Is that what they're saying?'

'Indeed it is.'

'He has black marks on his skin? Small black marks . . . mottled black . . . marks. It's what they're saying?'

'That's what I heard.'

'Small black marks . . .'

'Lola?'

'Lola?'

I'm not even certain who said it. Frances or Mary. I felt a hand on my shoulder. 'Sweetheart. Are you all right?'

'I'm fine.'

'Are you sure?'

'Oh, I'm fine.' I tried to collect myself. Looked around at the mess I had made of the table. 'I am so sorry. Did I splash anyone? Did I—I didn't get anything on the script, did I, Miss Marion? You know it's the only copy. I should hate to—'

'I just *wish* I'd been bothered to go to that damn party,' Anita continued, blithely. 'Imagine how one could dine out on that—I mean,' she added quickly, 'now that we know he's likely to survive. Only Barclay is a drag, isn't he? He's a dreadful man. The only reason one bothers to be friends with him is because he serves such good champagne . . . *tippety-top, every drop, good champagne hits the spot . . .*'

320

'Anita, are you soused?' Mary asked her. 'I think it's time we called for the check.'

'If Mr Ullman says he has been poisoned,' I asked Anita, 'then why hasn't it been in the newspapers? Are you sure you heard it correctly?'

'Absolutely sure,' she said, rather tartly. 'And it will be in the papers. Mark my words. Poisoned by arsenic at Barclay Warburton's party.'

'But—No. I mean to say, wouldn't he—he would have noticed it!'

'Apparently it's tasteless.'

'It's tasteless. Yes. '

'So it might quite easily have been slipped into a glass of Mr Warburton's excellent champagne . . .'

'His glass of champagne . . .'

'Lola—sweetie,' it was Frances, 'you know, you should never pay the slightest attention to anything Anita says. You do realise it, don't you? This woman,' there was quite an edge to her voice, 'lives for nothing but gossip. Nothing is real to her.'

'And when she doesn't have gossip,' added Mary, 'she invents it . . . and, sweetie, you look like you've seen a ghost. But you mustn't pay the slightest attention. I'm quite certain she's invented this.'

'I'll tell you something else, though,' said Anita, ignoring them, fixing her attention on me. '*The plot thickens*, Lola. He's been calling out someone's name . . . On the way to the hospital, he was calling it. Again and again, he was calling it. When he was half comatose—'

'Well, if he was comatose—'

'*Half* comatose, Mary. I said half comatose . . .'

'Whose name?' It spat from me like a bullet. 'Whose name? *Whose name has he been calling?*'

Anita looked at me. 'Take it from me, dearie,' she said drily (a little offended, I think, by my urgent tone. She didn't know. Of course. She couldn't have realised). 'I'm pretty certain it wasn't "Lola".'

Once again, I felt the tears stinging. 'Of course not,' I muttered. 'I was only—'

But she had already moved on. She was scowling, trying to remember. 'Funny enough—it was a name one wouldn't expect. A *silly* name . . . Not in the least Hollywood. Mr Ullman told Mr Schenk . . . who told Norma . . . who told *me* . . . Now what in heck . . .? God—I do declare I'm going the teeniest bit gaga.'

* * *

The check came, and soon afterwards Anita, without offering to contribute towards it, wandered off to join Dorothy Parker and the others at their famous round table. Frances drew our luncheon to an end. She took with her my new version of *Idol Dreams*, which she promised to read over the weekend, and she and Mary and I are to meet next week, or the week after, as soon as we have all returned to Hollywood.

Mary Pickford has given me the telephone number of her assistant, which I have already given to Mr Hademak in the message I sent to the boarding-house. I have told Mary about Mr Hademak's employment with the de Saulleses, and about how, when next she sees Rudy, she can ask him about Mr Hademak too, since I was confident he would remember him. Hademak's story intrigued her, she said—as well it might: she, like everyone else in the country, had followed the court case avidly.

'And you, Lola, you gave evidence too?'

'Yes, I did . . . I was the one who—' I stopped. It was a shock, just hearing myself speak about it after so much time had passed, and yet with Frances's and Mary's eyes fixed on me with such warm curiosity, I felt a terrible urge to speak. 'You perhaps remember—there was a child's nurse . . . But, you see, the press adored her so. All men do. Except—I think—Rudy never *quite* did. Well. In any case the press men didn't see her commit the act, as I did. They didn't see her holding up that gun, and the bullets piercing his chest one after the other, and her hand quite steady. They didn't see her face as she pointed that gun. They didn't see how she used to . . .' I fell silent. 'I'm so sorry . . .' I said at last.

A long pause followed. I could feel the two women's eyes on me, waiting for me to say more, and then, finally, Miss Pickford leaned forward, squeezed my arm. 'Don't you worry,' she said. 'And if Mr Hademak is half as good as you have said he is, then I know Doug is going to be delighted. It happens he's been looking for a decent valet for many months. So if your friend doesn't object to making a life for himself at Pickfair . . .'

I laughed—in spite of everything: the storm that was raging inside me. In truth, by then, I couldn't wait to be free of them. 'Actually, Mary, I

323

can't imagine there is anywhere in the world he would more like to make a life.'

*   *   *

The three of us—Mary, Frances and I—were standing in the lobby of the hotel by then, saying our *au revoirs*. I noticed, from the corner of my eye, how—even at the Algonquin—people goggled at Miss Pickford. I was leaving, saying thank you for the thousandth time, and Anita came bustling across to us—stumbling very slightly, I thought, with her purple cloche hat gently askew.

'Ah!' she said, waving her finger at me. 'Found you! Miss Dorothy Parker says she wants to meet you.'

'Me?'

'*Because* . . .' she smiled ' . . . I told her you knew Mr Valentino when he was just a gigolo . . . She wants *all* the dirt.'

'But he wasn't a gigolo.'

'Oh yes he was!'

'I think,' I said, 'that I had better go. Please say to Miss Parker . . . I am sorry to disappoint her. And I should love to meet her another time. But Rudy was never a gigolo. And I am a little busy this afternoon. I'm so sorry . . .'

'Aha!' she burst out. She wasn't listening. 'I've just remembered. That's it!' She turned her attention to Frances. 'It wasn't La Negri he was calling out for in the ambulance. *Obviously*. God forbid! It wasn't that Bitch of a Bitch Natacha Rambova. *Thank God*. No, no. Not a bit! He was rolling around in that ambulance, half comatose,

324

in terrible pain, and all he could do was to call out for *Jenny!*' She turned to Mary. 'So,' she said, teetering slightly, 'that's the million-dollar question, isn't it? Who the hell is "Jenny"?'

HOTEL CONTINENTAL

NEW YORK

Thursday, 19 August 1926

10 p.m.
It is evening now, I know that and I am exhausted. Half crazy with happiness because he has been calling for me. And half demented because I have read the late editions of the newspapers. I have been down to the hospital again. And the crowds are back. Rudy's temperature is up. He is—Rudy, my Rudy, whom I cannot get near—gravely, desperately ill. He is in great pain. Terrible pain. He lurches in and out of consciousness, and the pain in his intestines is eating slowly at his survival—perhaps even his will to survive. The lights are turned on, up there on the eighth floor, and I suppose the doctors are tiptoeing in and out, and his pain is terrible, unbearable. And I am Jenny. His Jenny. And he needs me. And I cannot see him tonight, and tomorrow perhaps he will die.

And if he dies, it is—it is perhaps—because I have poisoned him.

1923–4

HOLLYWOOD

Perry didn't like me to attend the castings. Occasionally, at the beginning, I was still brave enough to resist him. But he would always kick up such a fuss, and then insist on driving me to them, which meant I was always late, and always in a dreadful, nervous state by the time I got there. Nobody ever wanted to hire me.

Soon it became more trouble than it was worth. Perry wanted me one hundred per cent at his disposal. He paid for everything. I stayed at home and used the empty time to write. I wrote a lot. More than at any other time—partly because I had nothing better to do, of course, and partly because it kept me company. Kept me sane, I think.

From the very beginning, after the twins had left, there would be periods—days on end—when he disappeared from the bungalow altogether. And each time he left it was the same: I found myself torn between fear and hope that he might never come back again. But he always did.

In his absence he used, sometimes, to send his friend William to deliver me cash, ostensibly, but really to check up on me. He would appear at the door, sometimes alone, sometimes with friends— and, gosh, I resented it. I resented it so bitterly that one evening I decided not to let him in. The bungalow windows were open. Of course he knew I was inside (when wasn't I?) but I didn't care. I hid beneath the kitchen counter until he grew tired of leaning on my doorbell, and finally he wandered away.

Later that night I woke from a deep sleep to find Perry, pie-eyed and jangling with cocaine, glowering over my pillow. He dragged me out of the bed. I stood before him, shivering with shock. He pulled back his hand and struck.

William had told him what had occurred, he said. I didn't argue. Didn't do anything. Stood there, wondering whether, if I caught his eye, made the wrong move, tilted my head this way instead of that, he might take it as a reason to lash out again. I just stood there, trembling, waiting for the temper to subside, the moment to pass.

Looking back, I can only think it served me right. What a fool I was to have put myself in such a position—but the truth is, I depended on him utterly. With my work at the studios dried up, I had no other source of income. With the twins gone, I had no other friends. With no word from Frances Marion—or anyone else I sent my work to—there seemed to be no chance of escape.

*   *   *

Soon after that incident, which was never mentioned again, Perry invited a man who specialised in house décor to come round to the apartment. He banished all that was left of the cheerful frippery arranged with such good cheer by the twins and me what seemed like a lifetime ago. He painted the sitting-room walls black, and the floor a deep scarlet, and gave us glass-beaded floor cushions with long tassels to sit on, and some exquisite mirrored side tables, and a cowskin couch, and various other modern, expensive objects. He transported half a ton of furniture from a shop on Fifth Avenue, New York—which shop had itself imported the furniture from France. There were woven silk carpets, apparently from the court of Versailles, Perry said, and wall hangings from Peking, and a little escritoire from somewhere, God knows where, with legs so spindly I was afraid to look at the thing for fear it might snap under the pressure. The escritoire was Perry's. He never sat at it, but I was forbidden to go near it, and he always kept it locked.

I didn't care. Not about much, actually. Except for the writing, and—pathetically—about Rudy, whose memory in spite of everything simply refused to fade, and whose existence I was reminded of each time I opened a newspaper or magazine, and each time I walked down Hollywood Boulevard and saw the great hoardings, with his name up in lights. I read about his comings and goings, his sojourns to New York, his one-man actor's strike against his studio . . . I read that he and his beloved, soon-to-be-second wife were on some crazy money-raising dance tour around the country, and that they were due to leave for Europe, and that then they were to spend more time in New York . . . They were never at home, it seemed—or they came and they went; and the knowledge that he was mostly gone made Hollywood seem a wretched place. Sucked light and hope out of the city. Out of everything.

*   *   *

And then this happened.

I heard Perry's car pulling up outside the apartment and felt the usual tightening of apprehension in my stomach. On this occasion, though, he sounded cheerful. He called out to me to come and see what he had bought, and I found him at the door, grinning, weighed down by shopping bags.

'Hope you're feeling up for some fun tonight, my angel,' he said. 'We've got a big and beautiful night ahead of us. Dinner at the Cocoanut Grove! How about that? An invitation from Miss Clara Bow. None other. No less.' He bowed, with all the shopping bags. 'And it's no good you asking me how I came by it because on my deathbed I'm never going to tell you . . .'

'Oh, gosh, Perry.' I laughed. 'Trust me. I'm sure I don't want to know!'

He smiled at that. 'Want to come along?'

'Do I want to come along? To the Cocoanut Grove? With Clara Bow?'

'But I have a condition . . .'

He said he would take me with him only if I promised not to mention my photoplays. Not to anyone: not to any stars, not to any agents, not to any studio executives. 'You're not to embarrass me, you understand? Just sit quietly, poppet, and be delightful, and look pretty.'

Perry had bought me an evening dress of rich yellow silk, and a platinum necklace with a large, tear-shaped pendant at the end, which he assured me was a diamond. I had my doubts.

But the dress was perfect—a perfect fit, fortunately, because I had filled out. Too much sitting at my table, drafting photoplays and pleading letters to Frances Marion (which I never

329

dared to post). Too little to do. Too much eating. I seemed to do nothing but eat.

But the dress was perfect: a perfect cut, a perfect colour, perfectly designed to fit my unaccustomed new curves. I disappeared to the bedroom to change, and returned to the sitting room twenty minutes later.

He was waiting for me, an open bottle of champagne beside him, long legs sprawled elegantly over the couch, his new gold necklace—with the tiny golden spoon attached—dangling nonchalantly from the top of his open shirt. He watched me as I crossed the room towards him—in a way he had; approving, desiring, intense and yet detached. And it made its way inside me, as it always did.

He unclipped the tiny gold spoon from his necklace, dipped it into the gold box where he kept his cocaine and held a delicate heap to my nose. I didn't hesitate. There were certain advantages to living with a guy like Perry. Soul-destroying advantages, for sure. But he had his moments. Long, delicious moments.

There was, in fact, a funny kind of tenderness about him when the talking stopped, when we were naked, or preparing to be: an exquisite, delicate balance he held, of masculine power kept in check and, if not quite tenderness, then at least a fearless kind of intimacy. He was a generous lover—revealed a side of himself that made me, I admit it, love him. Just a small bit.

We were very late in the end—and my short hair was a mess and my beautiful yellow dress was crumpled, and my body was a little limp. But Perry said I glowed. He said I was ravishing. He said I

330

would outshine every star in the galaxy. Every star in the Cocoanut Grove—and he said it in such a way that I truly believed him.

Perry had his moments.

*   *   *

'Now, sweetheart,' he said, as we were chugging up Wilshire, en route to the most famous nightspot in the world. He put his hand on my knee. 'I don't want you to take this wrong, poppet, but these people are my bread and butter and . . . Understand? Don't go acting like a rube.'

I said nothing. It was rather insulting of him, I thought.

'You're going to see the stars wall to wall in this place . . . maybe even your long-lost friend Mr Rudolph Valentino.' He glanced at me with a wry, sweet smile, one I had long since learned not to trust.

I chuckled, as if I didn't care; as if Perry was ridiculous; as if it hadn't been the first thing that crossed my mind when he told me where we would be dining tonight.

'. . . but the secret, when mixing with the stars, babykins, is to absolutely pretend you haven't noticed. If Charlie Chaplin himself is standing right there, jumping on your left big toe, you don't acknowledge him unless he's acknowledged you first. D'you understand that? Don't even look twice.'

'Don't worry, Perry.' I smiled at him. 'I won't disgrace you.'

'You could never disgrace me, baby girl.'

I had been living in Hollywood long enough to

331

know the rules. Of course I had. I also knew, which Perry obviously didn't, that Rudy was in town—just back from Europe, with his new wife in tow. And I knew that very little—nothing—would prevent me scouring the crowd for him that night. He loved it at the Cocoanut Grove. I knew that well enough. I had read it in *Photoplay*.

*　　*　　*

I acted like a rube. I'm afraid I did. Couldn't help it. When I first walked through those doors, the sight of that place had just exactly the effect it was supposed to. I gasped, and my feet stopped walking. It took my breath away.

The room is colossal. There must be three hundred dining tables spread out before the dance floor, and at the end of the room, blasting out from a tremendous stage, sits the famous band playing the best jazz, so they say, it's possible to hear outside of Harlem. I don't know about that. I've never been to Harlem. But I swear it's the best, most exciting, most exhilarating jazz I have ever heard anywhere else.

Here and there in that seemingly unending room, spouting up like out of some crazy nightmare, life-sized cocoanut trees are nailed to the floor, with stuffed monkeys hanging from their branches; and embedded into the ceiling—that infinite, deep blue ceiling there are stars that, by some electrical magic, actually twinkle, or they certainly seem to, and they look so distant and irregular, it's hard to believe they aren't real.

Perry pinched me, not especially gently. 'Buck up, poppet,' he said. 'Or do you want me to take you back home?' I moved aside. Apologised. Followed him quickly through the endless room to our table. 'And for Christ's sake,' he muttered into my hair, as I tottered in front of him, 'don't dare goggle at Clara. Better yet, poppet,' he stopped, to be sure I was listening, 'don't even talk to her. Unless she talks to you. Just leave her to me . . . She doesn't,' he added, as an afterthought, 'much like girls in any case.'

The film colony despises Clara Bow. She smokes and drinks and swears—and, even by Hollywood standards, she is considered promiscuous. She didn't much like girls, so the story went, but she adored men. The way she pawed at Perry that night I could only assume— She adored him above them all. Too bad. Perry wasn't mine. He had made that abundantly clear. And the truth is, it didn't much trouble me one way or the other. Perry and I had what we had. Not a great deal, as far as I was concerned. But something. He paid the bills. I wasn't about to make a fuss.

We were a party of eight that night, around our silver-laden, circular table. Miss Bow—Clara—had organised for God only knew how many bottles of champagne to be placed in an old suitcase beneath her seat, for which waiters, with great solicitude and very little subtlety, put ice buckets at our hostess's feet. She tipped them each a hundred bucks. I watched her. And the champagne flowed. Miss Bow was nothing if not generous.

There were no other stars in our party, chiefly because everybody who was anybody tended to despise her so. Our company was made up of hangers-on (like myself), lackeys and dope-suppliers (like Perry). Not that it mattered—or not

333

to me. One star, one evening at the Cocoanut Grove, one new dress, and a pendant that looked like a diamond . . . a couple of pinches of snow . . . and a whole lot of French champagne: it was more than enough for one night.

The eight of us sat at our table. They served us dinner—mushrooms stuffed with crab, I think, or maybe the other way round. And asparagus tips, and something very special with celery—gosh, I don't remember. I was buzzing with cocaine, and gulping back the champagne, and too excited to have any appetite for food. But it kept on coming. Course after course. What a waste! Anybody who came close to Perry was too busy chewing his own jaw to touch a mouthful of it.

I had neighbours. Who were they? A couple of guys—maybe one said he was an actor. I hardly talked to him. The other one kept telling me he was a film producer. He said he was raising funds to make a movie starring Miss Bow. 'It's a perfect vehicle for her,' he kept saying, over and over. He was good-looking, wired and jumpy; on the make—just like everyone in that town. He didn't want to talk to me any more than I wanted to talk to him. But we went through the motions, mouthing words at one another above the music, while I looked over his shoulder in furtive, desperate, edgy search of Rudy. And he looked as blatantly past me—nowhere, really, except at Clara.

And then there was Clara: resplendent in scarlet satin, with a black ostrich feather boa about her shoulders, and a thick choker of black pearls around her forehead, which made her dark eyes burn and her pale skin glow. Gosh, but she is

334

beautiful, sexual: an amazing-looking woman. We other girls, we all disappeared beside her.

Unfortunately for my neighbour, Clara was a lot more interested in Perry than she was in him; and Perry, thank God, was a lot more interested in her than he was in policing the direction of my eyeballs. So, for an hour or two, things went smoothly. I wouldn't say that I enjoyed myself—I was too strung out for that—but I was thrilled, more than thrilled, so on edge that I could feel my heart against my ribcage *thump thump thump*. Was Rudy here, in the room? Was it possible?

*   *   *

I had reached a state of mind where I believed I might set eyes on him at any moment. Already I had spotted Gloria Swanson, shimmying her doll-like little hips on the dance floor . . . and Norma and Constance Talmadge, heads bent together in conversation, and beside them, Buster Keaton; and poor sweet Roscoe Arbuckle, finally acquitted, who'd been to hell and back since last I set eyes on him. I saw Mabel Normand, and the appalling Peggy Hopkins Joyce, all diamonds and gleaming eyes and idiotic giggles. I had read that Blanca de Saulles's younger brother had recently shot himself in the head for love of her. Not that it seemed to trouble her that night: she clung possessively to the arm of no less than Charlie Chaplin. *Charlie Chaplin!* They were all there with me that night, and I was drunk with it, I swear: cocaine and intoxicating glamour. Anything and everything seemed possible . . .

Clara and Perry got up to dance. They could

barely keep their hands off one another. I pretended not to see it. Immediately they reached the floor, my producer friend—my wired neighbour—asked if I would like to dance with him, and though I loved to dance, I was itching to dance, and even though the band was blasting out a Charleston, and my legs were jumping beneath the table, I knew quite well that to dance with anyone but Perry would be more than my life was worth. Regretfully, I told him I was tired. So he grabbed the girl on his other side and for a while I was left in peace, to look around in wonder.

Later, Clara returned to the table, followed closely by my neighbour and the girl. They sat down in a great gust of togetherness and exhaustion. Clara glanced at me—not unkindly or disdainfully, but not with any embarrassment either, given the way she and Perry had been behaving. She smiled, a brisk little smile.

'He's seein' to some business,' she said, in that crazy, dreadful Brooklyn drawl. 'Silly bastard ran out of dope.'

'Oh!' I said. Rather shocked. 'That's—'

She nodded before I had time to finish. 'Unfortunate. When ya take into considerin' what his profession is, 'n all.'

'Yes. I suppose . . .' I wasn't sure if it qualified as a profession, but there seemed little point in arguing about it at such a moment. And with such a woman. Her straight talking, combined with her glamour, her fame—and the fact, I suppose, that she was my lover's lover as well as my hostess for the evening—made me feel somewhat intimidated. 'Well . . . I hope . . .' What? I had no idea what I hoped. Or what else to say. I fell into awkward silence.

'He'll be here in a minute.'

She turned away. Back to the men. And I returned my attention to the dance floor.

The band had fallen silent, and most of the dancers were slowly meandering back to their tables. There wasn't much to look at. Except, that is, for a minor commotion, which seemed to be gathering steam in the furthest corner, just beneath the stage. There were a lot of heads knotted together, and a disagreement of some sort. The compère, on the edge of the stage, was crouched on his haunches, pleading—or so it seemed—and in the middle of the throng a man and a woman. I couldn't see their faces. Not until the crowd around them cleared, and the compère straightened up. And then I couldn't hear—

The blood was thumping so hard I couldn't hear— He was saying something but I couldn't hear—

'Ladies and gentlemen,' he cried. 'LADIES AND GENTLEMEN . . . We have a wonderful surprise. Tonight . . . we are privileged—we are truly, truly privileged . . . Please welcome home to Hollywood . . .'

. . . there she stood, his beautiful wife, beautiful lips uptipped in a smile of satisfaction, and there— his profile, his profile turned, half smiling, half frowning—bashful, unwilling . . .

'. . . MR AND MRS RUDOLPH VALENTINO!'

The band struck up—it was the music he had danced to in *The Four Horsemen*. How well I recognised it! As one, the crowd—this most sophisticated of crowds—burst into ecstatic applause. He turned to his wife, tilted his head to one side and, with a cool, polite smile, offered her his hand. She took it, with a little nod of her own, and together, to the music and the foot-thumping ovation, they glided to the centre of the empty dance floor.

What can I say? He was more handsome than I remembered. More handsome than in all my dreams. More handsome than any man I had ever laid eyes on. He moved—he floated—there is no mortal on earth who can dance with such mesmerising grace, such lightly, tightly held reserves of passion and strength. I could not take my eyes from him—his feet, his hips, his hands, his shoulders, his hands, his hips, the angle of his neck, his neck, his lips, his eyes, his mouth, his hands, his mouth, his hands . . .

She was invisible. To all of us, I think. And yet, from the expression on her face moments earlier, before the dancing began, one might have believed the entire show was put on for her. I think perhaps, in a way, it might have been. Because Rudy, when he took her hand, had seemed dismayed, unwilling . . . I'm certain of it. So I watched him, unable to breathe inside my yellow silk dress, unable to move . . . The years peeled away and it was as if I was standing in the garden at The Box, a young girl still, peering at him through the french windows of the terrace, falling in love with him for the first time . . . How much had happened since then! I remembered, at Coney Island, in the dance hall, how he held me when we went up on the stage to claim our prize, and how utterly, drunkenly happy we were . . .

The music stopped. The dance ended. The people roared. The star and his wife took their bows. He seemed in a hurry to melt back into the crowd, but his wife took another curtsy, and another . . .

Somebody laid their hand over mine; a woman's hand, small, with three vast ruby rings vying for attention on the chubby fingers. 'Sweetie, ya cryin' . . . And ya cold as a stinkin' ice block!' I looked up, at last, to see Miss Clara Bow, in all her scarlet magnificence. She was leaning across to me, a look of kindness—and curiosity—on her wonderful face. 'Honey, you OK? Look like y'jus seen a ghost.'

'Crying?' I said. 'I'm so sorry.' I wiped the tears away. There seemed to be lots of them. More and more. I wanted to stand up, run over to him, elbow my way across the room . . . *Hello, Rudy.* I would call out. *Hello, darling!* My *darling! Do you remember me?*

But my body was like lead. I could only sit and watch as the people closed in on him, hundreds of people, clapping him on the back, grinning and smiling, and then all I could see were the people, the great huddle of people, clambering to be near him, to catch a little of his stardust, and—

'Ya got taste, girl . . .' (Clara, again.) 'I'll say that for ya . . .'

'I adore him,' I heard me say.

She didn't laugh. 'I can see . . . He's a nice guy, too. A regular gentleman. An' it sure ain't many y'can say *that* about in this stinkin' town . . .'

'He is, isn't he?'

'Ya wanna meet him?' She was already standing up. 'C'mon. I'll do ya a favour. Why the hell not? Besides, he's about the only big star who's decent enough t'talk ta me nowadays. So I like him. Let's

339

get over there and say hi!'

'*No!*' I cried. 'I couldn't possibly.'

'Aw, don't be a stupid bitch! It's obvious ya want ta. *C'mon!*' She tugged on my arm. 'For once in my stinking life, I'm gonna make someone happy. Ha! Maybe I'll make two people happy. Maybe ya jus' the broad he's searchin' for. Anyone's gotta be an improvement on the Jezebel he's gone an' hitched hisself with for the moment. Come with me!'

I stood up. It was a little odd. She took my hand as if we were a pair of carefree children and, in her enthusiasm, half yanked me into the crowd. Thick, noisy crowd it was . . . terribly noisy. People screaming and yelling, and the jazz band had kicked up again . . . and people were heading back to the dance floor and, really, it seemed as if Rudy was a long, long way away . . . Too far, it seemed, and with every step I took, it seemed he was always moving further. My legs belonged to someone else, someone who had forgotten how to use them, so I stumbled one step, and then another . . . I glimpsed him through the throng—his head thrown back at something. Did I hear his wonderful laugh, over all that noise, or did I simply imagine it? . . . One step, and then another, and then another—an impatient tug from Clara, which almost lost me my balance . . . One more step, one more—I heard his laughter for sure, and the brittle voice of a woman: 'Rudy, darling, do let's sit down. I'm dreadfully tired . . . Do let's . . .' One more step, and then another: *Hello, Rudy, hello, darling! My darling—do you remember me?*

Would I say that? Would I dare? Would he remember me? Of course he would! Suddenly I knew it—better than I knew anything. I could see

it. The look of astonishment and recognition . . .
His face lighting up. His arms opening wide, just as
they had at Penn Station—just as they always
would, to greet his old friend, who had loved him
all these years . . . Clara pushed and shoved and
pulled and barged, and managed, in her perfectly
inimitable way, to elbow through the great throng,
until we were barely more than a few feet away.

'RUDY! BABY,' she bawled out. He glanced up.
'I WANTCHA TO MEET MY GREAT
FRIEND—' She realised she didn't know my name
and was turning, blankly, to ask me for it.

At the same instant I felt a vice grip on my other
arm, so tight, so harsh, I yelled out, beneath all the
music. Nobody seemed to hear. I barely heard
myself.

It was Perry. Holding me back again. Looking
down at me with an expression of bitter, violent,
horrible rage. I stared at his face. His hand
tightened on my arm but it took me a moment to
see it all, to understand what was happening. I
tried to turn back again, towards Rudy, but with his
free hand Perry grasped my cheek, then the back
of my head, preventing me from moving, and then
he bent down, without a word, and pressed his lips
to mine very, very hard. I could feel the pain of
that, and taste the blood, and I could feel Clara's
hand slipping from mine . . . I could hear her
greeting Rudy, kissing him noisily on each cheek,
and his greeting her—his warm, beautiful voice,
less Italian now . . . and she was saying, 'Rudy, ya
fat ol' bastard. Where you bin hiding all these
days? Hollywood ain't the same without you!'

And he laughed. 'Why, looking for you, Clara,'
he said. 'Always. Of course! Looking for you!'

And she laughed, and he laughed, and I could feel the blood from Perry's kiss, filling my mouth, and I could hear Rudy and Clara drifting slowly away, Clara's offer of a good turn lost in the moment, forgotten in all the exuberance of Rudy's greeting. He was introducing her to his wife, except then he couldn't find her—'She must have gone,' he said carelessly. 'Shall we dance?'

And that was it. I didn't hear anything else; the noise closed over them, and all I could feel was the pain.

*   *   *

He led me off the dance floor, holding me in such a grip that I could not move inside it. He led me off the floor to the table, he picked up my bag and my fur, and led me the long, long walk between the palm trees, under the glittering stars and swinging monkeys, to the exit.

Again. Pulled away again.

We drove home in silence—me, too stunned to speak; too stunned to be frightened; unable to hear or see anything but Rudy, his voice, his laughter, his dance . . . My arm ached where Perry had held it. My lips were swollen, but I was aware of nothing, none of it, nothing.

Outside the bungalow he switched off the engine and we sat in silence, listening to the night sounds and smelling the sweet evening scent of mimosa; and I suppose I waited, dumbly, to hear what was my fate.

Finally he said, 'I shall be kind. Because, in spite of every-thing—all I have done for you, and how little you care for me—I am rather fond of you,

342

Lola.'

'And I am fond of you.' God knows why I said it. There was a pause, I suppose. I had to say something.

He said, 'You can collect your stuff. Spend the night, for all I care. I shall return—probably tomorrow—and by then you had better be gone.'

That jolted me a bit. I suppose I had expected a storm. I think I was half braced for some kind of thrashing, and then I imagined he would have gone somewhere, disappeared for a day or two . . . And, really, I hadn't thought a moment beyond that. Really, I had barely *thought* at all—but his coolness, this lack of violence, this banishment, was something else; something much more chilling.

'Gone?' I said. 'But where?'

His face in the moonlight, his sunken cheeks, his glistening eyes, those white teeth, he looked quite cracked as he turned his gaze on me. 'What the fuck do I care?' he snarled, not so cool any more. Not so kind. 'Get out of my car. I'll be back in the morning some time. And woe betide you, little girl, if I ever set eyes on you in my place again.'

He leaned across me, his arm stretching across the stomach of my yellow silk dress, pulled open my door and shoved me out onto the driveway. And I stood there, dazed and stupid, still a little drunk, still a little wired, my body aching, my heart—stopped, so heavy with disappointment I could hardly comprehend what had befallen me.

If Rudy knew . . . was all I could think. *If Rudy knew, he would come and help me. If Rudy knew . . .*

But Rudy didn't know. He didn't know how close we had been that evening; how happy we could have been. As the sound of the motor-car faded, and the song of the crickets returned, I didn't think to glance back to watch Perry leaving. It was as if he had never existed.

*   *   *

I let myself into the apartment. Switched on the lights. Residue from our happy early evening was scattered across the sitting room: our champagne glasses, the discarded wrapping from my new dress and shoes, the box from which I had drawn my new, fake diamond pendant . . .

I took out a suitcase, Perry's suitcase, since I had none, and began to pile things into it—all the beautiful, expensive clothes Perry had given me, and all the useless signed photographs of Rudy, and my cheap little mah-jong set, which the twins had given to me last Christmas. Maybe even the Christmas before. It dawned on me that I needed to concentrate. I would never be coming back to this place. I needed to take everything I wanted now, or lose it for ever.

But then it turned out there wasn't much I wanted. It's a funny thing. Each time I move on from a place, there never is. My scripts, of course, and my letter from Rudy. But beyond that . . . So after I'd packed half a suitcase I lost heart in the job.

I had about a hundred and fifty dollars in cash stashed away, somewhere between Rudy's letter and his photographs. Hardly much. I began to wonder where in hell I was going to stay that night or any other night, and how I would survive, without cash, without a job, without friends . . .

I thought automatically of Lorna and Phoebe.

Would they take me in? Again? Probably not—why should they? In any case, I had lost contact with them entirely . . . I had no idea where I might find them.

Anyway—and then I suppose, my eyes fell on his little escritoire, home to all Perry's secrets, everything he wanted to keep from me. Even looking at the wretched thing made me nervous. I imagined opening it—forcing the lock, perhaps, if there was no key—and finding out once and for all what it was he guarded so closely inside. Suddenly I couldn't resist—I had nothing to lose, in any case. Perry had thrown me out. I wasn't ever supposed to see him again.

I crossed the room and stood before it. Paused, just a moment, just to be sure he wasn't returning; made a furtive, feeble tug on the roll-back cover— inlaid in walnut and God knows what else. It must have cost him a fortune. As I did so, something fell from the back of it and clattered to the ground. Almost gave me a heart attack! Lying on the floor behind one spindly leg was the key, tiny and irresistible. Perry must have been confident of his rule over me, I thought, or he might have made a better attempt to hide the wretched thing. I picked it up, unlocked the cover, pulled it back . . .

Inside were four drawers, each one wider than the one above. Having got so far I didn't hesitate. First, I opened the top drawer, the slimmest one: cocaine. Plenty of it, repacked into little paper envelopes. Not his main stash, I knew, because he kept that in a hole beneath the wardrobe in our bedroom. It didn't interest me. I considered helping myself to a quick pinch, just as a pep for the long hours ahead—but thought better of it. I closed the drawer. In the second I discovered a small pistol: not so small as the pretty little thing, with mother-of-pearl handle, that had been used to murder Jack de Saulles, but the sight of it gave me a start, brought unwelcome images flooding back, and for a while I think I stood there, transfixed, as the bullets punctured yet again, and the little boy screamed, and the little gun slipped neatly into her little handbag.

Was this the gun? Lawyer Uterhart had asked me, holding it before me as I stood in the witness stand. Was it? I had no idea. It looked the sort of gun a pretty society lady might have used, should she want to shoot her husband dead in front of everyone, including their son. *Was this the gun?* He had needed to ask me twice. I said, 'Why yes, I believe so,' just as Mr Uterhart had instructed.

I snapped the drawer shut.

The third drawer took a little more effort to open: its handle was loose and came off in my hand. I needed to reattach it and pull very gently before the thing would slide out.

Inside, there was cash. Plenty of it. Thick bundles of dollar bills, bound together with strips of paper. I hesitated. Oh, gosh, I hesitated. There must have been several thousand dollars sitting there, ready to be taken . . . More, even . . . I felt a sweat rising: if I took just one of the bundles, just one, it might at least pay for his cruelty tonight . . . I closed the drawer, still not certain whether I would go back to it, and opened the final one.

Nothing much in there, at first glance. Letters and bills, a couple of photographs—one of a girl, very beautiful, lying on a tiger-skin rug without a stitch on. She had signed the picture, surrounded by hearts and kisses, 'My darling, impossible Perry—an afternoon impossible to forget . . .' The writing was slightly smudged, but not where she had dated it, only a month earlier.

Beneath that photograph was another, curled and slightly ripped, of an elderly couple. The woman was seated, the man standing behind her, one hand on her shoulder. His parents, I supposed. Good-looking. Sour. Genteel and impoverished. They looked like hell.

I rummaged a little further in that final drawer, but in truth my mind was already returning to the drawer above it, from which one small bundle of dollar bills could so easily, simply be removed . . . Would it be so bad? Perry probably wouldn't even notice. But I knew it was impossible. I had more or less convinced myself of that, I think, when my fingers happened to touch an envelope—two envelopes—and, who knows why?, something compelled me to pull them out.

Both envelopes had already been opened, and both were addressed to me.

My dear Miss Nightingale [read the first],

I greatly enjoyed reading the two scenarios, which you may recall, you handed to me before a shelf of macaroni at a Piggly Wiggly grocery store on Santa Monica Boulevard many moons ago. I am afraid that for most of that time they have languished, quite forgotten, among the usual mountains of paperwork on my desk—and it was only by chance that my eye happened to fall upon them again last week.

*It was courageous of you to approach me, and
I am delighted that you did so. Your work—
most particularly in Catnip—reveals a good
deal of talent.*

*If you would like to arrange a meeting with me so
that we might discuss your future as a professional
scenarioist, please contact my secretary on the
telephone number below. I will be very happy to
help you.*

*In the meantime, I hope you will accept my
heartfelt apology in taking so long to write to you. I
know how time can drag when one is awaiting a
response from someone, and by now you may well
have given up on me entirely.
I sincerely hope not.*

*I look forward to meeting you again, at your
earliest convenience,
Frances Marion*

The letter was dated 17 March 1923. Eleven and a
half months ago. It had arrived only a few weeks
after the twins moved out—and Perry had hidden
it from me. He had opened it, read it, and locked it
away . . . Just as he had the second letter she wrote
me, four months later:

Dear Miss Nightingale,

*Forgive me for writing a second time, only I was
impressed by your courage and dedication when
you handed me your photoplays some time ago. I
have since written to you expressing my high
opinion of your work. You are a talented
scenarioist, and from the impression I received,*

348

one who is dedicated to the task. It would be a shame if all this were to go to waste, simply on account of a letter gone astray.

Do, please, at your earliest convenience, contact my secretary on the number below.

With very best wishes
From your supporter,
Frances Marion

She had written not once but twice! This, her last letter, was dated 12 July 1923. Eight months ago.

*   *   *

I rummaged through that drawer one final time—if he had hidden letters from Miss Marion, he might have hidden letters from— He had not. But there was the letter from Madeleine—the one I opened that first night he came to stay but never remembered to read. He had found it and hidden it! And a postcard from Phoebe, written to me a month ago, businesslike, telling me to get in touch. I folded the letters, the two from Miss Marion, the one from Madeleine, and the postcard from Phoebe—with her and Lorna's address at the top—and pressed them into the evening bag Perry had bought me for our evening at the Cocoanut Grove.

I also folded one medium-sized bundle of dollar bills from the drawer above. Then I picked up my suitcase and, without a backward look, I walked out on Citrus Avenue, leaving the front door—and the lid of that stupid escritoire—wide open behind me.

*   *   *

Three days later, I discovered the reason for my changed figure and my enormous appetite. I was pregnant.

HOTEL CONTINENTAL
NEW YORK

Friday, 20 August 1926

There is a message for me from Frances. There are four messages. And such long messages, too—and at any other time . . . Yet it isn't urgent. Nothing is urgent, except this. She has asked me to call her at once, but how can I do that?

She tells me what I knew to be the case all along. She tells me *Idol Dreams*, as I have rewritten it, is the best I have ever done, and of course it is, because it is real.

Except the ending is wrong! In my ending Rudy is not in hospital. Frances wants me to call her. But I cannot. I cannot. I cannot. I cannot lie here in this hot and noisy room a moment longer. I am leaving now and, somehow, I shall find a way to reach him. I cannot wait. I cannot be refused. I will not be turned back again. It is impossible. I cannot. I cannot.

Because Rudy is—

And I have to go. I simply have to go to him now.

350

1925

HOLLYWOOD

What happened next? What happened after I left that door swinging open and I never saw Perry again? He didn't come after the money. He might have tried as hard as he liked but I'd spent it. What other choice did I have?

Phoebe had been through it all before, of course. That was how she knew what to do, whom to see, what to expect. She and Lorna took the day off work and accompanied me to the place. Then they came in the evening, in their new auto, to drive me home again. Afterwards, when days had passed, and weeks—I think—and I didn't stop bleeding and I wouldn't eat and I couldn't get up, they told me they had been convinced I was trying to die. Perhaps I was, too.

So I slept, and bled, and stared at the ceiling. Phoebe and Lorna set me up in a spare room in their new apartment—they had done very well in the months since I had last seen them. It was on a spanking new block just off Franklin, filled with people as elegant as they were—actors and actresses on their way up. Beautiful, young people, full of hope and light. The apartment had—still has—its own little private garden out front, with its own little fountain.

I lay in that room for a long time before I found my voice again. Like Papa, I sometimes think: limp, half dead already, just as he had been, looking at the shade on the overhead electric light.

I could gaze for hours at the dots in the ceiling, with nothing on my mind; only a dull, deep longing for nothingness.

And they left me to that, my beautiful, kind friends. They allowed me to grieve somehow, though I don't remember how; and they made sure I didn't slip away from them for ever—just as I should have done for my father, but never did. And as I should have done for my unborn baby. But never did.

*　　　*　　　*

I turned up—gosh, it must have been five or so in the morning by the time I arrived at their gate—dragging Perry's suitcase behind me. It was already beginning to get light and it occurred to me that if the twins were working that day they might already have been up and gone.

There was a single bell for the front door, with a sign beside it: 'BELL OUT OF ORDER'. Beyond it, through the glass, I could see a porter's desk—deserted. I knocked loudly, just in case, but no one came.

Finally, utterly exhausted, I folded into a defeated heap by the edge of the fountain, rested my head on my knees and waited, listening to the soothing sound of the trickling water, the sound of my own breathing. I heard the footsteps just as I was sliding into sleep, *clippety-clip*, full of vigour; they were slightly deafening to me, in their clear sense of direction. I glanced up, saw the little feet, in their little shoes. Nice shoes. They stopped dead just before me. I heard the voice from above my head. She sounded shriller than usual: *'Well! Just look what the cat's brought in!'*

I didn't reply. Didn't even look up. I could tell from her tone how angry she was. Then, in a swoop, she crouched down beside me. Put a hand on my shoulder, and I began to sob.

'Threw you out, did he?' she said. 'Well, honey, you lasted longer than we expected. Ask Lorna. Just a couple of days ago, she said, "That little Lola must be quite the she-devil in the sack!" It's what she said, honey. 'Cause, so far as I know, you lasted a lot longer than any of the other girls ever did . . .'

'I saw him,' I said at last.

'You saw him? Doing what? What was he doing, Lola? Sweetie? What did you see?'

'She was going to introduce me. She said it. She said, "I want you to meet my good friend"—and he was there. He would have remembered. He would have . . .'

'Who, Lola? You're not making the slightest sense. Who's— OH! . . . Oh, *Lola* . . .'

'But then Perry pulled me away. Like he did last time only this time *it was him.* And he hid the letters. Perry hid the letters . . .'

'Which letters?' She leaned a little closer. 'Sweetie, which letters?'

'Your letter . . .'

'Oh.' She sounded disappointed. 'Well, that's all right, isn't it? You found us now. I thought you meant . . .'

'And other letters. Not from Rudy. I don't think so. I didn't find any . . . But two from Frances Marion.'

'. . . Frances—Frances Marion? She wrote, finally? Lola! What did she say? Lola, that's

353

terrific news. That's so exciting! What did she say?'

I fumbled in my evening bag, couldn't find anything through the tears. I tipped the full contents out onto the grass between us.

'Hey, hey, hey . . .' Phoebe said, plucking out the bandaged wad of dollars. 'What's this?'

'Oh . . .' I wiped my eyes. I had forgotten about the dollars. 'They're not mine, Phoebe. Only there was so much . . . and I hadn't anything saved, except a hundred and fifty dollars—and, apart from you and Lorna, and I know you're angry with me, and you have every right to be, I had nowhere to go.' Phoebe looked at me, I thought, with distaste. I began to feel quite frantic. 'And I don't suppose he'll even notice . . . In any case—I wasn't going to take it . . . but then after I saw the letters—I thought . . . Oh, God—well, if he'd given me the letters, I might have been in a position to earn the money for myself. Please, Phoebe. Don't be angry! Please don't tell him.'

'Are you crazy?'

'No . . .'

'Why would I tell him? The guy's a piece of crap. Jesus, you earned it, honey! I'm just sorry we ever brought him home with us that night. I should have known better. I *did* know better. But he was so damn insistent . . . in that charming way of his. Lola, if you knew how sorry I was. And Lorna. Both of us—we are so sorry . . .'

I tried to laugh. 'Nobody held a knife to my throat,' I said. Abruptly, I shoved the letters towards her. She took them and read them, and as she did so I watched her face, not changing in the least, and I wondered whether perhaps, in my madness and exhaustion, I had simply imagined

354

what was written inside them. Perhaps the letters weren't anything except letters—to Perry. From one of his jailbird friends . . . Or from one of his lovers . . .

She laid down the two letters and she hugged me—a warmer, sweeter, more welcome hug I could never have asked for. It was all I could do not to melt into tears all over again.

When she pulled away there were tears in her eyes too. 'How about that, Lola Nightingale?' she said. 'All that hard work of yours, all those late nights, sweating over your notebooks—they're finally going to pay off. Never mind the men, honey. You're going to be just fine.'

*   *   *

Except, of course, then I discovered I was pregnant, so I wasn't just fine. Not for a while. But those girls, my two wonderful friends, they nursed me through it. And finally, the instant I was strong enough to sit up and string a sentence together, they put me in front of the telephone, and they stood over me, and they wouldn't leave until I made the call.

'I've been sick,' I said to the assistant, when she picked up the telephone. My voice was shaking. 'Miss Marion probably won't remember me, anyway . . .' Lorna gave my shin a kick. 'I mean to say, she might remember me. She very, very kindly wrote to me—twice, actually. I gave her a couple of my photoplays, and she seemed to imply [another kick from Lorna]—that is, she was very enthusiastic about them. I would have contacted her at once, but the letters— It's a long story, but the letters didn't reach me until very recently. And now that I have them, it's as if my dreams had come—'

There was a click on the other end of the line. And then another voice. One I recognised at once.

'Lola Nightingale?' I could hear her smiling. 'Could it be . . . the elusive Miss Nightingale?'

'Why, yes—'

'We speak at last! It's wonderful to hear from you!'

'Oh!' I said. 'Oh! Miss Marion. If you knew—'

'What are you up to?'

'What? Now? In life? I'm not sure—'

'I mean this morning. What are you up to in the next half-hour or so?'

'Well, I—' Actually, it was nine o'clock in the morning, and I wasn't even dressed. 'I'm. Nothing. Strictly speaking. I'm doing nothing at all.'

'Neither am I. It so happens I just finished a piece of work last night, and I have nothing to do all morning. Except talk to you, if I'm lucky. I'm at Silverman Pictures currently—I'm just on my way in. Why don't you come by? Do you know where it is?'

Of course I did! Silverman Studios had produced two of the biggest box-office hits that year. 'I do,' I said. 'I certainly do! Poverty Row. Right beside Columbia, isn't it? But shall they—will they let me in?'

'I'll put your name at the gate. We can get some coffee. And there's a bunch of people I'd like you to meet. With a bit of luck, we'll be able to get you working right away.'

And that was how it happened. Phoebe and Lorna cajoled me into a chemise dress, lilac silk, bought for me by Perry. Pre-illness it had used to make me look quite chic, or so I believed. Now it hung off me. I looked pale and scrawny. But of all the many clothes I had brought with me, all far too big now, it was decreed to be the least unflattering among them.

'Everything else makes you look like a six-year-old,' Lorna complained. 'Lola Nightingale, it's a beautiful thing, in this town, to have a body like a ten-year-old boy. And we all know it. But you've taken the thing too far. Now you've got to fatten yourself up!'

'You're hardly so big yourself,' I said. The difference was, of course, as we all knew, she looked wonderful. They both did, in their fabulous new clothes, with their ultra-short bobs, razor-cut up the back. In the months I'd spent sitting alone in that apartment, their acting careers had certainly accelerated. Extra girls no longer, they were on the brink of being names in their own right. Hence the motor-car, albeit shared. Hence the beautiful, ultra-modern apartment—with a room to spare for their idiotic friend. Hence the fact they seemed to grow more beautiful every day.

*   *   *

They dropped me off at the Silverman gates, and I was led straight up to Miss Marion's office. She was working—temporarily, she was keen to remind me (Miss Marion never signs exclusively to any studio)—on the first floor of the main block, just a couple of doors up from Samuel Silverman himself. It was a nice office, with windows thrown wide open onto the busy back lot below. She was on the telephone when I arrived.

As she finished up her conversation I gazed happily out of the window onto the usual chaotic scene: I watched the Silverman porters, in their uniforms, and the Silverman office workers in their smart office shoes, strutting heedlessly between a large, unruly cow herd. I watched the gaggle of young extra girls, dressed as milkmaids, following the cows, and screaming each time a beast so much as turned its head towards them and, weaving between them all, a small army of carpenters, labouring beneath the bulk of a fifty-foot panel, done up to look like the interior of some sort of palatial ballroom. With all the commotion, and the cows and the screaming, they were struggling to keep the thing aloft.

A sight for sore eyes, it was to me! It had been many months since last I'd been anywhere near a studio and—honestly—the activity, the excitement, the inconsequential hotchpotch of it all made me feel like I was home. I sighed, a sigh of pure contentment, just as Miss Marion finished her call and came to stand behind me.

'You see that big handsome man in the greatcoat?' said she, following the direction of my gaze. 'The guy carrying the circus whip?' (I nodded. It was hard to miss him.) 'That's Ronald Colman. He's a fine actor,' she said. 'I have him in mind for my next picture. Tell me—Lola. Did you ever read the novel *Stella Dallas?* I'm convinced it would make an excellent picture. With a few changes. What do you think?'

'I have read it. Yes,' I said.

She looked at me. 'And?'

'And . . .' I stumbled. It seemed unfeasible that

the great Frances Marion should be asking my opinion on the matter.

'You mustn't be afraid to share your thoughts with me, Lola.' She laughed. 'It *is* Lola, isn't it? Lola Nightingale?'

'Yes, yes. Of course it is! Lola Nightingale! Thank you for seeing me. I can't begin to tell you what an honour it is . . .'

She smiled. 'Without an opinion on these matters, we writers would be utterly lost.'

We writers indeed! I managed not to smirk.

'Tell me. What do you think? Have you ever seen Mr Colman perform?'

'I have. I think he's a fine actor too. I think he would be excellent in the part of Stephen . . . But I wonder,' I couldn't prevent myself adding, 'have you perhaps considered . . .' and I blushed so hard I could feel every strand of hair on my head rising up in protest '. . . have you considered perhaps using Rudolph Valentino?'

She laughed. 'Ah! Rudy! Now wouldn't *that* be something? Unfortunately we simply can't afford him.' She stopped. 'But you're so thin!' she said suddenly. 'Were you so thin before? I don't believe so.'

'I've been rather sick.'

'Well, then. Well. I would have liked to introduce you to Mr Silverman. He's not an easy man—you probably heard. But he takes an interest in his writers. More so than any other producer I ever worked for. Which isn't, frankly, saying a great deal. But he's respectful. In his own particular badly mannered way. He's respectful of good work. And he approves of lady writers.' She smiled, a funny, enigmatic smile, as if, despite the gulf of

359

difference—her great stature and extraordinary achievements against my utter nothingness—there was a link between us in this world that belongs to the men . . . 'Anyway, it's too bad. He's not in today. You shall have to meet him some other time.'

'Oh!' I said. *Oh.*

'So I'm going to take you to the cafeteria instead, Lola. And who knows *whom* we shall meet in there?' She laughed. 'And I shall buy you some coffee and a very large bun. And you must promise me to eat the wretched bun . . .'

She led the way, small and elegant, walking with quick, efficient steps up and down stairs and along a maze of inexplicable corridors. As we whisked on by, deeper and deeper into that confusing building, she threw cursory pieces of information over her shoulder: 'That's the dreaded "vault", Lola, where we sit in misery and darkness to watch the rushes, and Mr Silverman is horrid to all of us, no matter what we show him, and all the actresses are reduced to tears. . . . Costumes in there! Oh, that room just goes on for miles. Step inside and you'll be lucky to come out before Christmas . . . Writing cubicles for contract scenarioists . . .That'll be you, Lola, one day! Enjoy the daylight while you can!'

We reached the cafeteria eventually. Heaven knows by what circuitous route. It was open to all who worked or performed at the studio—bar the extras, of course. And it was nothing much, noisy and functional—not very different from the extras' cafeterias I was used to, except in here the long tables were covered with decorative cloths, and sitting at them, all jumbled together, set designers ate beside carpenters, ate beside producers, ate beside writers and directors and actors—some of them very well known, some of them in full screen paint and costume, fresh from their sets. There was a handful of cowboys (isn't there always?) and two women in eighteenth-century evening dress and an Indian in a long dark wig and bear fur . . .

It took an age to work our way across to our places because the cafeteria was so full. By the time we were finally seated—me with my very large currant bun, Miss Marion with her cup of black coffee—I had been formally introduced to at least fifty people. Among them was a newly signed director from England, named Oliver King. Miss Marion paused to welcome him to the studio. She told him how much she had enjoyed his last picture—which picture, I must admit (and I always followed these things closely), I had never heard anything of. She said to him, 'And this is Miss Nightingale, a budding young scenarioist. Mr Silverman is quite determined to keep her here in the fold, at least in some sort of capacity, before she's snatched up by one of the other studios . . .'

'Uh-huh,' said Oliver King, chewing sullenly on his breadstick. Not in the least interested.

'Mr Silverman's secretary mentioned to me this morning that you might be looking for a secretarial assistant.'

He looked even less interested, if it were possible, and even more sullen, but confirmed that it was the case.

'Well, then, I have found you just the one! She's a fine stenographer—' Miss Marion stopped, frowning slightly, and turned to me. 'Aren't you, Lola?'

I confirmed that I was.

'And when she's not typing, you can give her all the scenarios that come in and she can read them and make her reports, and she can scout out novels for you to acquire, and generally make herself extraordinarily useful . . . What do you say?'

He looked positively annoyed. He scowled at me, shuffled about in his seat. He looked on the point of saying no.

I said, 'Mr King, I have been an assistant before—in a lawyers' office, and in a doctor's surgery. I'm really very—very . . .' What? Suddenly I couldn't think. I looked down at the currant bun. Hungry, actually. Ravenously hungry, suddenly, for the first time in many weeks. 'Well, I'm very . . .'

'Much in demand,' Miss Marion finished for me. I could have hugged her. 'So, Mr King, grab her while you can! Because I assure you, within half an hour of sitting in this cafeteria, she shall have found herself employment with someone. Trust me. It's now or never . . .'

He took a long, cool slurp from his water glass, scowled at me one more time, for good measure, and didn't seem to find anything in my appearance to lift his foul mood. Nor, apparently, to displease him sufficiently either, because finally he nodded.

'Very well,' he said. 'I shall be in my office from about two onwards. It's on the same hallway as Miss Marion's. No doubt one of the secretaries will be able to direct you . . .'

Miss Marion winked at me as we walked away. 'He's a *dreadful* man,' she whispered. 'A terrible bully, and quite talentless, in my opinion. I should be surprised if he lasts beyond his first picture here—if he lasts that long! But never mind. You have a foot in the door now, don't you, dear? Now it's up to you.'

And so it was. We drank our coffee. I ate my bun. Miss Marion asked me a little about my background. I told her I had grown up in London, and she seemed to be quite interested in that. She reiterated how much she had enjoyed my scenarios, but when I pressed her on what I might do with them next, or what action I should take, she only added vaguely, 'Yes, there is promise, without doubt . . .'

Finally, and for the first time since I had arrived, she fixed me with her, clear, blue clever eyes. She leaned forward. 'Nevertheless, Lola, you have some way to go. I suggest you use this time to read as many other people's scenarios as you can get your hands on and particularly any that have been—or are being—turned into pictures. When you are working for Mr King, try to spend as much time as he will allow you on the sets, so that you can get a true understanding of what it is to make a film. Watch as many movies as you can: *watch,* and see the tricks available to the director—there are new ones all the time, and it's vital to keep up. Make a note of how each new trick of the camera will allow him to find new, fresh ways to tell his story. Look out for devices other photodramatists employ. Most of all, Lola, get yourself known around the studio. You're a pretty girl. It helps. Ingratiate yourself with the script editors, and the directors, and the actors—you need to have them all on your side.

'And above all, Lola, more than anything else, *keep writing.* Whole photoplays, with continuity, by all means—but scenarios too. Give them to Damian Cook, over there, whom I just now introduced you to—and if he says he likes them, offer to write the continuity . . . That's where the real money is . . . It's hard work, Lola. And tough. Competitive. Especially for a lady. But it's wonderful, too. Even now . . .' she paused '. . . after however many pictures, it is hard to describe the thrill of seeing your work brought to life up there on the big screen.'

She fell silent. I longed to ask her so much—about herself, about the movies—but some wretched English reticence prevented me asking anything at all, for fear it might seem impertinent. What a waste! In any case, as a result of that, and my general awestruck shyness, I think she grew rather bored with me. Shortly after that long speech she drank back her coffee and stood up.

'It's been a pleasure to meet you, Lola. And I would like to keep reading your work, so be sure to keep showing it to me, won't you?'

I assured her I would.

'No doubt before long we shall see your name up in lights . . . I'm quite sure we shall. Good luck!'

She was gone before I had time to thank her.

*   *   *

I found my way to Mr King's room without much difficulty. He didn't ask me any questions. He simply offered the job (with a starting salary of $46 a week). Then he directed me, one door along, to the outer office, where there were two desks, one of which he said, was to be mine.

At the other sat a woman of fifty, perhaps a little older. She had a face like a giant powder puff, and half hidden somewhere in the midst of it, a pallid

364

pair of eyes and the sourest set of lips I had ever laid sight on.

'Tell her what's involved, would you, Jean?' he shouted across to her, from his own desk in the other room. 'She's to start on Monday.'

Jean looked me up and down. 'I hope you're healthier than you look,' she said, 'we can't afford a girl taking days to be sick all the time.'

It was the beginning of a friendship that never did take root, despite all the long hours we have spent together.

She gave me a begrudging tour. Our office, I learned, was quite at the hub of things. As well as the door to the hallway, there were four other doors, each one leading to a separate director's office. Our office, and its four adjoining offices were sandwiched between the outer office, which led on to Mr Silverman's, and, on the other side, a similar hub-like arrangement, where hired producers and their secretaries worked.

My duties, she explained, like her own, were to look after the needs not only of Mr King but of the various other directors who came and went. Back then, when I joined, two of the four offices were empty and there was only one other director to attend to. Today, Mr King is long gone, just as Miss Marion prophesied. But now all four offices are in use and, between them, we have three different movies due to go into production before the autumn. Really, it must be one of the busiest offices in Hollywood.

*   *   *

I didn't see Miss Marion again. That is to say—I

365

would glimpse her in the hallway from time to time, but nothing more than that. She always smiled when she saw me, always with a slightly glazed expression. Sometimes, she would say, 'Ooh, Lola. Very much enjoyed the last . . . think you're getting better!' Sometimes: 'Thought the ending of that one was rather weak.' But always it was in passing, on the move. She would never say any more, or ever give any sign that I might approach her for further advice. I wondered, sometimes, what was the point, since nothing ever seemed to come of her encouragement. But I did keep writing, rewriting, posting each new draft into the cubbyhole outside her office door. And then, perhaps once a month (against Jean's instructions), I would slip some new piece of work onto the desk of one of my directors, and sometimes, in the cafeteria, I would hand one to the assistant of a big star, with a plea that they pass it on.

The months passed, nothing changed: I moved officially into the spare room at the twins' apartment, and began to pay a decent rent. They were very welcoming, and it was almost like old times again. Better, in a way, because I enjoyed my job. And yet, in spite of living and working so much at the heart of the industry, still it felt as if I was dropping my precious work into the same deep, dark hole. Nobody—not the script editors, not the stars, not the directors, not one of them—even registered receipt of the damn things, let alone suggested they do anything further with them.

It seems extraordinary to think how long I persevered. And yet somehow I couldn't stop. If I did—if I stopped writing for too long—my fingers would start to itch, and my thoughts would clog, and I would quickly become despairing. So I continued. Sometimes I look on my need to write things down as an affliction of the mind, but then, on the other hand, I suppose if I am proud of anything in my life, I am proud that I have kept on writing. I do not give up easily. Not when something matters to me so much.

The job at Silverman Studio was—it remains, since I am still employed by them—the best job I have ever had. I loved it from the first, and that was in spite of Jean and Mr King, and all the other childish, egotistical directors who came strutting through our office doors. It is wonderful to work in a world that utterly absorbs you. I am very lucky.

*　　　*　　　*

And I must remember it. I must remember it, no matter what happens to me now, no matter what happened to me before today and no matter what will happen tomorrow; and even though I cannot speak to Rudy, and even though I am sitting here—crouching here, writing this—in this dreadful, humiliating place, surrounded by the stench of old urine and stale sex and filthy, stinking sweat, and I am condemned to remain here, with the police guard at the door, until— God knows when: somebody stands bail for me and I am finally released from here, I must remember that in a million ways I am one of the luckiest women alive.

Because one day all this will be over and I shall return to California, with Rudy, and I shall have everything I ever dreamed of, but never deserved. I am homesick. I miss the twins. I miss my bed. I miss my desk. I miss Jean's sour face, glowering across to me. I miss my old, safe, beautiful life . . . It's the smell in here, I think. I could bear it otherwise. And there is a woman behind me, giving me the evil eye. She has noticed my silk chemise, and that my shoes are good, and I suppose she is wondering what in hell I am doing in here. As well she might. I wonder myself . . .

She is making me a little afraid. But it's not important. I shall pretend my darnedest I haven't noticed—though she's— Oh—

She's coming over. She's addressing me. She's asking me . . . where I came by my beautiful hat!

It doesn't fit on her big fat head, and it happens I came by it at very great expense only yesterday. But she has mean little eyes, and I have given it to her. And now I wish she would leave me—I still have so much to write . . .

*   *   *

Of course, there were big stars coming in and out of the studio all the time and I quickly became rather blasé about all that. They used to sweep up past our desks on their way in and out to see Mr Silverman or the directors, and they were generally well mannered. Clara Bow came in once. I hadn't been in the job for long and I hadn't learned the etiquette, so I leaped up from behind my desk and greeted her like an old friend.

'Miss Bow!' I cried. 'It's good to see you again.'

She started, rather as if she'd seen a mouse. 'Hello, dear,' she said slowly. It was obvious—and she made no attempt to hide it—she had not the faintest idea who I was, nor any great interest in finding out. She began to walk on.

'Do you remember?' I said. 'We were at the Cocoanut Grove.'

'When ain't we, sweetie?'

'We were having dinner.'

'Ain't thinning the field so great.'

'I was with a gentleman named . . .' I remembered the bundle of dollars I had stolen and thought better of mentioning him. 'And then you were on the point of introducing me to—you were so kind, you were going to introduce me to Mr Valentino . . . Don't you remember?'

'Lola . . .' I heard Jean's warning voice from behind me. I ignored it.

Miss Bow glanced at Jean, then back to me. 'Sure I remember,' she said blandly. 'It was a great evening. Well. See ya! Give him my regards.'

Stars—most of them: they aren't like the rest of us. After that I learned not to expect anything from them at all.

*   *   *

Of course, there are stars and more stars; there are 'heart throbs' and there are superstars; there are American sweethearts . . .

And then there is Rudolph Valentino.

He had returned from his dance tour and a long journey through Europe, amid rumours I couldn't help but rejoice at: that his marriage to the dreaded Natacha was all but over. It was public knowledge that he had at last settled his contract disagreement with Famous Players-Lasky and

369

fulfilled his obligations to Ritz Carlton. He was home, free to work again, and being wooed by just about every studio in Hollywood. Everybody wanted him.

So it was that Mr Silverman's secretary, Margaret, informed us, in a memorandum to the entire staff, that Mr Valentino and his new manager Mr Ullman would shortly be paying us a visit. The memorandum requested that we all make it our 'personal responsibility' to ensure Mr Valentino and his party be made to feel as welcome as possible. And it soon became clear that Mr Silverman meant business.

First the studio's set decorators were ordered off their sets to give our hallway and offices a fresh lick of paint; next, those of us who worked on the same floor as Mr Silverman were delivered ultra-modern-looking new desks with matching chairs, and desk lights. Pot plants were placed at all the windows. Drapes in the colours of the Italian flag were hung at our normally bare windows. A new carpet was laid in the corridor and a pair of glass doors with large, gold-plated handles was installed in the front hall. For at least a fortnight before the great arrival, Silverman studios (and in particular our floor, where the great meeting was due to take place) was in a state of quivering hysteria.

It was nothing to match mine, of course. I was unable to sleep, or eat, or drink, or to think of anything else.

Would he recognise me? Would he even get a chance to recognise me? Or would he be whisked past our freshly painted offices, our snazzy new matching chairs and desks, directly into Mr Silverman's office, without time for so much as a

370

glance to left or to right?

The possibility tormented me. In the evenings, alone with the twins, I could speak of nothing else.

Night after night, we discussed what I might wear, how I should arrange my hair, what I would say if he happened to glance my way, what I would say if he happened *not* to glance my way. We envisaged every scenario, imagined a thousand pretexts, devised a million ways of saying: *Hello, Rudy. Remember me?*

Nothing sounded right. Or even believable. Somehow, after so long, it seemed impossible that we should even meet. And yet, with Phoebe and Lorna's encouragement, and my own feverish imagination, I began to dream of our reunion, picture the moment, frame by frame, when first he would glimpse me, throw his arms about me and lift me into the air . . .

Close-up . . . as . . . RUDOLPH VALENTINO and LOLA NIGHTINGALE's lips move together for tender kiss . . . *Dissolve to credits.*

'This could be the moment,' Lorna said very seriously one night. 'Are you sure you're ready?'

I was, I said, laughing. Just about as ready as a girl ever could be.

'Because it's perfect. It's perfect timing. *And* you're looking beautiful again,' she said. '*And* that dreadful wife is finally off the scene. Lola, this could be the moment you've been waiting for all these years,' she said.

*　　　*　　　*

The day arrived. I had been to the salon, of course, and restyled my hair in the ultra-modern fashion:

shingled at the back and with a sleek permanent wave at the front. I wore a white flannel suit with silver buttons, bought especially for the occasion, and white shoes with silver straps and—though I say it myself—the new suit flattered me: camouflaged a little of the scrawniness, brought out the green in my eyes and the peroxide blonde in my hair. Or I believed it did. At any rate, I felt pretty good. If Rudy happened to glance in my direction I believed he would be pleased by what he saw.

Phoebe wasn't working that morning. She dropped me off in the car. 'Now go get him.' She giggled. 'Mrs Rudolph Valentino Number Three!' I groaned. And she sped away through the dust, cackling merrily.

I wandered the building for a full twenty minutes before I could even remember where my office was. When I sat down at my desk and Jean offered up her customary 'Good morning, Lola. You are rather late,' I discovered that all I could do was to nod. Not that she noticed. But for a moment or two my nerves had robbed me of my voice entirely.

'And by the way it may be a Red Letter Day for the studio,' Jean clucked, 'but we still have work to do. Last I checked this was "Not Quite the Rudolph Valentino Film Studio".' She tittered, pleased with her little joke. "Not Quite the Rudolph Valentino Film Studio," she said it again. 'At least, not yet. We still have plenty of other stars to worry about and it's no good everyone thinking . . .'

. . . So began another day.

*   *   *

His Pierce Arrow drew up in front of the building at noon, sharp. We were lucky. Our office window looked out almost directly above the new glass gold-plated doors, and though Jean tutted and grumbled, even she could not prevent herself waddling over to peer as he and Mr Ullman climbed from their auto into the bright sun.

Our window was open. We heard their voices . . . polite greetings, well-mannered laughter . . . Rudolph Valentino smiled. Every inch the movie star. Mr Silverman grimaced and guffawed. Mrs Silverman writhed and fluttered. Minutes ticked by . . . What were they doing out there? Why didn't they come on in?

Just then a second car appeared on the driveway. A white Rolls-Royce. The four of them looked on as it drew up before them. The movie star stepped towards it; the chauffeur moved faster—leaped out from his driving seat, shimmied past Rudy and held open the car door. They waited. We all waited. It felt like a long time.

Finally there emerged . . . Mrs Valentino. She wore a gold turban and a fur boa of pure white, and I watched with utter wretchedness as she held out her smooth cheek for a kiss from her husband. My Rudy.

'But they are apart!' I cried.

'Sssh!' ordered Joan. 'Apparently not.'

'But they are apart! Everybody knows it!'

'Be quiet! What is the matter with you?'

They didn't seem to hear me anyway. Mrs Valentino offered a limp hand to the Silvermans. Finally somebody opened the double doors from

373

inside the hall and, together, the party of five disappeared into the building.

We returned to our desks. Mr Silverman and his guests would be coming directly to his office on the first floor. They would travel via the elevator at the end of our hallway, which meant, of course, that it would be impossible for them to reach Mr Silverman's office without first passing by our door.

It was to be my moment. Perhaps my solitary chance. I needed to be sure to do something—anything—to persuade him to look my way.

There . . . was the clank of the elevator door . . .

And the elevator grate being pulled open . . .

And the elevator grate being pulled back . . .

And the sound of voices: a man's voice I didn't recognise—it had to be Mr Ullman's, and then a warm, deep laugh, which I could never forget.

. . .I have missed you—your beautiful face, your courage, your humour, your spirit. I have missed you, darling, more than I can ever express . . .

Jean said something. I looked at her. Mouth moving. Stared at her. 'Lola? . . . *Lola?*' She was glaring at me. He was coming up the hall now. I heard his voice—softer, deeper than Mr Ullman's. Asking a question. What did he say? What was he saying? Why did Jean insist on talking so? '. . . LOLA!'

And then Mr Silverman's voice; and a high-pitched wheezy giggle—Mrs Silverman . . . Another laugh and Mr Ullman, *Blah-blah-blah.*

'LOLA, SIT DOWN!'

Jean had crossed the room and pulled me away

374

from the door. Was I standing at the door? I must have been. She pulled at me. I looked away. The voices came closer, and closer still . . .

'. . . very pleasant offices . . .' That was what Rudolph Valentino was saying, at the instant he passed right by our door, and my head was turned away, looking at Jean, yanking infuriatingly on my arm.

They walked on by. I glimpsed Mr Ullman's heel, and then the door to Mr Silverman's outer office opened . . . and it closed. Their voices grew more muffled. Another door opened—the door to Mr Silverman's private office . . . and then that door closed, and even the muffled voices were gone.

And then there was silence.

Jean said, 'Lola Nightingale, what in Heaven's name possessed you?'

I had no idea what she was talking about.

'Are you *trying* to get yourself fired? Because I could name a thousand young ladies who might kill for an opportunity to have this job . . .' I gazed at her. 'I could, you know . . . A thousand at least.'

I didn't react.

'What in Heaven's name is the matter with you, girl? . . .. *Sit down!*'

'Jean, I missed him.'

She stared at me. 'Missed who?'

'Do you suppose they'll come by this way on their way out? Oh, of course they will. But they probably shan't look in. Why would they? Why should they? Oh, dear God, Jean.' I sat. I dropped my head onto my desk, 'What is the point? Dear God . . . *what is the point?*' And I began to sob.

The moment had passed. I had missed it. In my fine suit, and my new hair, with the new ultra-sleek

375

permanent wave and the side parting. And the
simple, short line I had rehearsed—again and
again: *Hello, Rudy—do you remember me? From
The Box?* I would never have a chance to say it. Not
now. Not ever. And all was lost.

Jean said nothing for quite a while. I suppose she
was rather astonished since—up until that point—I
had never once presented her with anything but a
fairly professional front. Finally, she said—in a
voice of wonder, above all, but which I like to think
was at least a little kinder than any I had heard her
use before, 'You were about to walk out into the
hallway, Lola. You were walking into the hallway
. . . If I hadn't pulled you back, Heaven knows what
might have happened. Have you gone stark staring
crazy? Whatever's gotten into you?'

'Nothing,' I said, and continued to sob. When I
looked up some moments later, she was still
staring at me—and I thought I detected a hint of
fear on her face. I said, 'Oh, what does it matter
anyway? . . . I used to know him, years ago. On
Long Island. When he was just a dancer. And I was
just a girl . . .'

*. . . and wherever I go, whatever I do, there will
always be a place in my heart which waits for
you . . .*

She continued to stare. I couldn't be sure if she
believed me or not. Didn't much care either way.
She said, 'You're telling me you used to know Mr
Valentino?'

'He wasn't called Mr Valentino . . . He was only a
dancer . . .'

'Well, then . . .' she said at last. 'Why ever didn't

you say?'

I shrugged.

She couldn't take her eyes off me after that. I glanced at her: a slow blush was creeping from the top of her—new—chemise, up her neck and cheeks, behind the glasses, all the way to her forehead. 'You used to know Mr Valentino?' she said again. 'Well, then . . . Why ever didn't you say?'

I had nothing more to add.

'Well, then,' she said again, one more time. 'You had better go and clean yourself up. Because if he comes back this way he shall see quite clearly that you've been crying. And I don't see how that's going to help.'

'Help—what?' I asked.

It was her turn to shrug. 'It doesn't give a very smart impression. Of the way we run things,' she said.

'He's hardly likely to look.'

'Go and wash your face,' she said. 'And wipe some of that rouge off while you're at it, young lady. You have a little too much paint, I think. For the office.'

*   *   *

It provided me with an excuse to get out of the office and into that hallway. I didn't argue with her. Without another word, I took my purse and left the room. Washed my face, reapplied my rouge and lipstick—I thought perhaps if I lingered long enough I could time my return so that I bumped right into him, just at the instant he would be exiting Mr Silverman's office. I could do that, I thought. If I was clever about it. So long as Jean didn't come after me first. Only there was no telling how long he might be. Ages, probably. Or perhaps Mr Silverman would insist on giving him a tour of the studio before any business was conducted.

Well—so I lingered . . . and I lingered . . . and I lingered a little more. Until I couldn't stand it— what if I missed him? I edged back out into the hallway, closer to that door, the door that led to the office that led to the door that led to the office where I knew Rudy to be; and I stood there, gazing at it, closed tight against me, God knows for how long. It felt like hours, and all the time my heart was beating so hard I could feel it, pinching in my shoes.

I felt horribly conspicuous, tried to hide myself against the wall, but of course that was impossible since the wall was quite flat, and there was nothing in the long, white hallway, which smelled of fresh paint—there was nothing to hide behind. Finally I heard Jean's voice. I glanced up to see her head poking angrily out from our office door.

'Lola!' she said, in a deafening stage whisper. 'Get back here at once!'

And there and then I was faced with a choice. I could do as I was ordered—return to my desk and my excellent job—and kiss goodbye to this one golden opportunity, to the idle dream that possessed me, and I could regret it for the rest of my life. Or I could take a couple of steps forward, put out my hand, open the door just half a yard in front of me, and walk right into that room.

God knows. I had no plan. Nothing. A head filled with nothing and a heart beating so hard I couldn't see straight. I stepped forward, opened the door, and walked in.

'Oh!' Mr Silverman's secretary looked startled, not in the least pleased to see me. She's a nice girl, actually. We get along all right. 'Lola! *What are you doing in here?* You really shouldn't . . .' She glanced nervously at the door leading to Mr Silverman's sanctum. 'Don't you realise—'

And there! At that instant the door to that sanctum burst open wide! Mrs Valentino came first of course, as haughty and beautiful as any woman I ever laid eyes on. And beside her Mrs Silverman, perspiring at the armpits in her too-tight, too-orange silk frock. And then Rudy, his head turned away—saying something to Mr Silverman. And finally Mr Ullman. The three men were heavy in conversation. They stood at the threshold a moment. Margaret, Mr Silverman's secretary—in a panic due to my presence I presume—half rose out of her chair. She reached across to me, standing there frozen. She tugged at my sleeve, pulling to tuck me in behind her desk. I did that. Stood behind her chair, wondering what the line had been that I had rehearsed so often. I knew he would look at me in a second. How could he not? How could he not, when I was standing there before him?

. . .I have missed you—your beautiful face, your courage, your humour, your spirit. I have missed you, darling, more than I can ever express . . .

Well, I cleared my throat. But nobody seemed to hear me. Mr Silverman was saying something about—something. He mentioned Frances

379

Marion, I think. Or do I imagine that? Because Miss Marion came bustling in a second later, bearing a collection of bound folders. She glided across the room, not glancing at Margaret or at me, smiling very warmly, heading directly towards Rudy.

'Ah, Frances!' said Mr Silverman

'Joel,' she said. 'So sorry I'm late. Rudy, darling. *Wonderful* to see you, and looking so well . . . I must say we've missed you, Tom and I. On our mountain walks.' She laughed. 'Tom has a long message for me to give you. Something involving one of your horses, or one of his. Or possibly both. But I think he'd better relay it himself. It's terribly complicated and I don't remember a word of it . . .' They kissed each other affectionately. Then Miss Marion turned to Rudy's wife. 'Natacha,' she said, more coolly. 'Goodness. But what an utterly magnificent bonnet.'

Natacha looked livid. But Rudy gave a small, involuntary laugh. '*Frances!*' he said.

'What?' Miss Marion smiled. 'What have I said? It's a very, very fine bonnet. I'm only sorry you can't recognise it for yourself, Rudy. Rotten husband that you are.'

'Hardly a "bonnet", Frances,' Natacha snapped. 'I don't imagine Monsieur Fortuny would appreciate your use of the word.'

'Pay no attention, darling,' Rudy said to his wife, trying not to smile. 'She's saying it because she's jealous. She could never bring herself to wear anything even an eighth so daring . . . She's too afraid people would laugh at her. And by the way, Frances, may I say your silly new wig looks quite wrong on your tiny head? Also, I can't help noticing, it's completely skew-whiff.' The two of them melted into carefree, childish laughter. Mr and Mrs Silverman and Mr Ullman stood by, meanwhile, all rather nonplussed, and Natacha, beneath her golden turban, looked so disdainful it must only have spurred them on.

'I swear I can see your bald head underneath!' Rudy cried. It wasn't especially funny. Or I don't believe so. But something about Rudy's laughter was always impossibly infectious. He and Frances, patting her head of very decent, natural hair, began laughing so helplessly there were tears in both their eyes. I noticed Margaret laughing just beside me, and then Mrs Silverman, too. And me. Even Mr Silverman cracked a crooked smile . . . And still nobody looked at us. Rudy—utterly preoccupied with his ridiculous joke—seemed to be quite unaware that we were even in the room.

Finally Mr Silverman, discomfited as much by his almost-smile, I shouldn't wonder, as by the childishness of Rudy's humour, attempted to usher the group on. 'We have luncheon waiting for us,' he said. 'Shall we make our way . . . ?'

'Luncheon?' Mrs Valentino snapped. 'Nobody mentioned luncheon. Rudy, you never mentioned lunch . . .' She pulled out her delicate arm and glanced at her delicate watch. The diamonds on the wristband caught the sunlight, reflected onto her hard, beautiful face, and sent a shiver of pure hatred through me. Jealousy, of course. But something else, too. For an instant, that angry, spoilt, beautiful little face looked like no one more than Blanca de Saulles. I gave an involuntary gasp.

Frances Marion heard it. 'Oh! Hello, Lola dear. You look very nice. What are you doing in here?'

381

They all turned then. Mr and Mrs Silverman. Mr Ullman. Margaret. Mrs Valentino. Rudy.

He glanced across at me, still smiling.

I looked at him.

He looked at me. He looked at me, and the smile faltered. I know it did. The smile faltered. He frowned, just a little.

I tried to speak. My lips wouldn't move.

'Ooh, that reminds me,' Frances said. 'I've been rummaging about in the Silverman vaults all week for you, Rudy darling, knowing you were coming. I thought it might be fun . . . And I've brought you a select—a *very* select—collection of the finest scenarios I could find. All utterly perfect for you. And you must promise me to look them over. Will you do that? I must have read fifty thousand of the damn things. And out of all of those I have found you four. Just four. Two of which, I might add, I wrote myself, and have nothing whatsoever to do with Joel, unless he pays me handsomely for them, and in advance . . .' She glanced at Mr Silverman, who tipped his head in good-natured submission. 'In any case,' she went on, 'I'm convinced you're going to adore them all. I wouldn't bother you with them if I didn't. Will you take a peek at them? Will you, darling? Just the moment you can?'

She moved to hand him the bound files, but Mr Ullman stepped forward and took them from her.

'Well, of course I will look at them,' Rudy said. 'Frances, I respect your judgement above almost anyone's, as you well know. I should be delighted. Thank you.'

'Excellent, excellent,' Mr Silverman said, rubbing his hands together. 'Well, come along. We have caviar flown in by aeroplane from Persia this very

382

morning. And all in your honour, Mr Valentino! And Mrs Valentino, of course . . . But I really don't think we should keep it waiting any longer.'

Rudy had long since looked away from me and yet still my lips remained shut. I watched them walk away, across the office floor. Mr Silverman reached for the door. He held it open for his star. And just as Rudy was about to walk through it, he glanced back at me one more time, frowning again. He stopped. And I swear he was about to say something. He leaned a little forward. I swear, if I could only have spoken, if I could only have moved, or nodded, or smiled . . . He looked at me—

But I have changed! I am so much slimmer, and older, and blonder, and a woman now, in any case; I have changed—not just my name, but everything; with my dress to my knees and my hair all shingled and coloured and waved, I am not the English girl he knew all those years ago, but a woman, an American, a modern American woman. What did I expect?

His wife took his arm, muttered something into his ear and they left together, side by side, and our moment, my moment, was gone.

POLICE PRECINCT, NEW YORK

Saturday, 21 August 1926

At the door to the hospital I told the security man I was Jenny. 'Don't you get it?' I yelled at him. 'I'm *Jenny*. I'm *Jenny!*' He didn't get it. So then everything got crazy. I was hysterical. The security guy, Steffen, who missed his chance to take a swing at me last time—well, he finally got his turn. Laid me flat on the sidewalk, he did, and I guess I may have blacked out for a second because, next thing I knew, the cameras were flashing and the crowd was howling, though I couldn't quite tell whether it was in outrage at Steffen, or pleasure at seeing me floored, or just the general euphoria of witnessing a drama . . . and then, somehow, before I even stood up, the police were there. They rolled me over like a sack of meat, put the damn cuffs on my wrists and threw me in back of their van.

So, here I am. I spent last night in the police cell. Me and my black eye. And the funny thing is, it wasn't so bad. I mean to say, it was no worse than another night in the hotel. It doesn't matter much to me where I am, so long as I can't be with Rudy. In any case, after I gave the woman my hat she left me alone—more or less. And then when I made the call to Fat Larry back at the hotel, the policeman in charge seemed to take a fancy to me. He gave me a cigarette, which calmed me down; and before he put me back in the cell I

384

asked him if he would allow me paper and pen, so at least I could write while I was down there. And that was what I did. Write and wait. All night. Scribble and wait. And scribble and wait. For Larry the room clerk—of all the people in the world—to come and get me the hell out of here.

And now my skull throbs more than I can say, and my right eye is too swollen to open. It's Saturday, and I am still here, and I am running low on paper, and my friendly policeman has gone off duty and the new one will hardly even speak to me, so God knows what's to happen next. He's sitting there reading the morning paper and I can see Rudy's name on the front in big letters. But I can't see—however he holds it, I can't see what it says. I just asked him—shouted through the bars—if there was any news on Mr Valentino. That perked him up. He said, 'He's dying, you crazy bitch. Dontcha read the papers?'

So here I am, with a skull that feels like it's cracked in half. And I can do nothing now, but wait. And scribble. And wait.

I told Larry where I hid my cash. Told him to bring it down to the station and pay the damn bail. He said he couldn't come before his shift was over, and he said he didn't know when that would be. 'Maybe tonight, maybe in the morning, maybe not till afternoon . . . Mark ain't feeling so well . . .' Mark being who? I have no idea. The other lobby clerk, I suppose. But what else could I do?

'Couldn't you send the boy down with it?' I said to Larry. 'Casey! Couldn't you send Casey down?'

Larry laughed. 'Send the boy to a police station

385

with a handful of cash?' he said. 'I'll be down as soon as I can.'

And maybe he will, maybe he won't. Maybe he'll take the cash and stay right where he is. But I am not going to let it eat me, this uncertainty. They can't keep me in here for ever. They can't. Can they?

1926

HOLLYWOOD–NEW YORK

He didn't sign with us after all, of course. Despite all that fresh paint and caviar, he signed with Joe Schenk at United Artists, just as everyone, in their hearts, had always known he should and would. The contract he signed, thanks to Mr Ullman (I should love him for this if for nothing else), expressly forbade his hateful, meddlesome wife from being present on set at any point before, during or after filming. So I wasn't the only person who detested the sight of her. Truth be told, everybody did.

As a sweetener to his wife, Rudy had insisted that she be given a film of her own to produce and star in. And I have to report that that particular piece of pretentious nonsense—*What Price Beauty?*—came and sank without anybody noticing it one way or the other. I went to see it with Lorna, one idle Saturday afternoon. We were the only people in the theatre.

I suppose Rudy's deal with United put the final nail into the coffin of their marriage. She went off to Europe shortly afterwards: her royal tour of Silverman Studios, in that wonderful bonnet, was one of her last official appearances as Mrs Rudolph Valentino. Nobody was terribly shocked to hear the marriage had come to an end.

But I don't want to dwell on it. Gossip and tittle-tattle. When I think of Natacha Rambova, the second Mrs Valentino, I can only think of Mrs de Saulles, a little taller and with a golden turban on her head. Both of them were among the most poisonous women in the world—and Rudy bedded them both. But then—to quote Miss Clara Bow—it ain't thinning the field so great. Rudy does a lot of bedding.

He signed with United Artists and almost at once, or very shortly afterwards, he disappeared into the desert to shoot *Son of the Sheik* (written by Frances Marion, it so happens. I understand she was offered such a vast fortune to write it, and Rudy to star in it, that neither could resist). I think Mr Silverman was quite annoyed about that, after all the trouble he took. But there—Miss Marion has such power in this town she can do just about whatever she likes.

In any case there was quite a dull feeling about the studio for a while afterwards. The smell of fresh paint stuck in people's nostrils—especially Mr Silverman's, I should think. Everyone felt a little foolish.

Though not half so foolish as I felt. The moment he turned away from me that day, something inside me surrendered. I can't think of any other way to put it. It was as if I aged fifty years, right there on the spot. As soon as we were left alone, Mr Silverman's secretary asked me what had compelled me to barge into the office 'at a time like this?' and I said, 'Oh nothing very much . . .'

And I wandered back to my desk, one foot in front of the other. Jean delivered a reproachful lecture about girls-like-me remembering my place. I typed the letters I was supposed to type, delivered the tea I was told to deliver, packaged up the photoplays other people had written and sent them wherever I was told I should. And I went home, and I related to Phoebe and Lorna all that had happened during the day, and after that I didn't mention his name again. Nor did they.

*   *   *

One foot in front of the other. Several weeks passed. A month. Maybe even two. They passed very slowly. I returned, yet again, to *Idol Dreams*, rewriting it, this time, as if to rewrite my memory of our friendship. It was a bitter draft, and I am glad I never showed it to anyone. But I was angry with myself, and with Rudy, too, for failing to live up to my dreams. And I was tired. Tired, tired, tired—tired of everything; tired of trying; tired of loving; tired of hoping; tired of being such a fool. And so the days passed. Another and then another, and they were all much the same, only each was a little greyer than the previous one.

Phoebe and Lorna, I tried my best to avoid. I cooked for them sometimes, in a feeble effort to please or to make my dull presence in their sparkling, generous lives at least a little less of a terrible drag . . . Not that they ever said a word of reproach. Not one.

Other than that I lay low, cranked my thin face

388

into a smile when they entered the room, and slunk away as quickly as was politely possible thereafter. They had heard more than enough of my problems and, though I believed they would have helped had I asked them—had I the faintest idea how to be helped—I was determined not to bother them any more.

*   *   *

And then there came . . . one bright sunny morning just exactly three weeks ago.

There we were, Jean and I, sitting opposite one another, working away in our usual silence . . . and in walked William from the post room. He smiled at me. He always does. He said, 'Two wires for you, Miss Nightingale.'

Jean put out a hand to receive them.

'They're for Miss Nightingale,' he said.

'All wires come to me first, William. You know that.'

He hesitated. Looked from the envelopes, to me, to Jean, shrugged, and handed them to Jean. She opened them right there in front of me. First one. And then the next.

I watched the familiar flush creep slowly from chest, to neck, to ears and cheeks and forehead. I saw her mouth tighten. She removed her spectacles and wiped her eyes. Replaced the spectacles; shot me an irritable glance.

'You're not supposed to receive personal correspondence here at the office,' she said. 'I thought you understood that, Lola.'

'But I can't help it if people send me things, can I?'

'It's not really the point.'

'In any case, if they're personal, you had better pass them over.'

'I shall give them to you,' she said, folding them and putting them away in the drawer of her desk, 'when you leave this evening. Otherwise,' and I do believe she smiled at that point, 'there'll be no sense out of you all day. Have you finished the letter for Mr Dryden? It needs to go before luncheon. Do hurry up.'

It was another half an hour before she needed to go to the bathroom, and the silly woman forgot to take the telegrams with her. I hurried across the room the moment she stepped into the hallway.

LOLA NIGHTINGALE
SILVERMAN STUDIOS

DARLING GIRL CONGRATULATIONS ADORE MALICIOUS INTENT STOP AM HOLED UP IN FLORIDA BUT RETURN ALGONQUIN NEW YORK 14 AUGUST STOP SUGGEST ACT IMMEDIATELY REGARDING WICKED PLEASURES STOP GOOD LUCK SO HAPPY TO BE PROVED RIGHT STOP SEE YOU IN NEW YORK

FRANCES MARION

That was the first wire. Numbly I turned to the second:

LOLA NIGHTINGALE
SILVERMAN STUDIOS

MR RUDOLPH VALENTINO HAS ASKED ME TO CONVEY TO YOU HIS GREAT ADMIRATION FOR YOUR SCENARIO

390

WICKED PLEASURES WHICH HE IS KEEN TO DISCUSS
WITH YOU AT YOUR EARLIEST CONVENIENCE STOP MR
VALENTINO STRESSES HIS ENTHUSIASM AND URGENCY
THEREFORE TAKEN LIBERTY OF BOOKING YOU ONTO
TRAIN LEAVING MIDNIGHT 7 AUGUST LOS ANGELES
NEW YORK STOP A ROOM IN YOUR NAME IS BOOKED AT
HOTEL CONTINENTAL, BROADWAY AND 41ST STOP
ANTICIPATING YOUR ARRIVAL 12 AUGUST STOP ALL
EXPENSES BILLED TO MR VALENTINO'S OFFICE STOP
SUGGEST TELEPHONING MYSELF HERE AT AMBASSAD
OR HOTEL ON ARRIVAL STOP CONGRATULATIONS AND
BON VOYAGE STOP GEORGE ULLMAN MANAGER TO
MR VALENTINO

It was eleven thirty on the morning of 7 August.
Three weeks due to leave in less than twelve hours.

I shan't bother to write the details of my
negotiations with Jean, who was furious to
remember that I was owed plenty of leave, and
quite wretched at having to admit that, though the
office was busy, with none of our directors due to
start shooting before October, my request to take
it could not have landed at a better time.

Nor will I write of my own elation, which in any
case cannot be properly conveyed on a sheet of
paper. I remained at my desk for the rest of the
day, though I was utterly incapable of working,
until by five o'clock, Jean's pleasure at waylaying
me was outweighed by her irritation at the smile on
my face. She could find no decent reason to detain
me and so I left, promising to be back at my desk
before the end of the month. Her parting words, as
I left, were 'It may be that your replacement will be
too good to let go again, Lola. I sincerely hope it

works out for you.'

'That's very sweet of you,' I said.

*   *   *

Phoebe and Lorna were out when I reached home. They were filming, both of them, and weren't due back until late. I packed my bags, pulled my savings from the box beneath my bed—$457 in all—and left them a long, loving letter, promising that if all worked out I would set about writing any number of photoplays exclusively for them to star in. I don't suppose they believed me, but I will. I will.

There followed five long days across country. I'd not been back east since I'd left nine years ago, a different woman entirely, I thought. Not a woman at all, perhaps. And I wondered, on that endless journey, about the woman I had become.

I thought about Rudy, who hadn't recognised me, who had promised me he would never forget me, who had promised me that he loved me, and that there would always be a part of his soul that would miss me—who had promised me that, and allowed me to believe it; I thought about how he had looked at me and failed to see me in Mr Silverman's office, with his monstrous, gold-turbaned wife beside him, and his manager behind him, and everyone so desperate to please him: I thought of how I had written to him, one of the million fan letters he had received, and been fobbed off with so many damned portraits I could build a house with them—and of how I had come to Los Angeles, to the address he had sent me . . .

and finally, after all the years of constancy, a slow, cold, hard anger began to grow.

Had he known, when he had ordered Mr Ullman to wire to me, for whom he was really sending? Of course he hadn't! How could he? I have changed my name. The photoplay was given to him—in my presence—and with a handful of others, written by Miss Marion or by other strangers. How could he possibly know? And if he did, if he could recognise a small part of our shared story in the one I had written for him—would it mean anything to him at all? Or—that is to say—anything more than a warm laugh, a fond memory, a hug from an old friend?

I couldn't tell which might have been worse, more hurtful: nothing, no memory of me at all (but that seemed impossible, even in his cluttered, eventful life. We had been friends. We had loved one another when nobody else did). Would that be worse? Or a warm memory that meant nothing to him: 'Well, if it isn't Jennifer Doyle. Look at you! How have *you* been? You changed your hair! What a small world!'

The thought of that, of a fond greeting and nothing more, after all these years—I couldn't bear it. So much so, as the train rumbled forward, on and on, through the wide, empty, unchanging landscape, through an America I had all but forgotten, I wondered whether it wouldn't be better simply to leap out onto the track and head back home again to my safe and pleasant job at the studio, before my replacement stole it from under my nose. Before Rudy, with his easy touch, his warmth, the glow of light that shone from him, broke my heart once and for all, and all over again, just as I was learning to live without him.

I'm not entirely certain what prevented me doing it. Of course, there was the meeting with Frances Marion, and all that it promised for my work, but I'm ashamed to say that it barely featured in my considerations. Over and over again, I replayed the scene in my head, where Rudy recognised me at last and, with his easy, magnetic warmth, wielded his careless axe at my very being.

Good God, is it . . . is it really . . . is it Jennifer? JENNIFER! Of course!

Ha ha ha! How extraordinary! And to think—Why, I'd quite forgotten—but how lovely to see you!

Come here, old girl—give me a hug!

But what an altogether amusing coincidence!

And quite pretty too!

Do you know, Jennifer, what with all my wives and lovers and riches and stardom and the worldwide adoration and the vast fortune I have amassed and all that utterly silly stuff, I'd quite forgotten—I must admit I'd absolutely

entirely

and completely

forgotten

You ever lived!

It was with a mixture of rage, misery and dread that once again I stayed alone in my carriage for most of the journey. I didn't jump off the train. I did not turn around and scurry home. Of course not. How could I have done? But I did conceive of a plan.

Since I was en route now, to meet a man I had loved unceasingly for ten years, and who, when last we met, had looked me straight in the eye and failed to recognise me, it seemed there was only

394

one way I could make our inevitable reunion bearable. I have changed a great deal in any case of course since the days he first knew me: with my short blonde permanently waved hair, my Americanised accent and my Americanised walk, my stick-thin body and my lipstick and rouge and shaped eyebrows and kohled eyes. There are times when I wonder if I would recognise myself. With the help of a cloche hat pulled low over my forehead I realised I could get through our entire encounter as a stranger. It was not ideal, but it was preferable to the passionless, easy warmth he would offer me as an old friend. I couldn't have borne that.

I took the subway to the hotel, dropped my luggage and, before even taking a shower, set out along Broadway to fix myself up with some kind of a disguise.

But then with so many dollars in my pocket and New York at my disposal, I wound up getting a little carried away: I purchased several new dresses and two new pairs of shoes and various other things—a set of long beads with earrings to match—because a person can still want to look attractive even if she's in disguise, and then a wonderful hat, which I intended to wear pulled as far down over my face as possible; and finally (which purchase dismayed me rather, but I felt was essential if my heart was not to break) a pair of wire-rimmed eyeglasses. At length—and dripping with the August heat—I returned to the hotel and left my messages: one for Frances Marion at the Algonquin, though I knew she wasn't due in New York for several days, and, finally, one for Mr

395

Ullman at the Ambassador.

His secretary called back within the hour. I was to make my way to the Ambassador Hotel by five o'clock.

Mr Valentino would be waiting for me.

*　　　*　　　*

Two hours, then. Twelve blocks of hot and noisy New York streets to trample through. And two hours. I took a shower, and though the water ran hot, and the weather was sweltering, I couldn't prevent myself shivering. My hands shook so badly I could not do the buttons of my new dress, until finally I had to give up on it altogether and put on another instead. The problem (of my shaking hands) was even more acute when it came to painting my face, which was quite waxy with the heat. By the time I was ready to leave, my whole body shook. It took me several attempts before I could hold the bedroom doorknob firmly enough to turn it. And then, in the lobby, I realised I had come down without my purse and had to go back up again, and down again, and up again, because I had forgotten to bring a copy of the scenario.

I resisted the strong temptation to take a slurp from my hip flask. I resisted that. But then, as I knew time was ticking by and I was already late, and I had been up and down to the lobby twice already, and Larry at the desk was already giving me the queerest of looks, I sat on the edge of my small bed and smoked one last cigarette; the last cigarette—so it felt, though I'm not certain why— of a condemned woman. One way or another, I realised that my life, after this meeting, would probably never be the same.

Perhaps, I thought—it seemed unimaginable—but perhaps, perhaps, his stardom had distorted him or distorted my memory—or both. Perhaps I would spy him this afternoon, from beneath my disguise, and see straight through him—and wonder at whatever I had loved in him, whatever I had been dreaming about all these years. And what miraculous liberation it would be! To be set free at last! And not only free (lest I forget) but on my way to a successful career as a Hollywood screenwriter.

I considered the scenario I had written so long ago and which, out of nowhere, was about to change my life. It was my twenty-eighth, I'd calculated on the train from Los Angeles (if you only counted the completed ones) and until now a long way from my favourite. I had started it—written the first of innumerable drafts—while I was living at Citrus Avenue with Perry.

The story was about Rudy, I suppose. Indirectly. It occurs to me that everything I have ever written is about Rudy, or a version of Rudy, or Rudy and me, or Rudy without me. This one was a simple story—called *Wicked Pleasures*. It tells the tale of a young, ambitious immigrant arriving penniless in New York, whose talent as a musician—a violinist—leads to his falling in with a fast, rich, society set. Finding himself dazzled by the swirl of decadence and debauchery around him, he briefly abandons his ambition and falls in love with a rich man's beautiful wife—who persuades him to do something terrible to protect her from ruin. It saves her, but leads him to the brink of ruin instead, until finally his talent, ambition and newly acquired worldly wisdom combine to pull him back from the brink again . . . A simple story with a happy ending. He might just as well have been a talented and ambitious dancer. *Wicked Pleasures* was about loneliness, of course, and the perniciousness of glamour: two subjects that were bound to be close to Rudy's heart. Nevertheless, I wondered what it was about the story that had so drawn him to it, and with such urgency, too.

*   *   *

I was shown up to the suite at once. They sent a girl down, about my age, very pretty. In the elevator she looked at me, with her big blue curious eyes, and she said, 'It's not often Mr Valentino takes such a shine to a piece of work. You must have written something real special.'

'I'm not at all sure that I did,' I muttered.

'Well, Mr Valentino certainly thinks so. He's quite impatient to meet you!'

'Is he?'

She smiled. 'But, you know, you absolutely mustn't be nervous, and I can absolutely see that you are. Because he's quite the kindest man in the world. Believe me. He puts everyone at their ease. That's just what he does. Because he is so absolutely the kindest gentleman you will ever meet. And I should know, because I work for him.'

She chattered on, a little nonsensically, perhaps, but with plenty of verve, and the elevator climbed inexorably . . . one floor, two floors . . . to the eleventh, and I was very grateful to her. She led me along the wide, cool hallway towards his suite, over delicate Oriental carpets, past vases of lilies, beneath crystal chandeliers—I swear, even the air smelled expensive.

'I heard him saying to Mr Ullman,' she said, 'that reading your little photoplay had made him feel like its author was a "friend of the soul". That's what I heard him say!'

'He said that?'

'It's what he said! Imagine that! Rudolph Valentino saying that about a person! And that person being *you*! A friend of the soul! How about that?'

'How about that?' I mumbled. And the next thing I knew we had reached as far as we could go. We had stopped before a large mahogany door and her knuckles were poised to rap upon it.

'Stop!' I said. 'Please—if you would—please. I'm not sure that I can . . .'

But she had already done it, knocked softly and pushed open the door, and more or less shoved me inside. 'Friend of the soul!' she whispered—her final words—and winked at me, then closed the door between us and I was left there, standing quite alone in the longest, largest, swankiest drawing room I have laid eyes on. At the far end (though I could hardly see them, thanks to the eyeglasses, and the brim of my hat being pulled down so low) were the figures of two gentlemen: one, slender, elegant, lithe; the other a little round lump of a man. Each was seated on a separate couch of deep black velvet, low and immeasurably large. Between them was a third couch, which was empty, and at their feet, with piles of papers spread all across, lay a pair of perfectly symmetrical zebra skins.

The men were so far away and so engrossed in

their conversation they didn't notice me come in. So I stood quietly for a minute—for an age—listening and waiting, trying to drum up the courage to announce myself.

'Well, George,' Rudy was saying, 'you haven't read the damn thing! Not properly. In any case, we can discuss it later. She'll be here any minute and I want you to leave us. Please.'

'Leave?' He chuckled. 'Really? Whatever for?'

'Because, George . . . I am sorry to be rude. Only I must ask you to leave.'

'*Just because?*'

'Because the girl is bound to be shy—and I don't see how you sitting there looking miserable is going to make her feel any easier.'

'I'm simply telling you what you already know: Americans will be setting fire to their seats before the movie is even finished. They detest no one and nothing more than they detest the wops.'

'America hates a wop—you keep saying it. Again and again you say it—America hates the wops—as if it were immutable fact. But it's not quite correct, is it? I mean to say . . . In any case, the script isn't specific. He's simply an immigrant. An outsider. Anyone who finds himself alone in a new place . . . But why aren't you leaving, George? I thought we agreed you were leaving . . .'

'At the very least you must allow me to meet the wretched girl . . .'

'She is not wretched.'

'But she is unheard of.'

'She is not remotely wretched. She has written a remarkable photoplay . . .'

'Her story is drawn from nothing—nowhere. If she'd taken it from a novel it might have been easier—and the damned *title,* Rudy, *Wicked Pleasures!* The mere title doesn't stand a cat's chance of getting by the censors.'

'George, you are simply creating hurdles. And I keep asking you to leave. Would you please leave? It is vital that I see this girl in private.'

'I'll grant you, it's a fine scenario. Indeed. Very emotional. Got lots of heart. But it's a story about a wop. In a country with a million paid-up members of Mr Clarke's wop-detesting Klan. Americans don't want to hear stories-of-the-heart about the wops. They want to see you hanged for Bolshevism, mostly. If recent events count for anything. Or, failing that, packed off home back to Wopland.'

'Well, then, it's about time we showed them differently.'

'I'm telling you. It's a pancake. And you know it.'

'I don't accept that.'

'Rudy, I'm simply requesting—'

'I insist that you leave, George.'

'Fine. I'll leave. But can we simply agree that you *don't promise her anything*. Make no promises. That's all I ask . . .'

'I shall promise her,' Rudy said, standing up, 'that I will make every possible effort to get this picture of hers made, and that I— Oh!'

Ha. At last! The man—with eyes in the back of his head—had seen me.

I looked at the ground. I looked anywhere but at Rudy. Finally Mr Ullman spotted me too. And a thoroughly awkward silence fell. 'Well!' I said at length, far louder than was necessary, even in such an enormous room. 'Well, well . . . and here I am!'

'Yes indeed.' Mr Ullman nodded. 'Here you are.'

It didn't sound terribly friendly. He didn't bother to stand up.

I was aware of Rudy, from the corner of my eye, making his catlike way towards me. And I knew even without looking that nothing was changed. From his walk, from his hand outstretched to take mine, I knew I loved him still, just as much as ever I had.

'What a terrible welcome,' he cried, 'and when you have come such a long way!' I held out my hand. He took it with both of his. From beneath the brim of my rammed-down hat I saw his hands on mine—I saw his hands and smelled his smell and heard his voice, so familiar, so much a part of me, and yet so completely unreal. I dared not look up. Worse still, I could not let go.

So we stood there. Holding one another. Or me holding him. I couldn't be sure. And he with his second hand still covering mine. Yes. That was true. I could hear him breathing.

Rudy said quietly, 'Miss Nightingale? I can't quite see you beneath your hat . . . but it was you, wasn't it? In Mr Silverman's office that day?'

'In Mr Silverman's office?' I repeated.

'Frances told me the author was a secretary at the studio. And I was certain I had seen you—as we came out of Mr Silverman's office. Do you remember? It is you, isn't it? I remember clearly. She called you Lola . . .'

'She called me . . . Yes, well—I suppose she would have done.' My head was spinning. I'd not made any allowances for this.

'There's no reason why you would remember,' he said—absurdly. He stepped back from me, and our hands separated. He laughed, I think, rather

402

awkwardly, as if he were embarrassed. 'Well, Miss—Lola Nightingale. It's a pleasure to meet you. Again . . .'

Just then Mr Ullman, from his place on the sofa, shouted something about it being time for cocktails.

'Would you like a drink, Miss—Nightingale?' Rudy asked me. 'Can I order you something? A Manhattan, perhaps? Or perhaps,' he said, 'perhaps you prefer champagne?' Good God, that voice! As if I were the only person it was ever intended for, as if when he spoke, only I was ever meant to hear it.

I loved champagne—better than any other drink in the world.

'Since perhaps you agree with me,' that same velvet voice, talking only to me, 'there's really no finer drink in all the world. Can I get you some champagne?'

It was the last time we had seen each other, sitting side by side on that bench in Central Park on that ice-cold terrible night, and together we had finished both of our bottles. And afterwards he had leaned back and gazed at the stars and said, drink softening the edges of his words, 'Do you suppose, Jennifer, that there is a finer drink in all the world? Is there any drink so sweet, so helpful, so gentle on our wretched spirits than a bottle of the finest, crispest, coldest champagne? Do you suppose there is?'

And I had said there was not. That I loved champagne more than any drink, and that when I was rich I would never drink anything else.

And he had laughed. I could still hear it—the soft laughter as he had leaned back there, and how my heart had been frozen, and how, as he laughed, he had reached out to take my hand in his, and how he had squeezed it, since there was nothing to be said, nothing in the world to do after such a terrible night, except to laugh at the helpfulness of champagne.

I heard his voice again. Was he teasing me? Was it possible? 'Hello, Miss—Nightingale?' I heard him saying. 'Can I fetch you some cham—'

'Thank you. I don't care for champagne.'

'No?' he replied at once. And then, after a pause: 'Well, then, perhaps a cocktail? My valet makes an excellent Manhattan.'

'That would be nice. Thank you.'

I thought he had looked away and couldn't resist stealing a glance at his face at last: I peered at him, over the rim of the wretched eyeglasses—and found his eyes were on me still. I looked away.

'You know, it's better than anything I've seen in a year or more.'

'What is?' I said.

I could hear him smiling. 'The scenario, Miss Nightingale.'

'Oh!'

'You should know it. I would have picked it out *no matter what.*'

'Thank you,' I said, not really hearing him, not really listening. And it struck me as such a silly, inadequate response, I felt a terrible urge—I wasn't sure to do which—to laugh or to cry. I did neither. I kept my head down. 'You are very kind,' I muttered.

'Kind? Of me to have read it, or you to have written it?'

'Well, the truth is I've written so many,' I was

saying, 'and I'd had so many returned unopened, I had rather despaired of anybody *ever* actually reading one, I think—I'm not even sure why I kept on writing. I keep—kept—telling myself to stop, and then somehow . . . somehow, there I was again, writing another and another—' I stopped. Embarrassed. He was looking at me intently. I could feel it, his eyes burning into me. He was smiling, perhaps. I couldn't be sure. 'So, anyway,' I murmured, 'kind of you—to have read it, I guess. And then to pay for me to come all the way from Los Angeles. I am . . . very grateful.'

'I receive twenty or more photoplays every week, Miss Nightingale. And I read every one . . . approach each one full of hope . . . But they are all the same! Son of a Sheik, Uncle of Sheik, Grandfather of Sheik, First Cousin Twice Removed of a damned Sheik . . .'

A gurgle of laughter escaped me, in spite of everything.

'I had despaired of anyone offering me anything else! But then came *Wicked Pleasures*.'

'Are we to conduct this entire interview from the two furthest corners of the room?' Mr Ullman called out irritably. I think we had both forgotten he was there. 'Or am I being purposely excluded? Miss Nightingale, it's a pleasure to meet you at last. My name is George Ullman and I am Mr Valentino's manager. Why don't you come and sit down and allow me to introduce myself properly?'

'Well, George, since you're *still here*,' Rudy replied, without turning, 'why don't you haul yourself out of that couch and come over and greet Miss Nightingale yourself? Instead of bellyaching at us from two hundred yards away. Our guest has made it all the way from the other side of America. You might at least bother yourself to cross the room.'

Again, I found myself laughing. His accent was all but gone, I noticed, only the faintest trace of it left. Whether we liked it or not—and I suspect I liked it rather more than he did—Rudy and I were both Americans now.

Mr Ullman showed no sign of shifting himself, so Rudy and I made our way across the room to join him, Rudy calling to his valet for cocktails as we travelled.

'I insist that I stay for one short drink,' declared Mr Ullman. 'Mr Valentino is so enthusiastic about your work, Miss Nightingale, I would consider it positively negligent of me to leave without at least getting to know you a little.'

Rudy shot Mr Ullman a look that boded trouble, but chose not to fight.

'I asked George to find a room for you here at the Ambassador,' he said instead, as I took my place on the third couch, 'but I now understand he's put you up in some rotten hole somewhere else entirely. It's out of the question, of course. So, with your permission, Miss—Nightingale, if you prefer it, I will send my driver to collect your luggage at once, and we can arrange for you to get a room here. It would be much more comfortable.'

'Thank you. No,' I replied at once. 'No, I'm very happy where I am.'

'You see?' smirked Mr Ullman. 'She's perfectly happy where she is.'

'And in any case,' Rudy said, just as if neither of us had spoken, 'if we're to work together, it would be a good deal simpler for everyone if we were all

406

in more or less the same place. Wouldn't it?'

Would it? The thought of the two of us residing at the same hotel in separate bedrooms and as strangers filled me with nothing, I think, but horror. Or misery, actually. I couldn't have borne it.

'Not,' he continued hurriedly, 'that there is a great deal of work to be done. On the contrary, it's as near to perfect as any photoplay I ever laid eyes on. Only—if George and I are to take *Pleasures* . . .' The valet appeared with our three drinks. Rudy took one and handed it to me. 'The best Manhattan in Manhattan,' he said. 'But not as good as champagne . . . Congratulations, Miss Nightingale.' We drank, his eyes on me, I could feel them. 'If we are to take *Pleasures*,' he continued, 'and make it our first production together, in conjunction with United Artists—'

'Good God, Rudy,' burst out Mr Ullman, 'you would like us to *produce* it too, would you? You never mentioned that!'

Rudy laughed. 'We discussed it with Joe only a fortnight ago! Have you been paying the slightest attention?'

'To produce *something*, why, yes. But, Rudy, you only read the damn thing last week!'

'Well,' said Rudy, unruffled, 'then you must forgive me. Perhaps I neglected to tell you. I had a copy of *Wicked Pleasures* delivered to Joe the same day—and he adored it, just as I do. And he has as good as agreed that we will go ahead . . .'

I listened to this, not certain what part I was meant to play. So I sat primly on the edge of my enormous sofa, with my eyeglasses obscuring my vision, and my hat making my head itch. Rudy had

407

not changed then: still the same man, after all the extraordinary things that had befallen him, the same impulsiveness, warmth, optimism, thoughtfulness, energy, grace . . . the same man I had fallen in love with.

'I apologise,' he said to me, 'on behalf of Mr Ullman. But please, rest assured, I have not brought you all this way for nothing . . . I have not . . .' He fell silent. A long silence. 'No matter what else, Miss Nightingale, I am committed . . . to *Wicked Pleasures* . . .'

Mr Ullman took a slurp of his drink. Gave an offensive little chuckle. 'To her *Wicked Pleasures,* Rudy,' he asked, 'or to yours?'

'They are one and the same,' Rudy replied swiftly, softly, looking at me.

Another silence after that. I cleared my throat, but could think of nothing to say, with the air so thick.

He leaned across, a cigarette case open in his hand. 'Do you smoke?'

I took one without replying, and put it to my lips.

He took one for himself, and then he stood— bent over to where I sat, half lost on that ocean of couch—it took a moment for the flame from his lighter to meet the end of my cigarette, because my hands were shaking—and yet again a hush fell. A hush in which I felt his eyes upon me—burning into me, and I felt his attention upon me and I felt his closeness to me so intensely that I could recognise the beat of his heart—does it sound absurd? I could.

I told myself that it was nothing, perhaps, simply the power of his presence—his extraordinary charisma—and yet, at the same time, I knew. Just as I always had.

But, still, I couldn't bring myself to look at him. From between the brim of that hat and the rim of those silly eyeglasses, I looked anywhere—anywhere in the room but at him.

'Frances Marion is a great champion of yours,' he said suddenly. He returned the lighter to his pocket. 'It was she who gave me your script of course. You probably guessed.'

I nodded. 'Eventually. But Mr Ullman's wire took me completely by surprise. I thought perhaps there might have been a mistake—that the *Wicked Pleasures* you wired me about was another one entirely . . . written by someone else . . .'

'Impossible,' Rudy said without hesitation.

'Well—but it *might* be possible,' perked up Mr Ullman. 'Have we checked? Only imagine—if it had been written by someone we had all heard of how much easier our task would be!'

'Except it wasn't and it isn't,' Rudy said. He turned his eyes to me, 'Your script reminded me so much of my own earliest experiences in this country—it was almost as if it had been written by a friend . . . someone who had been through the same experience themselves. But you sound quite American, Miss—Nightingale . . .'

'Do I?'

'Or do I detect an accent—the faintest hint of an English childhood hiding in there somewhere?'

'Do you?'

'I don't know . . .' He smiled. 'Do I?'

A pause, during which I think Mr Ullman slurped at his Manhattan, and I felt myself melting, slowly, beneath Rudy's warm, unrelenting scrutiny.

'Frances told me only a small amount about you,'

he said at length.

'Well, I suppose she doesn't know very much.'

'So I discovered.'

'I accosted her in the Piggly Wiggly on Santa Monica Boulevard. With my photoplay. Did she tell you that?'

'She did.' Rudy chuckled. 'Courageous of you . . .'

'Crazy of me. And quite impertinent.'

'Crazy and impertinent, too, I suppose. But I admire you for it. I'm not certain I would have had the courage.'

'Well, of course you would!' I burst out. 'Rudy, you're the most co—'

He smiled. 'What? What am I, Lola? '

I could feel myself blushing. 'A well-known figure, Mr Valentino.'

'Ah, yes.' He sounded disappointed. 'So I am . . .'

Once again I was conscious of nothing but the searching warmth of his eyes. I reached for my cocktail glass.

'The best Manhattan in Manhattan,' he said again, as the alcohol hit my throat. 'I was right. Wasn't I? George, shall I order you another, and perhaps get it delivered to your room? I know you have plenty of urgent business to attend to.'

'None especially,' he answered casually.

Rudy said nothing, only he turned to look at his manager. Mr Ullman's comfortable expression altered as if an electric charge had been put through him. 'Nevertheless I must get on with it,' he muttered.

Suddenly the thought of Mr Ullman leaving, and of Rudy and me being left alone, after all these years, filled me with a dense panic. 'Please, Mr

Ullman, don't hurry yourself on my account,' I burst out. 'Besides, I'm not sure we really have anything more to discuss—do we, Mr Valentino? I ought to be going . . .' I began the awkward process of pulling myself up from that deep, low couch. 'And then,' I babbled, 'as soon as Miss Marion is in town—Tuesday, I think she said, yes, Tuesday— then we can all get together again and—'

'No,' Rudy said, with the same velvet soft voice.

I looked at him directly then. Couldn't stop myself. He was quite still—leaning back against the couch, long legs stretched out—languid, composed, a cigarette between his fingers, smoke curling, his eyes fixed on me, every part of him motionless, watchful. 'Not yet,' he said. 'Sit down.'

Mr Ullman looked from one of us to the other, back and forth. I looked at Rudy. Rudy looked at me. I don't know how many seconds passed.

At some point, in any case, I heard Mr Ullman heaving a great sigh. 'Oh, forget about the drink, then,' he said. 'I shall ask Dyer to send me one to my room. Call me, will you, when you're free? We still have a lot to discuss.'

Rudy didn't reply.

'Miss Nightingale. Pleasure to meet you,' Ullman said. Or something along those lines. 'I shall start work on some sort of contract right away . . .'

And then he left. Rudy stood up. He crossed the room—empty room—and nothing was said between us. And up there on the eleventh floor, beneath the hum of luxury and silence, we could just make out the rumble of city traffic.

He was bent over something, though I couldn't see what. I smiled to myself. It was all so familiar to me—so utterly natural: his silence, his presence,

411

the tilt of his head, the coil of cigarette smoke, which always surrounded him—it was as if he had only ever been in the next room all this time, not away for ten long years, turning himself into the world's most admired—

Smoking as much as you ever were, Rudy . . . I think I even opened my mouth to say it. I stopped—and laughed quietly to myself.

'It is—quite funny, isn't it?' he said, without turning around.

I didn't know what to say. I said nothing.

'After so much time. I think it's madness.'

'Maybe,' I said. Carefully.

Still, with his back to me, he said, 'I do wish you'd take off that ridiculous hat.'

Well, I didn't. 'It's not ridiculous,' I said.

'It's completely ridiculous. In the circumstances.'

'I don't think so. Actually, I think it's—'

He set the needle down then. And the song filled the air around us—and after that I had nothing to say at all.

> *You made me love you . . .*
> *. . . I didn't want to do it*

He had turned around. I took off the ridiculous hat, and the wretched eyeglasses too—I needed a moment, just a moment, to myself, to collect myself. Neither of us spoke.

> *. . .You made me want you . . .*
> *And all the time you knew it*

Idiotic song! He was leaning against the phonograph, watching me. I looked back at him.

412

. . . I guess you always knew it . . .
. . . I guess you always knew it . . .

The song played on . . . And he smiled—it was a
wistful smile—and I saw him suddenly, separated
from all this . . . elegance, success, luxury,
glamour—just as he had been at The Box, simply
as a man apart, like all men but unlike any other.
He stood there, as he had always stood: separate,
fearless, brimming at once with the joy and the
melancholy of existence, with that innate
instinctive wisdom that was always peculiarly his.
He stood there as he had always stood: with
perfect grace. It was why I ever fell in love with
him, and why I loved him still.
  'Been a long time,' he said.
  'Yes, it has.'
  'You haven't changed.'
  'Yes, I have.'
  'No. Not really.'
  'You haven't changed either. You haven't.'
  He shrugged. 'I wrote to you. A hundred times.'
  'You wrote to me once.'
  'Ha! Yes. I mean to say—I wrote to you. I never
mailed the letters.'
  I laughed.
  'But you don't believe me.'
  'Why would I?'
  He thought about it. Finally, he said, 'Absolutely.
Why indeed?' He shrugged again. 'On the one
hand, why would you believe me?' He left the
phonograph, came back towards me, stopped and
crouched right there, before me, by the edge of
sofa, so that our eyes were level, and I might never

413

look anywhere else. The music stopped, and it was only us. 'On the other hand, Jennifer, on the other hand, I don't see how you couldn't.'

And nor did I. 'Because I never received them,' I said.

'Because I never mailed them.'

'Because I came to Hollywood, and you were nowhere to be found.'

'Because I waited and I heard nothing.'

'And you married. Not once, but twice.'

'Oh! And you have lived like a nun, all these years?' He laughed, a deep, rich, warm laugh. 'Somehow I doubt that very much, Jennifer . . .'

'And you changed your name. And you left no forwarding address.'

'Because I waited for you. Month after month I waited, in that stinking boarding-house—but you never wrote. You never said you were coming.'

'And you left no forwarding address.'

'No.'

It was his turn to look away. 'Every day,' he said at last, 'I would say to that lousy bastard, I would ask him, "Is there a letter?" And he would shake his head with so much relish I could see the fleas fly out—and every day, and every letter you didn't send, and every other letter in the world I was ever sent, felt as if it had been designed by you, sent by you, like a poison dart, to remind me of how little you cared, how easily you had forgotten, how quickly you assumed the worst . . . I began to hate you.'

'Ah! How clever of you. To get to that so quickly. It took me so much longer. It took me years.'

'Which would no doubt explain,' he said, looking back at me again, 'why you sound so bitter.'

'Since you became the idol of everybody's dreams, Rudolph Valentino,' I could hear my voice rising, 'do you know how many times I have written to you? I must have received a hundred damned stupid "autographed" portraits of you to show for it. And nothing! Nothing else. Nothing.'

He gazed at me a long moment. 'That's the best you could do?' he said quietly. 'Do you have any idea how many "damned stupid" letters I receive every week? Do you?'

'Oh, plenty, I'm sure.'

'Plenty indeed. Two thousand on a quiet week, Jennifer. I detest them! Couldn't you have known that? This week, thanks to *Son of the Sheik*, maybe I have received five thousand. I don't know. I don't care. My secretary tells me as if it were— something to rejoice at. Was that really the best you could do? Was that *all* you could do? When I was so visible to you. And you were so lost to me. Was that *all* you could bring yourself to do?'

'I came to Hollywood.'

'You came to Hollywood. Much good it did either of us. How could I have known?'

I smiled. 'How, indeed?' A silence fell. Filled with our anger. 'Well. Rudy. Well. Well . . . We seem to be going in circles. I'm sorry. I'm very sorry. In any case . . . I think maybe I should . . .'

He was crouched in front of me still. To stand up and leave him, I needed somehow to get past him. Without touching him. Without his touching me. Without his trying to prevent me. Without his noticing.

'No,' he said. He put a hand on the edge of the sofa, a little way from me, not close enough. I could feel the warmth of him—his desire, his love:

415

it wrapped around us like something enchanted. 'Don't. Jenny. Do. Not. '

I couldn't, of course. Nothing on earth could have moved me.

There was a long, long silence. Not a word between us. I gazed at his hand, too close to me and not close enough—and he looked, I think, at me, at his hand, but at me really, because I could feel his eyes on me. He didn't move, didn't touch me. I didn't move—couldn't, actually. Absolutely—and then the other hand, just a single finger—and just the tiniest brush against my hip, and then a sigh, or a small, low moan, one from him, one from me. He moved away. Moved right away. To a silver box on the mantelpiece in front of us. Lit a cigarette for me, and another for himself, and we smoked in silence together, far apart but never closer—in our enchanted fog, where nothing else existed. Nothing at all, but each other.

'I have something to show you,' he said.

From his wallet he pulled a sheet of paper, worn at the edges from years of folding and unfolding— as worn as the letter he wrote to me all those years ago. He opened it out. 'I took it from your father's room after you were gone . . . the following morning . . . It was there—on the bed. When they took him away. He had been lying on it, they said . . . and I have been meaning to give it to you. But then . . . I carry it with me everywhere. You can probably see.' He passed it to me.

Papa must have drawn it while he was alone in that boarding-house—I knew it because of the pin. I was wearing the golden pin that Rudy had given me at The Box, on that last day, in the nursery, before he and Papa were sent into exile.

416

I gazed at it in silence, too emotional to speak.

'He caught you, though, didn't he?' Rudy said softly, finally. But my eyes had clouded. I couldn't really see. 'He must have loved you so very much,' he said. 'It's what I feel—it's one of the things I feel—when I look at it. And I look at it . . .' He smiled. 'There's not a day that passes when I don't.'

'May I, Rudy? Would you mind terribly—if I kept it now?' I said at last. 'Only I didn't know . . .'

He stepped towards me, took my hand and pulled me up from the couch, so that we stood before each other at last, with nothing and no one between us.

'Darling Jenny,' he said, 'you can keep it for ever. You can keep it . . . on one small condition . . .'

He kissed me.

'As long as you promise to stay with me, Jenny . . .'

I smiled. 'I never left you.'

'Never,' he said. 'Never. Never leave me again . . .'

We kissed, standing on one of the zebra skins, where it all began, where I found my dress in a messy heap last Friday night, which seems like a thousand years ago. We kissed and all the years, all the bitterness, everything was gone, everything but his scent, his hands, his tongue, his eyes, his body and mine . . .

And that was how it all began.

And that's how I know that he loves me. He loves me. And I love him. And he is mine. And he will be well again soon, because he loves me and we have found each other and he loves me. He loves me. He loves me. And I love him.

HOTEL CONTINENTAL

NEW YORK

22–3 August 1926

Larry didn't come with my cash. What did I expect? It wasn't until this evening that anybody came for me at all, and then two came at once: Justin Hademak first, about to post bail for me, with money sent expressly from sweet, dear Madeleine. She had not forgotten, after all this time.

And then, hot on his heels, came Frances Marion, who insisted she pay it instead. Both she and Mr Hademak had seen the photographs in different newspapers: one of an 'unknown flapper' being laid out flat by a security guard outside the Polyclinic Hospital; another of the same dim-witted girl, being bundled into the back of a police van. They had tracked me down to this cell, both, and acquainted themselves with one another in the waiting room. I think Mr Hademak, his new job at Pickfair almost but not yet assured, was a little dazzled to meet Miss Marion, whom he knew to be his idol's closest friend. He allowed her to post bail in his place.

She did much more than that.

We were standing on the steps outside the police station. I could feel the city sun on my face, smelled the petroleum in my nostrils—never so pleased to be free. I thanked her. Or I tried to thank her. But she stopped me mid-flow: 'It's you, isn't it?' she said.

'What's me?'

'I read *Idol Dreams*, Lola. Oh, I left you so many messages! Suddenly so much about your earlier work made sense.'

'I'm sorry?' I said. I was confused. 'I really—I hate to be rude after everything. And my work—it is so important to me. Please don't imagine it isn't. But I simply—I have to get to the hospital.'

'Because they're all about the same thing, aren't they? One way or another. All of them! They're all about Rudy! Aren't they?'

I didn't answer.

'And it's *you* who is Jennifer! Whom every one has been looking for! Mr Hademak just confirmed it. Lola, Lola—Jenny—I am so sorry.'

'It doesn't matter. It doesn't matter in the least. Only . . .'

'It was Anita Loos who wouldn't let it drop. I suppose we should all be grateful to her. She had a bee in her bonnet and she's been asking everyone, *Who is Jenny*? Like Prince Charming and the glass slipper, she's been carrying that question around with her: Where is Jenny? Where in the hell is this Jenny? Nobody knew. We have been racking our brains—but none of us knows a Jenny. Not one of us. But it's you! It was you. All along.'

'Miss Marion—can you tell me? How is he? Do you know? Does anyone know? Was it arsenic? Has he been poisoned? Shall he survive? *Tell me*. Please—does anyone know?'

'Lola . . .' The answer was there for me. In those two syllables.

'No. He is not . . .' I said.

'I have just spoken to George Ullman. Mr Ullman has not left his side in twenty-four hours. The doctors—he says the doctors seem to think—It's crazy down there. Thousands of people, and reporters—it's going to be hard to get to the door. . . Lola, he is dying. Unless some miracle happens—'

'It's not true! How can you know that? How can you know it, when you haven't seen him? There are so many rumours. Nothing but rumours. He is not. He is not dying!'

'He has been in and out of consciousness all day. And last night, too. You must come with me now. I have made the arrangements. Come with me now. There is still time—if we hurry.'

'Now? Is it really so terribly—don't I have time to . . . perhaps . . . Is it so bad? I should change my clothes. I'm filthy . . . Shouldn't I at least wash my face?'

'I have told Mr Ullman you are coming. And Mr Ullman has told Rudy you are coming. And Lola—Jenny—Lola, *Rudy is waiting for you*. Only we don't know for how long.'

* * *

The taxicab drew up at just about the exact spot I'd been bundled into that police van almost twenty-four hours previously. The crowds were still there, only they had swelled to five times the size or more and they were noisier, drunker, much more rumbustious. There must have been thousands of people out there, like vultures smelling death, come to witness the final moments. And there was a sense of celebration in the air too: like a public holiday, like a fairground—with news-stands and food stands, postcard stands and trinket stands—and the crowd breaking into snatches of song, and, by those doors, which I had grown to know so well, a whole host of reporters, twenty or thirty or more.

Mr Hademak led the way. He forced a path for us through the sea of hats, until we reached that same darned guard, Steffen, again. He saw Mr Hademak first, and then he saw me. He caught my eye and I winced.

'I'm not sure,' I muttered to Miss Marion, 'but I don't think he's going to let us in . . .'

'Nonsense. It's all arranged. Keep walking.'

I couldn't. He had stopped us.

'Ghoul,' he said. Arms folded, legs apart, nothing but dull aggression.

Mr Hademak said, 'Steffen. Good evening. Mr Valentino is expecting us.'

Steffen didn't move. Miss Marion, all five feet of her, appeared from behind the pair of us. 'Make way,' she said. 'At once. Keep us standing here one second more, I shall have you fired, man. Move out of the way.'

He hesitated. The crowd began to catcall again. Who knows on whose part? And then the reporters joined in, a couple of whom, by now, had come to recognise me: 'It's the nutso Sheba and the ghoul back again! Don't you ever give in, lady?'

'Out of the way,' Miss Marion said.

Steffen looked uncertain. 'Nobody said nothing about the ghoul,' he said.

'He is with us.' Miss Marion was about to fight.

'Please,' I said. 'Please—time is passing. Let us by.'

Miss Marion turned to Mr Hademak—he was already backing away. He wished me good luck, and then he was gone. The doors opened, and to the sound of cheers from the crowd—inexplicable, meaningless, stupid—I was finally allowed into the hall.

Miss Marion took me to the eighth floor, where Mr Ullman was waiting—a shadow of the man I had met ten days ago. Pale as the moon, cheeks sunken, his suit hanging from his shoulders. Ten days ago. Ten days ago. How things had changed. He shook my hand. 'Why didn't you come?' he said.

'Oh . . .' I laughed. 'If you knew . . . If you knew how I have tried . . .'

*   *   *

A large room, with mahogany furniture—a large, old fashioned mahogany bed; the open window and the curtains drawn back, and the hum of the air-conditioning and, beneath it, the hum of the crowd outside. I could hear individual voices—the reporters' laughter, the newsboys still shouting their headlines: *Film Idol At Death's Door*.

Had he heard that as he lay there? Could he hear it now? Could he hear me?

Mr Ullman had warned me that Rudy did not look as he had ten days before. 'You may be shocked,' he said. 'He is not quite as he was.' He managed a thin, most wretched smile. 'A little imperfect. He is a little more human now.'

422

I said nothing.

Rudy lay in the half-darkness, with only the light from West 50th shining into the room, shining onto his dreadful, pockmarked face. Speckled black.

It took a moment. Because he was not my father but my lover, and he, too, was dying, but he was not dead. And I could speak to him still. Perhaps he could hear me.

Rudy

Rudy

Darling

He breathed . . . in . . . out . . . in . . .

. . . out.

But nothing changed. His face, his eyes . . . I don't know if he knew me.

Rudy, it's me. Jennifer.

He breathed . . . in . . . out . . . in . . .

. . . out.

I rested my hand on the edge of the bed—too close, and not close enough—much, much too far. So I held his hand, but it was cool. It didn't respond to my touch. Nothing. Nothing.

In . . .

. . . out.

And after that, I sat. Listening to the crowd below, but not hearing it; listening to his breathing, and remembering. I whispered I was sorry. Sorry for so many things. Sorry, sorry, sorry.

And then there was nothing to say. He knew the rest.

I have no idea how long I stayed with him. All I know is that they led me away before he said anything to me. And I know that today it is

Monday, and Rudy is dead.

Mr Ullman delivered a letter to my hotel this morning. A note from Rudy, he said. For me to open when there was surely nothing left to be said. I have opened it. It lies here on the bed, beside my typewriter, and all these thousands of words. It is a scrap of cardboard, torn from a packet I know well. From the Warburton bathroom? I suppose. There is a picture of a glossy rat, legs up, with no black speckles on his glossy black coat. And on the back, my Rudy has left me a message, in shaking hand:

Cara . . . So much to look forward to . . .

That is all.

HOTEL CONTINENTAL

NEW YORK

Tuesday, 24 August 1926

He died yesterday morning, and the city has lost its mind. There are queues—thousands and thousands—to see Rudy in his bier. I have seen him. Mr Ullman allowed me to see him before the crowds arrived. They have covered his pockmarked face, and he looks peaceful. In spite of everything.

It is raining at last. I have never seen such rain. And still the people flock to see his body. I hear they take things from the bier—flowers, and buttons, and pieces of his hair—and then, this afternoon, a riot broke out, and the undertaker's window was smashed.

It is the same undertaker they used for Mr de Saulles.

They will move the coffin now, Mr Ullman has said. But the crowds won't leave. They are waiting for the stars to arrive, to pay their respects at the coffin. Pola came. With a black veil over her head. Wailing so loud they could hear it all the way down Fifth Avenue. Rudy would have laughed. She asked Mr Ullman to help her from the car, and then, before all the photographers, she gave a dreadful cry, like a dying animal, and she let go of Mr Ullman's hand and collapsed onto the sidewalk. They have photographs. Mr Ullman had to pick her up.

Well. It is Pola's show now. A show for the mob. It is madness. And Rudy is gone.

Mr Ullman has sent me tickets to the funeral. But I shan't go. They will all be there, of course— Mr Chaplin, Miss Pickford, Mr Fairbanks . . . And I suppose there will be another funeral in California. It makes no difference to me. I am going home.

It is Pola's show now. A show for the mob.

And Rudy is gone from all that. And I am still here. And I will always be his, and a small part of him will always be mine. Because he loved me.

He loved me.

He loved me.

And I love him.

And that is enough. How else do these stories end? I am the luckiest woman alive.

POSTSCRIPT

To: Nathan Wannermaker, Senior Executive Vice President, SilvermanCentury Studios
From: Andrew Meize, Executive Vice President, Production, SilvermanCentury Studios
Subject: Gabriella Nightingale
Date: 7 August 2010

ATTACHED Private Papers of Lola Nightingale

Nathan
As you will have read in the press, the attached manuscript purportedly arrived at Gabriella's private address last week, pursuant to the death of her father, who was the only child of the late, great Lola Nightingale, probably (my opinion) the most brilliant screenwriter of her generation.

The papers arrived with a bunch of stuff—letters and drawings etc—and a 1925 Remington electric typewriter, if you can believe! I appreciate it's been a while since Gabriella won her Oscar. Nevertheless, I'm guessing this is the real thing.

As it is, Gabriella's giving us a first-look—I think partly because of the

Silverman connection—which is nice. She's super keen to play Lola, and personally, I think it's a fabulous idea. I think everyone will. I suggest grabbing a read of attached material—and acting fast.

In the meantime . . . 4YRFUN . . . Call up RV's image when you get a minute and prepare to be amazed. The resemblance is actually freaky. Plus we all know how Gabriella can dance . . .

Enjoy.
Andrew

AUTHOR'S NOTES

Details of the murder of the politician and businessman, John Longer de Saulles at the hands of his beautiful Chilean-heiress former wife were on the front pages of newspapers across America for many months. Much of my description of the murder, murder scene, chief protagonists and circumstances leading to the crime, is drawn from the truly vast amount that was written at the time, and also from detailed reports of the court case.

The high-society murder gripped the public imagination to such a degree that in 1918 a feature film was made about it in Hollywood.

Professional dancer, Italian immigrant Rodolfo Guglielmi gave evidence on Mrs de Saulles's behalf during her divorce case. He testified that her husband, Democrat and former minister under President Woodrow Wilson, was an adulterer. He named his professional dance partner, Joan Sawyer, as Mr de Saulles's lover.

Rodolfo Guglielmi and Blanca de Saulles were well known to be close friends and regular dancing partners at this time.

Shortly after giving evidence, Rodolfo Guglielmi was arrested for graft. The charges wouldn't stick, and all paperwork related to the case has mysteriously disappeared. The experience led him to leave New York shortly afterwards.

In Hollywood, Rodolfo Guglielmi changed his name several times, settling finally on the name

Rudolph Valentino. In 1921, thanks to his performance in the hit movie *The Four Horsemen of the Apocalypse*, and most particularly thanks to a scene in which he dances the tango, he was propelled to international stardom. The release of *The Sheik*, a few months later, turned him from star to superstar, and he became the world's very first male international sex symbol.

During Valentino's final illness and for some time after his death, rumours were rife that he had been poisoned. His illness mirrored many of the symptoms of acute arsenic poisoning, including the marks on his skin, which were covered by makeup when his body lay in state at the funeral home.

Official cause of death was peritonitis brought on by a perforated ulcer.

Rudy's brother Alberto declined to allow an autopsy on the body.

Shortly after Valentino was admitted to hospital, so was Barclay Warburton. Barclay recovered shortly afterwards but the details of his illness remained a mystery. No details were ever released.

Public response to Rudy's death was as great or even greater than it was to the death of Diana, Princess of Wales. By Tuesday, 24 August, an estimated hundred thousand people lined the streets outside the funeral home hoping to get a glimpse of him in his coffin. When the doors to the funeral parlour opened the masses surged, and a riot broke out. Police on horseback charged the crowd. Windows at the funeral home were smashed and a hundred people ended up in hospital. At least two female fans, one of them in London, committed suicide, naming Valentino as the cause. 'The rioting was without precedent in

New York,' reported the *New York Times*, 'both in numbers concerned and in the behaviour of the crowd, which in larger part consisted of women and girls.'

Shortly after his Rudy's death, George Ullman wrote a memoir, *Valentino as I Knew Him*. In it he reported that during the final ambulance ride from the Ambassador Hotel to the Polyclinic Hospital, and also while he lay ill in hospital, Rudolph Valentino called repeatedly for an unknown 'Jenny'.

Natacha Rambova (born Winifred Shaughnessy, and about whom it is quite hard to find anything very positive reported) was adamant that 'Jenny' was the name of his spiritual guide from the Next World . . . The author begs to differ.

For many years, on the anniversary of his death, a veiled woman in mourning clothes would lay a wreath at Rudy's grave. Dubbed by the press (with imaginative flair) 'the woman in black', she was never identified.

*   *   *

Frances Marion, beautiful, clever, witty, and renowned for the help and support she gave to younger women in the film industry, married three times, had two sons, and won two Academy Awards for screenwriting in a career that spanned thirty years. She died in 1973, aged eighty-five. Her best friend was Mary Pickford.

Mary Pickford, a.k.a. 'America's Sweetheart', died at Pickfair in 1979, aged eighty-seven. For many years she was the most adored actress in America, and one of the most powerful women in Hollywood. In 1919 she founded United Artists with D. W. Griffith, Charlie Chaplin, and her second husband, movie star Douglas Fairbanks Snr.

Blanca de Saulles returned to Chile and married again in 1921. She divorced soon after, and died alone in 1940.

Jack de Saulles Jnr died in his early fifties while playing golf in Santiago, Chile.

Rudolph Valentino was a man of extraordinary sexual appeal not only to women. Rumours about him abound and many, but perhaps not all, are sheer invention. He was a rare human being: intelligent, humorous, elegant, warm and bold; an icon of grace and sensuality for us all.

Acknowledgements

Lynne Drew, Claire Bord and Clare Alexander thank you for getting the show on the road. Thank you Alona Mingueto for keeping it there. Sarah Ritherdon and Louise Swannell—what a joy it is to work with you. Thank you.

Thanks to Jonathan Foreman, Tim Geary, Natasha Galloway, Sally Rigg, Susan Douglas, Kevin Macdonald, Tessa Williams, Panda, Zebedee and Bashe . . .

And, above all, thank you Peter.

Actor Rudolph Valentino dancing with his wife
Natacha Rambova c.1923

Rudolph Valentino and Alice Terry hold each other in a scene from the 1921 film 'The Conquering Power'

Rudolph Valentino in the movie 'Cobra', 1925

Rudolph Valentino in 'The Sheik', 1921

Blanca de Saulles, c.1910–15

John de Saulles, 1914

ribune LATE CITY EDITION

★ ★ ★ ★ ★

TWO CENTS
In Greater New York | THREE CENTS
Within 200 Miles | FOUR CENTS
Elsewhere

Queen Marie Rejects Invitations From '30,000,000' in America

Royal Rumanian Says "No" to All, Because Her Visit Will Be Official; She Plans to Visit Whole Country and Call on President

By The Associated Press

PARIS, Aug. 24.—Queen Marie of Rumania has within a week received invitations from America, from individuals and organizations, in all representing 30,000,000 citizens, asking her to be their guest while visiting the United States.

The Queen cannot accept any of these invitations, as she intends to travel as a Queen and not incognito and thus will be the guest of the nation at large. In one portion of her trip she will probably be the guest of the State of Washington when she goes to dedicate a Rumanian room in a museum at Maryhill.

All reports that she has accepted any invitations to be a guest at private functions are held to be untrue, as her Majesty does not wish to tie herself up to any hostess. She plans to stay in

the United States less than two months and wants to see as much of the country as possible and to meet as many persons as she can.

A detailed itinerary of the Queen's trip will be made public by the Rumanian authorities on September 1 and until then nothing official will be known. It is understood, however, that the Queen will land in New York and go immediately to Washington to make a courtesy call on President Coolidge. She will then go to Buffalo to view Niagara Falls and cross into Canada to see one Canadian national park, to visit Yellowstone Park, Yosemite Valley and the Grand Canyon and to go to Texas, where she has many friends whom she made during the war.

Among the cities on her tentative list

(Continued on page seven)

100 Hurt as 30,000 Fight To View Body Of Valentino

Riotous Mob Holds Broadway Ten Hours; Women Trampled, Police Swept Aside, Windows Smashed

Throng Storms Door Four Times

Pavement Soaped to Fell Mounted Men; More Than 50,000 Pass Bier Before Halt at Midnight

A boisterous, unruly mob, seethed about the Campbell Funeral Church, Broadway and Sixty-sixth Street, from 2 o'clock yesterday afternoon until midnight, when the doors were closed, striving to force a way to the room where the body of Rudolph Valentino, motion picture star, lay.

Maniac Blows Up Bank, Kills 2, Injures a Score

Hall Witnesses Offered Bribes, Officer Charges

Top New York Herald Tribune, 25th August 1926

Bottom 1st September 1926: The funeral procession of actor Rudolph Valentino (1895–1926) coming up Broadway, New York

Daily News frontpage (8/25/26) Rudolph Valentino lying in an open casket

441